"From now
you'll spend t
your cabin.

Glory's eyes widened. Drawing herself up, she tilted her chin defiantly. "Why are you treating me this way?"

"Because, you little vixen, I'm trying to make you understand. The *Black Spider* is not a passenger ship. These men aren't used to having a woman on board—especially a beautiful woman. You're putting yourself in danger."

Nicholas cursed beneath his breath and hauled her against him. "This," he said, his voice cold, "is what I'm trying to make you see." Brutally, his mouth claimed hers. He felt her stiffen in surprise, her lips part in protest, and he deepened the kiss, thrusting his tongue violently between her teeth. Her slender fists beat at his chest, and she fought to pull away, but he only held her tighter . . . Mercilessly, he shoved her against the bulkhead, pinning her wrists above her head. One hand slid up her thigh to cup her bottom. He kissed her fiercely, savagely, without a thought for her pleasure . . .

"Now do you understand?" he asked, his voice ragged. "That's what will happen to you if you don't do what I say."

CAPTAIN'S BRIDE

KAT MARTIN

CHARTER/DIAMOND BOOKS, NEW YORK

CAPTAIN'S BRIDE

A Charter/Diamond Book / published by arrangement with
the author

PRINTING HISTORY
Charter/Diamond edition / September 1990

ISBN: 1-55773-382-1

Charter/Diamond Books are published by The Berkley Publishing
Group, 200 Madison Avenue, New York, New York 10016.
The name "CHARTER/DIAMOND" and its logo are trademarks
belonging to Charter Communications, Inc.

PRINTED IN THE UNITED STATES OF AMERICA

10 9 8 7 6 5 4 3 2 1

To my husband, Larry, who is always there for me.
And to the wonderful people of Charleston,
who, even in the face of disaster,
work to preserve their proud heritage
and welcome others to share it with them.

Chapter One

Charleston, South Carolina

April 2, 1840

The snap and crack of the lash, followed by a bone-chilling scream, echoed across the manicured lawns of the great plantation house.

Gloria Summerfield closed her eyes. Her slim fingers trembled as she tightened the sash of her ruffled silk faille wrapper and moved to the open window, gray with the first light of dawn. Outside, the birds had ceased their morning trill, which only amplified the quiet between the screams. Pulling the window closed, Glory secured the brass latch in an effort to block out the noises, but still she could hear them. Muffled now. Eerie, haunting sounds.

Her movements wooden, Glory seated herself before her gilt-framed mirror, determined to still her racing heart by immersing herself in the tasks of the day, but her hand shook fiercely. The silver brush seemed leaden as she fought to arrange her sleep-tangled hair. Pale blond wisps caught in the horsehair bristles, and it was all she could do to free the glistening strands. It will be over soon, she told herself. But when the screams didn't stop, Glory's fingers tightened around the handle of the brush and her usually bright eyes turned to angry blue flame. Whirling

around on the tapestry-covered stool, she jumped to her
feet and raced to the door, forgetting her slippers as she
hurried down the hall.

The sounds of her bare feet muffled by the thick Persian
carpet, Glory descended the two flights of stairs to the
cold marble floor of the foyer. She hurried past the elegant
receiving room, past the dining room with it's imported
crystal chandelier, and into her father's study, certain he
would already be hard at work on his ledgers. Instead, the
tall man stood staring out the window, hands clasped
tightly behind his back, a decided droop to his usually
straight wide shoulders.

"Papa, you've got to stop them," Glory pleaded, her
voice high and brittle. "They'll kill him if they keep this
up!" She slammed the heavy door behind her with a little
more force than she intended. As her father turned the full
force of his gaze on her, his stern features gentled for a
moment; then he stiffened, his face implacable once more.

"I wish it were that simple, Glory," he said. Kindly
blue eyes a shade lighter than her own seemed the only
softness to his features. "I'm afraid I have no more say in
the matter."

"Surely there's something you can do?"

"It's out of my hands, daughter. Ephram conspired with
a Negro from another plantation to run away. That makes
his crime punishable by the committee."

"But Willie is his brother. Surely that isn't the same
thing."

"It's still a conspiracy in the eyes of the law. Ephram
knew the chance he was taking when he left. The sentence
is fifty lashes and that's what he'll receive."

Glory gripped the back of her father's high-back chair,
fingers biting into the tufted brown leather. "Punishing a
man for wanting to be free isn't justice, Father. The man
is a human being. He deserves better treatment."

Her father left the window and strode the short distance
to her side. Lamplight shone on his once-blond hair, now
a glistening gray.

"We've argued this a thousand times," he said. "You know he's chattel in the eyes of the law."

Glory responded with silence, making her position clear.

"You like your life here," her father said. "At least admit that much. You like the parties and the gowns and the beaux."

How could she deny it? Of course she liked her life. What young woman wouldn't? "Those things are wonderful," she told him. "Summerfield Manor is my home. I love everything about it. But it isn't right for us to enjoy ourselves at the expense of others."

"Life isn't easy to understand, Glory. We all just do our best. Ephram had a good home here, far better than most. He shouldn't have run away."

"I know, Father, but slavery can't be the answer."

Julian Summerfield sighed. "I know how strongly you feel about this. I'm just grateful you have enough respect for me not to let the others know."

"Sometimes I think I should."

Julian lifted a lock of his daughter's pale blond hair and smoothed it between his fingers. "It'll all make sense when you grow up. In time, you'll get used to it."

"I *am* grown up," Glory said.

Her father only nodded. Stuffing his hands deep into the pockets of his gray serge morning coat, he turned back toward the window.

Glory thought he'd looked older for a moment, the lines of his face a little deeper than just the day before. Her father was a good man. Intelligent, considerate, and generous to a fault. Glory valued his judgment, and knew him to be correct in most things. But not in this. I'll never get used to human suffering, she thought. I don't ever want to.

Finally, the screaming ceased, the quiet almost as loud as the Negro's high-pitched screams.

Glory felt her tension ease. Life at Summerfield Manor would return to normal. Tomorrow evening she would at-

tend her gala nineteenth birthday ball. By then she would
have forgotten the terrible scene outside her window as
she'd taught herself to do. She would laugh and dance and
flirt—and enjoy herself immensely. She would remember
none of the cruelty of today.

But her heart would remember. Her heart would never
forget.

As if reading her thoughts, her father tilted her chin
with a callused hand. "It's over now," he said gently.
"Your mother has coffee in the dining room. Why don't
you bring us both a cup. After you're dressed, you can
help me with the ledgers."

Glory forced a smile she didn't feel. "All right, Father." With a breath of resignation, she swept from the
room.

Nicholas Blackwell swung his long lean legs over the
side of the bed and reached for his breeches, casually
draped over a spindle-legged chair.

"Surely you aren't leaving yet?" Lavinia Bond seemed
incredulous. "It's still early and Victor won't be home for
hours."

To Nicholas it seemed incredible he'd stayed through
the night. "Sorry, sweeting. Duty calls. I need to check
the off-loading down at the dock." Still sitting on the bed,
he pulled on his breeches, then grabbed up his shirt.

Lavinia ran her hands along the corded muscles of his
back and nipped playfully at his shoulder. "Are you sure
you won't change your mind?" Almost reverently, she
laced a finger through his curly black hair.

Nicholas turned to see one creamy breast spilling above
the sheet, the pink bud at the tip beckoning his touch.
There was no denying her body was beautiful and yet . . .

He scoffed at his lack of interest. A month ago he might
have been tempted to stay. Now he was eager to be gone.
He had sampled the lady's more than ample charms and
had not found them lacking. But, like all the others, she'd
become tiresome and demanding. He'd spent too much
time in Charleston lately. When he'd visited her for just

one night two or three times a year, he'd enjoyed her company—at least in bed. But his ship had docked in Charleston a week ago. And a week with Lavinia Bond was far too long.

"Not this time, sweet." He cupped her breast and kissed it quickly, then turned and pulled on his tall black boots. Lavinia slipped into her embroidered silk wrapper and walked him through the elegant single-house down the stairs to the front door.

"Will I see you before the party?" she asked, running her finger down his chest inside the front of his partially buttoned shirt. The stiff black bristles curled against her hand, evoking memories of their heated lovemaking. Lavinia licked her full red lips, a shade darker than her hair.

"What party?" Nicholas asked, his mind already on his duties aboard the ship.

"Why the Summerfields', of course. Julian's a friend of yours, isn't he?"

"It slipped my mind." But it hadn't. Julian had made a point of inviting him to spend a few days at Summerfield Manor, and Nicholas found himself actually looking forward to it. Though the older man had been his father's best friend, Nicholas had never visited the estate. But he'd been working hard these past few months; he deserved a rest. He needed one. The last thing he needed was more of Lavinia Bond.

"Do us both a favor, sweeting. Try to be a little discreet. I'd hate to have to shoot your husband just to satisfy his misplaced sense of honor."

"You don't think I'm worth it, darling?"

"I didn't say that, did I?" Nicholas opened the door. A heavy dray laden with barrels thundered down the narrow tree-lined street. Milk bottles rattled and clanked, and a stray cat hissed and rushed from beneath the wheels of a flatbed wagon. "Time to go, sweet."

Lavinia pulled his head down for a warm moist kiss, but his mind was already on the day ahead. He had more than enough to do if he intended to finish by tomorrow, in time for Julian's party.

"I'll let you know when Victor will be gone again," Lavinia called after him as he moved onto the street.

"You do that," he said. Without looking back, Nicholas strode down Tradd Street toward the three towering masts of the *Black Spider*, which swayed above the buildings along the Battery in the distance.

"How do I look, Plenty?" Glory took a last backward glance in her full-length cherrywood-framed mirror, doing a tiny pirouette that made the voluminous skirts of her new white organdy gown swirl around her.

Plenty pursed her thick lips as if she wasn't certain Glory would pass inspection. "Well . . ." She checked Glory from every angle, then her round face split into a wide bright grin. "You look lovely, chile. Jes' like always."

Glory leaned over to plant a light kiss on the old slave's cheek. "And you *always* say that. But—I have to believe, this time you're right!" Glory laughed, a soft tinkling sound, and postured in front of the mirror. "I shall absolutely devastate them this evening!"

Plenty chuckled, her vast girth rippling with the motion. "You always do!"

"I've got to go. I've kept them waiting just long enough." She snatched up her white silk fan, heavily beaded with the same seed pearls and silver thread that adorned her gown, and swept through the door. Strains of a Viennese waltz rose up from below as Glory descended the sweeping staircase from her third floor chamber to the second-floor ballroom. When she was halfway down, Benjamin Perry, a slim blond man in his early twenties spotted Glory and beamed up at her, delighted, it seemed, to be coming up from the foyer just in time to escort her into the ball.

"Hello, Ben." Glory extended a white-gloved hand, and the young man bowed over it with such reverence Glory feared he might lose his balance and topple over. She suppressed the tiny bubble of laughter that welled in her throat.

"Good evening, Miss Summerfield," Ben said. "You look absolutely"—his eyes dipped to the swells of her breasts, barely concealed by a sweep of organdy across the bodice of her gown—"beautiful." As he caught Glory's knowing glance, twin spots of color stained the youthful bloom of his cheeks. "Might I request the honor of escorting you?"

"Thank you, Ben, but Eric has already asked."

Eric Dixon—tall, brown-haired, and handsome—approached from a few feet away. He glared down at the younger man, but turned a warm smile on Glory. "I believe I have the honor, Miss Summerfield." Eric offered a frock-coated arm, his immaculate black evening clothes setting off his fine features, clear skin, and hazel eyes.

Ben Perry flushed and backed away. For a moment Glory wondered if Eric would deign to speak to Ben at all.

"Better luck next time, old boy," Eric called out as he led Glory toward the strains of the music.

The pair stepped into the ballroom, and the hum in the room dropped to a hushed murmur. A slight applause followed, which Glory acknowledged with a demure curtsy. Conversation and laughter resumed as Eric led Glory onto the gleaming black and white tiled floor. Other couples, all elegantly dressed, joined in, smiling at Glory and offering natal day felicitations.

It was Glory's night of nights. Her dance card had been filled long ago and the less fortunate young men seemed heartbroken when she turned them away. Most of them fawned over her, and Glory enjoyed every sugar-coated phrase, every platitude, every paean to her beauty. She whirled around the floor in the arms of one elegantly dressed gentleman after another, Eric always close at hand to offer a word of encouragement or see to her slightest wish.

Of all her suitors, Eric seemed the most likely. He was handsome and charming—and obsessively devoted to her. She wished she were in love with him, but then, maybe she was and didn't know it. She'd always imagined falling in love would be like falling off some towering peak, leaving her breathless, her heart in tatters, and her stomach doing tiny pirouettes. So far that had never happened.

Whatever did happen, Glory decided, life was a grand adventure. Each day brought her happiness and something new to learn. For Glory, life was as bright as a Christmas bauble—most of the time.

"Nicholas, my boy! Come in. Come in." Standing beneath the huge crystal chandelier in the foyer of the mansion, Julian Summerfield enveloped the tall lean sea captain in a warm embrace. "I'd near given you up."

Nicholas accepted the welcome, extending a sun-browned hand. "We had a few problems with the off-loading. Couldn't be helped." His own sure grip was matched in kind by the imposing man before him. "It's good to see you, Julian."

"I've been looking forward to this occasion for some time," the older man said. "Ezra, fetch the captain's bags up to his room and have one of the stable boys see to his horse."

The wizened old slave exerted a creaky bow. "Yes, sir, massa." Long, bent legs carried him out the carved double doors, between twin Doric columns, and down the broad steps to the sweeping gravel drive where Nicholas's hired saddle horse pawed the ground nervously. Dozens of horses, countless broughams, phaetons, and carriages, along with the noisy footmen, lined the drive.

"Come, my boy," Julian commanded, "let me introduce you." With a bulky arm across Nicholas's broad shoulders, Julian led him up the stairs to the ballroom. A frail brunette who, except for her still-dark hair, looked to be somewhat older than Julian stepped into their path. She snapped several commands to the servants, her posture erect, her mouth a narrow, uninviting line, then turned hard dark eyes to Nicholas.

"Louise!" Eyes wide, Julian appeared almost startled by her presence, but quickly regained his composure.

"May I present Captain Blackwell. Nicholas, my wife, Louise."

An announcement that the woman was really a pillar of salt could not have stunned Nicholas more. Louise Summerfield seemed the antithesis of her husband's warmth and charm. Cold, remote, and distant—that was Nicholas's first impression. For Julian's sake he prayed he was wrong.

"Mrs. Summerfield."

"It's a pleasure to meet you, Captain."

The words, said with little sincerity and even less enthusiasm, rang with a hollowness Nicholas could hardly have missed. "The pleasure is mine, madam."

"Julian," Louise said, "I'm afraid you must excuse me. I'm needed in the kitchen. The dinner preparations, you understand."

"Of course, my dear."

"Captain Blackwell," she addressed him, "I'm sure Julian and Glory will keep you well entertained. They enjoy this sort of frivolity much more than I. We'll have other opportunities to get acquainted during your stay."

"I look forward to it," Nicholas said, and wished he could mean it. He watched her leave, looking neither right nor left, saying little to the guests and they in turn saying little to her. She was not unattractive, Nicholas decided. Tall, willowy, fine-featured. But her pinched expression, the tightness around her mouth, made her seem older than her years.

"Louise doesn't care much for parties," Julian explained. "She usually spends the evening out in the kitchen or upstairs in her room."

"I see," Nicholas said, but he didn't. How could a man like Julian Summerfield, so vital and full of life, be married to a woman like that? Then again, why should it be such a surprise? His own father had married a woman much the same. Elizabeth St. John Blackwell, Nicholas's stepmother, was just as coldly aloof.

"You'll come to understand Louise after you get to

know her," Julian said, and Nicholas wondered if his thoughts had been that obvious.

Nicholas nodded. "I'm sure she has a lot on her mind this evening."

They moved into the main salon, where dancers twirled, dipped, and swayed beneath gleaming crystal chandeliers. Nicholas discovered he knew several of Julian's guests, and Julian introduced him to others. When Julian excused himself to speak with some banking associates from Charleston, Nicholas took the opportunity to stroll onto the balcony for a breath of fresh air. For the past three days a light spring rain had muddied the fields. The musky, earthen smell mingled with the sweet scent of honeysuckle, and Nicholas thought how much he had come to love the South.

Though he'd been born and raised a northerner, his business as a merchantman had made spending time in the South a necessity. His fleet of ships plied the coastal waters between Boston, New Orleans, and the Caribbean, transporting everything from cotton to molasses, shoes to pickled herring, venison hams to sperm candles. He loved the life of a seaman, loved the freedom, the exhilaration of fighting the elements, and the satisfaction of building his fortune.

"Nicholas!" Lavinia's syrupy voice drifted across the balcony.

How appropriate, he thought as she rushed to his side stirring a fresh wave of the honeysuckle scent. All sweetness and sugar and not a moment's regard for the man she had married. Yet how could he fault her when he'd been sharing her bed all week?

"Good evening, Lavinia, you look lovely." And she did. Her flame-red hair curled in delicate ringlets above her head, and her green eyes sparkled as bright as the emeralds at her throat. Even in the dim lamplight of the balcony, Nicholas could see the shimmering perfection of her skin, the fullness of her breasts.

"And you, Nicholas, look like one of Satan's own—

devilishly attractive. I blush just thinking of these past few days.''

"You never blushed in your life, Lavinia. Where's Victor? I think you had better go find him before he discovers you're missing.''

"Oh, bother. He never pays any attention to me at all.''

"I'm certain there are others inside who will.''

"Oh, Nicholas, you're no fun at all.''

One corner of his mouth lifted in what might have passed for a smile. "That isn't what you said the other night, sweeting.''

Lavinia batted her long black lashes and peeped at him over the top of her fan. With a mock bow, Nicholas excused himself and strolled back inside.

He was leaning against the doorjamb, one long leg crossed over the other, when Julian walked up beside him. Nicholas barely heard him. For the past few minutes, his gaze had been following a golden-haired woman gowned in white. No, not golden, he decided. Flaxen. Flaxen-haired. Until tonight Nicholas hadn't understood the difference. Her skin was the color of day-old cream, rich and smooth, with just the hint of an apricot blush. The radiant creature dancing in the arms of a handsome smiling young man was one of the most beautiful women Nicholas had ever seen.

"I see you've discovered my daughter,'' Julian said as he approached, his voice laced with pride and the hint of a smile.

"Your *daughter*!'' Nicholas nearly choked on the word. For the past five minutes he'd been scheming how to bring the girl to his bed, conjuring images of her naked body writhing beneath him while he trailed warm kisses along the curve of her neck. Now he felt a wave of guilt bordering on sacrilege.

"My pride and joy would be more apt,'' Julian said. "Lovely, isn't she?''

"Exquisite,'' Nicholas agreed, continuing to watch her graceful movements on the dance floor.

"I'm glad you approve. Glory is one of the reasons I invited you here."

"Oh?" Nicholas forced his attention to the powerful man beside him.

"My daughter is nineteen today. She's all grown up. Ready to make a life of her own. In fact, she should have been married before now."

"I'm certain she hasn't lacked for suitors."

"Quantity is not the problem, I assure you. It's quality I'm worried about." Julian glanced around to be certain they had the privacy he needed. "I planned to discuss this with you tomorrow. But I think maybe now is the time."

Nicholas's curiosity was piqued as he watched his friend's blue eyes turn serious.

"You see, I want my daughter to be happy in her marriage," Julian told him. "I want her to love and respect her mate. I want her to marry a man who is her equal."

"Surely among all her admirers there must be someone."

"Oh, they're all good boys . . . men, really. Each would surely give her a good home, treat her well. I've spoiled her terribly, pampered her in the extreme. Any of her suitors would be willing to go right on spoiling her, just as I have. I have no worries about that. But Glory has much more to offer than a pretty face."

Nicholas couldn't have agreed more. His practiced eye measured the gentle curves of her elegant figure, the full breasts swelling above her organdy gown.

"It wouldn't be long," Julian was saying, "before she'd have any one of her current suitors whipped into a cowering mass of jelly."

Nicholas felt the pull of a smile as Julian pointed to the group of admirers crowding around his daughter.

"Just look at them, Nicholas. Glory treats them as if they were pets, not men she is considering for marriage. What kind of life would she have? I want Glory to marry someone who is man enough to handle her." He looked hard at Nicholas. "I thought maybe you'd be interested."

"Me!" Nicholas's dark features blanched. "You would

consider *me* for your daughter's hand? You know my reputation, Julian. Most fathers would call me out if I so much as got near their daughters, let alone proposed marriage.''

''With your wealth and position, I hardly think so. But then, I've always seen more in you than you see in yourself. You're a good man, Nicholas. You'd make a fine husband.''

''I'm flattered, Julian. More than you'll ever know. But I'm not the kind of man to settle down. I live my life from day to day. I'm at sea most of the time. What kind of life would that be for a woman?''

''You don't have to spend your time at sea. We both know that. You have several estates up north. It's time you thought of marriage and family.''

''And your daughter thinks this is a good idea, too, I suppose.''

''My daughter would be furious if she knew I even mentioned the word 'marriage.' Getting Glory to the altar would be your job. I just wanted you to know that if you're interested, you have my blessing.''

''I've never been *interested* in marriage. You above all others should know that.''

''The past doesn't always repeat itself, Nicholas. Just because your father's marriages failed doesn't mean yours would.''

''And what of yours, Julian? Are you happily married?''

A frown creasing his brow, Julian sighed and looked away. ''My marriage to Louise was arranged. It was never right for either of us. But I did love someone once.'' For a moment he was lost in the past, his eyes distant. ''If Hannah could have been my wife, I'd have been the happiest man alive.'' The frown faded as he remembered those happy times, hours spent in front of the tiny fire in their small cabin, Hannah curled beside him, or the two of them lying in their old iron bed. When a laughing couple jostled him from behind, his thoughts reluctantly returned to the present, his attention to Nicholas. ''Give it some thought, my boy. But for God's sake don't mention it to Glory or Louise. I'd have my head taken off.''

Nicholas fought the pull of a smile, and instead arched the black slash of his brow. ''Your secret's safe with me. And again I thank you for the compliment, but I'm afraid I'm a dedicated bachelor. Spoiled young virgins are not my style.''

Julian smiled knowingly. ''Come along. I think it's time you met the guest of honor.''

Chapter Two

Julian skirted the dancers and headed toward the far corner of the room, where Glory was holding court. Nicholas had to admit she was a beauty, perfection in every way. The kind of woman who excited him in bed but elsewhere bored him to distraction.

He eyed the group of well-dressed men surrounding her. Her simpering beaux irritated him. Nicholas found it humiliating for a man to make a fool of himself over a woman—*any* woman.

Watching Gloria Summerfield being fawned over, virtually worshiped by her young admirers, raised the hackles at the back of Nicholas's neck. She would probably turn out just like Lavinia and all the other women he'd known: unfeeling, self-centered, with the morals of an anchor rat. He found himself determined to dislike her even before they were introduced.

Nicholas brushed past clusters of elegantly gowned ladies as he followed Julian around the room. He didn't miss their appreciative glances or the invitation in several pairs of dark-fringed eyes. As the two men neared the corner of the room, most of the young men stepped away from the girl gowned in white, and a last stern glance from Julian sent the handsome brown-haired man, who seemed to be the girl's most ardent suitor, scurrying to the punch bowl.

"Glory, I'd like you to meet Captain Blackwell. Nicholas, my daughter, Glory."

Glory extended a slim hand, and Nicholas Blackwell bowed slightly, bringing her gloved fingers to his lips. Though the gesture appeared gallant, it somehow lacked sincerity, and Glory wondered why.

"It is a pleasure to meet you, sir," she said, meaning it. Her father had been praising the virtues of Nicholas Blackwell for as long as Glory could remember.

"The pleasure is all mine, Miss Summerfield, I assure you," the captain said. His dark eyes roamed over her in a manner that sent bright color to Glory's cheeks.

"Father has spoken of you often," she said, her hand still in his, "always with glowing accolades. But I must confess, Captain, I expected a much older man."

"Then I'm sorry to disappoint you," he said. And Glory knew without doubt the captain knew he hadn't. Nicholas Blackwell was rakishly handsome, with angular features, curly black hair, and a swarthy complexion that gave him a slightly foreign appearance, though Glory knew him to be of English and French Creole descent. His black evening clothes fit his tall frame perfectly, outlining broad shoulders and tapering to narrow hips and long lean legs.

"If you two don't mind," Julian said, "I believe I need a drink. Maybe Glory could find it in her heart to grace you with a dance, Nicholas."

"I'm sure Miss Summerfield's heart is already overburdened," he said dryly, "what with every dandy from here to New Orleans simpering at her feet."

Glory bristled. Her father chuckled softly and walked away, leaving her to duel with the handsome captain alone. Still feeling the bite of his words and rising to the challenge—the first she'd had in what seemed like ages—Glory turned the full measure of her charm on Nicholas Blackwell, expecting him at any moment to crumble and join the others in their adulation.

"You speak of my admirers, Captain, yet it is you who have been ravaging the hearts of the ladies this evening.

Every woman in the room has been watching you; I've even caught myself a time or two.''

"Oh, really?'' He quirked a sleek black brow. "I can't imagine when you'd have had time.''

Glory refused to respond to the gibe. The captain might be a little more sophisticated than her other beaux, but he was still a man, and when it came to handling men . . . well, she hadn't found one yet she couldn't manage. "I'm beginning to think you don't approve of a woman being courted, Captain,'' she said with a pout as she lowered her lashes.

"What I don't approve of, Miss Summerfield, is a woman who leads men to believe she feels something for them when in truth she is merely using them to feed her vanity. I had hoped for more from the daughter of a man like Julian Summerfield.''

Glory felt the high color in her cheeks, which were suffused with an angry heat. *Why, the insolent ass,* she fumed. No longer enjoying the game, she turned toward Eric Dixon, who had been awaiting any indication his attention would be welcome.

Glory forced a smile in his direction, and Eric stepped forward, a possessive look in his hazel eyes.

"Eric Dixon,'' Glory said coolly, "this is Captain Blackwell. The captain's an old friend of Father's.''

"Yes, I can see exactly how *old* he is.''

Glory had told Eric of the captain's forthcoming visit, portraying him as a kindly older man whom her father virtually revered. No wonder that image didn't match the *other* stories she'd heard! The tall, dark-haired captain with the cool gray eyes was a far cry from the kindly middle-aged sea dog she'd expected.

Eric shook hands with an obvious lack of enthusiasm, and Nicholas smiled thinly, barely lifting one corner of his mouth.

"I believe this dance is ours, Glory,'' Eric said, drawing her toward the floor.

Nicholas stepped between them. "I'm sure, Mr. Dixon, since you spend so much time with Miss Summerfield, you won't mind giving up a dance for an old friend of the family.'' He emphasized the word ''old,'' and Glory secretly fumed. The man wasn't much older than Eric, who was twenty-seven, though the captain had a worldliness it took most men years to acquire.

Before Glory could protest, Nicholas Blackwell had gripped her wrist and led her onto the floor. His other hand settled on her waist with a casual possessiveness Glory found infuriating. It was all she could do to control her temper as he stepped into the strains of the waltz and whirled her unerringly around the dance floor.

''You're beautiful when you're angry,'' he said, ''but then, you were just as lovely before.''

''Surely, Captain, you can come up with something more original than that.''

''Temper, temper,'' he baited. ''You wouldn't want one of your lapdogs to think I've insulted you. He might call me out and wind up getting himself killed.''

Remembering whispered gossip about the captain's skill with the pistol, Glory stiffened and tried to pull away, but Nicholas only tightened his hold.

''My father may find you a paragon of virtue, Captain Blackwell, but I heard you were a rake and a rogue. I just didn't expect you to prove it so quickly.''

''And I heard, Miss Summerfield, you were pampered and spoiled and in need of a man who could take you down a peg or two.''

If he hadn't been holding her, Glory might have stumbled. It was all she could do to suppress the murderous glint in her bright blue eyes.

''Smile,'' he said. ''Remember your lapdogs.''

''Let me go,'' she said through gritted teeth. ''How Father could be so fond of you is beyond me.''

''We'll finish the dance, Miss Summerfield; then I'll escort you back to your . . . friends.''

''You are the most despicable . . .''

For the first time Nicholas Blackwell allowed himself a genuine smile. ''You and I are going to get along just fine,'' he said. A wave of relief swept over him, as welcome as an early spring rain. He had been drawn to the young woman from the first moment he saw her, even more so now that he had held her in his arms. If she had warmed to him in the least, he would have been hard pressed to stay away from her. Though he tried his best to keep them at bay, thoughts of the graceful blonde warming his bed still danced at the edge of his mind.

The girl was Julian Summerfield's daughter. The only way Nicholas could bed her would be to marry her—and that he would not consider. It was better she loathe him, stay as far away from him as possible.

The dance ended and Nicholas returned Glory to Eric Dixon's care. Her cheeks glowed with anger, but her demeanor remained courteous. She had taken his warning to heart. At least she wasn't quite the unfeeling tease she appeared.

"Thank you for the dance, Miss Summerfield," Nicholas said with a hint of sarcasm.

"My pleasure, Captain Blackwell," she replied with an equal lack of sincerity.

With a last appreciative glance, Nicholas turned on his heel and strode toward the gentlemen's bar. The syrupy voice of Lavinia Bond trailed him across the room.

"Good Lord, Glory, who was that man?" Miriam Allstor, Glory's best friend, hurried up beside her. Glory checked her appearance in the gilt-framed mirror in her chamber and pinned back a stray curl that had tumbled loose during a schottische she had danced in the arms of Jack Flanagan, another of her suitors.

"That's Captain Blackwell, father's friend."

"My, God! No wonder they say he's a rogue."

"He's also an arrogant jackass," Glory said, her temper heating up again. "The man is no gentleman, I can tell you that."

"He made advances to you! Oh, Glory, how exciting! I'd simply swoon if he did that to me!" Miriam's green eyes rolled skyward at the mere thought.

"He did no such thing. In fact, he doesn't even like me.

He thinks I lead men on just for my—Oh, never mind what he thinks. Captain Blackwell is an arrogant fool.''

"Maybe. But he's certainly an attractive man—in a wolf-ish sort of way.'' She grinned mischievously.

The girls left Glory's chamber and returned to the landing just outside the second-floor ballroom. Miriam located Nicholas Blackwell leaning against the far wall of the room in conversation with Lavinia Bond and several other married ladies, a bored expression on his face.

"Lavinia certainly seems to like him,'' Miriam said.

Glory followed the line of Miriam's gaze. "Well, I don't. I hope Father enjoys his company, because I certainly don't intend to entertain the man.''

Miriam leaned over to whisper in Glory's ear. "I heard a rumor the captain was seen leaving Lavinia's house early yesterday morning. Can you imagine?''

Glory's head snapped up. "Surely you're mistaken.''

"I didn't see him. Willard Darcy did. Willard told Sarah Hashim and Sarah told me.''

"You shouldn't pay attention to gossip, Miriam,'' Glory said. "Besides, I don't believe Father would invite a man like that to our home.''

"Men don't think like we do, Glory. I know you're a little naive, but—''

"I think we should change the subject, Miriam. Captain Blackwell is our guest,'' she said with feigned propriety, but felt a surge of temper as she watched Lavinia leaning over him, giving him an unfettered view of her lush bosom, and added, "even if he is a . . . *cocksman*!'' Relishing the shocked expression on her friend's cherubic face, Glory stifled a grin. "I'd better go now. Mark Williams has this dance. He'll be looking for me.'' With a swish of organdy skirts, Glory left the hallway—and her friend Miriam staring after her in wide-eyed astonishment.

At supper Glory was seated beside Captain Blackwell, with Eric Dixon on her right. The captain barely spoke to her. Most of his conversation was spent on Alicia Townsend, an attractive widow from Goose Creek whose late husband had been a close friend of Glory's father. Alicia was quietly attractive, with an elegant figure and thick dark brown hair. She was intelligent and a good conversationalist. Glory found herself straining to hear what Alicia had to say to Nicholas Blackwell. Worst of all, she found herself slightly pricked that he was paying the pretty brunette so much attention.

"Is something wrong, Glory?" Eric asked when the waiter lifted her untouched bowl of she-crab soup.

"What? Oh, no, Eric. I'm just not very hungry." The sound of the widow's soft laughter set her even more on edge, and Glory wondered if it really was her vanity making her so angry. Could one man's lack of attention upset her so? Glory didn't want to believe that about herself, but what other reason could there be?

Picking up her silver fork, she attacked her salad greens with a little extra zeal. Whatever there was about the infamous Captain Blackwell, Gloria Summerfield would not be daunted. She intended to ignore him, pay him not the slightest heed.

That was no easy task when his solid thigh inadvertently pressed against her, or when the deep cadence of his voice in whispered conversation with the widow drifted to her ears.

Morning at Summerfield Manor was a joy to the senses. Nicholas awoke to the fragrance of azaleas floating through the open windows, the heat of the sun on his cheek. He stretched and rolled to his side, meaning to caress the warm body next to him but, with a start that erased the last of his hazy sleep, realized he slept alone. No flaxen-haired beauty nestled beside him—she was only a dream. With his mouth curved in a rueful half-smile, Nicholas shoved back the satin cover and swung his long legs from the huge four-poster rice bed onto the floor. A thick Tartan carpet protected his bare feet from the coolness of the wide oak planks beneath him.

After pouring water from the blue porcelain pitcher into the basin on a marble-topped bureau, Nicholas performed his usual morning ablutions, dressed in riding breeches and a crisp linen shirt, and headed downstairs.

Glory Summerfield, in a light green chambray gown, was seated in the dining room beside her father, their discussion animated until Nicholas walked into the room.

"Nicholas." Julian stood up and indicated a seat across from Glory. Louise Summerfield was nowhere to be seen. "Plenty," Julian beckoned, "you may serve now." The buxom black woman swayed precariously, her pendulous breasts swinging with her jaunty gait as she moved toward the door to the pantry.

"Yes, sir, Massa Julian," the heavy slave called over her shoulder.

"Good morning, Julian, Miss Summerfield," Nicholas greeted them as he seated himself before an elegant service of porcelain and silver.

"Good morning, Captain." Bright blue eyes met his boldly and staunchly refused to glance away.

"Bah," Julian said, swallowing a sip of his rich-smelling coffee while a tall thin Negro poured Nicholas a cup. "I'm sure my daughter prefers to dispense with formality between friends. Don't you, my dear?" He shot her a hard glance.

"Oh, course, Father. Captain, you may call me Gloria."

Nicholas almost smiled. "I'm honored, Glory," he said pointedly and saw warm color brighten her cheeks to the same soft coral shade as her lips.

Julian grinned broadly and took another sip of his coffee. "Something's come up this morning, Nicholas. I'm afraid I won't be able to show you the plantation as I had planned. My daughter has volunteered for the task. I was certain you wouldn't mind."

Touché, Nicholas thought. Julian always was a sly old dog, but this time his efforts might prove his undoing. Sending the fox to guard the chickens was always a risky move.

"You're certain I won't be interrupting your plans?" Nicholas directed the question to Glory.

"Well, I had planned to—"

"Nonsense!" Julian cut in. "Of course you won't."

Nicholas fought the pull of a smile. The thin slave returned to the dining room with silver platters filled to overflowing: succulent honeyed ham, fried potatoes, fluffy scrambled eggs, and fresh hot biscuits. Porcelain gravy boats ran with thick red-eye gravy, and a big bowl steamed with grits.

"Dig in, my boy," Julian said with a satisfied smile, and Nicholas wasted no time in doing just that. Glory only picked at her food and said little. When the meal ended, Julian excused himself and so did Glory. She would meet Nicholas out at the stables.

Nicholas wandered the grounds of the plantation absorbed in the hustle and bustle around him. Women in bright-colored skirts, their kinky hair hidden beneath equally bright-colored turbans, chattered noisily while tiny children played at their feet. Some hooked laundry from iron cauldrons of boiling water with long wooden poles, while others dug in the huge vegetable garden that ran beside the main barn.

Nicholas passed through the dairy, where two Negro women butchered lambs, two more churned butter, and a young boy forked hay into the manger. Even after his lengthy perusal, Nicholas reached the stable ahead of Glory.

A barrel-chested, mud-faced Negro stood ready to serve him. "Massa Julian say you ride Hannibal," the man said. "He a mighty fine horse. One o' the massa's favorites." He sauntered to a back stall, his heavy-legged stride unhurried, and returned with a big black stallion. A second trip brought a dancing blood-bay gelding with four white-stockinged feet.

"This be Raider. He for the missy."

"They're both fine animals," Nicholas said, running his hand along Hannibal's sleek black withers. "Julian always did have an eye for horseflesh."

"I'm glad you approve, Captain," Glory called out from the doorway. "I take it you like horses."

"As a matter of fact, I do."

Glory eyed him thoughtfully. He looked exceedingly handsome in his snug-fitting breeches and billowy white linen shirt. At her father's urging—and for his sake alone, she told herself—she was determined to make a fresh start with the captain this morning. The fact that he liked horses at least gave them something in common.

She took the big gelding's reins in a slim gloved hand. "Thank you, Zeke," she said, smiling warmly at the thickset slave. "Looks as if you're taking very good care of them." The man beamed with pride as she turned her attention to Nicholas. "Horses are one of my passions in life," she told him, patting the bay's neck. "I've loved them since I was a little girl. Father had me riding almost before I could walk."

Glory smiled up at Nicholas, the first real smile she'd graced him with since Julian had introduced them. Her eyes sparkled and her cheeks bloomed, and Nicholas began to understand why so many men had fallen prey to her charms.

"Hannibal," she continued, "the horse you're riding, is a direct descendant of the Godolphin Arabian. His sons have raced and won at Plaquemine and Donaldsonville. I believe he could have been a champion—he has the stamina and the speed—but Father wanted him kept for breeding."

Nicholas arched a brow. "Your father said you were more than a pretty face."

"*Did* he?" This time she smiled mischievously, and Nicholas felt his resolve begin to slip. "What else did he say?"

"He said you'd probably turn your husband into a cowering mass of jelly. I believe those were his words."

Glory laughed aloud, a sparkling, crystalline sound Nicholas found enchanting. Sunlight streamed through the open barn door, lighting several tendrils of pale hair that had escaped from the smart chignon at the back of her head. A dark green veiled riding hat, which matched her habit, sat at a jaunty angle atop her head. Tiny kidskin boots peeped from beneath the hem of her skirt.

"Sometimes Father gets a little carried away."

Her anger was gone today and though Nicholas knew he should rekindle the flame, he simply hadn't the heart. He was entitled to a few hours of pleasure, he told himself. When the time was right, he'd spark her anger again, keep her at bay. For now he would indulge himself.

"Since we seem to be making better progress this morning than we did last night," he said, "I propose we continue our truce and enjoy the day."

"I believe that's a splendid idea, Captain." She smiled again, caught up in the excitement of the ride, perhaps, or the warmth of the sunshine after three days of rain.

Once the black groom had led the horses out of the barn, Nicholas lifted Glory into her sidesaddle, noting the way her tiny waist fit neatly into his hands, and handed up her riding crop. Hannibal, the stallion he would ride, pranced and pawed the earth in anticipation.

"Glory, chile!"

Nicholas glanced up as the buxom Negro woman from the house called to her mistress and waddled toward the barn carrying a wicker basket in her plump hands.

"I done made you and the cap'n some lunch. Cap'n need to keep up his strength if'n he's gonna ride with you." The old woman winked at Nicholas and grinned broadly.

"Thank you, Plenty," Glory said.

Nicholas packed the lunch in a leather bag the big Negro named Zeke found for him, tied it behind the saddle, and mounted. Glory set her booted heel to the bay's side and the horse broke into a trot. Nicholas caught them easily, the big black settling into a mile-eating gait.

They rode the muddy lanes in silence, enjoying the sun, the brisk morning air, and the smell of magnolias. Negro slaves worked among the rows of newly planted cotton, weeding and thinning, some of them singing softly as they worked.

"Summerfield Manor has sixty-five hundred acres," Glory told him. "Twenty-five hundred in cotton, twelve hundred in rice, three hundred in grain for our own use, and the rest is left fallow. Father feels it keeps the land from losing its strength."

"And I thought you only had time for your beaux."

Glory laughed. "I like helping my father."

They rode for miles along the lane, beneath sweeping oaks draped with whispy strands of moss, along marshy waterways, through dense yellow and loblolly pine forests. When they came to the rice fields along the river, Glory described the planting procedures and again Nicholas was impressed with her intelligence.

"After the land is cleared, a complex series of trenches called quarter divides and cross ditches is constructed to secure an even flow of water over each section during the growing season. We use floodgates to control the tides." She pointed toward the end of one of the fields. "You can see one over there."

Nicholas followed the line of her slender arm, her gloved finger indicating a massive wooden gate.

"To flood the field the operator opens the gate and the water rushes in. It's let off at the ebb tide."

"Sounds complicated."

"Most of the fields have already been planted, but if you look through the oaks, you can see some of the mules at work. The ground is so soggy they have to wear huge boots—kind of like snowshoes for mud. A square piece of heavy leather on the bottom, tied over the feet with raw-hide thongs."

Nicholas watched her closely, noticing the way she seemed to come alive as she spoke. "I thought women were supposed to run the household on a plantation."

"My mother takes care of all that. Actually I have very few responsibilities. If father didn't let me help with the ledgers, I'm sure I'd go out of my mind with boredom."

"I should think with all your admirers, you'd have more than enough to keep you occupied."

She shot him a fiery glance, but he looked as if he

meant no insult, so Glory decided to let the comment pass. "I enjoy frivolity, as my mother calls it, just as much as any other woman. But I also enjoy the challenge of working with Father. I'm really only involved in the book work—profit margins, buying and selling, things like that— but I enjoy it just the same." The captain only nodded. He seemed to be sizing her up, weighing her words, and Glory wondered at his thoughts.

The morning progressed far differently than Glory expected. At first the captain was attentive, bantering lightly back and forth with her. Though he rarely smiled, he seemed to be relaxed and enjoying himself. As the hours passed, Nicholas became more and more subdued, and Glory wondered at the cause.

"Look! There's a big blue heron!" She pointed toward the edge of the rice field. "And there's a snowy egret sitting on his left." As she finished speaking, she caught a movement just outside her line of vision. Turning, she spotted Jonas Fry, the head overseer, in what appeared to be a heated conversation with one of the slaves, a slender youth she recognized as a Negro her father had just purchased off the dock in Charleston.

"Would you excuse me a moment, Captain?" she said. "I believe I've forgotten something."

Before he could answer, she whirled the bay and headed toward the overseer. Just as she feared, his face was puffed up with anger. At any moment he would resort to the whip he carried at his waist, and the slender youth would suffer the biting sting.

"What seems to be the problem, Jonas?" Glory asked as she reached them. The boy glanced up at her with huge frightened eyes.

"Nothin' for you to fret about, Miss Glory. Boy's never planted before. He's thick between the ears and clumsy as an ox. Couple of good strokes'll set him to payin' closer attention." It was obvious by the overseer's even angrier expression the boy would suffer for certain now. She probably shouldn't have interfered, but it was too late to back down. She decided on a change of tactic.

"Oh, Jonas," Glory said, smiling at him sweetly, "I know he probably needs a lesson, but I do wish you'd let me borrow him. I forgot my oilcloth, and the ground is so wet that I'm sure to ruin my habit."

For a moment Jonas wavered, thrown off by the mistress's dazzling smile; then his dark look brightened, and his puffy face split into a satisfied grin. "It's a four-mile walk to the main house and back. Long walk for an oilcloth. But if that'll make you happy, Miss Glory, it'll be my pleasure to send this here nigger to do yer biddin'."

Glory felt a hint of annoyance at the man's coarse language, then a surge of relief. She smiled down at the overseer as if he'd had no choice but to gratify the silly whim of the master's daughter.

Glory was feeling secretly pleased with herself when Nicholas Blackwell rode up beside her. It was obvious from his disapproving scowl he'd overhead the conversation. For a moment Glory regretted her impulsiveness. The Captain already believed she was pampered and spoiled; now he would be more convinced than ever. Then Glory remembered the huge round eyes of the young Negro boy about to receive the lash and lifted her chin in defiance. Why should she care what Nicholas Blackwell thought!

Chapter Three

"Have him leave the oilcloth on the old log up on Honeysuckle Knoll," she told the overseer. "And, Jonas"—she batted her thick dark lashes in his direction—"thank you so very much."

Nicholas made no comment, just sat a little straighter in his saddle, his mouth set in a thin, disapproving line. They rode the lane in silence, Glory wishing she could explain, but refusing to give the captain the satisfaction of knowing she cared. If he wanted to think the worst, then let him!

"Are you getting hungry?" she asked after nearly an hour had passed.

"Think your *oilcloth* will have arrived?" he responded dryly.

"If it hasn't, I'll just have to manage somehow." Nicholas looked at her askance, and she stiffened at his continued withdrawal. "It'll be drier up on Honeysuckle Knoll," she told him.

Saddle leather creaked in rhythm to the horses' steady gait as they rode along the path, Glory determined to enjoy the warm spring sun, Nicholas growing more solemn by the moment.

"My brother and I used to come up this way when we were children," she said, hoping to draw him into conversation and make him forget the scene at the rice field.

"One of our tutors, Mr. Eisner, loved the out-of-doors. He would tell us the names of the different plants and animals we passed along the way."

"I didn't know you had a brother," Nicholas said.

And neither does anyone else, thanks to Mother. "He's away at school in the North. He wants to be a botanist. Mr. Eisner's lectures made quite an impression on him."

Again Nicholas nodded, but he seemed preoccupied. He cut a handsome figure astride the big black, and for the first time in years, Glory felt a little self-conscious. "You're a very good horseman, Captain."

"Thank you," he replied. "So are you. I wouldn't have expected a woman of your . . . *tastes* to enjoy so strenuous a sport."

Glory ignored the barb. "I never was much of a tomboy, but riding is like nothing else. Don't you agree?"

"What? Oh, yes, yes, I do."

Glory quietly seethed at his lack of interest. Why was she rambling on like an idiot when the captain was obviously bored with her company? For the past half-hour the only time he'd looked at her was when he thought she *wasn't* looking at him.

"Captain, if you'd rather return to the house—"

"That might be a good idea, Miss Summerfield. I—"

"Glory," she corrected.

"Glory." He reined the black to a halt and turned to face her. She sat astride her big bay like a countess, wisps of flaxen hair glistening in the sun. Again Nicholas felt the strain in his breeches that had plagued him off and on for the past two hours. "I'm afraid I'm a little preoccupied with my ship," he lied, then combined the words with an element of truth. "I probably shouldn't have left Charleston."

"Father says you work too hard," Glory said.

"Maybe so, but I think you may be right about returning early."

Glory fought a surge of temper. "I *am* beginning to tire," she told him, furious that he'd enjoyed the morning not nearly as much as she. "And there are several *important* matters I should attend to this afternoon."

It was clear she felt *he* was *not* one of them, and Nicholas fought a surge of anger. If she were anyone but Julian's daughter, he'd have spent the morning charming the spoiled little chit into his bed. As it was, all he'd managed to do was give himself a case of the discomforts. And he wouldn't be able to find ease for that until he returned to Charleston. Even Lavinia Bond was beginning to look good.

"Tell you what, Captain," Glory said as she turned her mount around on the path. "I'll bet I can beat you home. There's a shortcut we can take through the fields if you think you're up to a few hedges."

"I don't think that's a good idea. The ground's too muddy. Someone might get hurt."

"You're not afraid you'll lose, are you?"

"Look, Miss Summerfield, as long as you're with me, you're my responsibility. We'll go back the way we came."

"Father told me a little about you, Captain, but he failed to mention you were a coward." With that she spun the big bay and dug her small heels into its flanks. The horse leaped into a gallop, then settled into a low-necked run.

Nicholas cursed beneath his breath and urged the black stallion forward. At first he pressed the animal hard to catch the bay. Then the black picked up the challenge and hurled himself faster, hoofbeats thundering against the muddy earth.

Spoiled and pampered, he thought. Not a moment's concern for anything other than her whims. She'd probably break her fool neck, and Julian would never forgive him. He leaned over the black's mane, urging him faster, hoping to catch the girl before she reached the first hedge looming in the distance. As fast as the animal ran, Hannibal had gained only half the distance Nicholas needed. Glory sailed over the hedge, her body parallel with the neck of the bay, taking the jump with just as much grace as she'd shown on the ballroom floor.

Nicholas cursed her for the little fool she was, took the

hedge behind her, and continued his pursuit. She was still a few feet ahead when they approached a split-rail fence near one of the rice fields. As they drew near, the ground grew even soggier and Nicholas still wasn't close enough to stop her.

Just as she sized up the jump, the bay slipped in the marshy soil. The horse made the fence, but his landing was less than perfect, and Glory nearly pitched over the animal's head. She regained her balance and pulled the horse to a halt just the other side of the fence, jumping down from her sidesaddle in a single graceful motion.

Relieved but furious, Nicholas allowed the stallion to take the fence at his ease, then halted the animal on the opposite side. Glory stood ankle deep in the rich dark mud, examining the bay's foreleg, the hem of her skirt black and dirty.

Nicholas worked a muscle in his jaw, barely controlling his temper. Dismounting, he stalked to where the horse stood in the mud whinnying softly, and examined the leg. "I hope you're satisfied."

For a moment she looked up at him contritely, then she stiffened her spine. "How was I supposed to know the field had been flooded? I've taken this jump a hundred times."

"You're supposed to use that pretty little head of yours," Nicholas told her, his voice hard. "You're supposed to know better than to race across a muddy field!"

"I just wanted to . . ." *Teach you a lesson,* she thought. "Have some fun," she said. "I didn't mean for him to get hurt, and I'll thank you not to lecture me." As if to emphasize her point, Glory slapped her riding crop against the fullness of her skirts, her blue eyes snapping fire.

"You're willful and spoiled," Nicholas said, his temper barely in check. "Someone ought to take that riding crop to your backside."

Glory's cheeks flamed. "*You're* certainly not man enough to do it!"

Nicholas straightened, his hard look boring into her. "I think you would find I'm man enough, Miss Summerfield.

But I have neither the time nor the inclination to give young ladies lessons in deportment.'' Ducking beneath his horse's neck, he jammed a booted foot in the metal stirrup and swung a long leg over the low back of his saddle. With his mouth curved in a thin, mirthless smile, he reined the black away.

''Where do you think you're going?'' Glory called after him, incredulous. ''You can't just leave me out here!''

''Can't I?'' Nicholas threw back over his shoulder.

''But my horse . . . he's injured. I can't ride him like this!''

''Then I suggest you start walking.'' Nicholas set the black into a leisurely canter.

''Damn you, Nicholas Blackwell! Damn you!''

Nicholas whirled the big black and fixed his gaze on Glory, pinning her with his eyes. ''Keep that up, Miss Summerfield, and I may just come back and give you that lesson we discussed.'' Even at a distance he could see her eyes go wide. She didn't say another word, just started leading the bay through the muddy field toward the lane in the distance. Nicholas smiled to himself. He wouldn't mind giving her lessons—in bed, where they'd do the most good. Since that was not an option, maybe the long walk back to the plantation would teach her to mind her manners.

The trip back home seemed interminable. Glory fumed all the way.

She'd been right about Captain Blackwell in the first place. He was nothing but an overbearing, arrogant ass! How dare he leave her stranded out here! No gentleman would ever treat a lady that way. But then, Captain Blackwell was obviously no gentleman! Except for the first few hours, he hadn't even tried to make pleasant conversation. The man could not have cared less about what she had to say. He was just . . . just . . . *despicable*. That's what he was!

When she finally reached the main road, Glory hailed a wagon loaded with hay, which was headed toward the house. The old slave at the reins jumped down to help her onto the wooden seat, and Glory graciously let him fuss over her. Her feet ached, her ankles were rubbed raw from walking in the deep black mud, and her riding skirt hung in tatters from pushing her way through shrubs and vines she'd intended to jump. Again she damned Nicholas Blackwell. Why hadn't her father warned her about the man?

"Papa, how could you?" Glory railed, calling him by the childhood name she used whenever she lost her temper or became upset. "Surely you had some idea what he was like!" In her stockinged feet, she stood in his study in front of his massive rosewood desk, mud still dripping from the hem of her riding skirt.

"Tell me again, *what* exactly it is Nicholas has done? Did he make advances? Did he force himself on you?" She could hear the hint of amusement in his voice.

"Of course not! I told you what he did. He *left* me out there. He made me walk all the way back to the house!"

"Because you'd acted exceedingly foolhardy and endangered not only your own life and his but also the lives of the animals. Those are valuable horses, Glory. They deserve better treatment and you know it."

"I refuse to discuss this any further." Glory drew herself up to her full height which was quite impressive compared to most of the women she knew. "Nicholas Blackwell is a cad and a bounder. I wouldn't be surprised if Miriam is right and he is . . . *involved* with Lavinia Bond!"

"Glory!" Her father leaped from his chair.

"It's all right, Father. I'm a grown woman. I understand these things."

"What things?" Nicholas asked from the doorway, but his amused expression said he'd heard every word. With casual nonchalance, he leaned his tall frame against the jamb.

"I'm sure you would find them just as uninteresting as

you did the rest of our conversation today," Glory told
him bitterly.

"You look a little worn, Miss Summerfield," Nicholas
said, lifting one black brow and raking her from bosom to
toe with his hard gray eyes. "Maybe riding is too strenuous a sport for you after all."

"Why, you—"

"Stop it right now, both of you!" Julian warned.

Glory squared her shoulders, stared the captain straight
in the eye, and stormed past him as he moved farther into
the room. The noisy slam of the heavy walnut door marked
her exit.

"Well, Nicholas . . ." Julian indicated he should take
the overstuffed leather chair in front of the desk. "I guess
you were serious when you said you weren't interested in
marriage."

Nicholas stretched out in the chair, crossing his long
legs atop the matching leather ottoman. "I was serious,
all right. But I didn't intend to cause problems between
you and your daughter."

Julian chuckled. "How about a little bourbon and
branch water?"

Nicholas nodded. "I could use a good stiff drink."

Julian poured two fingers of fine Kentucky bourbon into
tall crystal glasses, added a dash of water, then handed
the glass to Nicholas. "I've never seen her this way,"
Julian said. "At least not with a man. With the others she
just smiles and bats her lashes, and you wonder what she's
thinking about because it certainly isn't the young man
who's in the room. She'll fight with me, of course, but the
others . . ." He shook his head. "At least you sparked a
little spirit."

"Oh, she's got plenty of spirit," Nicholas said. "God
help the man she marries. If she can't sweet-talk him into
doing what she wants, she'll shame him into it."

"I'm sorry you find her so unattractive." Julian eyed
Nicholas over the top of his glass.

Nicholas cocked a brow. "She's beautiful and you know

it. She's intelligent and charming. She's also pampered, spoiled, willful, stubborn, and selfish."

"Not selfish, my boy, never selfish. Glory would give away the clothes on her back if she thought someone needed them."

"I'm certain she has hundreds of good qualities," said Nicholas, not sounding as though he meant it. "She'd be a challenge, that's for certain. If she weren't your daughter, I'd like nothing better than to bring her to heel. But marriage? Not a chance. My father went through hell, and most of the married men I know aren't much better off. I intend to stay single. If you're as smart as I think you are, you'll keep your daughter away from me."

Again Julian chuckled, a vibrant, husky sound, just like the man himself. "You've seen how easy it is to keep Glory from doing anything she pleases . . . But you seem to be doing a fine job of making her dislike you, so I'll just leave it to you."

Glory soaked in the warm sudsy tub for over an hour. The heat helped drain some of her tension and ease a little of her temper. How could her father have taken that awful man's side? Eric Dixon would never have acted that way! He'd have given up his own mount and led the bay through the mud to the house.

But, she admitted grudgingly, her father and Captain Blackwell were right about one thing. She shouldn't have taken the hedges in that much mud. Of course she hadn't meant for the bay to get hurt. She loved the big horse and all the other animals in her father's stable. Well, it was over and done with now, and she'd be damned if she'd let Captain Blackwell know how she felt.

By early evening, Glory's temper had cooled. She took a little extra care with her toilette, determined to appear nonplussed. April, her maid, coiffed Glory's pale locks into ringlets on either side of her neck, then helped her slip into a daringly low cut pale blue watered-silk gown that enhanced the bright blue of her eyes. Neither her father nor her mother had seen the gown before—she'd been saving it for something special. Well, retribution was special enough. She intended to make Nicholas Blackwell squirm if it was the last thing she ever did.

By the time Glory entered the dining room, her father and mother and the tall handsome captain were seated at the long mahogany Hepplewhite table. Milk-white bayberry tapers lit the room from a crystal candelabrum, and the gold-trimmed porcelain dinnerware gleamed in the candlelight. Both of the men rose as Glory swept in.

"Good evening, Mother, Father. Captain Blackwell." The last name came out with a gush of sweetness oozing an insincerity Glory hadn't intended. It was not an auspicious beginning.

"Good evening, my dear," her father said.

Nicholas pulled out her chair. "You look lovely this evening." His gray eyes swept her boldly, then returned to her bosom, where the peaks of her breasts were barely concealed by the gown. Her father glowered for a moment; then a faint smile curved his mouth, and he picked up his wineglass as if nothing were amiss. Her mother frowned.

"Why, thank you, Captain," Glory said. "I'm surprised you noticed.

This time her mother smiled and her father frowned.

"Well, Captain Blackwell," her mother said while two tall Negroes served the meal: roast chicken, brook trout, corn, black beans, hominy, and fresh-baked bread. "Why don't you tell us what's going on up north? With all your travels you must have heard the latest Yankee slander on this part of the country." She smoothed a brunette strand into the tight coils of hair at either side of her neck and tipped her head back, which made it appear she was looking down her nose at Nicholas, even though he was a foot taller than she.

"I hardly think politics is a matter for discussion at the table, Louise," Julian said, passing Nicholas a steaming platter of chicken. Though the table was set for royalty,

the meal was served family style, and Nicholas felt warmed
by the gesture of acceptance.

"The *Yankees*," Nicholas said pointedly, "have been
too busy digging out after the flood to worry much about
the Southerns."

"Yes," Julian agreed, "we've been reading about it.
Terrible thing. Seems to be affecting half the country."

"Lots of goods have been damaged." Nicholas loaded
his plate with food, then hefted a forkful of hominy.
"Should strengthen the market for cotton and rice."

"It's about time something did," Julian grumbled.
Having been kept debt-free, Summerfield Manor had suffered far less from the depression of 'thirty-seven than most
of the other plantations, but the Charleston economy was
still languishing, as was most of the South.

Supper continued pleasantly for everyone except Glory.
Though the captain's glance strayed periodically to the
curve of her breast, he conversed not at all with her and
for the most part acted as if she weren't even in the room.
By the end of the meal, Glory's cheeks burned with indig-
nation. She sat quietly fuming as her mother rose from the
table.

"If you'll all excuse me," her mother said, "I have
some sewing to do upstairs."

"Certainly, my dear." Both her father and the captain
stood as Louise left the room. "Nicholas, what do you say
we retire to the billiard room for brandy and cigars?" He
glanced at Glory. "Since there's just the three of us, you
won't mind if Glory joins us, will you?"

Nicholas lifted one corner of his mouth in what might
have passed for a smile. "I would be honored."

"Well, I'm afraid *I* would mind, Father. Captain Blackwell owes me an apology. I was forced to tolerate his
boorish presence at supper, but I will not tolerate it one
moment more!"

"Glory!" Julian's temper fired. "Captain Blackwell is
our guest. You will treat him with respect!"

"Not until he apologizes!"

"You, Miss Summerfield," Nicholas said hotly, "deserve the lesson I mentioned this afternoon—not an apology!"

"Stop it! Both of you." Julian looked from one to the other. Glory's bosom heaved, threatening to burst from the confines of the gown. Nicholas's scowl was black and unyielding. They were both standing up, glowering furiously at each other, while Julian still sat at the table an equal distance between them. "I think you should *both* apologize!" Julian said.

"What!" Glory shrieked. "He's the one who—"

"And you, young lady," Julian interrupted, "are the one who risked injury to yourself and your horse on a dangerous jump."

A little of Glory's anger dissolved. The beautiful bay had very nearly broken its leg. "All right," she conceded at last. "I will if he will." She stood in front of her chair, her slim fingers biting into the tiny waist of her gown.

"Captain?" Julian asked.

"But of course," he said gallantly.

Battling her temper down, Glory pressed her lips together and took several steadying breaths. She turned her bright blue eyes—and all the false charm she could bring to bear—on the captain. "I apologize to Captain Blackwell for what happened this afternoon. It was a foolish thing to do. But Raider's taken that jump a hundred times and I just didn't think—"

"That is correct, my dear," Julian put in, "you didn't think." He turned his attention to Nicholas. "Captain?"

"And I, Miss Summerfield, am sorry you were forced to walk all the way home on foot. It's a very long walk, and I'm certain you were more than a little tired by the time you reached home."

"What! That's no apology!"

"I'm also sorry you're still angry," the captain added with a teasing note in his voice. "But as I said before, you look beautiful that way."

Julian Summerfield roared with laughter. Glory held her tongue, her color high. A tiny place in the back of her mind saluted the captain's quick wit. She decided to accept

his backhanded compliment and—for her father's sake—
concede defeat. At least for the time being.

"All right, Captain, you win. Consider your apology
accepted." She smiled effusively. "Billiards, anyone?"
Without a backward glance, Glory swept from the room.

Chapter Four

Playing the game of billiards was Glory's secret vice.

Until tonight, the fact that she played had been a closely guarded secret. No lady of quality would ever venture into the smoke-filled rooms where men secluded themselves to drink brandy and discuss business, but her father had amused himself by teaching Glory to play. In the beginning, Glory would have preferred to be upstairs dressing her dolls or perfecting her skills on the harp or pianoforte. But for Julian's sake, and for the extra time it gave them together, she had learned to play.

Glory's mother had been furious. Louise had done her best to end their boisterous camaraderie in the confines of the billiard room, but to no avail. Eventually, Glory came to love the game as much as her father did, and she was good at it. She appeased her mother by promising not to let anyone know she played, and until tonight she hadn't.

She'd been amazed when her father had included her in the invitation, but now that he had, she was bound and determined to play the best game ever.

Glory was rummaging through a window seat at the far end of the room when Nicholas entered. As she bent over, Nicholas noticed again her dainty waist, admired her full bosom, which teased the low neckline of her gown. He could easily imagine the tantalizing curves of her bottom and her long, slender legs. Beads of perspiration formed on his brow. Nicholas drew a kerchief from his gray brocade waistcoat to blot them away.

Damn the woman for the provocative creature she was! She was determined to make his stay a living hell, and she was damn well succeeding. She was all he'd been able to think about from the first moment he'd seen her.

Glory straightened and walked toward him, proudly holding a long teakwood cue beautifully inlaid with ivory. It was thinner than the others, which were kept on the wall, obviously custom made for her slighter frame, and Nicholas fought to suppress his amusement. She was full of surprises—delightfully so. And the more he felt drawn to her, the more he wished he'd never come to Summerfield Manor.

They were playing pocket billiards. Nicholas racked up the balls, and they lagged for the break. Glory won. Nicholas chalked it up to luck until he watched her sink the one ball on her opening shot. The two and three followed, but she missed the four—barely. A difficult bank shot Nicholas would probably have missed as well. He silently saluted her skill.

Nicholas sank the next three balls with ease but missed his fourth shot, and Julian sank only two. Glory ran the table. The smile she lavished on him was so exceedingly smug, Nicholas found his temper rising again. A woman playing billiards. It was unheard of. Unladylike. The girl should be taught her rightful place, and Nicholas was just the man who could do it! The thought intrigued him more than a little. If only she weren't Julian's daughter.

The evening wore on. They were excellent players, and all three won their share of games. In the end, Glory came out on top. Nicholas put her winning off to the advantage she held in her low-necked gown. He found it nearly impossible to concentrate on the game with the girl's beautiful bosom threatening to overflow as she leaned over the table to place her shot. No wonder women weren't encouraged to play.

"Well, Captain, I hope you've enjoyed the evening as

much as I." Glory smiled broadly, her even teeth pearl-like in her beautiful oval face.

Nicholas barely lifted one corner of his mouth. "I've never played billiards with a woman before. I'm not certain I could survive the experience again. But one thing I'll say for you, Miss Summerfield: You never cease to amaze me."

Glory wasn't sure whether his words were a compliment or an insult, but right now she didn't really care. She'd beaten Nicholas Blackwell this evening, and she felt exhilarated.

"Good night, Captain." She moved past him to where her father rested in a tufted leather chair and kissed him on the cheek. "Good night, Father."

He patted her hand. "Get a good night's rest, my dear," he told her. "We'll see you in the morning."

Glory nodded and left the room, a satisfied smile on her face.

Glory awoke the next morning feeling better than she had in days. She recalled her evening with Nicholas Blackwell as she stretched and yawned. April scurried about, opening the mosquito netting, drawing the curtains, and folding wide the heavy wooden shutters to allow the cool morning air to cleanse the room. At last Glory had won the upper hand with the captain. His mood had been black by the time they ended the games. Glory smiled at the thought. It was time someone bested the man at something. From the look on his face, it was not a common occurrence, and Glory reveled in her victory.

"Hurry up, chile." Plenty bustled into the room just as Glory finished dressing. "You got company. Mr. Eric down in the receiving room with your daddy and the captain."

Glory smiled. "Tell them I'll be right there." Dabbing a spot of cologne behind each ear, she turned to her maid. "April, you'd better hurry and finish my hair. We wouldn't want to keep our guests waiting."

Plenty waddled back out the door, and April began

brushing Glory's hair. She was going to visit Miriam today—she'd had quite enough of the captain—but a little of
Eric's flattery always gave her a bit of a lift. She'd flirt
with him outrageously, show the captain just how charming she could be.

After a final quick glance in the mirror, Glory headed
down the sweeping staircase dressed in a rose silk day
dress. While April had coiffed her hair in ringlets beside
her face, Plenty had brought her warm sweet rolls and
coffee, since she'd missed breakfast, which, from the look
on her father's face, he was none too happy about.

"Good morning, gentlemen. Captain," she said pointedly and caught the hint of a frown from her father and a
look of amusement from Nicholas.

"Good morning, Glory," Eric said. His hazel eyes
swept over her, his look of adoration unmistakable. "You
look ravishing, as always."

"Thank you, Eric."

"Glory, we've been waiting patiently down here for
hours," her father said. "Nicholas and I are riding over
to the rice fields. Since it's such a lovely day, we thought
you might enjoy coming with us."

"That's very thoughtful of you, Father," Glory said.
"But I have an engagement at Buckland Oaks."

"I'll be happy to escort you," Eric put in, his hazel
eyes soft.

"What kind of engagement?" her father wanted to
know.

"Miriam is planning a costume ball, and I've agreed to
help. Besides, her mother is sick, and I'm taking her some
of Plenty's special remedy."

Julian sighed in defeat. "Well, I suppose you have no
choice if Mrs. Allstor is ill."

Glory smiled at the captain, who hadn't said a word and
looked utterly bored by the entire conversation. "Have a
nice ride, Captain. I'll see you at supper."

He merely nodded, looked hard at Eric, who had rushed
to open the door, then returned his attention to her father,

who appeared not the slightest bit happy about this latest turn of events.

Outside, Glory called for the calèche to be readied, instructing them to leave the top open in concession to the beautiful weather, while she conversed lightly with Eric. He told her he'd thought of her every moment since the night of her birthday, told her how much he adored her, and asked her to attend Miriam's costume ball with him. As handsome and attentive as he was, Glory found it hard to keep her mind on the conversation. She suddenly wished she'd gone riding with her father and the captain—though for the life of her she couldn't imagine why.

Glory spent the day at Miriam's feeling the same disquiet she'd felt before she left. She'd sent Eric packing as soon as they arrived, telling him how much she and Miriam had to do and placating him with a tentative acceptance of his invitation to the costume ball. All the while she wondered what Nicholas Blackwell and her father were doing.

Miriam only made matters worse. "How are you and that roguish sea captain getting along?" she asked. "He is, without doubt, the most wickedly handsome man I've ever seen. Why, I'd positively die to spend the day with him. But then, I guess you have so many beaux you hardly need another." They were seated on the porch, looking out across manicured gardens toward the river.

"I told you before, Miriam, Captain Blackwell's an arrogant, despicable man. Why he . . . he's no gentleman, I'll tell you that."

"Did he kiss you, Glory? Did he?"

"Don't be a featherhead, Miriam. Captain Blackwell and I don't get along at all. If he weren't Father's friend, I swear I wouldn't so much as speak to the man. He's rude and overbearing; he's ill-tempered and inconsiderate; he's—"

"Absolutely divine," Miriam broke in. She rolled her eyes and fluttered her painted fan, and Glory fought down an urge to strangle her. She changed the subject to something safer, and the long afternoon rolled slowly to a close, Glory staunchly refusing to arrive at home before her father and the captain, no matter how tedious Miriam's usually sparkling company seemed.

She even forced herself to stay a little longer than usual. By the time she finally did leave, her driver, old Mose, was nervously wringing his bony hands.

"Your daddy don' like you comin' home late, Miss Glory. He gonna have my hide."

"Oh, horsefeathers," Glory said, paying the old man no heed. "If we hurry, we'll be home well before dark."

But they weren't. Halfway home the carriage hit a rut and one of the wheels broke off the axle. Mose was taking forever to fix it. His gnarled old hands were not as nimble as they used to be, and Glory hadn't the vaguest idea what to do to help him. She just sat quietly in the seat, waiting patiently for him to finish, and wondering how she was going to calm her father's raging temper.

"Damn that girl," Julian Summerfield raved. "She damned well knows better than to stay out this late!"

"She probably just let the time slip by," Nicholas soothed. They sat in the upstairs drawing room, sipping bourbon and branch water and smoking thin cigars, Julian's concern becoming more and more apparent.

"What that girl needs is a husband," Julian stormed. "And the sooner the better!"

"Listen, Julian, I'm sure she's all right, but just to be on the safe side, why don't I go make sure?"

"I'll go with you," Julian volunteered, leaping to his feet. He took several hurried steps, then suddenly stopped short, one hand going to the small of his back. "Damned if I haven't pulled a muscle," he said, but couldn't meet Nicholas's gaze. "Darned sacroiliac."

Nicholas almost smiled. "I know the road to Buckland Oaks. She's probably not far. I'll escort her the rest of the way home."

"Thank you, Nicholas. This damn back of mine picks the darnedest times to act up."

Nicholas just nodded. Crushing out his cigar, he headed for the door, setting his glass down on the piecrust table near the fireplace on the way out. Since the night air was still chilly, he stopped by his bedchamber to draw on his black wool cloak. Then he strode downstairs.

One of the stable boys saddled Hannibal for him, and Nicholas swung up into the saddle. He'd begun to worry about the girl himself, though he wasn't certain why he should. She was probably just indulging herself. She was willful and spoiled. A woman like that wouldn't be the least concerned for the worry she caused others. Julian should have taken the girl in hand years ago; now it was too late. Too late for a father, but not for a husband. In that Julian was correct.

Setting Hannibal at a mile-eating pace down the road to Buckland Oaks, Nicholas thought of his somewhat limited experience with the institution of marriage. His mother had been a beautiful French Creole woman. She'd been the darling of every party, the belle of every ball. Everywhere she went men fell at her feet. Alexander Blackwell, Nicholas's father, had been no exception. He'd loved his wife, Collette, with a limitless passion; unfortunately Collette did not love him. At least not in the same way. Collette Dubois Blackwell wasn't capable of that kind of love.

After Nicholas was born, Collette had lain with every dandy in New Orleans. His father had known of her infidelities, but had chosen to ignore them, hoping he could somehow regain her love.

When Nicholas was seven years old, his mother ran away to France with a wealthy merchant with never a thought for Nicholas or his father. A few years later, Nicholas was told she had died of some sort of plague. How he had missed her. How he had yearned for her love—just as his father had.

As always, thoughts of his beautiful, hedonistic mother darkened Nicholas's mood. Gloria Summerfield, with her soft laughter and flirtatious ways, would probably turn out just the same. Just like all the other women Nicholas had known. For the hundredth time that day, Nicholas vowed

not to get involved with the girl. Tomorrow he'd be leaving
Summerfield Manor, returning to his ship and the way of
life to which he belonged. Nicholas could hardly wait.

"Aren't you done yet, Mose?" Glory asked, glancing
up and down the dark, tree-lined lane. Only the lonely
hooting of an owl had kept them company until now, but
as the moon rose above the trees, Glory began to hear
other sounds. She couldn't make out just exactly what they
were, but they were ominous sounds, and Glory was anxious to be on her way.

"All set, Miz Glory." Mose tottered over to the calèche
and climbed into the driver's seat. He clucked the team of
matched sorrels into a trot, and the carriage rolled away.

At first Glory breathed a sigh of relief. But as they traveled farther down the lane, the ominous sounds grew
louder. She noticed old Mose glancing nervously from side
to side, and a chill of apprehension raced down her spine.
The noises sounded closer now—hounds baying, horses'
hooves thundering against the still-soft earth. As her worry
increased, her heart began to thud in rhythm to the gal-
loping beasts.

Old Mose slapped the reins a little harder, urging the
team forward at a faster pace. As the tall pine forest rushed
past in a moonlit blur, Glory gripped the velvet seat to
keep from being tossed around inside the open carriage.
Seeing a bend in the road up ahead, Mose slowed the
horses. At the same time, a small Negro youth rushed
from the side of the lane, forcing Mose to pull up on the
reins to avoid a collision. Just for a moment, the youth
froze in his tracks and Glory recognized Ephram's brother,
Willie. Then he bolted toward the woods.

"Willie, wait!" she cried out. "Not that way, they'll
catch you for sure!"

Willie turned and, recognizing Glory's voice, raced up
beside the coach, his slender body bathed in sweat, his
clothes in shreds, his arms and legs scratched and bleeding. "Please, Miz Glory," he pleaded. "Dey'll kill me
for sure."

The echo of the lash rang in Glory's ears. By some miracle Ephram had survived the whipping. Little Willie had neither his older brother's size nor his stamina.

The sounds were getting louder. Glory could hear men's voices as they called back and forth to each other, searching determinedly for the runaway slave. The hoofbeats of their horses were so loud she wondered how she could possibly hear the pounding of her heart.

"Please, Miss Glory," Willie begged. "You da only hope I got. Dey *ain't* nobody else."

Glory glanced at the woods, ringing with the terrible sounds of death, and back at the boy, who seemed nothing more than two huge white-ringed eyes. "We've got to find someplace for you to hide."

"There's a tool box under my seat," Mose offered. "The boy is small enough to fit."

Glory hesitated only a moment. "Get in!" she ordered, and Willie's flashing smile was all the thanks she needed.

"What the hell's going on here?" Nicholas Blackwell stormed onto the scene just as Willie lifted the canvas flap concealing the tool box beneath Mose's seat.

An expression of terror frozen on her face, Glory stared up at him, seated astride the big black. He looked ominous and forbidding in his dark cloak, his features drawn and angry.

"Please, Nicholas," she pleaded, hands clutching the folds of her skirt. "They'll kill him if I don't help. Just go back up the road a little. No one will ever have to know you were here."

Nicholas hesitated only a moment, his glance straying to the woods, then back to the anxious face of the girl in the carriage. "Do as she says," he commanded the boy, and Willie climbed into the box. "The dogs will pick up his scent," he told Glory. "Do you have anything we can use to distract them? Food scraps, anything?"

"I have some fried chicken Mrs. Allstor sent along."

Nicholas dismounted. With trembling fingers, Glory hurriedly handed him a small wicker basket from the seat beside her. She hadn't missed the word "we." Gratitude surged through her, so potent it made her feel weak.

Nicholas looked into the basket. "Pepper. Let's hope this works." He set the basket in the foot box of the calèche, sprinkled the pepper all over the tool box, rearranged the canvas flap, and climbed back on his horse just as twenty sweat-covered riders burst through the woods and onto the road. A short, stout man held five baying hounds by the end of their taut leashes, and the cacophony of snorting horses and heaving men threatened to overwhelm Glory's senses.

From the center of the group, Thomas Jervey, a muscular man in his mid-forties who owned a neighboring plantation, approached.

"Miz Summerfield." Though the air was cool, he lifted his felt hat and wiped the sweat from his brow with an elbow. "Sorry to bother you, but the hounds have been following that Nigra who ran from Buckland Oaks." The dogs strained at their leashes, baying and barking furiously at the driver's seat of the carriage. "They seem to have followed him here. Mind tellin' me what you're doin' out so late?"

"I was visiting Miriam Allstor. One of the carriage wheels broke on my way home. Mose just got it fixed." She pointed to the wheel, broken and lashed haphazardly back together on the right side of the calèche. "Since I was late getting home, Captain Blackwell came out to escort me back."

"Mind if we take a look?" Jervey asked, and Glory felt the color drain from her face.

"Not in the least," Nicholas put in, dismounting from the black and coming to stand near the front of the carriage. The stout man holding the dogs brought them around to the driver's seat, and Glory thought her heart would stop.

Nicholas lifted the flap, revealing the lunch, while the dogs, standing on their hind legs, took several deep sniffs. Then they sneezed and howled pitifully, turned tail, and ran in the opposite direction, pulling the stout man along behind them. Seeing the wicker basket Nicholas had opened to reveal the chicken and a bit of spilled pepper, the men chuckled softly among themselves.

"Sorry to bother you, Miz Glory," Thomas Jervey said. "But you can't be too careful." He turned toward Nicholas. "You'll see she gets home safely, Captain?"

Nicholas nodded. He swung himself up on the black, his dark cloak billowing out behind him. "Good luck with your hunt," he told Jervey. Then he signaled for Mose to take the carriage on home.

Glory leaned back against the seat, her heart still hammering wildly. The carriage rolled along the road in silence for several miles, until Nicholas motioned for Mose to stop. After dismounting, he tied the stallion to the calèche, and joined Glory inside the open rig.

"Mind telling me what that was all about?" he asked, settling his lanky frame against the seat.

If the day had been trying so far, Glory now found it exceedingly so. She could feel the captain's powerful presence—and his muscular thigh pressing against hers through the folds of her skirt.

"I wish I could tell you, Captain. But it all happened so quickly. I just did what seemed right at the moment."

Nicholas regarded her closely. "You risked your reputation and your father's standing in the community to help a runaway slave? Only yesterday you sent a man on a four-mile walk just so you wouldn't soil your riding habit."

"Things aren't always as they appear, Captain. Sometimes Jonas, the overseer, is a little too eager with the whip. I believed the boy would rather take a four-mile walk than nurse the cuts on his back."

Nicholas felt a little of his cynicism slip away. Maybe there was more to the girl than he thought. Moonlight filtered between the clouds, and Nicholas noticed the way the soft light glistened on her smooth cheeks and lit the blue of her eyes. "I don't think I've ever met a woman more full of surprises than you, love," he said softly. Glory's cheeks pinkened at his use of so intimate a word, and he felt that same pull of attraction he'd felt before.

"I'm grateful for your help, Captain. But I'm afraid I'm going to need to ask for more. Willie won't be safe until he reaches the North. You could take him there aboard your ship."

Nicholas stiffened. "I don't approve of the institution of slavery, Glory. But I have friends in the South. Men like your father. Men I admire and respect. I do business with these men. I won't interfere in their way of life."

"I appreciate your feelings, Captain. I feel much the same way. But just this once . . . ? No one need ever know."

He ran a long tanned finger down the line of her cheek. She looked so beautiful, so caring. He really had no choice—he'd known that the moment he came upon her in the road. "All right. Just this once. But don't ever ask it of me again."

"Thank you, Captain."

"Back there you called me Nicholas. I liked the way it sounded."

"Nicholas," she whispered softly.

It seemed so natural he should kiss her, so right somehow. What harm could there be in one little kiss? He lifted her chin and covered her soft coral lips. They felt full and warm, and Nicholas heard himself groan. When she parted them to allow his tongue entrance, Nicholas forgot the promises he'd made himself, forgot all but the warmth of her breath, the sweetness of her mouth. He deepened the kiss and felt her slender arms slip behind his neck, her fingers glide through the strands of his curly black hair.

Glory felt a rush of desire so poignant it made her dizzy. His lips were full and insistent, and a warm, pervasive glow spread through her limbs. She felt hot and languid, tense and shivery all at the same time. His hands cupped her face, his firm fingers guiding her in the kiss while they gently held her captive. Her nipples hardened against the fabric of her dress, felt heavy, and just a little achy. His tongue searched her mouth, tasting every corner, taking her breath away, making her head spin.

Glory had been kissed before, dozens of times, by

countless suitors. Sweet, chaste kisses, warm on her lips. Promises of things to come. The kiss she experienced with Nicholas Blackwell was like no other. She wanted the kiss to go on forever, but even that wouldn't have been enough. When his hands moved down the bodice of her dress to cup the weight of her bosom, when his fingers teased the stiff peak through the soft green fabric, Glory knew exactly what it was she wanted from Nicholas Blackwell, and the thought cleared her mind like a dip in an icy stream.

"Please, Captain," she whispered, pulling away, her voice a little shaky. "This is too . . . I mean, I didn't intend to . . . I mean, I don't think we should . . ."

"I know *exactly* what you mean, Miss Summerfield."

His voice sounded husky as he twisted away from her, trying to ease the bulge in his breeches Glory pretended not to see. Her face flamed scarlet, and she was glad a cloud had covered the moon.

Nicholas glanced at the side of the road. "I didn't intend to, either."

They rode the rest of the way in silence, Glory's lips still tender from the blush of his kiss, her heart still hammering uncomfortably. As she glanced at his angular profile, watched the wind blow strands of his curly black hair and moonbeams lighten his usually dark gray eyes, Glory began to understand why women like Lavinia Bond would risk their honor for Nicholas Blackwell.

Mose stopped the carriage some distance from the main house to let Willie out, with instructions as to which cabin belonged to Mose. In the morning Willie could slip back into the box for the long ride to the wharf in Charleston. From there Captain Blackwell would see that he reached safety in the North.

Glory and the Captain said a detached good-night, but Glory thought he looked at her differently somehow. She knew she saw *him* in a different light. She desired Nicholas Blackwell, desired a man for the very first time in her life, and Glory felt both stunned and a little ashamed. She'd always known her father was a man of lusty appe-

tites—at least he had been until Hannah died. After that
he'd gone to Charleston, she was sure, to call on the ladies
of the evening. He had never again visited the slave quar-
ters, as he had when Hannah lived there.

Until tonight, Glory had always been certain she'd inherited her mother's more delicate sensibilities regarding a
woman's duties in the marriage bed. To her mother, inti-
macy was an obligation. After Glory was born, Louise had
been thankful when Julian stopped visiting her room al-
together. Her mother had explained to Glory that what
happened between a man and a woman was for procrea-
tion, to bring new life into the world. Passion was something only a man enjoyed. Glory had always believed her
mother—until tonight. Surely she hadn't inherited her
father's passions instead of her mother's! But now Glory
wasn't so certain.

Julian spotted the change in attitude the moment they
entered the dining room early the following morning. Last
night both had pleaded fatigue and gone straight to their
chambers. This morning Glory watched Nicholas covertly
from beneath her thick dark lashes, an achingly wistful
look on her face.

And Nicholas smiled. Not a thin, narrow, mirthless
smile, but a real, genuine, full-fledged smile. At least
when he looked at Glory.

Julian wondered what could have happened between
them on the road last night, and part of him questioned
his judgment in throwing them together so much. The other
part said he'd had to give his daughter the chance at love
he'd known only briefly.

Now Nicholas was leaving. And if the look on Glory's
face was any indication, she was damned sorry to see him
go. Nicholas didn't look any too pleased himself.

"Good-bye, Captain Blackwell," Glory was saying.
They'd walked outside on the piazza to stand in the warm
spring sun.

Nicholas took her slim fingers in his hand and brought
them to his lips. His eyes, usually a dark gray, looked

lighter somehow. "It's been a pleasure, Miss Summerfield. More than you'll ever know."

"Will you be returning to Charleston soon?" she asked, almost willing him to say yes, it seemed to Julian.

"I'm afraid not." He didn't add anything further, and Julian wondered why he sounded so final while his expression seemed to belie his words.

Glory straightened. "Then I wish you well, Captain." She turned to go, her head held high, fair hair gleaming in the early morning light.

"And you, Glory. Don't settle for less than what you want." He glanced pointedly at Julian. Then he climbed aboard the calèche, his rented saddle horse trailing behind. The captain had found the animal lame that morning, so Mose was driving him into Charleston.

"Thank you again, Julian," Nicholas called out. "For everything."

As the carriage rolled into the distance, Julian moved to stand beside his daughter. She looked down the lane until the calèche turned the bend in the road and moved out of sight.

"You really liked him, didn't you?" Julian said softly, meeting his daughter's troubled gaze.

"Too much" was all she said.

Glory spent the next few weeks determinedly trying to forget Nicholas Blackwell. It was no easy task. She attended several soirees and finally Miriam's costume ball with Eric Dixon. But now the men who fawned over her seemed immature or dandyish. When she kissed Eric and felt nothing more than a pleasant glow, she thought of Nicholas's more passionate embrace. Whenever she saw Lavinia Bond, she fought the torturous image of Nicholas lying with the luscious red-haired woman, his hands caressing her, his warm lips brushing her eager flesh. Worst of all, she felt jealous that it was Lavinia and not she who had been the object of his ardor.

Not until the first of May did Glory's life return to some

semblance of order. She'd resigned herself to marrying Eric Dixon as her mother had strongly begun to urge.

"It's time you married," she'd say. "Eric is a fine southern gentleman. His family has lived here for generations. You two will make a splendid match."

It was just like her mother. Her marriage to Julian Summerfield had been arranged. Love was never a consideration. As far as Glory knew, her mother had never really been in love. She shared a home with Julian, but little more. Proud of the plantation she and Julian had built, Louise valued the land and the family name. Oh, she loved Glory, in her own detached way, and probably even Julian. But she revolved in a distant world, where closeness to others was not allowed.

Glory was seated in the upstairs withdrawing room practicing on the pianoforte, the sun streaming through the open window, when her mother walked in. Glory had never seen so bleak an expression, such utter despair on her mother's usually placid face.

"Mother! My God, what's happened?" Glory leaped from the piano bench and hurried across the room, the layers of her ruched skirts rustling with the motion. Plenty burst into the room behind Louise, while April entered sobbing.

"Get your mama over to da sofa, chile' " Plenty commanded, and Glory meekly did as she was told. "You sit down, too."

"Me! Why do I need to sit down? Plenty, what's happened?"

"It's Julian," her mother choked out. "He was riding Hannibal, taking the hedges. Hannibal went down. Julian hit his head." She sat there staring straight ahead, her face as pale as porcelain, her eyes bleak and vacant. "Glory, your father is dead."

Chapter Five

Glory was sure she couldn't have survived the ordeal if it hadn't been for her half brother, Nathan.

The tall light-skinned Negro arrived on a packet from New York just two days after her father's death. He'd been on his way home from school for the summer. A year younger than Glory, Nathan looked several years older. He was handsome and well built, tall and broad-shouldered like his father. Since his mother had also been of mixed blood, his features looked more Caucasian than Negro. Having spent most of his life in boarding schools, he was highly educated and well spoken.

"Oh, Nathan," Glory cried against his shoulder. "I miss Papa so much." They had walked down near the river, below the formal gardens. A sudden spring storm seemed imminent: clouds gathered and threatened, and the air hung thick and still.

"I just can't quite believe it," Nathan told her. "I keep expecting him to crest the rise on his big black stallion or walk up to my cottage." Nathan wasn't allowed inside the main house—Louise Summerfield wouldn't tolerate the presence of Julian's bastard son. So Nathan had been raised by Sara, one of the Negro women, in the small cottage Julian had built for Hannah. A place away from the rest. A place where he and Hannah could be alone.

Hannah had been a quiet-spoken young woman, the

child of a well-educated quadroon from New Orleans. As a little girl, Hannah had been taught to read and write, though by law it was forbidden. When her mother died, she'd been sold to pay their debts, though she was then only a child of fourteen. At the manor, she'd blossomed into a beautiful young woman, and Julian had fallen in love with her.

Everyone had looked the other way, even Louise. The affair had lasted a little less than two years, just long enough for Nathan to be born. Hannah died when a second child came early and complications set in. Glory's mother had wept with joy; Julian had grieved for weeks, and Nathan had been left alone.

"I never thought it could happen to him," Glory said to Nathan. "He was so strong. Like a rock. And always there when you needed him." She wept softly against Nathan's shoulder, his tall frame looming above her more slender one.

"I miss him, too," Nathan said quietly. Living on the edge of plantation society, belonging neither to the Caucasian race he was schooled in nor to the Negro, despite his curly black hair and cocoa coloring, Nathan had grown up fast. He held no illusions about life. He had loved his father. Now his father had been taken from him, just as his mother had. Nathan had always been alone—except for Glory.

"Why did it have to be him, Nathan?" Glory said. "He was so good and kind. He always worried about everyone except himself, always wanted the best for everyone."

"I know, Glory. I know."

At first Glory had been unable to cry, unable to accept her father's death as real. Once Nathan came home and they shared each other's grief, Glory couldn't *stop* crying. When the day of the funeral arrived, Glory was sure she had no tears left.

She stood inside the little wrought-iron fence that surrounded the family plot. All by herself. Her mother had relegated Nathan to a place among the Negroes, and, though Glory had cried and pleaded, threatened and cajoled, Nathan had finally persuaded his sister to leave the matter alone.

"Father would want you there, Nathan," she'd said.

"Father will know I'm close by."

After that, Glory had refused to stand beside her mother. Instead she stood a few feet away, a bitter spring wind billowing the heavy skirts of her black silk mourning dress. The cloudy day seemed appropriate. While the minister droned on, Glory stood with her head held high, but she was grateful for the dense veil she wore, which shrouded her drawn features from the scores of friends and relatives who had gathered to pay their last respects.

As Glory heard the low keening of the slaves on the hillside, saw the first shovelful of dirt pitched onto her father's casket, she felt a knot of despair that tightened like a noose and threatened to suffocate her. Head spinning, she swayed unsteadily. Tears filled her eyes, and she fought to keep them from spilling onto her cheeks. The mourners around her blurred into a single gray mass.

She sensed his presence even before he touched her, his strong, sun-browned hand sliding beneath her elbow to share with her a little of his strength. She didn't need to look up to know that Nicholas Blackwell stood beside her, but when she did, she found him staring straight ahead, his quiet support giving her the courage she needed. He said not a word, his expression carefully controlled, but his usually swarthy complexion looked wan, his mouth no more than a thin, grim line.

Glory knew in that moment that he shared her pain, and in realizing others had loved her father as she had, she felt a little of her own pain go away.

When the service was over, Nicholas led her from the graveyard beneath the oaks. "You know how sorry I am," he said, his voice heavy and low.

"Thank you for coming, Captain."

"I'm afraid I can't stay. I heard about the accident in a port just south of here. Your father was respected and admired. News of what happened traveled fast. I came as quickly as I could, but I have to return to my ship right away.''

"I understand.''

"I'm headed for Barbados. At the end of the month I'll be back in Charleston for three days on my way north. If there's anything I can do, anything you need, just send word.''

"Thank you.''

He didn't offer to see her, didn't want to see her again. Nicholas had battled images of Gloria Summerfield since the day he'd left the manor. He was just beginning to forget her when he received news of the accident. Now he felt the same intense attraction, the same pounding in his blood, and knew he'd again spend weeks fighting his desire for her.

Just like your father, a tiny voice said. The words plagued him day and night. Want of a woman had turned Alexander Blackwell into a drunken failure and finally been the death of him. It wouldn't happen to Nicholas. Not for Gloria Summerfield or any other woman.

He walked her up the hill to the house.

"Good-bye, Captain,'' she said.

He squeezed her hand, left her with a polite farewell, and made his way over to her mother, to whom he paid his respects. A few minutes later, he was mounting his hired saddle horse, riding out through the massive stone gates as quietly as he had come. With a last glimpse over his shoulder, he spotted Glory among the others dressed in black, looking pale and fragile. She didn't appear to notice those around her, just stood watching him as he rode off down the lane.

"Mother, you can't be serious!'' Glory stormed about the drawing room, her fists clenched at her sides, strands of blond hair tumbling free of her tight chignon. "Nathan is my brother. He's a member of this family, just as much as I am!''

"Don't say that! Don't you ever say that to me again!'' Her mother's features were distorted, her brown eyes glistening with rage. "Nathan is a slave. That is *all* he is. He belongs to Summerfield Manor. From now on he'll work in the fields just like the rest of the slaves."

"Father's not dead two weeks, and you're already trying to destroy his son!"

Her mother's hand connected with Glory's cheek so hard she felt the sting of tears. The echo of the slap resounded across the room.

"Don't you ever refer to that . . . that *Nigra* as my husband's son."

Glory swallowed hard, but held her ground. "Father meant for Nathan to be a free man of color. He was to receive his papers on his twentieth birthday. That's what Father wanted and you know it."

"What Julian wanted! Always what Julian wanted. What about what I want? Do you think I wanted your father to flaunt his affair with a Negro slave? Do you think I wanted him to raise his bastard right here under my nose? Do you think I wanted to hear our neighbors snickering at me behind my back?"

"I know it was hard on you, Mother. But it isn't Nathan's fault. Let him go back up north. Let him return to school. He can leave now instead of in the fall."

"No! Nathan is a slave. He'll take his place with the rest of his people as he should have years ago."

"Mother, please. Be reasonable. Nathan doesn't know the first thing about being a field hand. He wasn't brought up that way."

"Then he'll just have to learn." She swept toward the door. "I will not discuss this with you again, Glory. Ever. Go to your room. When you come out, I expect you to behave like the lady you've been taught to be. I never want to hear Nathan's name mentioned in this house again."

Her mother marched through the doorway, then stopped and turned to face her. "There's one more thing," she added. "I want you to stop consorting with the slaves. Your father allowed it. I will not. From now on, you'll keep to your rightful place." She left the room, and Glory remained behind, dumbstruck.

How could this be happening? How could the woman do such a thing to Nathan? Remembering her passionate words, Glory realized she'd never understood the depth of her mother's shame and humiliation. Never really understood her at all. Part of her felt sorry about the misery Louise had lived with all these years. Another part hated her for the terrible payment she intended to extol from Nathan, maybe even from Glory.

Nathan had been working in the rice fields for eight days before Glory was able to see him alone. His tall frame already looked gaunt; his hands and feet were covered with blisters, and his shirt was torn and bloody from the marks of the whip. Glory cried just looking at him.

"Oh, God, Nathan. What have they done to you?"

He raised himself up, a look of fierce pride hardening his features as Glory had never seen them. "Nothing that hasn't been done to my people for hundreds of years."

"But you're different from the others. You're educated. You're gentle and kind. You can't stand up to this kind of treatment. We've got to do something!"

"There's nothing we *can* do, Glory. Your mother has made up her mind. If I try to run, she'll have the slave catchers hunt me down. She owns me. She can do whatever she wants."

"That's not good enough. I won't stand by and do nothing. I've had time to think about this, Nathan, and I've come up with an idea."

"Glory, it's no use."

"Listen to me, Nathan! We have to try. Father would have wanted us to try."

Nathan took a deep breath and looked out over the still waters of the lagoon. They stood among the oaks, beneath wispy strands of moss that hid them from the prying eyes of Jonas Fry. "I suppose you're right, Glory. You usually are."

"Father had a friend," Glory said. "A sea captain. His name is Nicholas Blackwell. He'll be in Charleston at the end of the month. If we put the word out through some of the slaves, we can find out exactly when he arrives. He'll be in Charleston for three days. We'll go to him the day before he leaves. Surely we can get as far as Charleston without being caught."

"Will he take me north?" Nathan asked.

"I—I don't know. He helped me once before, but I don't think we should risk telling him the truth. I'm going to tell him there's a family emergency of some kind. I have several relatives in the North, so he should believe me. I'll play on his sympathies, his loyalty to Father."

"And just how do you persuade him to take me along?"

"I'll tell him I brought you for protection." She smiled up at him. "After this past week, you ought to be able to act like a slave."

This time Nathan smiled. "Yassum, Miz Glory," he said with a deep Southern drawl. "Whatever you say. You is shorely da boss."

"Then you'll do it?" she asked.

"Are you sure you'll be safe with this . . . Captain Blackwell?"

Glory felt a sudden warmth in her cheeks as she remembered the tall captain's kiss, the heat in his eyes that night on the road. "I'll be safe," she said. But she wasn't completely sure—and she wasn't sure she wanted to be.

Nathan clutched her hand. "All right, we'll try it. You just tell me what you want me to do."

News of the captain's arrival in Charleston reached Glory through the slave grapevine. He was headed to New York with a shipment of sugar and tobacco.

"Dat big boat o' his come in dis mornin'," Plenty told her after checking to make certain they were alone in Glory's room. "I surely don't like dis, chile." Plenty shook her turbaned head and clucked at her like a mother hen. "Don't like seein' you go off by yourself like dis."

"I'll be with Nathan," Glory reminded her. "I won't be gone that long. Once I get Nathan safely back to New York, I'll return on the first packet. I just thank God Father set up trust funds for Nathan and me. He'll have plenty of money to finish school, and I won't have to depend on my mother for anything ever again.''

"She gonna have plenty of trouble runnin' da manor without you, chile."

"She'll be fine. She knows as much about running this plantation as Father did. Besides, she doesn't listen to anything I have to say. She relies on Jonas Fry—the last man on earth Father would have listened to.''

"I s'pose you're right. I *know* you're right about helpin' Nathan. Dat Jonas Fry never did like da boy. Says he's nothin' but a uppity nigger. He'll do his best to break da boy. Your daddy wouldna liked dat one bit.''

"I just hope nothing goes wrong,'' Glory said. "Nathan and I have to be on that boat by the time the tide turns Thursday morning. That's when the *Black Spider* is supposed to sail."

But things did go wrong. The weather turned nasty. Though the air was humid and warm, black clouds rolled and thundered and slashes of lightning rent the sky. Glory waited till she was sure the others were asleep, then dressed in a crisp black pleated-faille traveling dress. She arranged her pale hair in ringlets beside her face, then covered her head with a wide-brimmed bonnet. Grabbing a lightweight mantle, she slipped down the servants' stairs to the back door.

"Good luck, chile,'' Plenty whispered, enveloping Glory in the folds of her thick girth. "Promise you'll be careful.''

"I promise,'' Glory said. "Don't you worry about a thing.''

Plenty just nodded. Holding open the back door, she watched Glory as she made her way to the stables in the light rain.

Wearing his ragged work clothes, a floppy-brimmed hat pulled low across his face, Nathan waited beside the barn next to a canvas-topped gig. The gig was small and manageable, needing only one horse to pull it the long way into town. They both climbed onto the seat and Nathan slapped the reins lightly against the animal's rump.

"At first I thought this weather was a bad omen," Glory told him, "but now that I think about it, maybe it's the other way around. It makes a great cover, and the lane is so dark and muddy we're not likely to pass a soul."

"Just as long as the rain doesn't get any worse," Nathan cautioned. "The road's barely passable as it is."

But the rain did get worse, and the wind began to howl. Several times Nathan was forced to stop the carriage to remove heavy tree limbs that blocked their way or to clear a mound of loose earth that had tumbled onto the road. He was thankful his weeks of backbreaking work in the rice fields had muscled his shoulders and legs and turned his blisters to calluses. When the carriage bogged down in a mud hole just outside of Charleston, he found he had strength he hadn't known about. Together he and Glory freed the gig and continued on. It was almost dawn by the time they headed down Meeting Street toward the Battery. When they turned on Tradd Street, headed for South Adger's wharf, the tall masts of the *Black Spider* beckoned in the graying light of dawn.

"Hurry, Nathan," Glory urged. "They're getting ready to make way." Glory's heart pounded. The rain had slowed their journey by hours. A few more minutes and they would have been too late. "Somebody is bound to discover the gig sooner or later, but by then we'll be well on our way."

They climbed out of the carriage and hurried to the gangplank, Glory walking in front, her dark clothes soaked and clinging to her body, her hair wet beneath her soggy bonnet, several long blond strands slicked against her cheek. Nathan followed, carrying Glory's big tapestry carpetbag as well as a smaller bag of his own, his hat pulled low. Despite his light skin, his ragged clothes and muscled body made him look just like any other black man.

Several sea gulls screeching above the tall masts, the sounds of creaking timbers, and the hustle of men at work drew Glory's attention as she walked along the narrow plank that crossed from dock to ship.

She spotted Nicholas Blackwell in an instant, though he

was no more than an outline against the lightening sky. His height, as well as his broad shoulders, long legs, and lean hips set him apart from the others. For a moment she hesitated, a little afraid to approach the intimidating figure who barked orders to his crew with a stern authority that brooked no argument. Then she thought of Nathan and squared her shoulders. After cautioning her half brother to remain in the shadows, she headed toward the captain.

The look of surprise on his lean, tanned face turned rapidly to one of concern as he strode across the deck to greet her.

"Glory, what is it?" he asked, taking in her bedraggled appearance. "Has something happened?" He grasped her wet hands in his and worriedly searched her face. The wind billowed the open front of his white linen shirt. She noticed he wore a thin gold earring in one ear.

"I need to talk to you, Captain," she told him.

"Of course. Come into my cabin."

They walked down the companionway and into the small room, and Glory untied and removed her cloak and bonnet. Nicholas draped them across a squat oak chair. She noticed the way his snug black breeches, wet from the rain, clung to his lean hard thighs as he pulled up another chair for her to sit in. Two long strides carried him to a whale oil lamp beside his bunk.

The captain lit the lamp, though dawn was beginning to break outside the low portholes above his wide berth. The bed had been neatly made and was as orderly as the rest of the room. Only a few open ledgers on the captain's oak desk and several bound volumes near his chair spoke of the work that went on in the cabin.

From a crystal decanter the captain poured a little brandy into the bottom of a snifter, handed her the glass, then sat down at the end of his berth to face her. "Now, tell me what this is all about."

"I need your help, Captain Blackwell. My aunt in New York is ill, and I must reach her right away."

"Surely you're not traveling alone?"

"Not exactly." She took a sip of the brandy to steady

her nerves. "I brought one of the servants along for protection."

"Where is your chaperon?" he asked, arching a fine black brow.

"I . . . I didn't have time to find one," she lied.

He regarded her closely. "You're telling me you've traveled in the rain all night, without a proper companion, because you want me to help you reach your sick aunt." His gray eyes said he didn't believe a word she said. "Why me? Why not a regular passenger ship? The *Black Spider* is a merchant vessel."

Glory took a steadying breath. This was going to be harder than she thought. "The truth is, Captain, my mother and my aunt don't get along. My mother has forbidden me to go to her. I hoped you would help me."

"I'm not about to go against your mother's wishes, Miss Summerfield," he said, beginning to get angry. "You had better have your servant take you back home where you belong."

Glory rose to her feet, playing her final card. "I'm going to New York, Captain Blackwell—with or without your assistance. I came to you because you and my father were friends. I felt I'd be safe on board your ship. If you won't take me to New York, I'll find someone who will. If anything happens to me, it will be on *your* conscience." She swung toward the low door, praying he would stop her. She'd taken only a few steps before she felt his hand on her arm.

"You're that determined to go?"

"I am."

"You understand we'll be stopping at ports along the way. It will take you days longer to reach New York."

"I'd still feel safer traveling with you, Captain."

"Then you leave me no choice. I'll take you to your aunt, but I'm sending word to your mother."

"I don't need my mother's permission, Captain. I'm a grown woman. But then, maybe you hadn't noticed."

Nicholas Blackwell raked her with his eyes. Wet and soggy, her expensive black traveling dress clung to every curve of her body. It outlined the points of her thrusting breasts and hinted at the shapely line of her hips and legs. Even damp and windblown, her flaxen hair gleamed in the lamplight.

He'd noticed all right.

He'd noticed the first time he saw her. Though he hated to admit it, he'd imagined bedding her a hundred times during his weeks at sea.

"I've noticed, Miss Summerfield. As I'm certain my men will." Her cheeks flushed at his words, and he remembered the smooth feel of them cradled between his hands. "If you're sailing with me, I'll expect you to follow my orders. You'll do exactly as I say. Is that understood?"

"Of course, Captain."

"There are two other women aboard."

For a moment she looked relieved. Then she eyed him suspiciously. "Are these women *passengers?*" she asked, "or *personal* acquaintances?"

Remembering what she'd said about Lavinia Bond, he felt the pull of a smile. "They're passengers. Though I believe you'll find them . . . *different* from the other women you've known."

"I'm sure I'll enjoy their company."

One corner of his mouth curved upward. "You'll find them educational, of that I have no doubt. You can bunk with Rosabelle." He started toward the door.

"And my servant?"

He turned to face her, his expression hard. She was lying and he knew it. But he owed it to Julian to discover just exactly what she was up to.

"I have money to pay for our passage," she added before he could answer.

"I see." He studied her face a moment more, recognizing the determined look in her eye. The same look she'd worn before she raced him across the muddy fields. Spoiled and willful, he thought, and wondered if this episode would end in disaster as well. He ignored the tiny voice that reminded him of the way she'd saved the Negro boy—and the sweetness of the kiss they'd shared on the road.

"Come along, Miss Summerfield. I'll show you to your cabin."

Glory lifted her soggy skirts and muddy petticoats and followed him into the corridor.

"Captain?" an attractive blond man in well-tailored clothes called out from the top of the passageway. "We're ready to cast off whenever you give the order."

Nicholas turned to face him. "Make way, Mr. Pintassle. I'll join you on deck just as soon as I get our new passenger settled in." The young man eyed Glory oddly for a moment, then turned and headed back up on deck.

Nicholas knocked lightly on one of the cabin doors. After receiving permission to enter, he swung the door wide, just as the ship began to creak and sway. It was an odd sensation, and Glory braced herself against the bulkhead.

"I hope you don't get seasick," Nicholas said with a scowl.

"I'll do my best," she told him, and prayed she wouldn't embarrass herself. She'd traveled by ship only once before, on a coastal packet to Savannah with her father. During that much shorter trip, she'd gotten just a little woozy, but the sea had been smooth, the sailing easy. Today the waters still churned from last night's storm; whitecaps pounded against the sides of the ship even while it sat in port. But the storm was ebbing, by the look of it. Already the sun was beginning to peek through the clouds. Glory could see a bright dawn breaking outside the tiny porthole, and she read it as a good sign,

"Miss Summerfield, meet Rosabelle," Nicholas said.

"Pleased to meet you, Miss . . . ?"

"Rosabelle," the girl reminded her, as if she weren't too bright. "Just plain Rosabelle."

Glory glanced up at the captain, who looked amused, then back to the girl on the bunk. "Rosabelle," she corrected. She could barely make out the girl's features in the still-early light, but she appeared to be short and slightly pudgy, with long mouse-brown hair. When she leaned forward into the sunshine, Glory noticed she was very young, with apple-round cheeks and full scarlet lips. Her nightdress was of thin, worn muslin.

"I'll have your servant bring your bags," Nicholas told Glory. "After that, one of the men will show him where he can bunk."

"Thank you, Captain."

Nicholas nodded and closed the door. He headed down the narrow passageway already regretting his decision. It was almost as if Julian Summerfield's presence hovered above him, smiling triumphantly. Two weeks with Glory. Two weeks with nothing, no one, to keep him away from her but his own somewhat frayed conscience. Seeing her today, he realized again how many times he'd thought of her these past few weeks. He could still remember their kiss, the feel of her lips beneath his, with such clarity it might have happened only minutes ago, instead of weeks. The fact was, he wanted Gloria Summerfield in his bed. Badly. But bedding her meant marriage—the ultimate nightmare for Nicholas. Marriage was out of the question.

As captain of the ship, he reminded himself, he had an obligation to treat her with at least a minimum of courtesy. But above that, he decided, he would force himself to stay clear of the blue-eyed girl—or make her dislike him so much she'd stay away from him!

"Looks like me and you is cabinmates," Rosabelle said in a soft voice that betrayed her lack of education.

"I guess so," Glory agreed, attempting to be polite when all she really wanted to do was get out of her wet garments and into her bunk. "You're traveling all the way to New York?"

"Nah. There's a settlement near Cape Fear. But it'll take us a while to get there. Cap'n's got some stops along the way."

A knock at the door interrupted them as Nathan delivered Glory's big carpetbag. He said nothing, just grinned and winked at her, then fled the room. Glory hung up her several black dresses as best she could on a peg beside the door, removed her soggy clothes, and gratefully climbed into the top berth. Asleep in minutes, she didn't awaken until ten hours later, when she heard someone pounding on her door.

"Just a minute," she called out. After slipping into a light silk wrapper, she ran her hands through her rumpled blond hair. She knew she looked a fright and suddenly prayed the man at the door wasn't the handsome captain.

It was.

The hard lines of his face seemed to ease a little as he took in her sleepy appearance, the tangled mass of her hair.

"I didn't mean to wake you," he said. "I thought you'd be up by now."

"You'll have to forgive me, Captain. I didn't mean to sleep so long. What time is it?"

"Almost three o'clock."

"I guess the trip into Charleston took more out of me than I thought."

"I'm sure it did," he said dryly. "I stopped by to ask if you wanted a tour of the ship, but I see my timing was off."

"If you'll give me a few minutes to get ready, I'd like that very much."

She looked perfect just the way she was, he thought. For the place he would most like to take her was back to his bed. A single ray of sunlight reflected on her hair, turning it a silvery gold, and her clear complexion still carried the rosy tint of sleep. Though she held her wrapper in place with a long, slim-fingered hand, he could see the mounds of her breasts, and almost ached to know whether they really tilted upward, as they appeared. Instead he let her close the door, and returned to his place on the deck. A few minutes later, he glimpsed her pale hair ruffled by the wind as she climbed the aft ladder to join him on the holystoned deck.

Chapter Six

Glory breathed deeply of the clean salt air. The wind whipped her crisp silk skirts with their layers of petticoats while sea gulls screeched overhead.

Fortunately the sea had calmed; the sky had turned a clear azure blue. As a brisk wind puffed the white canvas sails, several crewmen smartly made fast the lines. When Glory approached, they stopped their work and stared at her with what could only be described as awe. Glory smiled at them warmly.

Their tall sea captain stood at the rail, his long legs spread against the gentle roll and pitch of the ship. He glanced toward his men, then at Glory, his look a little sterner than before.

"Welcome aboard the *Black Spider*," he said. But the words rang false, and Glory wondered why.

"*Black Spider*," Glory repeated, eyeing the man dressed more like a pirate than the gentleman he'd been at the manor. She corrected herself: Not *exactly* a gentleman. "The name seems appropriate," she said only half teasing.

"She's a triple-masted, square-rigged ship," he told her, and a hint of pride laced his voice. "She measures two hundred twenty feet, and she's one of the older ships in the fleet, but she's reliable. We use her mostly for transporting merchandise to and from the secondary cities along the coast.''

"Father said you had quite an armada.'' Her eyes turned sad as she spoke of her father, but the clear ocean breezes were already beginning to soothe her, to lessen the ache in her heart.

A nearly imperceptible tightening around his mouth said the captain had noticed the change in her mood, but he only glanced out to sea. "The *Black Witch*, my flagship, is the fastest ship in the fleet.'' He led Glory toward the bow. "But she's been in dry dock for the past few months.'' Nicholas waved to the fair-haired man she'd seen before, and the man hurried toward them, a broad white-toothed smile on his face.

"Miss Summerfield,'' Nicholas said, "I'd like you to meet Joshua Pintassle, our first mate.''

"How do you do, Mr. Pintassle.''

"I'm honored, Miss Summerfield.'' Glory recognized the familiar warmth in his cheeks, the wistful look she'd seen on her suitors' faces so many times before. Joshua Pintassle looked every bit the gentleman, his hair and clothing immaculate, his handsome face smooth-shaven. She smiled up at him. She could always use an ally.

"If there's anything I can do,'' he was saying, "anything at all to make your trip more pleasant, just let me know.''

Glory smiled again and watched him through the thick fringe of her lashes. "I'll do that, Mr. Pintassle.''

Nicholas scowled. "I'm sure Miss Summerfield will get along just fine.'' He glanced toward the two men who were unfurling canvas. "That rigging looks a little slack,'' he said to his first mate. "Take care of it.''

"Aye, Captain,'' Joshua Pintassle said, his cheeks coloring. With a slight bow to Glory, he beat a hasty retreat.

"Maybe you'd like to take a turn at the wheel, Miss Summerfield,'' Nicholas suggested a bit curtly, returning his attention to Glory.

Her head came up. "Miss Summerfield? I thought we'd dispensed with formality back at the manor.''

With a narrow smile, Nicholas raked her with his eyes,
his slow perusal settling on the swell of her breasts, partly
exposed by the cut of her neckline, the rest oulined by the
wind against the fabric of her gown. "I think it would be
in both your best interest and mine if we weren't too
friendly in front of the crew." He glanced toward several
men in duck pants. One wore a red checked shirt, unbuttoned to expose his broad tattooed chest; another, shorter
man with a black patch over one eye lifted his canvas hat
in mock salute. Each watched Glory with bold interest.
"They're a tough lot," Nicholas warned. "Remember to
keep your distance."

Glory stiffened. His mild rebuke seemed a gentle way
of telling her just exactly what distance *he* intended keeping, and Glory felt a flare of temper. Maybe she no longer
held his interest. But then, maybe she never had. They'd
only shared a single kiss--one that had left Glory breathless and more than a little enamored of Nicholas Blackwell. Obviously the kiss had meant less than nothing to
the roguish sea captain.

"I'll remember that, Captain." She could have sworn
she saw his jaw tighten before he returned his attention to
the sea.

Nicholas escorted her up the ladder to the massive
carved teakwood wheel on the aft deck and even allowed
her to take a turn at steering. Then he introduced her to
the brig's second mate, a man named MacDougal. Mac,
as his shipmates called him, was a stocky red-faced Scotsman in his middle years. He'd known his captain since
Nicholas was a boy.

"Me and the cap'n go back a long ways, lass," he told
her. "Nicky signed on as a cabin boy aboard the *Sovereign
Lady* bound fer England. He was no more'n a boy. I took
him under my wing. Why, I taught the lad everythin' he
knows."

Glory was amazed at Nicholas's indulgent smile, one of
the few she'd ever seen. He looked younger, almost boyish, and Glory suddenly wished *she* could make him smile
like that.

"Don't listen to a word this old sea dog says," Nicholas teased. "He's got a barnacle for a heart and salt water in his veins."

Glory smiled at the old sailor who sat on the deck braiding hemp into rope. His nimble fingers worked the line with such speed and dexterity it made the task look easy. Glory could see that it wasn't. When they got out of earshot, Nicholas told her the older man was a rarity among men of the sea.

"In a way, the second mate holds the most difficult position on the ship," he explained. "He's neither an officer nor a member of the crew. He gets double a sailor's pay for walking the fine line between the two. Mac is one of the few men able to bridge the gap. He's admired by officers and crew alike."

To Glory, it seemed Nicholas said the words almost reverently, and it was obvious he felt more than a little attached to the old Scottish sailor.

Glory returned to her cabin in time to do a little reading before the evening meal. Nicholas had given her strict instructions not to be up on deck without Joshua Pintassle, Mac, or himself.

"I've got a lot of new men in the crew," he said, "and I'm not sure which of them I can trust." His smoke-gray eyes turned dark. "Where a woman like you is concerned, sometimes a man can't even trust himself."

As always with the captain, she wasn't certain whether she'd been complimented or insulted. She wondered if the man he spoke of could be himself and found herself hoping it was so. She wondered if the other two women had received the same instructions. She hadn't seen Rosabelle since she arrived, but Nicholas said she'd meet Madame LaFarge, the other woman aboard, at supper. The way he'd arched his brow and given her a mocking half-smile, she wondered what he had in store.

The ship creaked and rolled with a gentle rhythm Glory at first found soothing, but after reading awhile in the tight confines of the cabin, she found that her stomach had begun to disagree. She needed some fresh air before things got out of hand. Leaving the room, she headed toward the aft ladder, hoping to find one of her three appointed protectors up on deck. The salt breeze revived her the minute she climbed the stairs, and Glory breathed deeply of the clean fresh air.

Though her gaze searched the deck, she spotted none of the three men she sought. Certain that one of them would be along soon, she made her way to the rail.

"Ain't you a perty little thing," came the husky voice of a man behind her.

Glory spun to face him. He was a big man, almost as tall as Nicholas, barrel-chested, with a thatch of thick red hair. Glory smiled up at him. "Have you seen Mr. Pintassle or the captain?" she asked, but he didn't seem to hear her. His eyes were locked on the peaks of her breasts, and Glory felt herself color beneath his lengthy, too-bold gaze. "I said, have you seen Mr. Pintass—"

"I heard what you said, angel. Name's Jago. Jago Dodd, what's yours?"

"I really need to find Mr. Pintassle," Glory said.

He wasn't surprised at her evasion: He hadn't expected any words at all. He was surprised she hadn't turned tail and run. With a scar across his cheek and a three-day growth of beard, Jago Dodd was not exactly your parlor gentleman.

"My name's Gloria Summerfield," she told him, extending her slender hand. "I'm from Charleston."

Jago Dodd had never been more surprised in his life. His homely face split into a wide grin, and he took a second, even more appreciative look at the elegantly garbed woman in front of him. He had never conversed with a real lady before, and the fact that this one would speak to him at all changed his attitude toward her completely. He had planned to get an eyeful, maybe even a feel or two as he brushed past her somewhere on deck. Now he felt a surge of protectiveness for the trusting young woman who smiled into his knife-scarred, beetle-browed face as if he were just as good as the next man.

"I'll help you find him," he said, knowing he shouldn't leave his oakum-picking task. But the next sailor she smiled at might not be so understanding.

They walked toward the bow of the ship, Jago Dodd beside her, looking to his right and left as they passed more sailors at work along the way. The hard look on his face dared any man to look at her sideways. When they reached the bow, they found the captain instead of the first mate, and his expression said he was none too pleased.

Jago handed her over, a bit reluctantly it seemed to Glory, then spun on his heel and returned to his post.

"I thought I told you not to come on deck alone," he snapped.

"I needed some air. I thought I'd find one of you on deck and I did."

Nicholas scowled, thinking of Jago Dodd. Of all the men she could have asked for help, Jago was probably the most dangerous. Would the woman never understand what these men were thinking? He cursed beneath his breath and wished to God he'd never brought her along. "I'm a little busy right now. Come on. We'll find Josh." He gripped her arm none too gently and led her toward the stern where Joshua Pintassle volunteered to escort her with unabashed enthusiasm. Nicholas frowned and stalked away.

By the time they'd taken a turn around the deck, Glory and Joshua were friends. "It feels good to be on my own," she told him, thinking about home for the first time since she'd left. "I had no idea freedom could be so heady. I almost wish I didn't have to go back at all."

"I know what you mean," he said. "It's one of the reasons I decided not to work for my father. At least not right away. I wanted to be on my own for a while. I needed some time to find out about myself."

"Yes," Glory agreed. "Now that Father is gone, it just isn't the same at the manor. Something's missing. It doesn't hold the same appeal for me it did before."

"I knew your father only briefly, but he seemed a fine man, and I know the captain admired him."

"I know." Glory looked away. The sun was dropping into the flat blue line of the horizon, turning the sky a burning orange. "It'll be dark soon," she said, not wanting to dwell on a subject that always made her sad. "I think I had better go below." They headed toward the aft ladder, and Glory spotted Nathan along the way.

"Excuse me just a moment, Mr. Pintassle," she said. "I'd like a moment with my . . . servant."

"Of course."

Making certain no one was close enough to hear, Glory pulled Nathan aside. "Is everything all right? Are they treating you well?"

Nathan grinned, his teeth a flash of white against his cocoa complexion. "Yassum, Miz Glory. Dey's jes' fine. Filled me up wiff salt pork and gruel. Ain't Virgini' ham, but it'll do."

Glory fought a grin herself. "Don't get carried away, all right?"

"Yassum, Miz Glory."

Glory glanced over her shoulder, then poked him squarely in the ribs. "Will you behave?"

"I'm fine, Glory, really I am. I'm bunking in with the crew." He glanced across the deck to where the handsome blond first officer waited. "Another conquest?"

"Mr. Pintassle is a very nice man."

"I'm sure he is, and I can see by the look on his face, he's already joined your flock of admirers."

Glory looked askance. "Nathan, I swear, you're sounding more like Papa every day."

Nathan smiled at her words, and Glory could have sworn his chest puffed out a little. "I'd better not keep him waiting," she said. "I'll see you tomorrow."

"Yassum, Miz Glory."

Shaking her head in vexation, Glory returned to the first mate, who escorted her back to her cabin. She felt better now that she'd seen Nathan; he certainly didn't appear to be any the worse for wear. And as long as he was fed and not mistreated, he was far better off than he would have been back at Summerfield Manor. Glory wondered what her mother had done when she discovered the two of them missing. She'd be angry—furious, in fact. And there'd be the devil to pay when Glory got home. But as long as Nathan reached safety in the North, all the trouble would be worthwhile. Glory was sure she could make her mother see reason, once Nathan was off the plantation and out of Louise's life for good.

Nicholas came to her cabin a little after dark to escort her in to supper. She was pleasantly surprised to see he'd worn a tailored dark gray frock coat over a pair of navy blue breeches. The earring was gone from his ear. She wondered if he'd removed it in honor of her presence aboard the ship. He looked exceedingly handsome, and she found herself suddenly a little self-conscious. She wished she was wearing something that would catch the captain's eye instead of her drab mourning clothes. When he turned to close the door, she settled the neckline of her dress a little lower.

"Joshua will be joining us," Nicholas said. "And of course Madame LaFarge." As they strolled amiably along the companionway, the captain seemed a bit detached—except when he thought she wasn't looking. Then he either frowned or indulged himself in one of his mocking half-smiles.

"Good evening," the captain said to the others as they entered the cabin. The room was small and simply furnished with a cloth-covered wooden table and stout oak chairs. The table was set with heavy porcelain plates, and a brass whale oil lantern lit the room. "Joshua, you've already met Miss Summerfield."

"A pleasure to see you again." The first mate gave her a warm, appreciative smile.

Glory accepted the compliment with a smile of her own. With a nod to Joshua, she turned her attention to the other guest seated in the room. The smile froze on her lips.

"Miss Summerfield," Nicholas said, his voice heavy with amusement, "may I present Madame LaFarge?"

It was all Glory could do to choke out a polite hello.

"Pleased to make yer acquaintance." The full-figured woman waved a perfumed handkerchief in the air, the scent so overpowering that Glory had to fight to keep from sneezing. Glory had worn another of her crisp black mourning dresses while the broad-hipped Madame La-Farge was gowned outlandishly in bright red satin. The neckline dipped so low Glory was sure the woman's huge bosom would spill onto the table at any moment. With her painted face covered with a heavy layer of rice powder, she looked like a grotesque caricature of the woman she was beneath her makeup.

Nicholas seated Glory across from the buxom woman, and without ado, a simple supper of fish chowder and biscuits was served.

"Captain says you're headed north," Madame LaFarge said as Glory took a bite of flaky white cod.

She was surprised to find it delicious and suddenly realized she hadn't eaten since she left the plantation. "Yes. I'm going to New York."

"Me an' Rosabelle is getting off at the Cape," the garishly dressed woman told her. "You need a job, girlie? You're welcome to come along."

Glory's head snapped up, her pewter fork poised midway to her lips. "What . . . what kind of work do you do?" She prayed her instincts were wrong. Surely Captain Blackwell wouldn't allow *that* kind of woman on board his ship! But when Joshua Pintassle cleared his throat and glanced away red-faced, Glory wasn't so sure.

Madame LaFarge laughed heartily. "Now, ain't she a sweet one, Nicky boy? Fetch a high price on the Cape, she would." She turned her puffy, made-up face to Glory. "Me and Rosy work the oldest profession in the world— we play the whorepipe, dearie." With a great guffaw, she slapped her fleshy thighs, and Glory blushed to her toes. If she'd had a pistol she'd have shot Nicholas Blackwell in a place where'd he'd have no more use for women of the oldest profession—or any other woman for that matter!

For the second time since she'd known him, Nicholas Blackwell really smiled. His gray eyes danced with suppressed mirth, and Glory silently fumed. The man was infuriating! He'd known all along the two women were . . . were ladies of the evening, yet he hadn't had the decency to tell her! A gentleman would never have suggested she journey north with them, let alone share a cabin with one. Then a tiny voice reminded her he'd hardly *suggested* anything. Traveling aboard the *Spider* had been Glory's idea, not his.

Determined to ignore him, and somehow gain the upper hand, Glory deliberately turned her attention to the buxom Madame LaFarge. "Where is Rosabelle this evening?" she asked, carefully controlling her voice.

"She's feeling a mite poorly, if you know what I mean." She grinned and looked conspiratorially down her long nose at Glory, who pretended she knew exactly what the painted woman meant—which she didn't.

"She helped Cookie for a while this afternoon, but now she's back in her cabin."

"Cookie?"

"That's the shipboard name for cook," Joshua told her.

"I see."

"She's a good girl, Rosy is," Madame LaFarge continued. "Not real quick, but a good girl jus' the same. Too bad what happened to her, but it happens to the best of 'em. She's just lucky the captain's the kind of man he is."

Nicholas leaned back in his chair, watching the group with detached amusement. Glory smiled inanely, wishing she knew what in the world they were talking about. Everyone else seemed to know, yet it was obvious by Joshua's embarrassed expression that it was not a subject she wanted to pursue.

"Weather's warming up," Glory said, and even Nicholas seemed thankful for the turn in conversation.

"Yes, it is," Joshua chimed in. "We're due for a hot spell."

Nicholas added a few terse comments, and Madame LaFarge launched into a discussion of how much tougher it was to make a living on one's back in the heat.

All in all, once she conquered her embarrassment, Glory

discovered she liked the buxom woman after all. Nicholas graced her with only a few words throughout the meal, so after dinner, still angry at being the butt of his joke, Glory focused her attention on Joshua Pintassle. She was pleased to note that the satisfied curve of the captain's mouth quickly turned to a hard, unpleasant line.

Sipping a licorice cordial, Glory smiled sweetly and batted her thick dark lashes. "Tell me, Mr. Pintassle, how did a gentleman of your obvious breeding happen to end up in Captain Blackwell's employ?" The way she said the words implied a man like Joshua Pintassle deserved a far better master than the roguish sea captain he worked for. Glory felt a thrill of satisfaction when Nicholas's gray eyes darkened. Her barb had not gone unnoticed.

"Mind if I smoke?" he asked, reaching into his waist-coat to extract a thin cigar.

Glory arched an eyebrow. At home after supper, a gentleman would retire to the drawing room for his brandy and cigars. But then, shipboard etiquette might be alto-gether different. "Not in the least," she said, not really meaning it.

Nicholas made a grand show of offering one to Joshua, who declined, then lit the end and inhaled deeply, releas-ing a cloud of thick gray smoke into the room. It was all Glory could do to keep from coughing, though she found the aroma not unpleasant after all.

Joshua seemed oblivious to the exchange. Instead he warmed to his subject. "I've always loved the sea. I've probably spent more time on the ocean than I have on land. My father was a captain for nearly twenty years. Now he owns a fleet of passenger ships that sail from New York to Liverpool. Eventually I'll take over the company, but in the meantime, I wanted to be on my own. I've been with Captain Blackwell for the past three years. He's taught me a great deal."

"I'm certain he has," she said sweetly. Then, thinking of the young *lady* ensconced in her cabin, she suddenly wondered exactly what Nicholas Blackwell *had* taught the young officer. "I just feel fortunate that the captain was kind enough to look after me in my time of need," she said, not meaning a word of it. So far, the captain's hospitality had been thin at best.

"It's a pleasure to have such a beautiful woman on board," Joshua said.

"Why, thank you, Mr. Pintassle, you're only too kind."

"Quite the contrary, Miss Summerfield. There are few words that testify to beauty such as yours." His eyes traced the line of her neck, and Glory noticed the heat in his gaze. Nicholas glowered at them both. As if sensing his captain's disdain, Joshua turned his attention to Nicholas. "Don't you agree, Captain?"

"I assure you, Joshua, I'm well aware of Miss Summerfield's charms . . . and so is she."

Glory stiffened. This was the man she remembered, with his backhanded compliments and arrogant attitude.

Joshua seemed embarrassed. "I only meant to express our pleasure in her company."

"I'm sure you did, Josh." The captain's gray eyes hardened even more. If Glory hadn't known better, she might have thought he was jealous.

"Well, I hate to break up a party," Madame LaFarge put in. "It never pays!" She chuckled, the sound a throaty rumble. "But I for one could use a little rest. Won't get near enough sleep once we reach the Cape." She winked and grinned broadly. "If you gentlemen—and the pretty miss—will excuse me . . ." Her words trailed off as she hefted her ample body from the chair.

Glory wholeheartedly agreed. She'd had just about enough of Captain Blackwell. His obvious lack of interest in her disturbed her more than a little. Was it just her vanity that smarted, as the captain once said?

"I believe I'll retire as well," she told her dinner companions.

Joshua Pintassle rushed to pull out her chair, which scraped against the heavy plank floors. "I'd be honored to accompany you to your door, Miss Summerfield," he said, his gentle voice husky with anticipation.

"Miss Summerfield and I have a few things to discuss,"

Nicholas broke in, giving the younger man a hard look that made it clear the remark was an order and not just a statement.

"Of course, Captain." Joshua glanced at Glory a bit sheepishly. "Have a good evening, Miss Summerfield."

"I'd be pleased if you'd call me Glory," she said, sugar-sweetness dripping from her lips. The captain would clearly *not* be pleased, and Glory felt an inner thrill of satisfaction.

"Why, thank you, Glory," Joshua said. "And you'll call me Josh?"

"Why, of course." Fighting the pull of a smile, she felt Nicholas's none-too-gentle grip on her arm. It was only a small victory, but a victory just the same. If Nicholas Blackwell wasn't interested in her, Joshua Pintassle was. She meant to enjoy his attention whether the captain liked it or not!

Nicholas guided her up on deck in silence. Jago Dodd passed them, and Glory smiled at him warmly. Nicholas scowled and tugged her toward an isolated spot by the rail.

"I thought you understood. I don't want you getting too friendly with the crew."

"Does that include Mr. Pintassle? He certainly seems trustworthy enough."

"As a matter of fact, it does. Joshua is a fine officer and a gentleman. But the others might not understand. Need I remind you"—he lifted her chin, forcing her to face him squarely—"that you agreed to follow my orders?"

Glory stiffened. "Being courteous is hardly going against your orders, Captain."

Nicholas felt his temper flare. She was willful and spoiled, he reminded himself, and an outrageous tease. Not only was he positive she had lied to him about her reason for wanting to go north, but now she was determined to make trouble along the way—to say nothing of the trouble she was causing him just by her presence. Nicholas groaned inwardly. Why in God's name had he let her stay aboard?

"You're my responsibility now, Miss Summerfield," he said. "These men have been at sea for weeks. Our short stay in Charleston only whetted their appetites. Look around you." He indicated several tough-looking men who worked near the main mast. "Most of these men are used to taking what they want. If they decide they want *you*, there'll only be Josh, Mac, and me to stop them. You keep flirting with Josh and we'll have to count him out."

"Flirting! How dare you accuse me of flirting. I was merely making conversation. *You* hardly spoke to me, and I haven't much in common with Madame LaFarge."

His eyes bored into her; then he released a long slow breath. "I almost wish you did."

Glory's eyes widened at his words, but it was the tone in which he said them that sent warm color to her cheeks. For the first time she noticed the heat in his storm-gray eyes, the heavy pulse, fueled by his anger, throbbing at the base of his throat. Though his mouth was set, his lips curved invitingly, and Glory recalled the feel of them, warm and firm against her own. Her heart thudded uncomfortably, and she cursed herself for her weakness.

Nicholas Blackwell was a rogue and a bounder. Women meant nothing to him—he'd made that perfectly clear. Her fingers gripped the hard wooden rail, and she was grateful for something on which to vent her temper. "You are just as despicable as you were at the manor!"

"And you, Miss Summerfield, are just as spoiled and willful." He glowered down at her, his face only inches away. For a moment they stared at each other. Then, unable to stand the tension, Glory nervously licked her lips.

Nicholas Blackwell groaned.

Heavy male voices, whispering and laughing just a few feet away, drew his attention. The men were watching her, and he knew what they were thinking—he was thinking the same damned thing. Glaring down at her, he settled a firm hand at her waist and led her away.

They descended the aft ladder into the passageway. Only a dim whale-oil lantern lit the corridor. Nicholas stopped outside the door to her cabin and turned her to face him.

"I don't want any trouble, Miss Summerfield, and whether you mean to or not, you seem determined to stir it up. From now on you'll do as I say, or you'll spend the rest of this voyage in your cabin."

Glory's eyes widened. Drawing herself up, she tilted her chin defiantly. "How dare you threaten me?" Her ramrod-stiff posture made her seem inches taller than she had been only moments before. "Why are you treating me this way?"

"Because, you little vixen, I'm trying to make you understand. The *Black Spider* is not a passenger ship. These men aren't used to having a woman on board—especially a beautiful woman. You're putting yourself in danger." Nicholas watched her face. Her expression clearly said she didn't believe him. Ready to continue their contest of wills, she parted her lips, and he could see her delicate pink tongue. Lamplight glistened on her milky skin, gleamed against the flaxen ringlets of her hair.

Furious at the tempting picture she made, Nicholas cursed beneath his breath and hauled her against him. "This," he said, his voice cold, "is what I'm trying to make you see." Brutally, his mouth claimed hers. He felt her stiffen in surprise, her lips part in protest, and he deepened the kiss, thrusting his tongue violently between her teeth. Her slender fists beat at his chest, and she fought to pull away, but he only held her tighter. She tasted of the licorice cordial she'd enjoyed after supper, and the heady sensation only hardened his resolve. He'd demonstrate in no uncertain terms the consequences of her actions!

Mercilessly, he shoved her against the bulkhead, pinning her wrists above her head. One hand slid up her thigh to cup her bottom, pressing her against the hard length of him. He kissed her fiercely, savagely, without a thought for her pleasure—just as one of his men would. His hand moved from her hip to her breast and he kneaded the fullness roughly. When the thrusting peak stiffened against his hand, his own masculinity hardened in response. For a moment he had trouble remembering just why he was kissing her so cruelly when what he wanted to do was gentle his assault and make her respond as she had that night on the road.

His hand molded the heavy weight it caressed, and his thumb gently teased the peak. Then the sound of her tiny whimper returned him to his senses. Forcing himself to be brutal, he crushed her soft lips against his mouth until he tasted the metallic flavor of blood. Then he pulled away.

"Now do you understand?" he asked, his voice ragged, his face a cold taut mask. "That's what will happen to you if you don't do what I say."

Torn between humiliation and rage, trembling all over, Glory swallowed the bitter, angry lump in her throat. Her bosom heaved against the fabric of her dress, and her eyes flashed bright blue flame. "How dare you?" she snapped, playing the offended well-bred lady, but tears glistened on her cheeks. "How dare you treat me that way!" She hauled back her hand to slap him, but he caught her wrist midway. "I'm not one of your harlots!" she flung at him. "I am not your whore!"

"What I did was a suitor's touch compared to what my men would do to you. I don't want you to get hurt, Glory. Maybe now you'll understand."

With a shaky finger, Glory brushed at her tears. She bit back the angry retort curled on her tongue and summoned all the dignity she could muster. "You've made your point, Captain Blackwell. Now, if you'll excuse me . . ."

Chapter Seven

Moving blindly, Glory stepped into the narrow confines of her room and closed the door behind her. For a moment she just leaned against the heavy wooden planks, her eyes shut against the terrible pain in her heart. She could hear Nicholas's footfalls receding as he stalked down the passageway.

Stumbling across the room in the darkness, Glory could just make out Rosabelle's bulky figure curled up in the bottom bunk and was careful not to wake her. Though her fingers shook so hard she could scarcely unbutton her garments, Glory didn't ask for help. She didn't want to face the younger woman, at least not yet. Not until she came to grips with her raging emotions.

As she thought of Nicholas, she felt sick and betrayed, battered and discarded—so unlike the time before. She remembered a brisk spring evening, a carriage ride down a cloud-covered, tree-lined lane. The man who had kissed her that night, her gray-eyed champion, no longer existed, and Glory suddenly felt lost without him. With a flash of clarity, she discovered that the man her father had admired and respected meant more to her than she could have guessed—more than Eric Dixon, more than any man she had ever known. If only he'd been real.

Even her father had been fooled. He'd always believed Nicholas to be a man among men, a man he could trust and rely on. How disappointed he would have been to discover the captain was nothing more than the rake he appeared to be.

Struggling free of her garments at last, Glory pulled a cotton nightdress over her head and climbed into her berth. Though she tried to hold them at bay, warm tears rolled down her cheeks. How could she have been such a fool? The man was a libertine, a rake, and a rogue. Everyone in Charleston knew it. Why hadn't she believed them?

For a while she conjured images of the tall sea captain who had come to her rescue on the road. Of the way he had kissed her, the way he'd made her feel. Then the image changed to one of the cruel, arrogant, devil of a man who had brutally taken liberties with her tonight.

Lying in the darkness, thinking of the way he'd touched her, Glory felt her cheeks burn—because even as she struggled in his arms, even as he bruised her tender lips and roughly caressed her body, she had desired him. Wanted him as she hadn't known she could want any man. As she never wished to desire a man again. Nicholas Blackwell was a devil. A callous, unfeeling brute—and Glory was bound and determined to hate him.

After tossing for what seemed like hours, she drifted into a fitful sleep. Storm-gray eyes, dark with passion, hovered in her dreams.

Nicholas Blackwell snuffed out the lamp beside his bed. Resting on top of the sheet clad only in his breeches, he shoved his hands behind his head. The creak and sway of the ship, which usually lulled him to sleep, only grated on his tightly strung nerves. For the past two hours his mind had replayed the scene in the passageway and each time he remembered, he felt a little more rotten than before. Not that he'd had any choice, he reminded himself. Gloria Summerfield was as stubborn a woman as Nicholas Blackwell had ever had the misfortune to meet—and damned naive, if he read her right.

At first he'd thought she was teasing the men on board in an attempt to stir up trouble. After he'd kissed her—

pawed her would be more like it—he'd spent hours sorting out his thoughts. Now he believed the girl didn't know enough about men to realize the danger she was putting herself in. Oh, she'd had more than enough male admirers. Men like Eric Dixon, who'd probably done little more than hold her hand. To Glory, Nicholas was sure, her flirtations were nothing more than a parlor game: She was just playing by the same rules she'd been taught back home on the plantation.

But his crewmen weren't. Every time she smiled at one of them, or even at Josh, they read it as an invitation. When he'd found her in open conversation with Jago Dodd, Nicholas's stomach had tightened into a worried knot.

He'd had to do what he did; her safety was more important than her pride. And after the way he'd manhandled her, he had no doubt she'd finally gotten the message. But he would never forget the look of utter betrayal on her face. She had come to trust him, he knew. Too much. She seemed to trust every man she met, and for a woman traveling with only a servant to protect her, that could only mean disaster.

He turned on his side and punched his pillow, determined to get some sleep. He wondered what he would say to her on the morrow, if she would understand why he'd done what he did. At least he had accomplished one thing—he wouldn't have to worry about getting too deeply involved. From now on Gloria Summerfield wouldn't give him the time of day. He wondered why the thought of her scorn made him feel so bad.

Glory awoke to a sticky, humid dawn that only added to her dismal mood. The hot weather had been building since they'd left Charleston. Today looked to be the hottest yet. Glancing out the porthole, she saw the ship was anchored just off the coast. Tall pine forests reached nearly to the water's edge, and short stiff marsh grass dotted the shallows. Several dinghies heaped with so much cargo they nearly hid their four-man crews made their way back and forth to the shore.

Slipping down from her bunk, Glory washed her face and brushed her hair, then swirled the gleaming mass into a tight knot at the back of her head. She felt restless and more than a little melancholy, but she approached the day with a quiet resolve: She would do just as the captain suggested—remain in her cabin for the balance of the trip. She wasn't about to face him. She wasn't up to his dark mocking looks or the smug expression she was sure to see on his face. Instead, she picked up the new book of poems she'd brought along, Henry Wadsworth Longfellow's *Voices of the Night,* and sat down in the cabin's single tiny chair. Rosabelle stirred in the bunk beside her.

"Mornin', Miss Summerfield," she said, stretching her chubby arms above her head.

"Why don't you call me Glory?"

"Glory. That's a pretty name. It sounds like a sunrise."

Glory smiled. "Rosabelle's a pretty name, too. It almost rings when you say it."

The younger girl giggled. She sat up on her bunk a little too quickly and the color drained from her apple-round cheeks.

"Are you all right?" Glory asked, standing to assist her.

"I'm fine. Just a little dizzy. Got a touch a mornin' sickness."

"You mean because we're anchored?" As they sat anchored in the shallow waters of the coastal inlet, the roll and pitch of the ship was more pronounced.

"No, because I just get sick in the mornin'."

Glory nodded, but she still didn't understand why the girl would be sick only at one particular time of day.

"I'll be all right once we git to the Cape. Cap'n has friends there, a place where I kin have me babe."

Glory's bright eyes widened. She stared hard at the girl on the lower bunk. "You're going to have a . . . a baby?"

Rosabelle giggled again. "I ain't got a whole lotta choice."

When her eyes flew from the girl's round face to the plump mound beneath the thin muslin cover, Glory saw

that Rosabelle was indeed with child—*very* with child. She
licked her lips, which suddenly felt dry. "Captain Blackwell is helping you?"

"He's a good man, he is."

"How long have you known him?"

"Since I was fourteen, near as I kin recollect. He was
one o' me first."

"Oh, my God," Glory whispered. Her face paled, and
she sank back down on the small oak chair beside the
bunk.

"Cap'n says he'll make sure I'm taken care of. Says
he's proud o' me for wantin' to keep the babe."

"He's being awfully kind," Glory said softly. But her
mind said the babe might be his. In fact it *must* be his!
The hard man who had assaulted her in the passageway
last night wouldn't be that generous. Nicholas Blackwell
was transporting the mother of his bastard child, dumping
her in some unknown place, and the poor illiterate girl
seemed grateful. Oh, Lord, it was the most sinful thing
Glory had ever heard. How could he!

While Rosabelle performed her morning ablutions,
Glory pretended to read. It was all she could do to keep
the paper from trembling as she sightlessly turned each
page. When Rosabelle had finished, she smiled wanly at
Glory and fled the room for the fresher air up on deck.
Glory didn't blame her. But she'd be damned if she'd face
Nicholas Blackwell now—or ever!

Glory spent all of that day and half of the next in the
confines of the cabin. She sent Rosabelle in to the dining
room with myriad excuses ranging from headaches to seasickness. Joshua Pintassle had stopped by to see her, but
Glory refused to open the door. Only Rosabelle was allowed entrance. And Cookie, the whiskery old cook who
brought down her meals. And of course Nathan. He'd
stopped by when he heard she was ill. She assured him it
was just a bout of seasickness.

"Are they still treating you all right?" she asked, during their few moments alone.

"Good enough. Mostly they ignore me, and that's just fine with me. Scuttlebutt has it that most of the regular crew took sick with malaria. The captain picked this bunch up in Barbados. They're a scurvy lot."

Glory smiled. "You're beginning to sound like a sailor yourself."

Nathan grinned, his handsome face taking on a winning, boyish expression. "I've been spending most of my time with Cookie, helping him with the meals, that kind of thing. Helps to pass the time."

"We'll be in New York before long, thank God." She rolled her eyes skyward.

Nathan watched her with a bit of suspicion. "You sure there's nothing else wrong with you? Besides being seasick, I mean."

Glory glanced away. "I'll be fine in a day or two."

"And Captain Blackwell?" he pressed. "He's behaving himself? I've heard rumors about him. The men say he's quite a ladies' man."

"Nathan, I told you, everything's fine." A sharpness she hadn't intended had crept into her voice.

For a moment Nathan looked as though he didn't believe her; then he turned toward the door. "I'd better get back up on deck before they think something's amiss. Mos' us darkies," he drawled in his thick black accent, "don' spen' much time alone in da missy's cabin."

Glory stifled a grin, rose from her chair, and kissed him on the cheek. "I'll see you tomorrow," she assured him as he ducked through the low wooden door.

Three hours later, Glory was lying on her bunk wishing they would get to New York when she heard an insistent pounding on her door.

"It's Mac, lass. Let me in."

"I'm . . . I'm not feeling well, Mac." By now she really wasn't. The confines of the cabin combined with the now stifling heat and the roll and pitch of the ship had her stomach rolling as well. She cursed Nicholas Blackwell for the hundredth time that day.

"You'll let me in now, lass, or I'll have this door broke down!"

Glory leaped from the chair. In two quick strides she reached the door and swung it open. Mac stood in the passageway, his ruddy face split by a white-toothed grin.

"Now, that's better. It's fine ye be lookin' to me. All ye need is a little sea air, and I mean to see ye git it."

She opened her mouth to protest, then snapped it shut. They were still a long way from New York, and Mac was right—she needed some fresh air. Badly. As long as Mac was with her, she rationalized, she'd be safe from Nicholas Blackwell.

Mac eyed her from head to toe, taking in the long leg-of-mutton sleeves of her dress and her full black skirts. "And git rid o' them petticoats. It's too blasted hot fer 'em. Sometimes ye women got no sense at all."

Glory looked down at her very proper day dress. Mac was right. How much cooler she would be if she shed her mass of petticoats. She grinned up at him. "I'll just be a moment."

Mac waited in the passageway. When Glory had finished, she opened the door wearing a grateful smile and fewer petticoats. She accepted his arm, and they swept from the cabin. The cooler air brightened her mood—and her constitution—the moment they arrived on deck.

"Oh, Mac," she said, realizing how good it felt to be out-of-doors again. "Thank God you came." The wind blew wispy strands of pale hair that had escaped from her chignon, and Glory felt reborn. She'd been a fool to let Nicholas Blackwell intimidate her. The man was nothing more than an ill-mannered lout. She wouldn't let him bother her again.

They walked along the deck, and despite herself, Glory found her glance searching for the tall figure of the man she was determined to dislike.

"He's below," Mac said, and she blushed to know he'd read her thoughts. "You two must've had some spat. I never seen him like this in all the years we been together. He might fool the others. They just think he's in a mean temper. But he kinna fool me; I've known the lad too long.''

Though she'd vowed to hate him, Glory's spirits soared. "You really think he's upset?"

Mac nodded, a lock of sandy hair tumbling across his ruddy brow. "Downright miserable. Want to tell me about it?"

Glory shook her head. How could she ever explain to Mac what Nicholas had done to her?

"I be thinkin' I've a fair idea," he said, and Glory's cheeks pinkened again. "You're a nice girl, Glory. I could see that the minute ye come on board the *Spider*. But the others—the crew, I mean—they don't care nothin' about how nice ye be. All they see is a lass in pretty skirts. Captain was real worried ye'd get yerself in trouble. He can't be there to watch ye all the time."

Glory bristled. "I can take care of myself."

"Way the cap'n tells it, there's plenty o' things ye kin do, but I don't think that be one o' them." He watched her closely. "Seems to me, livin' on that big plantation and all, somebody's always been 'round to look out for ye."

Glory sighed. "Yes, I guess that's so."

"Nicky thinks a lot o' ye, lass. I never seen him in such a temper as when ye wouldna come outta yer cabin."

Glory stared at the deck. "He just wanted to embarrass me."

" 'Tis not so, lass."

They strolled along the deck to where a pile of lumber formed a natural barrier against the wind. "There's something in yer eyes, lass. Somethin' tells me I kin trust ye—and so kin Nicky." He squinted his own eyes against the sun as if making some momentous decision. "The cap'n's had a hard life. His mother run away and left him when he was only a little boy. His father never got over it. He married again, more to give Nicky a mother than anythin' else, but it didna work out—not for Alexander nor for Nicky. He run away to sea when he was twelve. That's

when I met him. He was the hardest-working lad I'd ever
seen.

"Time he was twenty-one he'd made first officer. About
the same time his father died. When Nicky left home,
Alexander Blackwell owned the biggest fleet o' vessels on
the eastern seaboard. When he returned, there was just
one old harbor scow left. Nicky took over the company.
Worked eighteen hours a day to build it into the fleet o'
ships it is today. He's built his own fortune along with it."
Mac patted her cheek and glanced out to sea. "But he
needs a lass to share it with. One he kin trust—and learn
to love. One who'll love him in return."

Glory felt a stab of bitterness. "From what I've heard,
Nicholas Blackwell gets more than his share of *love.*"

"Oh, he's got plenty o' women, if that's what ye mean.
But it isn't hardly the same."

"He could have a wife and child if he accepted his
responsibilities and married Rosabelle."

"Rosabelle!" Mac seemed incredulous.

"How can he stand to let someone else raise his child?"
Glory's blue eyes snapped with angry fire.

"I don't know what that little lassie in yer cabin's been
sayin', but the cap'n had nothin' to do wi' that. He felt
sorry for the lass is all. He's done his best to see that she's
cared for, but not because o' his conscience. He's just that
kind o' man."

Glory heard the truth in his words. She felt as if a weight
had been lifted from her chest. The breeze seemed suddenly fresher, the sun a little brighter than before. "Thank
you, Mac," she whispered. "Thank you for helping me
understand. You won't be sorry."

"I know that, lass. Deep down, Nicky knows it, too.
He wouldna be so damned miserable if he didna."

"Where is he, Mac?"

"In his cabin."

She hesitated a moment. "What if someone sees me?"

Mac chuckled. "Yer learnin', lass. Yer learnin'. C'mon,
I'll walk ye down."

He escorted her down the passageway, checked to be

certain no one else was around, then waited near the stairs while she knocked on the captain's door. With her heart knocking against her ribs, she licked her suddenly dry lips. When Nicholas, naked to the waist, opened the door scowling, she almost turned and ran.

"Hello," he said, quickly hiding his surprise. A glance down the hall told him Mac had brought her, and he pulled her inside. "You shouldn't have come here," he said, "even with Mac."

"I . . . I know," she said. Then, seeing his bare chest and broad shoulders, she backed away. "Please, Captain, don't misunderstand my intentions. I only came because I wanted to apologize for any trouble I might have caused."

He could see she was a little afraid of him and cursed himself for the hundredth time that day. As he grabbed up his shirt, he indicated she sit down in the squat oak chair while he took a seat on the foot of his neatly made berth.

Glory remained standing. "Of course, that doesn't excuse your actions," she added with a surge of spirit. Nicholas almost smiled. "You behaved despicably, and I for one shall never forget it."

He'd had the very same thought himself.

"On the other hand," she was saying, "I suppose you were trying to make a point." Her eyes slid away from his, and he read her embarrassment. "I may be a little naive, Captain, but I'm not a fool. Things are different where I come from. Women have little to fear. I've never been around men like these. I just didn't understand."

"And now you do."

"Yes." Her voice was soft. "Now I do." She turned to go, but he rose and caught her arm.

"Glory?"

"Yes?"

"I'm sorry, too."

She scoffed, remembering the last apology he'd made. "Sorry I didn't listen to you sooner?"

"No. Sorry I hurt you. I lost my temper and . . . well, I just didn't know any other way to make you understand."

He looked more than a little contrite, and Glory remembered the way he'd looked that night on the road—caring and gentle and protective. Her glance moved to his mouth, no longer harsh, but full and inviting. She wished he would kiss her as he had before. Instead, she nodded and turned to leave.

"Will you join us at supper?" he asked, and Glory felt a bubble of happiness swell inside her heart.

"I'd be honored," she said, facing him again. She could have sworn his gray eyes lightened.

"Until tonight, then."

"Until tonight."

The moment the door closed, Nicholas regretted his impulsiveness. Why in blazes hadn't he kept her at a distance? He had been stunned to see her outside his door; he'd felt sure she would never speak to him again. He was the one who should have initiated the apology. Never had a woman deserved one more. But saying he was sorry was not something Nicholas did well—and certainly not often. Besides, he didn't want her friendship. He didn't want to be near her again. Now he had no choice.

In the end he missed supper on purpose. Sent Josh Pintassle in his place. After supper he'd seen the two of them walking on deck, though he watched them from the shadows and they hadn't seen him. Glory seemed more reserved, and she rarely even glanced at the crew. He guessed his lesson had done some good after all.

"Tighten that halyard—the fore royal is luffing!" he snapped to three men on the starboard watch. "Look alive, soggers!"

"No use takin' it out on them, lad." Mac MacDougal sauntered up beside him with an easy loping gait born of years at sea.

"What in blazes is that supposed to mean?"

"It means, if ye wanted to stroll the deck with the lass, ye should've asked her."

"Damn you, Mac, the girl's got nothing to do with this."

"No?"

"Of course not. I'm changing course for Bull's Head Bay. I want to make the inlet by tomorrow night."

"Goin' to see Mistress Ginger, are ye?"

"Why not? We're making good time. The men could use a little shore leave and so could I."

"But the lass has nothing to do with it."

"Dammit, Mac, I told you before she hasn't."

"Aye, so you said." He ambled toward several crewmen who were hauling in line. "Bull's Head Bay. Sounds like a fine idea to me. Good night to ye, Cap'n."

A blustery wind ruffled the sails and a full moon bathed the waters in glistening light as the ship approached Bull's Head Bay. Glancing at the tree-lined shore clearly visible in the moonlight, Nicholas breathed a heart-felt sigh of relief. Off to one side, tiny lights Nicholas recognized as the Bull's Head Tavern beckoned him ashore.

On the second floor of the house next door to the tavern lived Ginger McKinnes, a buxom wench with hair as black as the night sea and skin as fair as the whitecaps above it. An evening in Ginger's willing arms ought to soothe a little of the tension he'd been feeling of late. He'd leave only a skeleton crew aboard, and Joshua Pintassle had already volunteered to watch after Glory. After a night ashore, they'd weigh anchor at dawn and with any luck be back on schedule by the following day.

"Furl the sails and heave to," Nicholas instructed. The ship slid silently through the water; then he gave the order to drop anchor. The great chunk of metal plunged into the sea, caught, and the rode groaned as it tightened, bringing the ship to a shuddering stop in the quiet swells of the cove.

Since supper had been served several hours earlier, Nicholas having supped in his cabin, the men were eager to take their leave. "I'll expect to see you all back here before first light," Nicholas told them. "It'll go hard for any man who tarries." He watched as the men hustled to lower the shore boats, most wearing broad, knowing grins.

There was no more notorious den of cutthroats and scoundrels than Bull's Head Bay—nor a prettier lot of whores. Ginger was one of the most expensive and most sought-after, but she always made time for Nicholas. Tonight would be no exception. Nicholas could hardly wait.

"We're going ashore?" Glory asked, strolling up beside Nicholas as more of the crew climbed over the side and down the rope ladder to the small boats bobbing beside the ship.

"The men are."

"Madame LaFarge is going, isn't she? And Rosabelle?"

"Rosy's been sick. She needs some time ashore. Madame LaFarge intends to ply her trade."

"I see." Glory felt her cheeks flame. But Nicholas seemed preoccupied, and she wondered if it had something to do with the reason he'd missed supper the past two nights. It galled her that he'd been ignoring her again.

"Joshua will be staying aboard," he told her. "You'll be safe enough."

"Why can't I go ashore with you?" she asked, and Nicholas glanced away, a little shamefaced, it seemed to Glory.

"Because I have business ashore. Besides, Bull's Head Bay is no place for a lady."

"But surely I'd be safe with you," she persisted.

"I'll be too busy to protect your virtue."

"But that's not fair. The other women get to go. They said we could all have a nice hot bath and—"

"Fair or not, you're staying aboard and that's final." He turned to Nathan, who was sitting on the deck finishing his lesson with Mac on how to braid hemp into line. "Your mistress is to remain aboard. Is that understood?"

"Yassa, Cap'n Blackwell."

Glory silently fumed. Wordlessly, she turned from the men and stormed toward the bow of the ship.

"Ah, let 'er go ashore, Nicky," Madame LaFarge cajoled. "She really wants to go. She kin have 'erself a nice hot bath upstairs, then sit in the tavern with Rosy whilst I earn a little pocket change.''

''Not a chance. That place is nothing but a den of thieves.''

''She could wear one o' me dresses,'' Rosabelle put in. No one would notice. She'd just be one o' the girls.''

Nicholas groaned aloud. ''Just one of the girls. That's all I need. Julian Summerfield's daughter parading like the queen of Cock Alley.''

''Come on, Nicky,'' Madame LaFarge pressed. ''Loosen up. Let the girl have some fun.''

''I said no, and that's the end of it. I left strict instructions with the night watch: Once we're gone, no one's to leave this vessel.''

''Wouldn't be you're plannin' on meetin' Miss Ginger, now, would it?''

''What I do with my time ashore is none of your concern.''

Rosabelle giggled. ''Kin hardly fault a man fer wantin' to relieve his need.''

''I guess not,'' Madame LaFarge reluctantly agreed. ''That pretty little blond piece prob'ly has him plumb tied in knots.''

Nicholas's dark look blackened.

''Don't seem right, though,'' Madame LaFarge added, ''leavin' Miss Glory behind jus' so's you can relieve the ache in yer breeches.''

Nicholas stalked away.

From her place behind the galley, Glory fought the urge to shove him overboard. So the black-hearted rake was meeting his harlot on shore! He hadn't meant a word he'd said. *Sorry.* That was a joke. Nicholas Blackwell hadn't been sorry a day in his life!

Standing alone in the darkness, Glory watched the captain's boat depart, carrying Mac and the last of the crew, while Joshua made a final turn around the deck. One small boat still bobbed near the anchor rode. Through her haze of temper, Glory made a decision: She was going ashore at Bull's Head Bay. She would dress up just as Rosabelle

suggested, then find the girls at the tavern. She'd show
Nicholas Blackwell he couldn't order her around just to
satisfy his lusty appetites. It wouldn't be difficult—with
Nathan to accompany her.

Secretly she hoped against hope she'd run into the tall
sea captain. She'd let him know once and for all he was
not going to dominate her the way he did his crew!

Chapter Eight

"Nathan, you *have* to take me! If you don't I'll go alone."

"I don't like this, Glory. The captain says you're supposed to stay aboard."

"The captain says, the captain says. I'm sick and tired of doing what the captain says. Don't you want to see what it's like? Where's your spirit of adventure?"

"Since when did you develop this yen for excitement?" Nathan wanted to know, and Glory grudgingly admired his perception.

Adventure was the furthest thing from Glory's mind. She wanted a bath, but mostly she wanted to see for herself the kind of woman Captain Blackwell preferred to her.

"Will you take me or not?" Glory asked.

"No. It's against the captain's orders."

"Fine, then I'll go alone." She lowered her chin and glowered at him furiously.

"You would, wouldn't you?" When she opened her mouth to answer, Nathan cut her off. "Never mind. I'll take you. I've never said no to you in my life. Why should I start now?"

Glory smiled in triumph. "I'll meet you near the bow as soon as Joshua retires for the night."

Nathan sighed resignedly, nodded, and slipped into the darkness.

Joshua Pintassle returned to Glory's side.

"I'm awfully tired, Joshua," she told him. "Would you mind terribly if I turned in early?"

He looked disappointed. "I suppose not. Though I was really looking forward to your company." When she didn't weaken, he walked her down the aft ladder to her cabin. She smiled up at him angelically, walked quietly into her room, and closed the door. The minute she heard Josh enter his cabin, Glory rushed to where Rosabelle's few tattered dresses were hung. Two had been let out to accommodate her now large girth, but one, a gaudy orange and white satin creation with stiff white petticoats, awaited the day she'd be small enough to wear it again.

Glory slipped out of her stylish black day dress and into Rosabelle's colorful gown. The gown was a good deal too small, pushing her breasts suggestively above the bodice and showing too much ankle beneath the hem. Glory swallowed hard. Knowing what she must look like, it was all she could do to keep her resolve. But she let her pale hair down, fluffed it out, and grabbed her cloak. She'd stay hidden within the folds of the cape, and as she walked, the color and fabric of her gown would imply she was no more than a working girl. Satisfied with her plan, she refused to dwell on the other implications.

Climbing the ladder to the deck, she glanced around, but took no more than a few steps before a masculine voice stopped her.

"Evenin', Miss." It was the night anchor watch, a youthful man with shaggy brown hair who stood a good four inches taller than Glory. Pulling her cloak around her, she prayed he hadn't noticed the odd clothing she wore beneath.

"Good evening." Glory's heart pounded. Of all the rotten luck. Now that the man had seen her, there was no way around it—she'd have to enlist his aid or forget their plan. The man could be prowling the deck half the night.

"My name's Glory," she said, batting her thick dark lashes. "What's yours?" The man smiled so broadly Glory counted two missing teeth, though the sailor looked no more than twenty.

"I'm called Ripley. Ripley Sterns."

"A pleasure to meet you, Mr. Sterns." She extended a slim-fingered hand, and the sailor accepted it almost reverently. "You know, Mr. Sterns—" she began, then paused for effect. "May I call you Ripley?"

Mutely he nodded.

"I feel so foolish, Ripley. Why, I hardly know you, yet here I am, about to ask for a favor."

"A favor?" He seemed almost pleased.

"Yes. You see I have to get to shore."

Instantly on guard, the sailor stiffened, his warm manner dissolving. "Cap'n Blackwell says nobody's to leave the ship."

"I know, but you see he didn't know about my special circumstances."

"What circumstances?"

"Well, Rosabelle left her medicine for the . . . ah, for her delicate condition, if you take my meaning . . . and she's going to need it. My servant and I will take it to her and come right back. The captain won't even know we've been gone."

He looked skeptical. "That'd be breakin' the cap'n's direct orders. No, ma'am. I don't think I could do that."

"Glory," she said sweetly.

The sailor swallowed hard. "Glory," he repeated. The word came out on a breathless sigh.

"We'd be back in an hour. Two at most. Mr. Pintassle's asleep. No one would know except you and me"—she touched his arm, her fingers cool against his flushed skin— "Ripley," she added softly.

"Can't your man go alone?"

"I'm afraid he's not very . . . I hate to put it indelicately, but I don't believe Nathan would be smart enough to find her. Besides, there are certain . . . *female* problems she and I will need to discuss."

The young sailor actually blushed. Then he glanced from bow to stern, noting the deck was quiet, the stars bright above. Soft moonlight grazed the coral in Glory's cheeks. "You're sure you'll come right back?" he asked.

"Of course."

"I know I shouldn't do this." Though he shook his shaggy head in a negative gesture, Glory knew his answer was yes.

"Thank you, Ripley," she whispered softly.

Just then Nathan appeared on deck. Seeing the sailor, he hesitated a moment, then came forward.

"We'd better get going," Glory said. "Mr. Sterns has been kind enough to let us go ashore."

Nathan nodded dumbly, but Glory spotted his knowing glance. He wasn't a bit surprised she'd been able to talk the sailor into letting them leave.

With some assistance from the sailor, and several words of caution, Glory climbed over the side and began the descent down the rope ladder. Nathan waited below in the tiny shore boat. As Nathan shoved off, she waved back at the sailor and settled on the seat, pulling her cloak around her, though the evening was warm and humid.

Once they reached shore, Nathan beached the craft and secured it to a nearby pine tree. Glory climbed out, barely wetting her kidskin shoes.

"Hurry up, Nathan," she whispered. "Rosabelle and Madame LaFarge are supposed to be in the tavern." She glanced at the amber glow of lamplight coming from a nearby cluster of windows.

"Are you sure you don't just want to peek in the window?"

"Maybe we should. That way we'll be sure they're inside." She wondered if Captain Blackwell would be there too—or already wrapped in his lover's arms.

Nicholas Blackwell flipped over his final card. Ace of spades. This was turning out to be his lucky night—except that Ginger, it seemed, had gone to the country to visit a sick patron. Her girlfriend Nina had assured Nicholas that Ginger would be home soon, adding she'd be happy to fill in for her friend if she didn't arrive on time. So far Nicholas had been content to play cards with some of the crew-men from the *Fleet Lady*, a schooner bound for Charleston laden with Havana cigars, rye whiskey, and buckshot, among various and sundry items.

"Looks like I win again," Nicholas said. Grumbling, the four sailors at the table watched as he raked in his winnings. The low-ceilinged tavern was noisy and crowded. Thick black smoke hovered in patches over the small, dimly lit tables. Several rowdy sailors sang sea chanties in one corner of the room while others were con-tent to pinch a barmaid's bottom or steal the quick feel of a soft breast.

"Ye can't seem to lose, Cap'n," Mac said, shaking his sandy-haired head. "Think I picked the wrong night to play wi' ye."

Nicholas almost smiled. He liked winning. At just about anything. As long as he was winning, he'd wait for Gin-ger. Well, maybe not that long. He'd come ashore for fe-male companionship and the hour was already growing late. He glanced at the pretty little redhead, Nina. She was looking prettier all the time.

"Let's go around back," Glory suggested once they reached the tavern. Along the way they'd passed only a couple of drunken sailors who eyed her briefly, then stag-gered on down the dirt lane.

"I don't like this, Glory. I don't know how I let you talk me into this in the first place."

"Probably because you thought it would do me good to see how the rest of the world lives. You're always telling me life's no fairy tale."

Nathan chuckled. "Yeah, maybe this is a good idea at that. But I still don't—"

"Well, well, well. Lookee what we 'ave 'ere." The cockney accent was unmistakable as a short, pigeon-shouldered man sauntered around the corner of the tavern.

Glory took a step backward, drawing deeper into the folds of her cloak. She took two more steps and bumped into the thick chest of a second, bigger man who had moved behind her. With a meaty hand, he pulled the hood from her head, exposing a mass of shiny blond hair.

"Whooee!" his skinny companion sputtered in surprise.

"You're right there, Smitty," the bigger man said with a low-country drawl. "Looks like that trip to the necessary's gonna pay off."

"I'll say, mate," the Englishman agreed. "Ain't she just about the pertiest piece o' baggage ye've ever seen?"

Nathan tugged at her arm. "We best be goin', Miz Glory," he said in his thick accent, and Glory couldn't have agreed more. She took a step toward Nathan, but the beefy sailor grabbed her arm.

"She ain't goin' anywhere, boy," the big sailor warned. "She's gonna conduct a little business. Me and Smitty got three months' wages in our pockets, and we mean to buy us the best piece of fluff in Bull's Head Bay. Near's I kin tell, she's it."

Nathan straightened, all pretense of the illiterate slave gone. "Back away and leave us alone." Again he pulled Glory toward him, and again the beefy sailor held her arm, tugging her in two directions at the same time.

"Well, now, ain't that somethin'? A nigger who kin talk like a white man."

Nathan swung a solid punch that thudded against the big sailor's jaw, and Glory stifled a scream. Jerking free of the sailor's grip, she turned to run, but the second sailor caught her around the waist and pulled her into his bony arms. Brandishing pistols, two more men stepped from behind. They moved behind Nathan, and before Glory could utter the words that would warn him, one brought the barrel of his weapon down on Nathan's skull with a loud, resounding crack.

Nathan slumped into the dirt.

Glory screamed in earnest and tore free of the little man who held her.

The big sailor caught her up and swung her clear off the ground. "Don't you fret, none, darlin'. Yer nigger boy'll be jus' fine. He'll be comin' 'round 'bout the time we're done with you.'' He chuckled heartily, and Glory felt suddenly sick. She tried to scream again, but he clamped his large hand over her mouth. ''You keep that up and I'm gonna git mad.''

Glory forced herself to be calm.

The big sailor untied her cloak and tossed it away, then marveled at the tempting sight she made. ''Would ya look at that, Smitty.'' Beads of perspiration formed on his brow. ''She's got legs all the way to hell and gone.''

The Englishman lifted her skirt and appraised the turn of her calves outlined by Rosabelle's black fishnet stockings. ''Guess we could take turns with her right 'ere, but I got me a feather mattress in m' room upstairs.''

''I ain't taken a woman betwixt the sheets in a coon's age,'' one of the other sailors, apparently a fellow crewman, put in. ''I say we have at her upstairs!''

A chorus of agreement followed, and Glory found herself tossed over the man's wide shoulder. He slapped her bottom soundly to the accompaniment of raucous laughter, and then she was jounced all the way up the street.

Kicking and pounding the man's broad back did not an ounce of good. Her only chance was to wait until they entered the tavern, then scream for help and pray one of the men from the *Black Spider* would recognize her and come to her assistance. Maybe Mac would be there. Or even—God forbid—Nicholas. She felt sure she would prefer to defend her virtue on her own rather than face Nicholas Blackwell under such humiliating circumstances.

After another bawdy slap and more laughter, she decided it didn't matter who her rescuer was.

As they moved down the dirt lane toward the tavern, Glory made a try at persuasion. ''Please, gentlemen,'' she pleaded, ''I know you think I'm a lady of the evening, but I assure you I am not. This is all a mistake. If you'll put me down, I'll see there are no repercussions.''

''Reper . . . reper . . . what'd she say?''

''I don't know,'' the big sailor said, ''but she'll be too busy to be talkin' once she's on her back!''

They all laughed uproariously, and Glory fumed. Riding upside down, she felt all the blood rush to her head, and she was beginning to feel dizzy. Maybe she should try screaming again. She decided against it. Her best chance lay inside the tavern. Rosabelle and Madame LaFarge were supposed to be there. She prayed to God they were.

"Put her down, bucko," a soft voice warned. Glory raised her head to see Jago Dodd standing just outside the tavern door.

"Thank, God," Glory whispered. "Gentlemen, please, Mr. Dodd will explain everything."

"Can't you keep that chit quiet?" one of the sailors demanded.

"Stay outta this, mate," the Englishman warned Jago. "Ye kin have her when we git through."

"I said put the lady down."

"Lady? Now, there's a laugh." As the big sailor strode toward the tavern, Glory spotted the gleam of metal in the Englishman's hand.

"Jago, watch out!" she warned, kicking her long legs in another attempt to free herself. "He's got a knife!"

"Shut up!" the man warned with a harder whack, and Glory braced herself against his shoulders to see. The three other men circled Jago, each brandishing a knife. Jago held a long gleaming blade of his own. Oh, God, she thought, this is all my fault. If something happens to Jago, I'll never forgive myself.

Nicholas slipped an arm around Nina's slender waist. "Let's go. I've waited long enough."

She smiled seductively up at him, green eyes bright with anticipation. "Ginger's told me all about you. I can't say I'm sorry she's busy tonight."

Nicholas smiled coldly. "You just make sure *I'm* not sorry." Guiding her along, he headed toward the staircase leading to her room at the top of the landing, but before he got halfway there, a commotion behind him drew his attention. Several men rushed past them toward the door.

Nicholas grabbed the arm of a one-eyed sailor who was hurrying behind the others. "What's going on out there?"

"Jago Dodd's takin' on four men from the *Fleet Lady* in a knife fight over some new whore."

Nicholas stiffened. He had hired the barrel-chested sailor in Barbados. Dodd had a terrible reputation for fighting, but a shortage of crewmen made hiring the man a necessity. So far he'd caused little trouble, but Nicholas didn't know him well enough to trust him. He didn't want to see one of his men killed in an unfair fight, either.

"Wait here," he told Nina. "I'll be right back."

Nicholas strode to the door, uncertain of what to expect. Outside, Jago Dodd stood surrounded by cheering men while he held three other knife-wielding sailors at bay. He was slashed in several places; red streaks stained his clothing, but he seemed to be holding his own.

Nicholas didn't like the odds. He took two long strides forward before the sight of a ruffled fanny and a pair of long, shapely black-stockinged legs stopped him cold. When the beefy sailor who held the girl turned sideways, Nicholas caught his breath. Silvery tendrils of pale blond hair hung almost to the ground. Her milk-white bosom bulged from the top of her skimpy orange satin gown.

"Nicholas!" she cried, propping herself up to see. "Thank God you're here! You've got to help Mr. Dodd!"

If Nicholas hadn't been so stunned—and so furious—he might have laughed. A crowd of drunken sailors were fighting to see which would bed her first, while spoiled and pampered Gloria Summerfield, dressed like a whore, worried about the safety of the toughest man of the lot.

"I'll see what I can do." Nicholas raised a booted foot and slammed it against the wrist of the first sailor he could reach, sending the man's knife flying. He punched a second and noticed Jago had sheathed his knife and kicked a third, joining him in the donnybrook.

With the odds more evenly matched against his friends, the beefy sailor set Glory on her feet and joined in, landing a smashing blow to Nicholas's stomach that doubled him over. Then a blow to his jaw sent him sprawling. Jago

Dodd punched the sailor so hard he buckled to his knees. Nicholas grinned at Jago and regained his feet, beginning to enjoy the fray.

After landing a solid left-right combination that sent a short, skinny sailor careening against a tree, Nicholas turned and punched another in the nose. The man's blood sprayed the front of Nicholas's white linen shirt. Glory wrung her hands, her blue eyes bright with uncertainty, and Nicholas vowed she should damned well be afraid— of him, instead of the men who were brawling over her!

A few more blows and the battle was over. All four crewmen from the *Fleet Lady* lay prostrate in the dirt. Nicholas and Jago Dodd stood above them, feet apart, fists clenched against any newcomers. None came.

Taking a deep, steadying breath, Nicholas turned to Jago and extended a hand. "I'm pleased to have you on board, Jago. You can sail with me anytime."

Jago grinned, creasing his beetle-browed, knife-scarred face. "Aye, Cap'n." He took Nicholas's hand in a bone-crushing grip.

Only then did Nicholas go to Glory. She seemed unable to speak. "Are you all right?" he asked, giving in to worry for the first time.

"Ye-yes," she stuttered, beginning to shake. Her full breasts threatened to spill out over the top of the gown. Her shiny hair tumbled in silken strands to frame her face.

Nicholas had seen her in mourning clothes, seen her in stylish day dresses, even seen her in elegant, daringly low-cut gowns, but he'd never in his wildest dreams imagined the pagan beauty that lay beneath her expensive fashions. His heart hammered and his blood boiled. It was all he could do not to carry her off, just as the sailors had intended to do.

"How did you get here?" he demanded, his tone harsher than he intended. The girl had the most infuriating effect on him. One he didn't like in the least. It made him all the angrier. He grabbed her by the arms and shook her— hard. "I said how did you get here!"

"Oh, my God, " she whispered. "Nathan!" She tore

free and began running madly down the dirt lane, her pale hair flying out behind her. She rounded the corner of the tavern to see Nathan sitting up, swaying, holding his head.

"Nathan!" she cried, rushing to kneel beside him. "Are you all right?"

He groaned. "My head hurts something awful, and there are two of you, but I guess I'll live . . . Are you all right?"

"I'm fine." She poked him gently in the ribs—a reminder to change his manner of speech—as Captain Blackwell knelt beside her.

He examined Nathan's head. "He's got a nasty lump and probably a slight concussion, but I think he'll be all right."

"Thank God."

Nicholas stood up, then jerked her none to gently to her feet. "I want to know just exactly how you got here. And I want the truth."

Glory swallowed hard. "I—I . . ." Noticing that the scowl on Nicholas's face was growing blacker by the moment, she licked her suddenly dry lips. "I told the night watch I had to see Rosabelle. I persuaded him to let us come ashore."

"Do you have any idea what you've done?"

She straightened her spine and lifted her chin defiantly. "Nothing so terrible. I came ashore, that's all. Just the same as you."

"Not quite the same," he said softly. "You caused one of my crewmen to disobey a direct order. Because of you, he'll be punished. As will your servant."

"What!" Glory shrieked. "But they've done nothing. It was my idea to come ashore, not theirs. Surely you can't blame them?"

Nicholas didn't answer. Just tugged her along to the shore boat, roughly handed her in to Jago, and climbed aboard himself. No one said a word as Jago and Nathan manned the oars. Glory's hands trembled so badly she had to clutch the folds of her skirt to still them. Surely Nicholas was only trying to scare her. He'd see reason once they reached the ship. She would persuade him to forgive the three of them somehow.

"Nicholas, please," she begged, the moment they set foot on the deck.

"Jago, escort the lady to her cabin. Lock the door. When Rosabelle returns, tell her she's to bunk with Madame LaFarge."

Jago nodded.

"When you've finished, escort her servant to the brig. "He'll make the balance of the voyage below decks."

"Nooo!" Glory screamed. "You can't do that! It was my idea. I made him do it!"

"Mr. Dodd."

"Aye, Captain." Jago wrapped a huge arm around her waist and effortlessly hauled her down the stairs to her cabin. He opened the door and gently but firmly deposited her inside.

"Sorry, Miss Glory. Try to understand. Captain Blackwell's got no choice. The whole crew knows he told you to stay behind. He told the night watch and your man directly. His word is law. He has to stand by it or the men won't work for him. You've left him no choice."

"Oh, God," Glory said. Tears coursed down her cheeks. "I didn't mean to hurt anyone."

"Captain knows that. He hates this as much as you." Jago closed the door, and Glory heard the key turn in the lock.

Still dressed in her orange satin garb, she sank onto the lower bunk and gave herself up to deep racking sobs. She'd never felt more miserable in her life. The last thing she'd wanted was to hurt someone else. Now Nathan would spend the rest of the voyage in the brig, and she still didn't know what would happen to the young sailor. And all because she'd wanted to have her way. She was spoiled and willful, just as Nicholas said. A fresh wave of tears spilled down her cheeks. The lump in her throat threatened to choke her.

After tossing and turning for what seemed like hours, she finally fell asleep. She awoke sometime later, feeling leaden and achy all over. Rising from the berth, she forced herself to wash her face and brush her hair, then pulled on a white cotton nightdress.

There was always tomorrow, she told herself. She'd try again tomorrow. Then she remembered the hard cold look on the tall sea captain's face. And felt like crying all over again.

Chapter Nine

Exhausted and worried, Glory awoke later than usual. The day was already hot and humid, leaving her nightgown clinging to her skin. The ship creaked and swayed beneath her so she knew they'd made way, and she longed for the cooler air up on deck. After performing her morning ablutions, she dressed in one of her black day dresses, leaving off all but her thinnest petticoat, her one concession to the heat. She was brushing her hair when a knock at the door interrupted her.

The ship's cook requested permission to enter. The wizened little man came shuffling in, carrying a tray laden with biscuits and coffee, his eyes downcast. "Mornin', Miss Glory," Cookie mumbled so low she could barely make out the words."

"Good morning, Cookie," she answered, just as half-heartedly. As he set the tray down and turned to leave the room, Glory caught his weathered hand. "Cookie, I have to speak with Captain Blackwell. Do you think you could—"

A loud crack stopped her in midsentence. Her eyes flew wide at the second crack, and her heart knocked against her ribs. She'd know that sound anywhere. "Cookie, tell me what's happening."

"Nothin' fer you to worry about. Had to be done." The lash sounded again.

"Tell me!"

"Man disobeyed the captain's direct order. He's—"

Glory didn't wait to hear the rest. Brushing past the grizzled old man, she raced out the door and up the ladder. The whole crew stood in silence, assembled in front of the mainmast. Mac MacDougal wielded the braided leather whip that sliced across the young sailor's bare back.

"Oh, God." Glory raced across the deck toward Nicholas, who stood arrow-straight, facing his men. Tears blurred her vision; she stumbled once, but kept on going. Nicholas's already dark expression darkened even more.

"Go back to your cabin," he commanded, his tone harsh.

"Please Captain," Glory pleaded. "Please don't do this. This was my fault, not his."

"Mr. Pintassle!" he called out. "Escort Miss Summerfield to my cabin. Make certain she doesn't leave. I'll see to her when I'm through here."

"Nicholas, please," Glory shrieked. "You can't do this!"

Joshua's arm slid beneath her elbow. "Please, Miss Summerfield," he said softly. "You'll only make things worse."

She just stared at him. The lash echoed. She thought of running to Mac, pleading with him to see reason, but, as if reading her thoughts, Jago Dodd stepped in front of her, forming a wall against the grisly sight and her intervention.

"Go with him, miss," he warned, and she knew he meant to take her below himself if she refused.

Nodding dumbly, she started back toward the ladder, Joshua Pintassle trailing along behind. He opened the captain's cabin door for her, but didn't follow her inside. She knew he kept watch in the corridor.

In minutes, the snap of the whip ceased its eerie rhythm, and Glory closed her eyes, thankful it was over. Wringing her hands, she stood nervously in front of Nicholas's desk waiting for him to appear. She didn't have long to wait.

He entered the room striding angrily toward her, his

gray eyes dark with fury. "That's twice you've disobeyed me in front of the crew!" he roared. "I'll not stand for it again!"

His anger fired her own.

"You had no right to punish that man. I was the one you should have punished. I was the one who disobeyed your damnable orders!

She faced him squarely, her blond hair tousled and swirling around her face as it had the night before. Nicholas regarded her darkly, his temper barely contained.

"I have *every* right. I am the master of this vessel. It is my duty to see the *Black Spider* reaches her destination safely. In order to do that, I must have a crew who will obey me. The night watch disobeyed my orders. Thanks to you, I had no choice but to punish him." Her bottom lip trembled, and Nicholas read the pain in her eyes. He hardened his heart against it.

"I'm the one you should punish," she argued. "Not Nathan, not that poor sailor. I'm the one who disobeyed your orders."

"For once in your life, Miss Summerfield," Nicholas said coldly, "you're right. Unfortunately, you're a woman. I can't—"

"That makes no difference. That is not the question here. How many lashes did the boy receive?"

"Ten," he said softly.

"Then give the same to me!"

Nicholas stared hard at her. Though she faced him with defiance, she couldn't disguise the guilt she felt, her terrible need to make amends. Combined with the rage he felt at being upbraided in front of his men, it was all the prodding he needed. "There's a leather pointer beside my desk. Get it."

For a moment she looked uncertain. Then she straightened, lifted her chin, and went to fetch the stiff leather rod. She handed it to him with trembling fingers and Nicholas almost weakened. "Turn around and put your hands on the desk."

She did as he told her. Raising the rod above his head,

he swung a stinging blow across the tender flesh of her bottom. She didn't even flinch. He forced himself to think of the man he'd had whipped on deck and brought the rod down in another stinging blow. Three. Four. Five. His hand shook so hard on the sixth he could scarcely hold the rod. Seven. He heard her whimper, and tossed the rod away as if it burned his palm.

"Enough!" He pulled her into his arms. "You've had enough."

"Nicholas, I'm so sorry." Her warm tears wet his cheeks where they pressed against him, and soaked the front of his shirt.

"It's over, love," he whispered. "You've paid for your mistake the same as the others. What's done is past; you don't have to feel guilty anymore."

She slid her arms around his neck and clung to him. "I didn't mean to hurt anyone."

"I know, love." He smoothed the silvery strands of hair from her cheeks, then kissed her forehead, her eyes, her nose. "I know." As she tilted her tearstained face to look at him, he kissed her lips, gently at first, tenderly, wanting to take away the hurt, wishing none of it had happened, wishing he could hold her forever. When she opened her mouth to allow his tongue entrance, Nicholas forgot their heated words, forgot all but his desire for her. With a soft groan, he deepened the kiss. Her mouth tasted sweet, her lips felt warm and full. Cradling her cheeks between his hands, he brushed away the last of her tears, and a surge of protectiveness wrapped itself around his heart.

Mindlessly he moved his mouth along the line of her slender throat while he lifted her into his arms and carried her to his bed. As he lay down beside her, his tongue traced a fiery path along her skin and his hands slid down the bodice of her dress, cupping her breasts, teasing the peaks through the heavy silk fabric. He wanted to rip the offending barrier away. Instead, he carefully began to unfasten the buttons at her back.

Glory was in the place she most wanted to be—wrapped in Nicholas's arms. Never had she felt like this, never had

she experienced the burning desire, the building need for
another human being. She wanted Nicholas to caress her,
wanted to feel his hands on her most sensitive, most intimate parts. His lips were a drug, seducing her, leaving
her breathless and thirsty.

He moved his mouth to the curve of her neck, and Glory
arched against him. Though she reveled in his touch, part
of her remained uncertain. She was acting like a wanton,
wishing he would touch her, wanting even more. His hands
worked the buttons at her back, and she only wished he
would hurry, that nothing lay between them. She could
hear her mother's words: "It's vile and dirty." But it didn't
seem vile to Glory. It seemed wonderful.

As his lips returned to her mouth and his tongue found
its way inside, Glory softly mewed with pleasure. Unbuttoning his shirt, she slipped her hands inside and marveled
at the feel of the stiff hairs curling on his chest, the flat
hard circle of his nipple. He groaned, and she reveled in
his response.

Miraculously, the bodice of her dress fell away, leaving
Glory's full breasts straining against the top of her corset.
Nicholas cradled each one and stroked her nipples, his
kiss warm and sensuous, his tongue probing and tasting,
sending tiny shivers across her flesh. She couldn't get
enough of him, couldn't stand the thought of his pulling
away. She felt a surge of love that bordered on madness,
and prayed he felt it, too.

The ship strained and surged, perfectly matching the
rhythm of their movements. Nicholas slid her skirts up and
cupped her bottom, forcing her even closer. She could feel
his manhood pressing determinedly against her and wondered how it would feel inside.

Conscious of her still-tender flesh, he gentled his touch,
but not before a tiny sting brought a moment of clarity.
Remembering the last time he had kissed her—the brutal
lesson he'd taught—she began to have her doubts. What if
he meant this as another means of punishment? What if
he was only demonstrating his power in a way words never

could? She felt him working the buttons of his breeches, and a soft sob caught in her throat.

At the sound, Nicholas pulled away to look at her. "Don't be afraid, love. I'm not going to hurt you."

"Nicholas," she whispered brokenly, "if this is one of your lessons, I'll never forgive you." The uncertainty on her face gave him pause.

Like a splash of cold seawater, reality surfaced, bringing with it the knowledge of where he was—and just exactly what he was doing. With a groan of resignation, he rolled away from her, raking a hand through his curly black hair.

Dress held modestly over her bosom, face flushed prettily, lips lightly bruised from his kisses, she sat up beside him, but couldn't meet his eyes. Waves of flaxen hair spilled across her shoulders.

Taking a calming breath, he turned her face with his hand, forcing her to look at him. "I've wanted you from the first moment I saw you. I've tried to stay away, but I can't do it anymore. The only lesson I want to teach you is how to make love."

"Oh, Nicholas." She slipped her arms around his neck, and he cradled her against him. Then he captured her lips and kissed her thoroughly. It took every ounce of his will to pull away.

"There is nothing I want more than to make love to you, right here and now. But my men are outside, sure I'm torturing you." His mouth curved up in one of his rare warm smiles. "If you don't go out there soon, I'll probably have a mutiny on my hands." His voice sounded husky, his breathing a little ragged, and Glory felt a tiny thrill that she could affect him so.

She smiled back at him, loving the gentle light in his storm-gray eyes. His features looked softer, almost boyish, and her heart swelled with love for him. Love. There was no way to deny it. She was in love with Nicholas. She prayed to God he felt the same.

A loud knock on his cabin door brought Nicholas to his feet. He adjusted his breeches and buttoned the front of his white linen shirt. As he approached the door, he glanced at Glory, who worked feverishly to rearrange her clothes, her face aglow with an enchanting pink blush.

"Who is it?" Nicholas called out.

"It's Mac, Cap'n. The men are worried about Miss Glory. They want to be sure ye've done her no harm."

Nicholas smiled ruefully and winked at Glory. "She'll be out in five minutes. None the worse for wear." Unfortunately, he thought. But *he* was. He had an ache in his breeches that wouldn't soon be soothed. With a sigh of resignation, he walked back to where Glory waited, her hair pulled aside, her back presented so he could do up her buttons. Such a simple gesture, yet one he felt so right in doing.

He thought of Nina, the woman he'd been determined to bed last night. Though he hadn't admitted it then, he'd been relieved to return to the ship. It wasn't Nina he wanted. It wasn't Ginger. He wanted Gloria Summerfield—and no one else would do. Somehow he would reconcile his conscience. Hell, if he had to, he'd marry the girl. The idea made him a little green around the gills. Finishing the last of her buttons, he kissed the slim column of her neck. When he turned her to face him, she looked troubled.

"What are you thinking?" he asked.

"I—I was wondering . . . I've never done anything—I'm not sure . . . what to think."

"How do you feel?"

"I'm not sure about that either. Kind of edgy or something. And I feel as if I want you to kiss me again."

Nicholas grinned delightedly. "That's exactly how you're supposed to feel. But once we make love, you'll feel different. You'll feel wonderful. I promise you."

"Make love?" Glory's heart raced. Was he speaking of marriage?

"That, sweet, is the natural result of what we were doing."

Glory swallowed hard. "I see." She thought the natural result of what they were doing was a marriage proposal.

He kissed the tip of her nose. "For now you'd better be going outside. The mutiny, remember?"

She blushed crimson and nodded. He placed a hand behind her neck and pulled her against him for a last brief kiss. Then she straightened her garments, paused a moment to regain her composure, and headed out the door.

Later that day they stopped briefly at Cape Fear, and Jago Dodd and a tall skinny sailor rowed Madame LaFarge and Rosabelle ashore. Discovering she'd developed an affection for the two ladies of somewhat dubious virtue, Glory hugged them before they left.

"I hope everything works out for you both," she said. "Give the baby a kiss for me."

"I promise," Rosabelle said tearfully. "If you ever need a friend, ya know where we'll be."

Glory handed her a bright yellow painted scarf. "Think of me when you wear it," she said. "I'll miss you both." Rosabelle accepted the gift with a tearful hug.

To Madame LaFarge Glory handed a small crystal vial, which held the dollop of expensive French perfume she'd managed to bring along.

"Thank ya, dearie. I won't forget ye. And I'll wager you'll have the captain in the same fix by the time he gets to New York!" She laughed uproariously, winked at Glory, and slapped her beefy thighs.

Glory hoped Madame LaFarge was right.

"Have a good trip, dearie. I'd tell ye to drop us a line, but neither Rosy nor me kin read, so's we wouldn't be able to write ye back."

Glory only nodded. She hugged the buxom woman again, then let the two climb over the rail to the shore boats waiting below. It was no easy task for the heavyset woman—or the pregnant one—but eventually they were seated, and Jago and the skinny crewman rowed them to shore. Glory watched till they'd climbed the hill out of sight."

"What will happen to them, Nicholas?" she asked as he walked up beside her.

"Rosabelle will be well provided for. I have friends on the Cape, a young couple who can't have children. They've been expecting her. She's agreed to stay on and work for them after the baby is born, and they'll be happy to have a child in the house."

"And Madame LaFarge?"

"She'll do whatever makes her happy—just as she always has."

Glory smiled up at him. For a moment his eyes met hers. He seemed to look at her differently somehow, the way he'd looked at her that night on the road. As if he wanted to say something, but couldn't quite find the words. And he watched her almost protectively, it seemed. She smiled to herself, secretly delighted with this latest turn of events.

Nicholas didn't appear at supper again that night.

"Good morning, Captain," Glory said to him a bit stiffly the following morning. He was standing beside the rail, handsome in snug black breeches and his usual snowy white shirt, looking out to sea as if pondering some weighty problem. Turning toward her, he graced her with a warm smile, and Glory's pique began to fade.

"Good morning, love. Sleep well?"

There was a suggestion of something intimate in his words, and warm color rushed to Glory's cheeks. "Yes, thank you, I did." It was a lie. She'd been out of sorts all evening, angry that the captain had ignored her again. She smiled and lowered her lashes. "I missed you at supper."

"I had some thinking to do."

"Some thinking?" she asked.

"Yes."

"I see."

"Do you?" he said.

"It's really none of my business."

"Ah, but it is. I thought maybe tonight, after supper, we might discuss it."

Glory's pulse raced. Nicholas Blackwell was the only man she'd known who could make her feel uncertain and shy and womanly all at the same time. "Fine" was all she could manage.

"I'm afraid I have some work to do, so I won't see you until then." His glance strayed from her face to the curve of her breast.

Recognizing the heat in that look, she felt a rush of embarrassment—and a warm glow in the pit of her stomach. It was a struggle to remember why she'd sought the captain out in the first place. At the moment all she could think of was the way he'd kissed her and the feel of his strong tanned hands on her breasts. She swallowed hard, glanced out to sea, then met his look squarely.

"Would it be all right if I went below to see my servant?" she asked before he could walk away.

"I'll have Joshua take you down." Nicholas smiled again, then left without further comment. The first mate arrived a few moments later.

"It's really not as bad as it looks, Glory," he told her as they walked to the aft ladder. "Nearly all of us have spent a day or two in the brig at one time or another. Besides, we'll be in New York in less than a week."

The brig turned out to be a tiny room at the aft end of the hold. The heavy oak door had a large opening obstructed by metal bars; a whale-oil lantern lit the room. Glory could see Nathan seated forlornly on a splintery wooden bench.

Her heart went out to him. "Can I go in? I'd like to speak to him alone."

"Of course." He unlocked the door and let her in. "I'll come back for you in a few minutes."

"Thank you, Josh."

Once inside, Glory waited until Joshua's footsteps faded away, then threw herself into her half brother's outstretched arms. "Oh, Nathan. I'm so sorry. I would never have talked you into taking me ashore if I'd known what would happen."

"Hush now, Glory. It really isn't so bad. The captain's been down here to check on me personally. He brought me a deck of cards and some hemp so I could practice bending line. Of course he doesn't know I can read.''

''We're still almost a week away from New York: maybe I can talk him into letting you go.''

''I don't think you should try, Glory. He might get suspicious if he thinks you're overly concerned about your servant. We can't take the chance of him finding out about us.''

Glory hugged him again. ''I suppose you're right. I just want you to know how sorry I am.''

''Everything's going to be fine just as soon as we reach New York.''

Glory nodded. ''I love you, Nathan.''

''I love you, too, Glory. Now get out of here. Cookie will be down with my dinner soon. He's challenged me to a game of gin rummy.''

Glory heard the jangle of keys as Joshua Pintassle approached. She kissed Nathan's cheek and left the cell.

Nicholas Blackwell stood in the darkness of the hold, clenching and unclenching his fists. What a fool he'd been! He watched Glory leave on Joshua's arm, then through the bars on the door watched the tall handsome Negro pace the confines of the brig, his long, powerful legs carrying him from one side of the room to the other. Why hadn't he seen it before? The man was no field hand. No house servant, either. His manner of speech as he'd spoken to Glory said he'd been well educated—and he was handsome to a fault.

Nicholas burned with rage at the way he'd been duped. He'd known the girl was up to something from the start, but he would never have guessed she was running away with her dusky-skinned lover. Not that the color of the man's skin made any difference. It didn't. The men Nicholas sailed with came from every corner of the world: every race, every creed, every color. He'd kept a beautiful mulatto mistress in New Orleans for two years, a woman who was perhaps the most gracious he'd ever known. Educated, charming, just as this man, Nathan, appeared to be.

Prejudice was not the issue.

Gloria Summerfield had played him for a fool, used him to take her north—even pretended passion. And the whole time she was in love with another man. Nicholas closed his eyes against the blinding fury that swept over him. How could he have been foolish enough to think Gloria Summerfield was different? She was a woman, wasn't she? Just like his mother. Just like Lavinia Bond and most of the other women he'd known. Glory Summerfield had wormed her way into his affections, then played him for a fool at every opportunity.

Somehow, some way, Nicholas decided, he would make her pay.

Nicholas had little time to ponder his revenge. The day turned blustery; sharp winds snapped the sails and strained the rigging, and the sky darkened ominously.

"Mr. Pintassle," he ordered, "furl the skysails, the royals, and the topgallants. Double-reef the topsails." That would cut their surface area by a third.

"Aye, Captain." Joshua hurried to carry out the order while the winds continued to build.

"She's a real freak storm, Cap'n," Mac MacDougal warned. "I've seen the likes o' her before—as have ye. Come on so fast ye kinna make cover, so strong ye wonder if she's bound to snap the ship in two."

Nicholas well remembered a storm like this. He'd been billeted aboard the *Stark Wind,* bound for the Bahamas. The ship had broken up off Grand Cay. Only half the crew had come out alive. The gold earring he sometimes wore marked the sinking he'd survived. He shuddered to think it could happen again.

"Nicholas?" The sound of Glory's crystalline voice whipped him around.

"Go below. It isn't safe for you up here."

The wind beat at her skirts and tore at her hair, and her face looked drawn and haggard. "I'm afraid I'm not feeling too well. Would it be all right if I stayed up here a moment?''

He wanted to say no. He wanted her to suffer, but her wan expression gave him pause. "Stand beside the wheel and stay out of the way. Only a few minutes. If these seas get any rougher, the decks will be awash.''

Glory nodded. She did as she was told and felt better with the stiff wind rushing past her cheeks. She had never seen the ocean like this. There were troughs the ship dropped into and foamy whitecaps the size of small hills. The clouds rolled with the same heavy movement as the sea.

Jago Dodd stood at the helm. "Sea's building pretty fast now, missy. You'll have to go below pretty soon.''

Glory nodded. A quarter of an hour passed before she saw Nicholas again.

"I thought you'd gone below.''

"I was just going.''

"I'll take the wheel, Jago. You see she gets there safely.''

"Aye, Captain.'' Jago took her arm.

Glory looked back over her shoulder, hoping Nicholas would give her one of his reassuring smiles. He didn't even look in her direction.

"Is everything going to be all right?'' she asked Jago as they made their way down the narrow, listing passageway.

"Hard to say for sure. Storm come up too sudden. Real unusual this time of year. Something ain't right. Captain can feel it; so can the crew. But he's a good man, the captain. If anyone can pull the *Black Spider* through, he can.''

"It's that bad?''

"Not yet, but from the looks of it, it may well be.''

"Thanks for being honest with me, Jago.''

"Never could see lying. But no sense to worry yet. The *Spider*'s a sturdy ship, and her captain's a damned fine seaman. Now you get yourself strapped down tight, and put in a good word for us with the Man above.''

"I'll do that, Jago." Glory smiled. "Watch out for Nicholas, will you?"

"He helped me, didn't he? Jago Dodd don't forget. I'll be watching 'im."

"Thank you, Jago." Glory went inside and battened down whatever loose possessions she could find.

Chapter Ten

On deck Nicholas, Mac, and Joshua watched the weather.

"Josh," Nicholas instructed, "you go below and try to get some rest. It's going to be a long night." He turned to Mac. "Shorten the topsails to their last row of reef points." That left only the fore and aft triangles of canvas rigged between the masts to help steady the ship, keep her from turning broadside to the wind, and running before the storm.

"Aye, Cap'n." With a worried frown, Mac stalked away.

By supper it was blowing so hard and the ship was rolling so heavily that the crew ate hardtack and drank cold chowder from their mugs.

Nicholas stood beside Jago at the wheel, fighting the blinding wind and watching the water race over the decks. With a great cracking sound, one of the stay sails split in two and then tore away; the fore and main topsails ripped away, flapped for a moment in the wind, then hurled themselves into the churning water to disappear beneath the foamy crests of the sea.

"Lower the upper yards," Nicholas commanded, hoping to ease the strain on the masts. The yardarms dipped into the sea with every roll to leeward. "Douse the spars."

Men fought the water-washed decks to do the captain's bidding. Jago fought to control the wheel.

"Bring down the royals," Nicholas ordered, while another wave broke over the decks. When the men had finished, he ordered the topgallant yards brought down.

By now the troughs were so deep that the ship raced downhill, then fought to climb up the terrifying wall of water on the other side. The *Spider* surged and heaved, fighting wind and water to stay upright. Huge waves exploded across the deck.

"She's takin' on water, Cap'n," Mac informed Nicholas, shouting to be heard above the roar of the wind, "faster than the men can pump her out."

Nicholas followed Mac to check the men working the pumps. The scene below decks made his blood run cold. Having broken free of its lashings, the cargo had shifted and smashed against the hull. Seawater rushed in from a rent in the planking. A team of men worked feverishly to repair it and pump out the flood.

Nicholas stayed below only a moment, returning to the deck just in time to see the mizzenmast snap like a twig.

"Look out below!" he shouted, cupping his hands against the wind. The young sailor who'd disobeyed his orders stepped away from death just in time. He grinned back at the captain, and Nicholas felt a wave of relief.

It was short-lived. The *Black Spider* was doomed. Now Nicholas's main concern was the safety of his crew.

"Ready the shore boats, Josh."

"Captain?"

"We've no other choice. We're not far off Hatteras. Have the men make for shore. It's their best chance."

"Aye, sir."

"Bring the man up from the brig. I'll see to the girl."

Joshua nodded and began to relay the necessary orders.

In her cabin below decks, Glory clung to the bottom bunk, praying the ship would stay afloat. Her stomach rolled along with the ship; she'd thrown up several times already. Only her fear had kept her from being totally bedridden. A fierce knock at her door set her heart to pounding. When she lifted the latch and swung the door wide, she found Cookie standing in the passageway.

"We're abandoning ship, Miss Glory. The cap'n will be down fer ye in just a minute. Don't take more than you can carry."

Before she could speak, he was gone. Frantic with worry, Glory rushed from the cabin. Nathan was locked in the tiny room below decks. She had to be certain he was safe.

Clutching the lantern from her room in her hand, she raced down the passageway toward the ladder that led to the aft end of the hold, and climbed down. When she reached the hold, she made her way to the tiny brig. The door was open; Nathan was gone. Breathing a sigh of relief, she turned to make her way back up on deck. She'd taken only a few hurried steps when she saw the heavy crate coming at her. Though she tried to sidestep, she couldn't duck out of the way in time. Her scream died in the roar of sea against hull. With a resounding thud, her head hit the bulkhead and blackness engulfed her.

The last of the men climbed over the rail and into the waiting shore boats. "You're *sure* she's in one of the boats?" Nicholas asked Mac for the third time.

"Dammit, lad. I wish I could say aye, that I was certain, but I kinna. Her man wouldna board Jago's boat till someone told him she'd already been loaded on another. But I didna see her. Cookie says he told her we were abandoning the *Spider*. Where else could the lass be?"

"I don't know, but I don't like it. You go on. I'm going to make another pass through the ship."

"Time's runnin' thin, lad. I'd best come wi' ye."

"You just try to keep that boat close enough to the ship for me to reach it." The small craft were nearly impossible to manage in the storm and Nicholas knew it. With the ship taking on water as fast as she was, listing till the rails were already touching the sea, he was taking a dangerous chance. But a nagging voice said something was wrong. He couldn't see all of the shore boats, so he couldn't know for sure if Glory was aboard one of them—but something told him she wasn't.

"I'll do my best, lad."

Battling the elements and a greater enemy, time, Nicholas fought his way across the sea-washed decks to the aft ladder. The passageway stood knee deep in water, but all of the cabins were empty. He tried to think where she might have gone, what or who could have been more important to her than her own safety. And suddenly, sickeningly, he knew. Frantic with worry, he made his way down the ladder toward the brig, holding his lantern high. Several heavy crates had toppled over near the door. As he pushed a smaller crate away, he noticed the glistening black silk at his feet.

The voice had been right. Glory lay unconscious beside the crate. The hull tilted crazily, and the hold was already half full of water. Kneeling beside her, he set the lantern down and laid a hand against her forehead. Her eyelids fluttered open.

"Nicholas . . . What . . . happened?"

"There isn't time," he told her. "We've got to get out of here."

She tried to sit up, but her dress was caught fast beneath the crate. Nicholas used both hands to rip the fabric away. Her sleeve was caught as well, so he ripped the buttons down her back, and she pulled free of the dress. When he helped her to her feet, she swayed against him.

"This way," he told her. Ignoring the pounding in her head, she followed him blindly, clutching his arm, letting him lead her to the deck. Realization of their terrible predicament hit her like a second blow.

When they reached the rail, Nicholas heard Glory gasp, felt her grip tighten on his arm. He glanced at her only briefly, then looked back out to sea, his worst fears confirmed. The last small shore boat had drifted yards away from the ship, and though Mac, Josh, and the men waged a furious battle to bring the boat back alongside, the task was hopeless. The other shore boats tossed and rolled even farther out to sea.

"Oh, God, Nicholas. What are we going to do?"

"We'll have to swim for Mac's boat. We'll be sucked under if we're near when she goes down."

Glory blanched. She turned her head slowly from side to side in denial, her blue eyes, huge with fear, dominating her pale face. Nicholas paid her no heed, just turned her back to him and hurriedly split the laces of her corset with the knife he had strapped to his waist. Wearing just her lacy chemise and thin cotton petticoat, she clutched him as another massive wave washed over the deck. Nicholas held on tight to keep her from being swept overboard.

"Nicholas . . . I'm . . . frightened," she told him, wetting her lips, though her whole face glistened with sea water.

"We have no choice." He grabbed a piece of line. "I'll tie this around your waist so you won't get too far away from me. I'll help you if you tire."

She just stared at him.

Catching her slight shoulders in an iron-hard grip, he shook her. "Dammit, Glory, there's no other way!"

Her voice came out in a whisper that was almost lost in the wind. "I can't swim."

Nicholas groaned. "You can play billiards, but you can't swim!"

The taunting words snapped her back to life. "I'm sorry, Captain Blackwell," she said defiantly. "I didn't know we were going to have to swim for our lives when I came on board."

Nicholas almost smiled. "All right, we'll try something else." He glanced around the debris-strewn deck. "We'll make a raft of these three barrels, then strap ourselves on top." He didn't tell her their control of the raft would be almost nil. She was frightened enough as it was.

"What can I do to help?"

"Just stay where you are—and hang on. I don't want you going over the side until I'm ready."

He set to work on the barrels, securing them with the

sturdy knots he'd learned from Mac as a boy. Glory clung to the mast, fighting each new wave, trying not to think about braving the vicious seas on only a makeshift raft.

It didn't take long before Nicholas had the barrels lashed together. "Come on. The longer we wait, the worse our chances." He dragged the barrel to the lower rail, which dipped in and out of the water and Glory climbed on top. Nicholas tied a line around her waist, tied the end of the line to the raft, and crisscrossed another section of line back and forth across the barrels for handholds.

"Whatever you do," he told her "try not to fall off. But don't panic if you do. Remember, you'll still be tied to the raft. If the barrels tip over, which I don't think they will, pull yourself to the surface and climb up on the other side."

It all sounded horrible to Glory, who'd never set foot in anything deeper than a bathtub. She clutched the ropes, which she knew might mean the difference between life and death, and said a small prayer for their safety. Nicholas climbed up beside her, a line around his own waist.

She clung to the ropes with all her might as another huge wave loomed above the top rail on the opposite side of the ship. When the water crashed over the deck, Glory screamed, and the small raft launched itself beneath a churning wall of water. Only the feel of Nicholas's strong arm across her shoulder gave her the courage to hang on.

Glory held her breath till the stale air seared her lungs, then held it even longer. Praying the end would be painless, she fought the terrible urge to breathe until the raft popped above the water like a cork in a barrel. Glory filled her burning lungs with the heavy, foam-laden air.

Another wave crashed over them, and the ritual repeated itself, but this time the seconds underwater were shorter.

Flattened against the barrels, using a length of splintered wood for a paddle, Nicholas tried his best to maneuver the raft toward the pitching shore boat, but the craft only seemed to move farther away.

"Is there anything I can do to help?" Glory offered.

"You just hang on." He might feel like throttling her

for the fool she'd made of him, but he'd do it after they were safe. He looked at the bedraggled woman clinging to the raft in her all but transparent garments. Even near-drowned and terrified, she looked beautiful. With a fresh surge of worry for her safety, Nicholas paddled even harder.

"Keep after it, lads," Mac instructed as the men fought to row the shore boat in the direction they had last glimpsed the captain's makeshift raft.

"Mac." Josh Pintassle laid a gentle hand on the old Scot's arm. "It's been hours since we've seen them. We've got no idea where to look. Neither has he. He'll be making his way toward Hatteras. The winds are pushing the seas that way. If they stay aboard the raft, they'll have a good chance of making it. We've got to do the same. The men are tiring. We've got to make shore if we can."

For a moment Mac wanted to argue, wanted to keep up the search as long as he had an ounce of strength left. He knew that was what Nicholas would do. But there were others to think of. The safety of the men had to come first.

"Aye, Mr. Pintassle." Heart heavy, eyes still searching the whitecapped seas, Mac ordered the men to make for land. It was nowhere to be seen, but it lay to the west, and if they could keep the tiny shore boat from swamping, they just might make it.

The hours blurred and ran together, just a series of aching muscles and burning lungs. Glory's fingers had gripped the braided line so long she couldn't bend them. She and Nicholas hadn't spoken for hours in an effort to conserve their strength. Eventually they'd fallen into an exhausted half-stupor that passed for sleep and had awoken to find the seas had calmed. A cloudless sky and a burning sun were their companions now.

Nicholas removed his torn and soggy shirt and draped it over Glory's head and bare shoulders. His own sun-browned torso had long ago become immune to the sun's searing rays. Glory managed a grateful smile then faded back into her exhausted sleep.

They drifted for hours. Nicholas scanned the endless horizon, hoping to spot land or at least one of the shore boats. When his eyelids became so heavy he couldn't stay awake, he, too, succumbed to the drug of sleep.

When he awoke hours later, it was to the rhythmic, grating crash and roar of sea against sand. At first he couldn't identify the sound; then he realized the raft wasn't moving. He turned to see a sandy beach and the short, stiff marsh grass that marked the shore.

After untying himself with brittle, wind-chafed fingers, he untied the line around Glory and shook her gently. "We made it, love," he told her softly.

"Nathan? Nathan, is that you?" She lifted her head but stared at him blankly, as if he weren't even there.

Nicholas felt as though he'd been kicked in the stomach. In the long hours at sea, fighting for survival, he'd almost forgotten her lover. In truth he wished he could forget. "Sorry to disappoint you," he told her bitterly. "It's only me."

She blinked several times and started to speak, but he turned and stalked into the shade of a nearby pine tree. He watched as she untied the rope from around her waist with trembling fingers, climbed from the raft, and walked toward him. "Nicholas?"

"Stay here," he said sharply. "I'll scout around, try to find out where we are." It was all he could do to be civil. He'd risked his life to keep her alive, and all she could think about was Nathan. Damn, how many times would he play the fool? Of course, as captain of the ship and her father's friend he'd had no choice but to see to her safety, he told himself. But every time he looked at her, his temper fired again.

Though he still felt weak, his strength returned a little more with every step he took. He scouted the sandy beach and found the tiny island they'd been washed ashore on was separated from a larger strip of land by a swampy marsh nearly a quarter-mile wide. He sloshed through the marsh, careful to watch for alligators and poisonous snakes, and finally came out on the other side. The terrain on the gradually sloping strand was much more inhabitable than the island.

There were tall pine trees, soft grassy flats, and even a string of rain-filled freshwater pools. Following a game trail inland, Nicholas felt satisfied he could find plenty of game for food. The strand was the perfect place for the two of them to rest and recover, and await a rescue party.

Nicholas knew the searchers would come sooner or later. When the *Black Spider* didn't make port on time, or certainly within a few days thereafter, a search vessel from his company would be launched. It would be easy to trace the *Spider*'s movements as far as Cape Fear. And the storm off Hatteras would be common knowledge. With the help of a signal fire, someone would find them. Of that Nicholas had no doubt.

In the meantime he had days, maybe even weeks, alone with the lying little vixen he'd rescued. The isolation of the island would provide the perfect opportunity to teach the pampered Miss Summerfield the lesson she'd been needing for so long. Then he'd bed her—one way or another.

Nicholas returned to the beach where Glory lay asleep beneath one of the island's few pine trees. The island was an inhospitable stretch of land made up of sand crabs and prickly marsh grass, with very little shelter from the wind. The only drinking water was a small rainwater pool covered with a silty scum.

Nicholas smiled to himself. He couldn't wait to see how Miss Pampered and Spoiled Summerfield survived the next few days.

Propping himself against a rock a few feet away from where Glory slept, he waited for her to awaken.

When the sun had moved far enough toward the horizon for her shade to be gone, Glory felt the heat and bright light in her eyes and awoke. She didn't move for a moment, searching the cloudless sky visible in patches through the branches overhead; then she looked out at the flat blue-green surface of the sea. She lay still, remembering the shipwreck and her perilous escape from death, when something moved against her arm and something bony touched her leg.

She bolted upright. Dozens of huge crabs, some nearly two feet long and each with a red horseshoe-shaped shell, surrounded her. Stifling a scream, she leaped to her feet and ran, threading her way through the minor invasion till she reached safety some distance away.

Trembling all over, she searched the island for Nicholas, until she heard his low laughter, bitter and amused.

"What's the matter? Your little friends bothering you?"

"You . . . bastard!" she stormed. "Why didn't you wake me up? One of those . . . those horrible creatures could have bitten me."

"They won't hurt you," he told her. "They're horseshoe crabs. Harmless. They've come ashore to mate."

She shuddered and looked back to where the creatures clustered and crawled. "Harmless or not, I don't like them."

"I'm sure you'll find a lot of things here you don't like." He leaned nonchalantly against the trunk of a pine, shirtless, one long leg crossed over the other, a smug expression on his face. "You'll just have to adjust."

Glory regarded him closely. His manner seemed almost hostile. "I assure you I'll do my best not to inconvenience you." Another chilling laugh, unlike anything she'd heard from him before. She forced herself to ignore it. "What do you think happened to the others?"

"If they kept their boats afloat, they probably made shore."

"Near here?"

"I doubt it. We were all pretty spread out." His voice sounded brittle, and again Glory wondered at his anger.

As she glanced at her surroundings—the barren shoreline, the lack of shelter, little or no water—realization dawned. Nicholas was shipwrecked on this dismal stretch of land because of her. If he hadn't stayed aboard the

Spider to search for her, he could have been on one of the
shore boats with his crew. They might have reached a port
or city by now. Instead, he was stranded on this lonely,
barren chunk of land because once again she had disobeyed his orders. He blamed her for what happened, and
now he was angry. Furious, in fact.

Damn him! Damn him to hell, Glory silently raged. It
wasn't her fault that crate fell on top of her. She'd been
headed back to her cabin, intent on waiting just as he'd
said. The nerve of the man! Good Lord, she'd almost
drowned out there, and here he was acting the injured
party. How she could ever have thought she loved an arrogant ass like Nicholas Blackwell was beyond her.

Glory sought the shade of another pine some distance
from the rattling, crawling crabs and settled in. She was
thirsty and hungry, and her body ached all over, but she'd
be damned if she would say a word to the almighty Captain Blackwell. Instead, she sat down and pulled her legs
up beneath her chin. Ignoring her, Nicholas stalked away.

For the first time she noticed the scars on his back, thin,
light lines that had faded over the years. She'd seen those
same scars too many times not to recognize the marks of
the lash. Though she tried to ignore it, she felt a rush of
sympathy for Nicholas. Then she thought of the boy he'd
had whipped on the deck of the *Spider* and wondered what
crime Nicholas had committed. The thought sent a chill
down her spine.

When he returned, he carried an armful of driftwood
and with the help of flint and steel made a small fire. The
evening air was warm, but the beckoning light of the fire
drew her from the lengthening shadows.

"I don't suppose you found any water while you were
out there?" she asked peevishly, still angry at his mistreatment of her.

"There's a pocket of rainwater near that far pine tree."

Surely he'd known she was thirsty. Without a thank-you,
she padded barefoot across the sand toward the water. It
looked brackish and undrinkable, but it was all they had,
so she'd have to make do. Holding a floating layer of scum

aside, Glory filled her hand and drank until her thirst was slaked. With a sigh of resignation, she returned to the fire.

Nicholas had something roasting over the spit he'd fashioned from fallen branches. "You've found something to eat?" she asked, her mouth beginning to water from the succulent aroma.

"Cottonmouth water moccasin," he replied.

"A snake!" The word came out in a hiss. "I can't eat a snake. Why it's . . . it's barbaric. What about a nice fish or something?"

"Did you catch one?"

"Well, no, but—"

"Then I guess it's snake or nothing." He seemed almost pleased.

"Oh, Lord," Glory said, sinking down on the sand beside him.

When the meat was cooked, he thrust the stick toward her until she finally pulled off a tiny, tentative bite. Nicholas cut off a chunk with the big knife he still carried at his waist. He ate with relish, licking his fingers noisily. Glory took a tiny bite that lodged in her throat. The taste was not unpleasant, but thoughts of the slimy creature turned her stomach, and she nearly gagged.

"I think I'll wait until tomorrow, if you don't mind," she said primly. "Maybe one of us can catch a fish."

"Suit yourself" was all he said. He rolled away from the fire, laid an arm across his eyes, and quickly fell asleep.

Hunger gnawing at her stomach, Glory tried futilely to do the same. The stars were bright, and the constant sea breeze kept the mosquitoes at bay, but still she tossed and turned. The ground was hard and uncomfortable, and it seemed she had sand over every part of her body. She thought of Nathan and wondered if he'd made it to shore. If anything had happened to him, she was sure she would have felt it. That was the way with them. They'd always been that close. She turned on her side, ignoring the grit in her teeth, and finally fell asleep.

* * *

Nicholas woke early and headed toward the strand. He needed a bath and a shave and a good solid meal beneath his belt. Upon reaching the strand, he noticed an added bonus. During the night, the current had carried some of the remains of the *Black Spider* to shore. The beach was littered with crates and boxes, lines and spars, trunks and sea chests. He smiled to himself. Once he'd repaid the spoiled little blonde for her treachery, he would build a modest shelter and they'd be able to live a fairly comfortable existence. Until then he would enjoy his revenge, make the girl as miserable as he possibly could.

He thought of the way she'd looked when he left. Petticoat hiked up to her thighs, blond hair tangled about her face. Her smooth skin looked gritty with patches of sand. She was exhausted and hungry, and though she'd tried to stay in the shade as much as possible, her skin had taken on a rosy burnished hue. She looked bedraggled and wilted—and lovely. It was all he could do not to take her right there on the sand.

He stayed on the strand all morning, unbraided some of the line he'd found among the litter on the shore to set rabbit snares, then bathed and shaved with his knife. A fat gray squirrel had the misfortune to cross the path of the first snare he'd set, and Nicholas dispatched it readily. After skinning it, he made a small fire, cooked, and ate it.

On returning to the island, he felt only a twinge of guilt when he saw Glory knee deep in the sea fishing with a strip of lace attached to a hairpin.

"Catch anything?" he asked, his voice thick with sarcasm.

"Just a sunburn," she told him, and Nicholas almost smiled.

"I brought you a nice sea gull. That should fill you up."

She groaned aloud and tossed her makeshift line back into the sea. She'd pulled the back of her petticoat between her legs and tucked it into the waistband, leaving her calves exposed. Nicholas felt a tightening in his loins. Damn the girl for the vixen she was. He prayed the next few days would soften her up for him. He'd hate to bed her against her will, but looking at her now, he knew he would only wait so long. She deserved whatever she got, and that included a stint on her back, tending his needs.

With an inward smile, Nicholas sauntered to the shore behind her. "You don't have any bait," he said. Pulling off his boots, he sloshed through the low waves till he stood calf deep in the water. While Glory fished, he unsheathed the knife at his waist, dug in the sand till he found several small clams, and pried open their shells. Walking up beside Glory, he lifted her slim hand and dumped the slippery shellfish into her palm.

"Here. These ought to do it."

Glory shrieked at the slimy feel and tossed the clams into the sea. Nicholas howled with laughter.

"Not much of a fisherman, are you?"

"Damn you, Nicholas Blackwell. If I didn't know better, I'd swear you were enjoying every moment of this."

"Come on," he said, pulling her toward shore. "I'll fix your supper."

Chapter Eleven

Nicholas returned to their makeshift campsite, made a fire, and prepared Glory a "tasty" meal of roasted sea gull.

Glory choked and gagged and downed enough of the meat to keep her from starving, while Nicholas pretended to relish the delicious taste of the tough, stringy meat; his earlier meal of succulent squirrel had been enough to keep him till morning.

"I'm going to bathe and wash my hair," Glory announced after supper. "I'll still be salty, but anything's better than all this sand."

"Don't go out past your knees," Nicholas warned. "Tiger sharks prowl the waters this time of year."

"Sharks?"

"Big enough to swallow a man whole. Tigers have been known to weigh eight hundred pounds."

"Oh, Lord, what next?" Dejectedly, Glory sank back down cross-legged on the sand. "I can't wash my hair in water up to my knees. The waves churn up the sand too much. Surely it's safe to go out farther than that."

"I wouldn't if I were you." He lifted one corner of his mouth. "You wouldn't want one of those long, pretty legs of yours to wind up shorter than the other."

"Oooh," Glory growled beneath her breath. "I don't know how much more of this I can stand. When do you think the rescue boats will be looking for us? Shouldn't we make a fire or something?''

"It'll be a week before they've had time to discover we're missing and organize a search, even if one of the shore boats made port. We'll worry about a signal fire before then." Nicholas leaned back against the trunk of a tree, as relaxed as if this whole episode were just the merest of adventures. He had shaved during the day, and his black hair glistened in the firelight.

"How did *you* do it?" Glory asked.

"Do what?"

"Wash your hair."

"I can swim, remember?"

"But what about the sharks?"

"They prefer pretty young girls."

She could see the arrogant curve of his lip profiled in the firelight. "I know you're trying to make me miserable, Captain Blackwell. And I just want you to know I expected nothing less from a rogue like you." With that she stalked away from the fire and settled at the base of a distant pine tree. The hot sun and lack of food had taken their toll, and she finally fell asleep.

Sometime after midnight, the wind began to howl. The sting of sand against her skin brought Glory fully awake. Scanning the island for Nicholas, she found him resting beneath a tree, his broad shoulders turned against the needlelike blasts. She wanted to go to him, to nestle in the curve of his arm, to feel safe and protected the way she had before. But all that was past. He'd made clear exactly how he felt about her, so instead she curled up against the stinging fury of the wind and tried futilely to go back to sleep. On the morrow, she vowed, she would build some sort of shelter—with or without the captain's help.

The breeze had abated by the time Glory awoke late the following morning. Nicholas had a fire going.

"Hungry?" he asked, again looking refreshed. She wondered how he managed to look so well groomed while she was a pitiful, bedraggled mess. Her lacy petticoat hung in tatters, her chemise was dirty, ripped, and torn, and her hair . . . God in heaven, would her pale hair ever look beautiful again?

"What?" she asked listlessly. The heat, wind, and sand were continuing to take their toll. "Oh, yes, I suppose so."

"I cooked some crab." He broke off a claw and handed it to her. "All you have to do is figure out how to get it out."

Glory felt like crying. The tantalizing crab made her mouth water, but the determined little claw wouldn't part with its bounty. "How did *you* get it out?" she asked.

"I cracked it with my teeth."

"Your teeth?"

"My teeth."

Why didn't she believe him? Desperate for a bite of the succulent meat, Glory bit down on the stubborn shell. The shell split apart, but so did a tiny chip from her tooth.

Nicholas chuckled softly. Taking his knife to a second claw, he broke it open and handed Glory the snowy white meat. Nothing had ever tasted as good. She ate every bite he gave her, paying no attention to the juices running down her arms. When she was full, she felt better than she had in days.

"God, that was good," she said. As she wiped her mouth with the hem of her petticoat, Nicholas watched her, but he didn't say a word.

"I thought maybe we could build a shelter today," she told him, and waited for his reaction.

"What for?"

"What for! Because that wind last night was miserable and sooner or later it's bound to rain."

Nicholas only shrugged. "Suit yourself, but don't expect any help from me. I like sleeping out in the open."

"Would you at least cut some branches for me? I'll tie them together with strips of lace from my petticoat."

Try as he might, Nicholas couldn't stifle his grin. "Better watch out, Miss Summerfield. You keep using up your skirt and you'll be sleeping out here in the raw."

Furious, Glory kicked her slender foot in the sand, stubbing her toe on a pebble buried beneath. She gritted her teeth against the stab of pain. "You are the most infuriating, most despicable cad I've ever met."

Nicholas raked her with his eyes, his look traveling with deliberate slowness from the top of her tangled locks to the toes of her slender feet. They came to rest on the high curves of her bosom above her lacy chemise.

"And you, Glory, are without a doubt the most delectable morsel on the island. Be careful what you say or it's you I'll be having for supper, instead of another sea gull."

Glory blushed crimson. It was the first time he'd paid her the least attention since they'd reached the island and she wasn't sure whether to be insulted or relieved. Without another word she stalked indignantly to the opposite end of the island. She didn't return until he'd accumulated a pile of branches large enough for the task she'd set herself.

"Have at it," Nicholas said dryly. "I think I'll take a swim."

Her eyes went wide. "But what about the sharks? What if something happens to you?"

"I'll do my best not to get eaten." He walked to the shoreline and pulled off his boots; then his long brown fingers worked the buttons of his breeches.

Glory couldn't look away. He slid his breeches off and, naked, walked immodestly toward the water. His long legs, narrow hips, and muscular buttocks held her like a spell. The scars on his back intrigued her, and again she wondered how he got them. Waist deep in the water he turned to face her. Glory quickly averted her eyes, but her rosy blush betrayed her, and Nicholas chuckled mirthlessly at her embarrassment.

"Join me?" he called out. "I promise I'll keep the sharks away."

How she would have loved to. She could have washed her hair and gotten rid of this endless sand. But there was no way in the world Gloria Summerfield was going into the water with a naked man.

"No, thank you," she called back stiffly as she set to
work on her lean-to.

She had no idea where to begin, so she started by tearing the lacy strips from her petticoat. Next she bound the
branches together as tightly as she could. She'd use the
area between two trees. If only she had some rope and a
few blankets. Sighing resignedly, she continued with her
task.

By dusk of that day she had finished. Her fingers were
cramped and sore, and her back hurt fiercely. Nicholas
had watched from afar. She cursed him endlessly. As she
took in his smug expression, she prayed the wind would
blow up a gale tonight. She wouldn't share an inch of her
shelter with the captain.

The wind did indeed come up. And to Glory's chagrin,
her shelter blew apart like lint in a whirlwind. Nicholas
slept nearby, never even looking up. Tired and discour-
aged, she slept off and on until Nicholas called her to a
breakfast of large tough mussels—all he claimed he could
find. Afterward Glory set to work to rebuild the shelter
and again Nicholas looked on, but today he seemed out
of sorts.

Nicholas's amusement had waned. He had watched
Glory for days, expecting her to break long before now.
So far she'd amazed him. She'd made do with the foulest
bit of water, eaten whatever he put in front of her, albeit
grudgingly, and generally held up better than some men
he'd known. In truth his conscience was beginning to prick
him sorely.

He'd already stayed on the inhospitable island a day
longer than he'd intended. The girl looked ragged and
weary and forlorn. He'd been certain that by now she'd
have thrown herself at his mercy, begged him to take care
of her. But things hadn't worked out as he'd planned. She
wouldn't give up. Wouldn't come crawling. He didn't know
how much longer he could stand to watch her suffer.

By afternoon she'd rebuilt her shelter. Tiny bits of lace
waved in the gentle breeze, and Nicholas found himself
smiling at her ingenuity and determination. He decided it

was time to put aside his anger and make peace with her. He intended to bed her. He preferred she be willing, but it really didn't matter. She had deceived him, made a fool of him. He owed her nothing now. He wondered if she'd fight him. She hadn't before. Tonight he'd find out.

He glanced toward her just as she tied the final branch in place. Out of the corner of his eye, a movement near the marsh caught his attention. Nicholas turned to see the sharp tusks and bristly snout of a feral boar searching the brush for the only pool of water on the island. For a moment the animal sniffed the air, and Nicholas spotted blood on an injured shoulder. Then the great beast lowered its head and charged—straight toward the young woman sitting beneath the pines.

"Glory!" Nicholas cried out, drawing his knife and racing toward her. With a glance at the boar, she screamed and scrambled to her feet, eyes wide with terror. Clutching her petticoats out of the way, she raced toward Nicholas. He caught her in his arms and pulled her aside, just as the boar reached them. Spinning away from the flashing tusks, Nicholas plunged his knife into the animal's back. The wild pig screeched and squealed, then charged into the makeshift shelter. Pine boughs went flying; blood covered the branches and turned the lace red.

Nicholas tugged his knife free of the wildly charging animal and sank the blade again, this time into the boar's neck, just beneath the skull. The animal thrashed and rooted, tearing the shelter to shreds and finally falling on its side, kicking and snorting in its final death throes.

Taking several steadying breaths to calm himself, Nicholas shuddered at what might have happened. The wild boar was deadly; its razor-sharp tusks could rip a man apart. He closed his eyes against the haunting image of Glory mutilated and dying, covered in the animal's blood.

Close. Too close. His glance searching, he found her slumped against the base of a tree, arms wrapped around the knees drawn beneath her chin, her body shaking with the fury of her sobs. Nicholas had never felt more rotten in his life. As his long strides carried him across the sand, he cursed himself for the fool he'd been, knelt beside her, and gently pulled her into his arms.

In a feeble attempt to free herself, she pushed against his chest. "Go away and . . . leave me alone," she ordered raggedly between breaths.

"No."

"It doesn't matter anyway. I don't care if you see me cry. I'm tired of being brave." A trail of tears rolled down her cheeks. "That horrible creature tore up my shelter. I need a bath—and I'm hungry. Oh, God, I wish Papa were here."

Nicholas tightened his hold. He hadn't meant for things to go so far. He certainly hadn't meant to endanger her life. Seeing her like this, her pride gone, her face pale, her body shaking with sobs, he felt a surge of protectiveness that twisted his heart and constricted his chest until he could barely breathe.

More tears rolled down her cheeks. "Papa would know what to do."

"I know what to do," he whispered beside her cheek. Scooping her into his arms, he carried her toward the marsh, a quarter of a mile through the ooze, and up onto the strand without even noticing her weight. She clung to him, crying all the while. He didn't stop until he'd waded to the middle of the freshwater pool he'd been using each morning to bathe. Only then did she lift her head from his chest to look around.

"Nicholas?"

"It's all right, love," he told her. "Everything's going to be all right from now on." Still she clung to him. He let go of her knees, and her toes sank into the soft sand at the bottom of the pond. With firm but gentle motions, he pulled her chemise over her head, slid her filthy petticoat and ragged drawers down her thighs, and helped her step free of the clinging garments.

With his hands around her tiny waist, he steadied her while she slipped beneath the surface to cleanse the sand from her face and hair. When she stood up, beads of water trickled down the wet strands of pale hair that clung to her neck and shoulders.

Nicholas thought she had never looked more beautiful. His gaze fixed on her full breasts, which pointed upward, just as he remembered. He ached to hold them in his hands. His arm circled her waist and he pulled her against him. Still a little dazed, she didn't resist. He hadn't planned to take advantage of her—at least not now—but feeling the warmth of her body, the smoothness of her skin, he groaned and covered her lips with his. The heat he felt sent a ripple of pleasure the length of him—and a surge of blood to his loins.

Deepening the kiss, he felt her lips part beneath his, and the first tentative touch of her tongue. When her arms slid around his neck, Nicholas felt a wave of desire like nothing he'd known. He kissed her cheeks, her eyes, the place beneath her ear, then moved along the slender column of her neck.

Feeling warm and cared for, nurtured and protected for the first time in days, Glory didn't care that she was nude, didn't care where she was or how she had gotten there. Nothing mattered except feeling clean and whole again. Nothing mattered but being in Nicholas's arms. A small voice said, *Remember what he's done to you,* but try as she might, she could only think of the way his lips felt, the gentleness of his touch.

Instead, she laced her fingers through the strands of his curly black hair and arched against him, feeling tingly and hot all over. His lips moved over her flesh, trailing warm kisses until he captured the crest of her nipple and circled it gently with his tongue. Glory moaned and tilted her head back, giving him better access to the breast he cradled in his hand. His mouth caressed, tasted, and sucked the stiff peak, and Glory's blood fired with the delicious sensations.

He kissed her again, this time demandingly, and Glory responded in kind. When his hands traveled down her body to cup her buttocks and pull her more firmly against him, she felt his hardened manhood pressing against her, demanding release from the confines of his breeches.

His arm slid beneath her knees, and he lifted her from the water, carrying her to a grassy spot at the edge of the pool. He left her only long enough to shed his own clothes and return to her side, easing himself down beside her.

"God, how I've wanted you," he whispered against her ear, his voice husky.

Though her hands pressed against his chest in feeble protest, he captured her lips and plunged his tongue into her mouth. Fiery sensations engulfed her. Glory writhed against him, forgetting her fears, blotting her doubts, wanting him to touch her, feeling achy and taut and consumed. Careful to keep his weight above her, he covered her body with his and parted her thighs with his knee.

It was all Nicholas could do to go slowly. He wanted to drive into her, wanted to plunge inside. From the tension in her body, he knew she wanted it too. Instead he guided himself within her until he reached the obstacle he only half expected. The proof of her virginity stirred in him a disturbing jolt of guilt—and an unwelcome surge of joy.

"Only a moment's pain, love," he told her, forcing his conscience aside. "Then all the pleasure I've promised."

She pulled away a little, afraid for the first time. "Nicholas?" she whispered hesitantly.

"Trust me," he told her.

And she did. She wrapped her arms around his neck and clung to him, seeking his mouth, opening her own to his tongue. Slipping his hands beneath her hips, he drove himself inside her. Only the pressure of his lips silenced her cry of pain. A tear slipped down her cheek to nestle in the tiny hollow at the base of her throat.

"Are you all right, love?" he asked, holding himself back until her pain subsided.

"Yes," she whispered, still a little uncertain.

Cradling her buttocks in his palms, he kissed her again, his tongue teasing the walls of her mouth; then he began to move in a slow, rhythmical pattern that made her forget her discomfort, made her think only of the tall man who held her in his arms. Responding to the ancient instincts of a man and woman, she moved against him, met his thrusts again and again until his muscles bunched with the sheen of their efforts and he called out her name.

Something powerful and frightening seemed to be building with his last few powerful strokes, but before she could discover what it was, Nicholas shuddered fiercely, held himself above her a moment more, then rolled away, drawing her with him into the curve of his arm. His eyes remained closed until his breathing slowed to normal.

Glory stroked the line of his jaw and wondered how she could possibly want him to kiss her again. She wished she felt as relaxed as he did. When he touched her breast, she jumped as if she'd been burned and heard his low soft laughter.

"I've disappointed you. I'm sorry." His teasing smile said he only half meant it. "I've wanted you so long I couldn't wait."

"How could anything so wonderful be disappointing?" she said, denying the tiny voice that reminded her the intimacies they'd shared belonged in the marriage bed, that women weren't supposed to feel the wondrous sensations she'd experienced. Instead, her glance moved from his gray eyes, now light and teasing, to the width of his chest, to the flat spot beneath his navel. Color flooded her cheeks when she noticed his softened manhood resting in its nest of protective black curls.

She turned her head away, but not before the forbidden object began to strengthen.

With a throaty chuckle, Nicholas teased the palm of her hand with his tongue, brought her fingers to his mouth to lick and suck each one. Glory felt a jolt of desire that tightened the muscles in her stomach and set her heart to pounding again. She rounded her gaze on his face and saw his eyes had darkened, hungry once more.

"It's your turn now," he told her, and before she could ask what he meant, he had covered her mouth with his and rolled on top of her, pressing her into the soft grass beneath them. Feeling his tongue warm and moist against her own, she moaned and felt the same heat as before, this time even more intense.

He was less gentle, more demanding this time, firing an ardor she wouldn't have believed. With every thrust of his hardness, every powerful impact inside, she slipped a little deeper into his spell. The thickness of his shaft amazed her, filled her with blazing heat that set her body on fire. She writhed against him, meeting each of his thrusts with fierce abandon—until a bubble of pleasure swelled inside and a thousand tiny pinpricks of light burst behind her eyes. Crying out his name, she clung to him, and he followed her to release.

They slept for a while on the soft green grass, she in awe of what had happened, he in contentment, it seemed. When they awoke, they made love again; then Nicholas carried her into the coolness of the pond.

"How do you feel?" he asked as the water trailed sweetly around her hips. She remembered he'd asked her that before.

"Like a cat in a window," she told him truthfully, with a light smile that denied a tiny thread of guilt. "As if I'd just lapped up the last of my cream and the sun was beating against my cushion."

He laughed good-naturedly and she thought how few times she'd heard the sound.

"You should do that more often," she said as they climbed from the pool.

"Do what?"

"Laugh." They sat in the sun till the warm air dried their skin, then pulled on their now clean and dry garments. Now that the sand had been washed away, Glory reveled in the freedom of her scant clothing, even if she did feel a bit exposed. Nicholas wore only his breeches. Glory loved to watch the muscles of his chest tighten and flex with his movements, loved the rich mahogany hue of his swarthy complexion. He seemed not the least uncomfortable in their primitive environment.

When she tried unsuccessfully to untangle her mass of

pale hair with her fingers, Nicholas grabbed her hand and tugged her toward the beach.

"Come on. There's something I want to show you."

She let him pull her along the overgrown path beneath the chatter of chipmunks and several frolicking squirrels, then stopped in amazement when she saw the dozens of crates and trunks that rested at the edge of the sand. At first she laughed delightedly and raced toward the trunks, throwing open the lids of several to discover blankets and tools, flour, coffee, and slabs of salt pork. Several crates held cones of sugar the *Spider* had been transporting from Barbados.

"There are some oranges in one of the other crates," he told her. "Rope, canvas from the sails, maybe even something that could pass for a comb. There's just about everything we need, except of course our clothes." He actually grinned. "But then, we needn't worry much about that from now on."

Glory felt a rush of color to her cheeks, but with a glance back at the boxes her features turned serious. "When did you find all this?"

Nicholas glanced away, suddenly unwilling to meet her gaze. "This morning," he said, chiding himself for not being honest enough to tell her the truth. He just couldn't bear the thought of losing her trust after the way she'd given herself to him this morning.

He wasn't a good liar, Glory thought. He'd found this stuff days ago. She felt a surge of temper that reddened her blush even more and fought the urge to punch him smack in the nose. Then she thought of the way he'd saved her from the boar, the way he'd made love to her, and couldn't bring herself to stay mad at him. If he could forgive her for getting him stranded on this lonely stretch of land in the first place, she could surely forgive him for a few days of ill treatment.

In truth, she admitted, she loved him so much she'd forgive him almost anything.

She smiled at him, and his dark expression warmed. "How about handing me an orange," she said. "I'm starved.'' He peeled one for her. The fruity smell made her mouth water. Their fingers brushed as he handed it over and a tiny shiver raced up her spine. She broke the fruit in two and fed half of it to him, the sweet juices running down her fingers. He licked them clean, his eyes turning dark.

''I think we'd better set up camp,'' he said. ''Before we get *sidetracked* again.'' The way he said the word made clear what he was thinking.

She lowered her lashes and nodded her agreement. ''Could I have another orange first?''

As he fetched her another of the delicious fruits, he seemed a little guilty. ''Tonight,'' he said, ''I'm going to cook you the best meal you've ever eaten.''

Glory silently prayed it wouldn't be a new version of sea gull.

After setting up a comfortable campsite near one of the pools, Nicholas went back to the island and dressed out the boar. On the strand he dug a pit, lined it with rocks and burning wood that soon turned to coals, wrapped the pork in leaves, and buried it beneath another layer of coals. Finding several pots and a tin mug among some of the tools, he cleaned them with sand and headed toward the beach, returning later with the potful of clams. A salad of tender watercress from one of the ponds completed the meal.

It all tasted delicious to Glory, who ate until she couldn't possibly stuff in another bite.

''You'll get fat if you keep eating like that,'' Nicholas teased. ''But then there'd just be more of you to love.''

Glory straightened. She prayed he did love her, if only just a little. She wondered if he intended marriage. Surely he wouldn't have taken her as he had if his intentions were less than honorable. After all, she'd been vulnerable and he knew it. Besides, he was her father's friend. She wished she could be certain, but Nicholas Blackwell was not a man to be hurried. He would let her know in his own good time. Meanwhile what was done was done. Glory planned to enjoy every minute they had together.

"Tomorrow," he was saying, "I'll build that shelter you've been wanting."

"Why the change of heart?" she couldn't resist asking.

Again the glance away. "I just decided you were right, that's all."

She didn't press him further. That night they made love beneath the stars, and Glory felt such a rush of happiness she thought she might burst. Nicholas seemed to feel it, too. He held her all night, one arm protectively around her as if he didn't want her to get too far away.

Game was plentiful on the strand, and wild onions, watercress, and other wild vegetables abounded. The shelter Nicholas built turned out to be a small one-room lean-to. It took him two days to complete, but finished, it provided a cozy retreat from sun, wind, and sand. They still cooked out-of-doors, but inside the shelter, pine needles covered a sandy floor and, shielded with a layer of blankets, afforded a wide, comfortable bed. *One* bed, Glory noticed with a rush of embarrassment. It was obvious Nicholas intended not the vaguest semblance of propriety, and the thought confirmed her conviction that he meant to propose marriage. Except for her worry about Nathan, Glory was coming to think of the strand as the next best thing to paradise.

They were seated beside the breakfast fire sipping coffee from their single tin mug when Nicholas offered to teach Glory to swim.

Chapter Twelve

"What do you say?" he prodded. "I'll be there right beside you every step of the way."

"I don't know. Maybe tomorrow." She glanced away.

"Why not now?"

"I . . . I've always been a little afraid of the water." She twisted the now ragged folds of her gray-white petticoat. "I guess I'm not much of a tomboy. When I was a little girl, I preferred playing with dolls or embroidering to being out-of-doors—except for riding, of course. Papa persuaded me to try riding, and I loved it right away. But that was different, or at least it seemed so to me."

"And what of billiards?" he teased. "Hardly a feminine pastime."

"Playing billiards was Father's idea, too. I'd never have dreamed of doing anything so unladylike." She turned to face him more squarely. "What about you?" she asked, hoping to keep the subject directed away from the matter of swimming. "What did you like to do as a boy?"

One corner of his mouth lifted in an indulgent smile, and she knew she hadn't fooled him a bit. "I was too busy looking after my father to have much of a childhood." He poked the dying fire, sending a shower of sparks into the warm morning air. "He drank to forget my mother's unfaithfulness. Then he drank to hide from my stepmother's nagging and because he felt guilty for allowing her to treat me so badly. She used to invent things to punish me for. Once she told Father I purposely trod on her daffodils when she knew I'd only been playing on the porch and lost my balance. She locked me in my room for two days with no food and just the smallest amount of water.

Glory touched his cheek, glad he was beginning to confide in her.

"I used to lie in bed," he told her, "praying she would die and Father and I would be free. Then I'd feel guilty for wishing such a terrible thing."

Glory felt tears welling as she thought of the little boy who had never known a mother's love. She wanted to put her arms around him, absorb some of his pain, but she also wanted him to trust her, tell her the things he hid in his heart. "Mac said you left home at twelve."

"I ran away to sea." He jabbed the fire again. "It was a hard life, but I came to love it. I still do."

"And your back?" She traced a finger down one of his almost invisible scars.

Nicholas surprised her by smiling. He seemed relieved his childhood was no longer the subject. "I made the same mistake your young sailor did. I disobeyed the captain's orders. I was young and hot-headed. I got into an argument with one of the mates from the larboard watch. I challenged him to a fight. The captain forbade it. We met after dark and the other man wound up with a broken arm. I won the fight, but the captain lost the services of a valuable man. I got exactly what I deserved—and so did that sailor who helped you."

"I never thought of it that way. On the plantation, the slaves were whipped for wanting to be free. I never thought it was right."

"On a ship, a man is whipped when his actions endanger the safety of the ship or the people on board. It doesn't happen often. When it does it's usually well deserved. The boy should have said no to you."

Glory nodded. "And I should have stayed aboard."

"As I recall you paid for your mistake as well."

Glory glanced away, a little embarrassed to think of the

discipline she herself had received. Nicholas, it seemed,
was a man who meted out justice in a stern but fair manner. "Do you always discipline your women with such a
heavy hand?" she teased.

"Only when they need it." He smiled, and a hungry
gleam darkened his storm-gray eyes. "From now on I plan
to keep your sails trimmed smartly and a firm hand on
your rudder."

Glory blushed to her toes. As if to prove his point,
Nicholas pushed her down on the sand and kissed her
soundly. "I can't remember wanting a woman as I do
you," he said. "I never seem to get enough."

Glory knew exactly what he meant.

The days on the strand passed in a hazy blur of lovemaking, improving their primitive home, and watching for
the rescue ship Nicholas felt sure was soon to arrive. He
had readied a huge signal fire, but would light it only when
sail had been spotted.

"Nicholas?" Glory approached him quietly, brushing
aside the heavy palmetto leaves that blocked her path.
Nicholas knelt beneath the leaves, setting a rabbit snare.

"Yes, love?"

"I'm ready to learn to swim."

Nicholas smiled delightedly. "You're going to love it, I
promise you."

"If you keep this promise as well as you did the last, I
have nothing to worry about."

They spent the day in the warm waters of the ocean and
once Glory got over her panic—and Nicholas vowed to
watch for sharks—she caught on easily. Not comfortable
swimming nude, she wore her chemise and thin cotton
drawers. Nicholas held her waist while she floated face
down in front of him, legs kicking out behind. Her shapely
bottom wiggled alluringly with every stroke, and it was
all he could do to concentrate on the lesson.

The thin fabric of her drawers, all but invisible in the
water, clung to the curves of her bottom and added to his
discomfort. Holding her dainty waist in his hands, deter-

mined to continue, he swallowed hard and tried to look somewhere else, but his traitorous eyes returned again and again to the tempting flesh wriggling in front of him. With a low groan of defeat, he gave in to his desire, carried her protesting to the shallows, and made passionate love to her.

The swimming lesson continued some time later.

Eventually Glory was able to swim by herself, though Nicholas warned her against going out too far. Occasionally, she would even go in without her garments, if Nicholas promised not to watch. Swimming, she declared, was far too unladylike a sport to indulge in without one's clothing. Today was one of those rare occasions. After extracting Nicholas's promise, Glory had removed her clothes and was paddling close to shore, ducking her flaxen-haired head, then breaking the surface and splashing delightedly when he heard her cry out.

Her high-pitched scream sent chills the length of him. He was on his feet and racing down the beach before her second scream reached his ears. His gaze searching the tranquil water, his knife unsheathed and gripped in his hand, he saw the deadly tentacles and cloudy mass of the Portuguese man-of-war's body just before he rushed into the surf.

Shoving the knife back into its scabbard, he plunged through the waves and pulled Glory away from the stinging tentacles of the jellyfish.

"Nicholas?" she whimpered, her voice choked with sobs. "What—what happened? I . . . hurt so . . . much."

"You're going to be fine," he said, wanting to reassure her, wishing he could ease her pain. Holding her in his arms, he sloshed ashore. "You've been stung by a jellyfish. A Portuguese man-of-war. They're rare in these waters. I . . . " His voice trailed off, but his gaze remained on her face. Her tortured expression twisted his heart.

Nicholas laid her on the sandy beach and began to examine her wounds. One whole side of her body looked as if it had been burned with a hot iron. Red welts marred the delicate flesh, and Nicholas cursed beneath his breath.

"I should never have let you go in alone," he said softly, blaming himself.

Glory moaned and tried to sit up. "I . . . I'm going to be sick." He held her while she retched up the fruit and fish she'd eaten for breakfast, her body shaking, trying to rid itself of the pain. "I'm so embarrassed," she whispered.

"Don't be absurd. This isn't your fault." The words came out a little more harshly than he intended. If he hadn't insisted she learn to swim, she wouldn't be suffering now. With a shudder of regret, he carried her back to their camp, where he made a pallet of pine needles beside the pool, covered it with a blanket, then made a poultice of mud for her burns. People had been known to die from the sting of the vicious man-of-war, but more often they just suffered in agony until their body could ward off the poison.

Nicholas applied the mud poultice while Glory bit her lip until it bled. She tried to stifle her tears, but still they came, in salty rivulets that trickled down her cheeks.

Nicholas cradled her head in his lap. "I'm sorry, love. So sorry. There's nothing to do but wait for the pain to go away."

She nodded weakly. "Talk to me. Tell me about . . . about . . ." She swallowed hard and wet her dry lips. "Just talk to me."

"I'll tell you about Bradford." He smoothed the hair from her cheek. "He's my stepbrother. I've been thinking about him lately." Though he brushed the tears from her cheek with a trembling hand, more followed in a wet cascade that tore at his heart. He swallowed hard and forced himself to go on. "Brad goes to school at Harvard. I can't imagine how my stepmother managed to have a son like Brad, but she did, and it's the one thing I'm grateful to her for."

Glory smiled. Tears spiked her long dark lashes, but

she ignored them. "What . . . does he . . . look like?" It was a battle to keep her mind off the agonizing pain.

"He's shorter than I am, though he's still quite tall. He has fair skin and brown hair—and the kindest hazel eyes you've ever looked into. He's nothing like me. Brad's gentle and caring. Everyone loves him."

"You can be gentle," Glory said.

Nicholas shook his head. "I'm overbearing, arrogant, and demanding. You ought to know that by now."

She gave him another weak smile.

"I'll grant you, I'm not without a certain amount of charm when I want to be," he teased, "but I'm certainly not lovable."

That's not true, she wanted to say. I love you. Instead, she kept silent. He hadn't said those words to her, and a proper southern lady would never be the first to admit such a thing. Of course a proper southern lady wouldn't be living on an isolated strip of land, wearing nothing but her petticoat, and making love to Nicholas Blackwell without benefit of marriage.

"I think you're . . . quite often . . . lovable," she told him instead, then moved too suddenly and felt a white-hot, searing stab of pain. Clenching her teeth, she closed her eyes and gripped his hand until her nails dug into his skin.

"Just lie quiet, love." He eased her head from his lap. "I'll make you some broth. We've got to get something in your stomach."

With a nod, she turned away, knowing she would rather rest in his lap than eat any day.

By the end of the fifth day, Glory had, for the most part, returned to normal. She bathed in the pool and washed her hair, though she hadn't as yet been in swimming again. Watching her around the camp, Nicholas felt the familiar surge of desire for her he hadn't experienced since her accident. He'd just been too damned worried until today. Seeing her leaving the pool, her thin white garments clinging to every curve, he groaned and glanced away.

Grudgingly he admitted he was falling in love with the elegant blonde. He hadn't meant to. Hadn't wanted to. In fact he'd done everything in his power to avoid it. But the evidence was clear. He thought of her day and night, worried about her—and wanted her endlessly.

She hadn't mentioned her lover, and since Nicholas had been the first to bed her, he decided she'd probably only *thought* she was in love with the handsome Negro. The man was just an infatuation, he told himself. As soon as they reached civilization, he decided, he would offer marriage. They'd move to his estate near Tarrytown in the New York countryside. He would be close enough to oversee his shipping company, but the estate would be the perfect place to raise a family. *His* family. The thought warmed his heart.

With a flash of clarity, Nicholas realized he actually *liked* the idea of being married to Glory.

Until now he had never believed it could happen to him, not after the way marriage had destroyed his father. But Gloria Summerfield was different from any other woman he'd known.

He trusted her. Why—after the way she'd tricked him—he couldn't say. But he did.

And she trusted him. Of that he was sure. She loved him, too. If he was any judge of women, and he was.

Thinking of the future they would share, he put aside his worries about her relationship with the man called Nathan. She had probably forgotten all about him by now.

At least he hoped so.

But his experience with women and his one small lingering doubt were enough to keep him from speaking his heart.

Chapter Thirteen

Eighteen days after the *Black Spider* went down, Glory spotted sail just south and east of where they were stranded. Jumping up and down and pointing excitedly, she flashed Nicholas a bright smile and rushed toward the beach. Nicholas headed straight for the signal fire. Glory waved her arms and loudly called out to the ship, though it was much too far away for the crew to hear her. Once the fire began to blaze, Nicholas joined her on the beach.

Glory slipped her arm through his. "Just think, Nicholas, at last we'll have clean clothes."

"And a hot bath," he said.

"And food we don't have to catch first."

"And a feather bed," he added with a warm note in his voice.

She tilted her face to look up at him. "In some ways I'll miss this place."

Smiling warmly, he ran a finger down the line of her jaw. "Me, too."

The huge signal fire shot flames into the air, marking their location, and the ship headed straight for their position. Nicholas brought a blanket for her to wrap herself up in, and Glory blushed prettily, conscious of her skimpy garments for the first time in days. Neither spoke for a while; they just stood quietly on the shore, listening to the waves breaking at their feet and watching the big ship approach.

"That's the *Black Witch*," Nicholas told her, ending the silence, a proud glow warming his gray eyes. "She's my flagship."

"She's beautiful."

"She can carry only half as much cargo as the *Spider*, but she's as fast as they come. A man named John Griffiths designed her. She has a sharper bow and a leaner hull than most ships; that's what makes her so fast. If they've picked up the rest of the crew, we'll make New York Harbor in four days."

Glory looked out at the graceful ship and, for the first time since the sinking, allowed herself to think of Nathan and the crew. During the time she'd spent on the island, she had refused to believe Nathan wasn't safe. Now that the resolution of her fears lay only minutes away, she was worried. Was he all right? Was he safely aboard the *Black Witch* with the rest of the crew? She prayed he was and in her heart felt almost sure. Still . . . She couldn't wait till she reached the ship and could put her fears to rest.

In the end she didn't have to wait that long. Two shore boats were launched from the *Witch* as the ship drew near, and shading her eyes from the sun, Glory could just make out Nathan's handsome dark profile in the bow of the second boat. Heart racing wildly, she rushed into the surf, waving and calling out his name. Jago sat at the helm, and she could see Mac and Josh Pintassle in the bow of the lead boat. Relieved at last, Glory wrapped her arms around herself and gave up a silent prayer of thanks.

Josh beached the first boat, and he and Mac jumped into the water at the same time. Glory rushed to Mac's open arms, hugging him first and then Josh.

"Thank God ye're both all right," Mac said, grinning and looking relieved.

"I knew the captain would make it," Josh added with a touch of admiration. The second boat pulled ashore just as the men turned to greet their captain, and the rest of the crew swarmed around to welcome him back.

Before the boat had run aground, Nathan jumped into the surf, and Glory rushed into his arms, laughing and crying at the same time. "Oh, Nathan . . . Nathan. Thank God you're all right. I was so worried."

Nathan buried his face in her hair, stroking her cheek and cradling her against him. For a moment he set her away, combing her from head to toe with his glance to assure himself that she was all right. Then he hugged her again.

"When the *Spider* went down, I thought you were on one of the other boats," he said. "I kept hoping and praying you were safe. I didn't find out what happened until the *Black Witch* picked us up on a beach way south of here. I've been sick with worry ever since. I'd never have forgiven myself if something had happened."

"I'm fine, Nathan. Captain Blackwell took very good care of me." Feeling a blush creep into her cheeks, she turned her glance toward shore and saw Nicholas walking away from her toward their makeshift camp, Josh and Mac close behind.

For the hundredth time since they'd been shipwrecked, Glory wondered if she should have told Nicholas who Nathan really was and why they were heading north. She'd been waiting for him to speak of their future. But she'd waited long enough. As soon as they reached the ship, she would explain everything. After what they'd shared these past few weeks, she was certain he'd understand.

"Gather up anything we can use and load it aboard the shore boats," Nicholas commanded several sailors as they reached the primitive campsite. It was all he could do to control the edge to his voice.

"Are you all right?" Josh asked. "I know things have been rough—"

"I'm fine!" Nicholas snapped. "I just want to get off this miserable stretch of land and back to the ship."

Josh eyed his friend closely. Nicholas stalked some distance away, then leaned against a pine tree as if to steady himself. His face looked pale beneath his swarthy tan, the skin stretched taut over his angular cheekbones.

Josh gave the necessary orders, and the men loaded the supplies and headed back to the boats. As they marched along the sandy beach, Josh heard several of the sailors snickering among themselves while another made lewd remarks. None had missed the implications of the tiny shelter with its single wide bed.

Worried at the turn of events, Josh drew his blond brows together until they formed a narrow line. He wondered if Glory could be the reason for the captain's distress. When it came to women, Nicholas Blackwell had never been one to stand on principle. He'd wanted her from the start. On the island she had been at his mercy. But Glory Summerfield was no easy conquest. Her father had been a powerful man and one of the captain's closest friends. Surely Nicholas knew he would be forced to marry her. Whatever the cause, the look on his friend's face said something was definitely wrong.

"Mr. Pintassle!" Nicholas's harsh command broke Josh's reverie. "Look alive, man! Get those goods loaded and let's make way."

"Aye, Captain."

Mac McDougal slapped Nicholas on the shoulder. "Simmer down, lad. Ye've been stranded here fer the better part o' three weeks. A few more minutes will make no never-mind."

Nicholas only nodded. He found it nearly impossible to speak in a normal tone of voice. Even now he could see Glory climbing aboard the second shore boat, holding another man's hand. When she'd rushed into Nathan's arms, Nicholas felt as if she'd thrust a knife into his heart.

Not since his childhood, not since his mother deserted him, had Nicholas cried, but he fought to keep the tears from welling now. His chest felt so tight he could barely breathe. How could he have been such a fool? He wasn't some green youth just off the boat. He was a grown man. One who was supposed to know women—he'd certainly pleasured more than his share! He had only been with Glory a few weeks. How could he have let her get so close to him? Let her convince him she cared?

How could he have come to love her so much?

Nicholas and the others returned to the beach and climbed aboard the shore boats. As the men rowed toward the ship, Nicholas glanced across the waves to where Glory sat beside the man called Nathan. He'd draped one arm over her shoulder as if protecting her from the sailors' questioning stares. She smiled up at him, her eyes filled with love. She didn't even try to disguise it.

Nicholas turned away, cursing his own stupidity. Why had he let himself believe she was different? Why had he dared to fall in love?

Nicholas set his jaw and clenched his fists. And slowly, as he'd taught himself to do, he turned his agony into rage.

The woman had duped him, tricked him into loving her. To her what they'd shared meant nothing more than physical pleasure. The man called Nathan was the one she loved. He'd seen it as she rushed into his arms. He saw it now as she smiled into the man's handsome face. She'd been a virgin, all right. But she had given him her virginity just to insure her protection. She'd used him, made a fool of him in every way. She had probably been laughing at him all along, thinking what an easy mark he was, what a lovesick fool.

In that moment, if Nicholas could have put his hands around her slender neck he would have choked the life out of her. The rage he felt surpassed anything he had ever known. For the first time he understood how a man could kill someone he loved in a fit of temper—and how his father could have turned to drink to forget the woman he loved.

Nicholas forced his gaze to the sleek ship bobbing at anchor just a few hundred yards away. The pain he felt settled into a slow aching throb as he forced himself under control. She isn't worth it, he told himself. She's just a woman, like all the others you've known. Just like your mother. All the hatred, all the loneliness and despair he'd bottled up inside for all these years, Nicholas now turned on Glory.

A quiet calm washed over him, and he turned in her direction. She was laughing softly, the crystalline sound he had loved suddenly grating on his ears. His mouth narrowed to a cold, thin line, and Nicholas felt his icy calm turn to brutal resolve.

Taking a deep steadying breath, he braced himself against the side of the boat and watched the *Black Witch* growing closer with each stroke of the oars. A slow, mirthless smile curved one corner of his mouth.

"Bring up the anchor rode, Mr. Pintassle. Let's make way." Nicholas turned from Josh toward a man who stood beside him. "I'll be taking command from here on out, Captain Durant. And I thank you for all you've done." A tall, spare man with a seaman's full beard, Captain Durant stood at the helm in his immaculate navy blue uniform, the brass buttons and gold braid flashing in the afternoon sun.

"I wish I could have brought them all back safely," Durant said. "But Mac saw the missing boat go under. He couldn't reach them, but he's sure none of them survived. There's no point in searching farther. All in all the casualties were exceedingly low."

Nicholas nodded. "A sinking's always disastrous. I just thank God there weren't more."

"Nicholas?" Glory stepped forward, holding the stiff wool blanket over her ragged garments. Mac and Nathan walked up behind her.

"Ah, if it isn't my pretty roommate, Miss Summerfield." He turned his attention to his second mate. "Mac, I'll be escorting her ladyship to my cabin. You take her . . . *servant* below. If memory serves, he's to spend the balance of the voyage in the brig."

Nathan's head snapped up, and Glory sucked in a breath. "Nicholas, you can't be serious! After what he's been through, surely he's more than paid for disobeying your orders.''

''Mac,'' Nicholas repeated.

Mac gave the captain a lengthy stare, then sighed resignedly. ''Aye, Captain. Ye best be following me, lad,'' he said to Nathan. ''It won't be fer long.''

Nathan touched Glory's arm in a warning gesture, giving her a look that clearly told her to let the matter be. Then he followed Mac below decks.

''Come with me,'' Nicholas commanded, his attention focused on Glory.

''Nicholas, there's something you don't understand,'' she told him as she followed him along the deck.

He turned to face her. ''I think it would be best if you addressed me as Captain.'' Before she could speak, he walked off toward the aft ladder, descended, and continued down the passageway. Glory trailed behind. Wordlessly, he opened the door to the captain's cabin, a splendidly furnished room much more spacious than the one he had occupied aboard the *Spider*.

Glory stepped inside. ''I hate to put you out, *Captain*.''

''Believe me, you aren't.''

Glory couldn't believe his tone of voice: harsh, brittle, almost jeering. ''There's something I need to tell you,'' she said simply.

''Really? I hate to miss your theatrics, but I already know about you and Nathan.''

''You do?''

''I've known almost from the start.''

She felt a rush of relief. ''I've been afraid to tell you. Afraid you wouldn't understand.''

''Ah, but I do, so you needn't concern yourself any further.'' He strode across the room and opened an ornately carved mahogany wardrobe. ''You'll find some dresses and underthings in here. There's a needle and thread in the top drawer of the bureau if you need to make alterations. Now if you'll excuse me, I have work to do.''

''But what about Nathan?''

''He stays where he is.'' Without a backward glance,

he turned and left the room, slamming the door just a little harder than necessary, it seemed to Glory.

Stunned, she stared after him. What on earth was the matter with him? Surely he was just preoccupied with his duties. Their relationship couldn't have changed that drastically in one short hour. She would talk to him after supper, she resolved. Once the ship was under way, he might be more relaxed. Perhaps he'd see reason and let Nathan go.

Then she remembered the stern sea captain who had commanded the *Black Spider*—a man far different from the warm, giving man she'd come to love on the strand— and began to have her doubts.

Nicholas didn't come in to supper. Glory fidgeted throughout the sumptuous meal served in the elegant officers' wardroom. It was obvious the *Black Witch* was Nicholas's most prized possession. His flawless taste was evident from the massive carved wooden beams to the ornate brass sconces on the walls. Wishing he would join them, she let her gaze stray toward the door, watching for him, waiting for him to come into the room and grace her with one of his secret warm smiles.

Earlier, after he'd left the cabin, she had found the dresses, just as Nicholas had said, and though they were several inches too short, she was able to nip them in at the waist and make them fit. She wondered what they were doing in his cabin and felt a stab of jealousy that another woman had once shared his room. Necessity forced her to wear the dresses, so she shoved thoughts of whom they belonged to from her mind.

The gown she had chosen for supper was an elegant green brocade. Worn off the shoulder, the dress had a soft sweeping ruffle that trimmed the low neckline and nearly touched her elbows. The dropped-V bodice accented her tiny waist. Glory had twisted her pale blond hair into smooth chignons at either side of her neck and the effect was astounding. She'd almost forgotten how pretty she could look. She didn't miss Josh's appreciate glance, or the way Captain Durant's eyes drifted to the swells of her cleavage.

She hoped Nicholas liked her appearance. She was worried about Nathan and more than a little worried about what Nicholas planned for their future. She refused to dwell on the way he'd treated her earlier. He was just preoccupied, nothing more.

Josh and Captain Durant were excellent company throughout the meal, which was also attended by the *Black Witch*'s first mate, William Allen, a dark-featured, broadfaced seaman in his mid-thirties.

As interesting as the men were, Glory had trouble following their conversation. She was anxious to speak with Nicholas, to settle things between them. Maybe tonight he would offer marriage. She knew by now every man in the crew was aware they'd shared a bed on the strand. She'd seen the looks and the lewd smiles that passed between them. Surely Nicholas had seen them, too.

Toward the end of the meal, Glory gave up watching for him. She declined a glass of sherry, pleaded a headache, and returned to her cabin. Disappointed and more than a little frustrated, she began preparing for bed. She had just finished brushing out her hair when a key grated in the heavy metal lock and the door swung open.

Nicholas stood in the doorway, a brass whale-oil lantern in his hand. Feeling the familiar rush of warmth he always stirred, Glory smiled warmly and rose from her seat in front of the ornate cherrywood-framed mirror. "I'm so glad you came," she said, walking toward him.

"Are you?" He lifted a winged black brow. Looking away from her, he began unbuttoning his shirt.

Glory's eyes widened as he tugged the shirt from his breeches. "What are you doing?"

"Getting ready for bed," he told her calmly.

"But . . . but where are you planning to sleep?"

"The same place I've been sleeping these past few weeks. With you."

"Nicholas, you can't sleep—"

"Captain," he corrected.

Glory's mouth went dry. "You can't mean to sleep with me on board the ship. Why the whole crew would know."

"They already know." He sat down in a tufted leather chair and pulled off his boots.

"Nicholas, I can't believe you mean to humiliate me this way. It's only four days to New York. We can be married, and then—"

"Married!" His brittle laughter rang across the room. In the glow of the lamplight, she could make out the hard angles and planes of his face. "What on earth gave you the idea we were getting married?"

Glory's hand inched to her throat. It was suddenly hard to breathe. "When we were shipwrecked . . . when you made love to me, I thought . . ." She swallowed hard. "I thought . . . you loved me."

"Love," he said with a sneer. "You're beginning to sound like Lavinia."

Glory sank down on the bed. No words would come. She shook her head slowly, unwilling to accept the hateful words.

"Get undressed," Nicholas commanded.

"What?"

"I said get out of that dress or I'll tear it off you."

Glory licked her lips, her throat so dry she could barely speak. "I don't believe you're doing this."

"I'll just bet you don't. Now do as I told you."

She only shook her head.

Nicholas stepped out of his breeches, kicked them aside, then, naked, strode immodestly up in front of her.

"Fine," he said. "Have it your way." He grabbed her arms and roughly jerked them above her head, pushing her back on the bed at the same time. She tried to cry out, but his lips silenced her. Using his body, he pressed her into the thick feather mattress, shoved up her brocade skirts, then the white froth of her petticoats. Glory struggled against him, a feeble effort at best. Her mind refused to grasp what he was doing. She loved Nicholas Blackwell. She didn't want to fight him. He deepened the kiss, thrusting his tongue between her teeth—and against her will, Glory felt the stirrings of desire. She moaned and arched against him.

Nicholas pulled away. "That's right, pretty little whore, I'm going to give you just what you want."

The words stung like a slap, bringing her to her senses. She tried to get up, but he pressed her back into the mattress. This time Glory struggled in earnest. This wasn't the man she loved. This was a stranger. A madman. She writhed and twisted beneath him, felt his fingers clutching the band of her lacy cotton drawers, then heard the fabric rip away, leaving her exposed, vulnerable. She could feel the cool air against her heated skin and a tiny sob escaped before Nicholas captured her lips in another brutal kiss.

His hands moved over her body, along the curve of her hips, until he reached the pale triangle at the juncture of her thighs. For a moment he coaxed and teased, heating her blood, making her ache with wanting; then he slid his fingers inside her. Glory cringed as he found her wet and eager for his touch.

He laughed softly, the sound almost demonic. "Such a beautiful traitorous body."

"Stop it, Nicholas," she whispered. "Please don't do this." But he only parted her thighs and positioned himself above her. She could feel his manhood, hot and swollen, and remembered the pleasure he could give. His lips covered hers, his mouth open and warm, tasting and savoring, forcing a response. Though her mind rebelled against his savagery, her body begged for more. His hardened shaft teased her womanhood, found the entrance, and drove inside, filling her until she forgot the violence, forgot the cruelty of his words, and thought only of their passion.

Gripping his wide shoulders, she felt his muscles bunch beneath her hand while again and again he plunged into her. With a will of its own, her body arched against him, meeting every thrust, aching for him to bring release as only Nicholas could. She felt his muscles tense and her own tensed as well until a thousand pinpricks of pleasure skimmed across her heated flesh. A few more violent strokes, and Nicholas followed her to climax.

He rested above her only a moment, then rolled away and climbed from the bed. Glory swallowed the ache in her throat, the bitterness, the pain. Though she closed her eyes against her welling tears, a tiny trail of wetness slipped down her cheek.

"Why, Nicholas?" she whispered.

"Why not? It's what we both wanted." Pulling on his breeches, he buttoned them up the front, dressing casually, as if she weren't even in the room. Then he left without a word.

Glory hugged her knees to her chest and wrapped her arms protectively around them. She fought the aching sadness that seeped through her very bones, until she heard his footsteps recede down the hall. Then nothing could stop the terrible racking sobs that shook her slender body.

Nicholas watched the ocean slip beneath the ship in a surge of frothy foam. He stood at the rail in darkness; only a sliver of moon between the clouds glistened on the passing waves.

"So this is where ye be." Mac MacDougal stepped quietly up beside him at the rail.

"I don't feel much like talking, Mac," Nicholas said, staring straight ahead, his hands braced on the solid wood as if it were all that kept him from hurling himself into the sea.

"I havna often meddled in yer affairs, lad. But I kin see by yer face somethin' isna as it should be. The lass is a good girl, Nicky. You're bound to do right by her."

"Stay out of this, Mac, I'm warning you." He turned a hard look on his friend. "This is none of your business."

"Ye've been like a son to me, lad. I've always been proud o' ye. Don't make me ashamed o' ye now." A flash of moonlight lit the Scotsman's ruddy face.

Nicholas didn't miss the tight lines of disapproval he'd seen only a few times before. Glancing away, he stared back out to sea. He heard Mac's deep sigh and felt his friend's weathered hand as it rested on his shoulder. Mac said nothing more, just turned and walked back toward his cabin. His heavy footfalls thudded against the deck, adding their burden to Nicholas's already heavy heart.

Chapter Fourteen

Glory didn't leave the cabin all the next day. Josh came by with a tray of food at noon and then again at supper. Glory smiled and thanked him, but told him she needed to rest from her ordeal on the strand. Josh's worried expression said he didn't believe her, but he made no further attempt to draw her out.

As the hour grew late, Glory began to worry. Would Nicholas come to her again tonight? She had no way of knowing. Whatever closeness they'd once had no longer existed. The man who had come to her room last night had been a stranger, as foreign to her as the land to which she traveled.

Unable to read his thoughts and afraid of what he might do next, Glory watched the door to the passageway with growing alarm. She tried to stitch up another of the remaining gowns, but her hands shook so badly that she had to put her needle away.

A flash of foreboding made her shove the heavy bureau in front of the door, just in case. It took all her strength to move the massive piece, but once the task was complete she felt a little better.

Though she would have preferred something more modest, she found a sheer silk nightdress in the wardrobe and pulled it over her head. Again she wondered whose it was.

Had Nicholas seduced the woman in this very bed? Had he spoken the same words of passion he'd said to her?

She climbed onto the wide berth, but sleep seemed elusive. Every time she closed her eyes and began to drift off, she saw Nicholas as he had looked on the strand, tall and handsome, laughing and smiling, his gray eyes alight with what she'd been sure was love. The memory swelled a hard lump in her throat and kept her tossing and turning on the lonely bed.

"You're beginning to sound like Lavinia . . . like Lavinia . . . like Lavinia." The words echoed like a litany. She closed her eyes and tried to blot out the bitter sound of his voice. Every noise in the passageway set her already taut nerves even more on edge, until the grating of a key in the lock made her sit bolt-upright.

The latch lifted and the door banged loudly against the bureau. Nicholas's low sardonic laughter seeped through the narrow crack in the door. For a moment Glory couldn't discern the soft thudding she heard next, but when the bureau shuddered and began to move, she recognized the sound as Nicholas slammed his muscular shoulder time after time against the wooden door.

Glory raced from the bed and threw her weight against the bureau. "Go away, Nicholas. Leave me alone."

"Get away from the door, Glory," he warned. "I'm coming in one way or another. If I have to, I'll bring the whole crew down here to help me break in."

Glory's shoulders slumped. As she backed away from the bureau, Nicholas made a last heave, opening the door enough to allow him entrance. When he stepped inside, she faced him squarely, fighting back tears, her chin lifted in defiance.

"I can't stop you, Captain. I am only a woman. If you intend to force yourself on me against my will, do what you must."

Nicholas regarded her closely. "Against your will, my sweet? I hardly think so."

Glory didn't move. Nicholas stepped closer, his stormy eyes devouring the curves of her breasts through the sheer

silk garment, the crests of her nipples two dark circles
beneath the cloth. Another step and he settled the palms
of his hands on either side of her face. Ever so slowly he
lowered his mouth to hers, and the heat of his lips scorched
her soul. She steeled herself against the familiar yearnings
and willed herself not to respond.

Nicholas used the side of his thumb to open her mouth,
then forced his tongue inside, employing it with practiced
skill. He teased her lips, then gently licked the corners.
Glory closed her eyes. She was back on the strand; the
man she kissed was Nicholas. Her Nicholas. The man she
loved. The hands that cupped her face were the gentle
hands she knew so well, hands that knew every part of her
body. Hands that had cared for her, protected her, saved
her very life.

When he moved his lips to the place beside her ear, it
was all she could do to stifle her moan. He trailed warm
kisses along her neck while slipping the gown off her
shoulders. When he moved his head to capture the hard
bud of her nipple, Glory swayed against him. Her fingers
slipped through the black hair curling at the nape of his
neck. She didn't know she was crying until Nicholas lifted
his head to look at her.

For a moment she hardly recognized him, his expression seemed so hard. Then, with a trembling hand, he
brushed away her tears and swept her into his arms. Her
blond hair trailed over his shoulder as his long strides carried them to the bed. He left her only long enough to shed
his clothes, then returned to the place beside her.

"So lovely," he said. "Will I ever be able to forget
you?"

The words mirrored thoughts of her own, and she whispered his name. I love you so much, she thought. In her
mind she couldn't stop saying it, but her lips would not
move.

Though they made love passionately, as though for the
very last time, he was gentle with her, just as he had been
on the strand. She felt his tenderness in the touch of his
lips, felt his caring, felt his need. It didn't matter what

happened on the morrow; tonight she had her Nicholas back, if only for these few precious hours. If only for tonight, her love was there beside her, showing her his feelings, giving of himself. His hands moved over her body, touching her, caressing her, urging her body to passion while her heart sighed with grief. How would she ever live without him? She didn't even want to try.

She wondered at his thoughts, wondered if he would miss her as she missed him, wondered why he was destroying her so completely. This time when they finished, he pulled her into the crook of his arm as he'd done so many times before. He didn't leave her, even when she feigned sleep, just kissed the pale strands of her hair and softly stroked her cheek. Exhausted, she stubbornly refused to fall asleep, though in his arms she could have. She didn't want to waste these few priceless hours, which might never come again.

Once during the long night when she was sure he'd drifted off, she opened her eyes and found his were open, too, gazing at her with a look Glory could only believe was regret. She wished he would make love to her one last time.

As if reading her thoughts his lips touched her cheek and Glory turned toward him. She touched his cheek and whispered his name. He kissed her then, with all the feelings she had ever believed he'd felt, and Glory thought her heart would break. She kissed him back and clutched his neck and wished the sun would never rise to tear them apart again. She prayed a huge wave would swamp the ship and end her misery.

They made love once more and this time, afterward, they both slept. When Glory woke up, Nicholas was gone.

He didn't return to her cabin that night or the next. Glory didn't see him again until the ship sailed into New York Harbor. Standing on deck beneath a gray sky, she clutched the light pelisse she wore over her borrowed rose silk dress to keep the wind from whipping it away. The stiff skirts swirled around her legs as she stood near the wheel making a sad farewell to her friends.

"Good-bye, Jago."

"You're a fine woman, Miss Glory. I've been proud to know you."

"Thank you, Jago, for all you've done."

"If there's anything you ever need," Josh Pintassle told her, "just let me know."

"Thank you, Joshua." She kissed his cheek. "I'll never forget you."

For a moment she thought he might say more, but he turned and walked away. Her glance followed his retreating figure until she spotted Nicholas standing near the rail. After snapping several orders to the crew, he turned in her direction, and though he didn't see her, her heart did a queer little twist. He noticed her moments later, watched her, but didn't make a move. His eyes swept her as if he wished to memorize each feature.

An ache wrapped itself around her heart, a pain so fierce Glory feared she might faint. She swallowed hard and moved to the opposite rail, clutching the smooth wood for support. Sea gulls screeched and turned overhead, and the South Street docks swarmed with activity. Through her tears, the sounds and sights faded to a merciful blur. She blinked hard, not wanting anyone to see.

Nicholas walked up beside her, but she didn't look at him. She was afraid of what she might see in his face. Would he look at her with derision—or with the love she yearned to glimpse just one last time? Though he stood beside her, she already missed him, as if she'd left him back on the strand.

"I'll have . . . Nathan brought up," he told her, a crisp yet plaintive note in his voice. "You can leave whenever you're ready. Mac will escort you wherever you wish to go."

"I have an aunt here," she said, keeping her voice carefully controlled. "Florence Summerfield Stacey. My father's sister. She lives not far from the Battery. She stared out at the bustling dock. They'd shared so much on the strand, yet each knew so little of the other. On the strand life had seemed so rich and full with just the two of them; there was no need for talk of others to intrude.

He didn't speak for a moment as if choosing just the right words. "I'll be returning to Barbados as soon as our stores are reprovisioned."

"Barbados?" Glory squeezed her eyes closed against the crushing pain. She hoped he wouldn't hear the tremor in her voice. It was all she could do to turn and look up at him, but she couldn't leave without knowing what she would see.

"Yes," he said, staring straight ahead. "I'll be working in the Caribbean for a while. The weather's so much more pleasant." His eyes looked vacant, carefully blank, his mouth a thin, narrow line. There was a sadness around the edges that hadn't been there before.

"I'll see the dress is returned," she said softly.

"Consider it a gift."

"Good-bye, *Captain*," she whispered, for her Nicholas was gone. Then before she could stop herself, she stood on tiptoe to kiss his cheek. In a whirl of stiff rose-colored skirts, she turned and walked to Mac's side. Joshua Pintassle came up the forward ladder with Nathan, who looked none the worse for wear, though he blinked several times in the bright sunlight. Glory rushed into his arms.

"Glory." He hugged her hard.

"Are you all right?" she asked, her voice unsteady.

"I'm fine." He glanced toward the captain, then back to her. "You don't look well. Are you ill?"

"No. I'm just a little tired."

"What about what happened on the strand? Has the captain offered marriage?"

She thought of Nicholas Blackwell's reputation with pistol and cutlass and imagined gentle Nathan dueling for her honor. "Yes," she lied. "I turned him down."

"You did what! Are you sure you want to do that? There's bound to be a scandal."

"I don't care about the scandal."

"Father would have forced you to marry the man."

"I don't want to marry him, Nathan. Surely that's all that matters."

"Your happiness is all that matters, Glory."

"What he did to *you* is reason enough to turn down his suit," she told him.

"A few days in the hold is not much of a price for a man to pay for his freedom." His soft brown eyes looked at her questioningly. "What happened between you two on the strand . . . You realize there might be . . . complications."

Glory felt warm color rush to her cheeks. "What happened on the strand was my fault. I could have said no. As to . . . *complications*, we'll just have to hope their aren't any."

"You're sure you know what you're doing?"

"Nathan, please. Let's just get out of here." Squaring her shoulders, she lifted her skirts and walked toward the gangway where Mac waited patiently, a dejected look on his face. Knowing her own expression must look much the same, she lifted her chin. She wouldn't give Nicholas Blackwell the satisfaction of a backward glance, she told herself as she walked down the gangway to the dock.

Careful to keep her eyes straight ahead, she clung to Mac's arm while they navigated crowded South Street. But when they rounded the corner onto Wall, Glory couldn't resist a last look at the *Black Witch*. Nicholas stood with his booted foot propped against the rail, his hand gripping one of the shrouds. The wind billowed the sleeves of his white linen shirt, and even from a distance she could see the dark thatch of hair on his chest, exposed in the V of the shirt. She knew he was watching and wondered at his thoughts. Why couldn't he love me? Oh, God, how she wished he did.

She knew she should hate him, but all she felt was love. And pain. Terrible, shattering, agonizing pain. Pain like nothing she had ever known. And a sadness even more profound than she'd felt when her father died. How would she survive it? Why would she want to? Feeling as if her knees might not continue to support her, she clutched Mac's arm and let him pull her along the bustling streets.

They passed drays and wheelbarrows, horses and pedestrians. An auctioneer stood amidst barrels and bales and lumber outside the Tontine Coffee House, his rapid-fire speech ringing above the noisy crowd gathered around him. Inside the building, Mac explained, brokers and underwriters negotiated shipping contracts and insured cargo.

Glory had trouble following his conversation, trouble in fact forcing one foot in front of the other. Since they had no trunks, and her aunt's home was only a few blocks away, they had decided to walk, and Glory was grateful for the time to collect her thoughts. Her aunt didn't know she was coming, but she rarely left the city, so she would more than likely be home. They had spent little time together, but Glory had always been fond of her aunt Flo. In some ways she felt closer to her aunt than she ever had to her mother. Maybe it was because they had both loved Julian Summerfield so much.

She had seen her fragile, gray-haired aunt at the funeral, but Glory had been so distraught she'd hardly spoken to her. Aunt Flo seemed to understand. Glory knew she would understand about Nathan, too, and why they'd run away.

They finally reached the stoop of the huge brick mansion, and Nathan rapped the heavy brass knocker against the ornate wooden door. A small, thin-faced, rather stuffy-looking servant opened the door.

"Please tell Mrs. Stacey her niece is here," Glory said, her voice sounding small.

Without so much as a smile, the little man motioned them into the receiving salon. The high-ceilinged room, decorated in the once-popular Federalist style, had wide carved moldings and ornamental doors that led nowhere, but lent balance to the room.

"I'd best be on my way, lass," Mac said. "Will ye be all right?"

Glory appreciated the deep concern in the Scot's eyes. She nodded. "I'll be fine."

"Why is it I dinna believe ye?" He concentrated on the toe of his boot, scuffed and ragged against the gleaming parquet floor. "The lad's behavin' like a fool, lass. It isna like him. I'm sorry things dinna work out."

"Thank you, Mac, for your concern." She kissed his ruddy cheek. The Scot turned and fled before her aunt came into the salon.

"Glory! For heaven's sake, what on earth are you doing in New York?" Florence Stacey's kindly blue eyes, so much like her father's, sparkled with pleasure. "And, Nathan, too!" She hugged them briefly. "Is your mother with you?" She glanced around until Glory's next words stopped her.

"We need your help, Aunt Flo. Nathan's returning to school, but I need a place to stay for a while . . . until I can catch a packet home." She hoped her aunt would let her stay for at least a few weeks. She wasn't ready to return to her life at Summerfield Manor. She needed some time to sort things out. "It's a long story, I'm afraid."

"Well, I've got nothing but time. Jeremy will show you up to your rooms. You can freshen up and then we'll talk. You're both welcome to stay just as long as you like."

Glory hugged her aunt fiercely. It was all she could do to pull away. Fighting a rush of tears, she turned and headed toward the stairs behind the thin-faced little butler.

Florence Stacey watched her go. She almost hadn't recognized the girl in the salon as her niece. The too-short gown, the tired droop to her shoulders, the forlorn expression. Something wasn't right and Florence knew it. She took a long, steadying breath. It wasn't the first time someone in the family had come to her in trouble. She was glad she inspired that kind of trust.

She watched as Glory climbed the stairway, taking each step as if her legs were leaden. She loved that girl like the daughter she never had. Florence Stacey was determined to find out just exactly what was going on.

That night Glory told her aunt about her mother's plans for Nathan, about leaving Charleston on the *Black Spider,* about the terrible storm at sea and how Captain Blackwell had saved her life. She kept her story impersonal, leaving out the part about Nathan's time in the brig and what had happened between her and Nicholas on the strand.

After supper, sensing Florence's need to speak with Glory alone, Nathan pleaded a headache, excused himself, and went upstairs to his room.

"Why don't we go into the parlor?" Florence suggested. "We'll have a nice glass of sherry."

"All right," Glory agreed.

When they were seated on the comfortable Queen Anne sofa, Florence came to the point. "You've told me all that's happened these past few weeks. We'll get you some new clothes to replace the ones you've lost. We'll get Nathan situated in school, and I'll write your mother, try to convince her to see reason. Maybe she'll give Nathan his freedman's papers, as your father would have wanted. In the meantime you can stay with me. I have a feeling you're not ready to go back home yet."

"No, Auntie Flo. I don't think I can face those people yet. So much has happened." She took a long swallow of sherry and glanced away, feeling the warmth of the liquid as it burned a path down her throat, fighting the sting in her eyes.

"Yes, it has. But nothing you've explained so far accounts for the terrible sadness I see. Won't you tell me about it?"

Glory's head came up. Her blue eyes searched her aunt's kindly face. "Is it obvious?"

"Yes, my dear, I'm afraid it is."

Glory took another deep swallow, smoothed the rose skirts of the gown Nicholas had given her, and leaned back against the seat.

"The man who saved my life, Captain Blackwell . . . We were stranded together on an isolated stretch of land for almost three weeks. I came to love him." She ran her finger around the rim of the stemmed crystal glass, for a moment seeing Nicholas as he was on the strand, handsome, smiling, loving. She felt the pull of a smile. "Actually, I think I fell in love with him almost from the first moment I saw him. At my nineteenth birthday ball. He was so arrogant—and dashing. All of the women were in love with him. Except me, of course. I was determined to dislike him. He was a friend of Father's. I think Father hoped I would marry him." She swallowed past the hard lump in her throat. "By the time we left the strand, I wanted that more than anything in the world."

"So why didn't you?" her aunt asked softly, resting a veined hand over Glory's supple one.

"He didn't want me after all. I guess I was just a convenience. Someone to satisfy his passions until he could reach civilization. I don't know. When we were on the strand, our time together seemed like a dream. A perfect fantasy. He cared for me, protected me. I was sure he felt as I did." Glory lifted her face, and tears washed down her cheeks. "He smiled all the time, and he taught me to swim, and he took care of me when I got sick and . . . oh, Auntie Flo, I loved him so much." She couldn't go on for the tight sobs clogging her throat. Slipping her arms around her tiny aunt's neck she cried against the frail woman's shoulder, deep, painful sobs that racked her slender body.

"My poor, dear child." Florence held her, patting her head and encouraging her to let the tears fall. Glory didn't resist. She couldn't have stopped if she'd wanted to. Her aunt rocked her as if she were a small child and let her weep out her sorrow until she had no more tears to cry.

"You can stay here as long as you wish. I always wanted a child, but your uncle Leonard and I were never blessed. You're the closest I've ever come." She stroked her niece's cheek, soothing her, wishing she could take away the pain. "I can't bear the thought of this man hurting you as he has. But you must have seen something good in him, or you would never have loved him. Someday you'll get over him and find someone else to love. Until then, we'll work through this together."

Glory sniffed and looked into her aunt's narrow, aged face. "I don't know if I can get through this at all. I wish I'd died when the ship went down."

"Don't talk like that. Not now, not ever. Do you hear me?"

Glory bit her lip to keep it from trembling. "Yes, Aunt Flo."

"Good. Now dry your tears. It's time you got some sleep."

Glory just nodded and let the older woman lead her up to her room. In the bedchamber, an airy room with a canopy bed and crisp chintz curtains, Florence undressed her, ordered her to drink the glass of warm milk Jeremy brought up, then tucked her into bed. The older woman sat quietly beside her until she finally fell asleep. Dreams of Nicholas kept her tossing and turning. She woke up feeling more exhausted than she had the night before.

The weeks passed in a blur for Glory. Nathan returned to school, and her aunt did all the things she'd promised. Glory had beautiful new clothes and all the love and understanding she could have wanted. Still it wasn't enough. All she thought about was Nicholas. At first she remembered the good things: the way he'd cared for her and protected her, the way he'd made love to her, the way he'd made her feel. She imagined him laughing, sunlight glistening on his curly black hair. Or swimming in the surf, water trickling in rivulets down his wide dark chest, the stiff hairs beckoning her touch. How she missed him.

Oh, Nicholas, she would agonize, how could I have been so wrong? How could I have loved you when you didn't love me? She wondered where he was, wondered what he was doing, remembered with fondness the way he'd stood on the deck, feet apart, shirt billowing as he rode the roll and pitch of the ship.

But the warm memories only made her more miserable, and so little by little she compelled herself to forget them. Purposely she dwelled on the night he had forced himself on her, the terrible things he'd said. She remembered the way he treated her those first few days after the shipwreck. His brooding disposition. His arrogance, his terrible betrayal in the end.

Though she tried to build a new life with her aunt, her heart wasn't in it. Since she had no desire to attend the numerous soirees and balls she would have been invited to, it took her weeks before she realized no invitations had been sent. No one had called at the house after the first few weeks. Not even her aunt Flo's closest friends. But it wasn't until she overheard some of the servants gossiping below the stairs that she realized how firmly she had been cast out.

"They say she's a woman of easy virtue." Glory recognized the scratchy voice of the upstairs maid. "They say she slept right there in his cabin, that she had no shame."

Gripping the banister to steady her suddenly shaky legs, Glory felt her heart wrench.

"They shared a bed on some deserted island," another voice said. "Gussy Simpson told me all about it."

"They've got a name for her, they have." Glory bit her lip. " 'The captain's tart.' That's what folks call her."

"It doesn't matter *what* they call her," Jeremy Wiggins defended. "Miss Summerfield's a fine young lady. She treats us with kindness and respect. It's that sea captain's fault. The man's nothing but a scoundrel and a rogue. It's obvious he took advantage of her innocence. I hope someday he gets what he deserves."

Stomach in knots, her knees trembling so hard she feared they wouldn't support her, Glory sank down on the stairs.

"You're right, Jeremy," Flora Whitman, the house-keeper chimed in. "The bloody bastard ought to be horse-whipped."

Oh, God, how could this be happening? How could Nicholas have done this to her? He must have known what would happen. Either he did it on purpose or he just didn't care.

She blinked hard, fighting back tears. The loyalty of her aunt's staff touched her. She felt a surge of affection for Jeremy Wiggins—and the first real stirring of hatred for Nicholas Blackwell.

"How long have you known what people are saying?" she asked her aunt one night after supper. "That's the reason you never go out, isn't it? It's because of me."

"It isn't as bad as all that. They're all a bunch of puffed-up snobs anyway. They made me choose between them and you, and I chose you. That's all there is to it. If my niece isn't good enough for them, then neither am I."

Glory sank down on the plush velvet sofa. "How did they find out?"

Florence sat next to her. "I'm not sure. The shipwreck was written up in all the papers. Some journalist interviewed several surviving crew members. They gave him the details. It didn't take much deduction to discover you'd been alone with the captain for almost three weeks. The man has one sordid reputation, I can certainly tell you that."

This time Glory felt closer to anger than to tears. "Nicholas Blackwell is a rake and a rogue. I was a fool to think he cared for me. I know that now. Unfortunately it's too late."

"To make matters worse," her aunt added, "people have found out that Nathan is your half brother. Apparently you introduced him that way to someone on the street."

"Mrs. Wentworth, the day after Nathan and I arrived. I was just so tired of lying. I'm proud of him. I won't lie about him again."

Florence patted her hand. "The gossip will die down," she said. "It always does. The Summerfield name is not to be taken lightly. By the time you go home, it'll all be forgotten."

"I'm afraid it isn't going to be that easy."

"Oh? Why not?"

When Glory didn't answer, Florence sucked in a breath. "Oh, my God. You don't mean you're . . ."

"I'm with child, Auntie Flo."

Less than a month later they were on their way to Boston. Glory was just beginning to thicken in the waist. At first she'd felt as if Nicholas had played one final lewd joke on her. But as the weeks crept by and the child began to move, her resentment toward the baby faded away. The child was hers, too. He or she was just an innocent victim of the destructive game Nicholas had played. The only person she hated was Nicholas. The man who had destroyed her life.

Florence owned a brownstone in Boston. Her late husband, Leonard, had inherited it from his German parents. He'd loved the old mansion so much that even after he died Florence hadn't had the heart to sell it. Now she was thankful she hadn't.

"We'll change your name. Say you're a young widow. That your husband was killed in a hunting accident. Since you've got a little of that soft southern accent, we'll say you're my niece from Savannah—that's close enough to the truth. You can be Mrs.—"

"Hatteras," Glory put in with a perverse sense of drama. "That seems more than appropriate, since the strand was the start of all my troubles."

"Mrs. Gloria Hatteras it is." Aunt Flo flashed a tiny supportive smile.

Glory found she liked Boston, even with its cold weather. The days were crisp and clear and the fall air exhilarating. As the weeks passed, the weather grew colder, but Glory found her mood improving each day. She had the baby to look forward to now.

She only worried a little at the doctor's warning: "The baby seems situated a bit oddly," he told her. "It may only have a tenuous hold. You must rest and take extra care. And your health could be better. From now on you are to eat three meals a day and get plenty of sleep."

She did exactly as he directed, and Aunt Flo doted on her endlessly.

The first few weeks had been the worst. She'd been sick every morning, looked wan and pale, and lost too much weight. Though she no longer fought the morning sickness, she still didn't look as strong as she would have liked.

Wearing a comfortable black crepe mourning dress, she sat in the downstairs drawing room while she practiced her crocheting, a skill she'd learned just before leaving the manor. Outside the window, she could see children playing ball on the street. A warm fire crackled on the marble hearth.

"Hello, dear." Her aunt entered the room on the arm of a tall brown-haired man, elegantly dressed in dark gray frock coat over a burgundy waistcoat and navy blue breeches.

"Glory, dear, this is George McMillan. He's an old friend of your uncle Leonard's."

George McMillan looked to be in his mid-thirties. A few gray hairs, which made him look more distinguished than old, betrayed his age, nothing more. He was lean and fit and exceedingly handsome. His smile was warm and inviting, and for the first time in weeks, Glory felt her interest stir.

"How do you do, Mr. McMillan?"

He brushed her fingers against his lips in a show of gallantry, and Glory felt the pull of a smile. How long it had been since someone had treated her like a woman. No. Like a lady. She realized she had missed it.

"Please," he said, his voice rich and warm. "I'd be honored if you'd call me George."

They sat in the drawing room for hours, discussing everything from the weather to the politics of the day. With so much time on her hands, Glory had become a devoted reader of the *Boston Transcript* as well as the *Liberator*, a fiery abolitionist publication. When she'd lived at Summerfield Manor, her most important concern had been which gown she would wear to the next ball. After what she'd been through, all that seemed superficial.

She found her interest sparked by concern for the Negro and was particularly interested in a group headed by William Lloyd Garrison and Frederick Douglass who called themselves the Underground Railroad. They helped runaway slaves along the route to the North, or assisted them in making a new start once they'd reached freedom.

As it turned out, George McMillan had strong antislavery feelings of his own.

"I'd be pleased, Mrs. Hatteras, if you'd accompany me to the next meeting. They're held at the Park Street Church. Helping runaway slaves is not a popular sentiment these days, but if you've the courage, the cause needs people like you. Especially Southerns. It's comforting to know they're not all chained to the same obsolete mentality."

George came often after that, and they did attend a few meetings, until her body became cumbersome and she no longer looked just a little overweight. Pregnant women were not encouraged to be seen in public, and Glory certainly didn't need to offend the people of Boston as she had those of New York.

Though she rested excessively, she often took carriage rides through the streets of Boston. The brownstone stood on Beacon Street, not far from the Common. She'd have the driver head down Tremont, past King's Chapel, and turn west toward the Charles River. She had visited the harbor only once. The tall masts of the schooners and packets wagging in the gentle breeze dredged up painful recollections of Nicholas, memories she thought she'd successfully buried. She could almost see him pacing the deck or standing at the helm, his gray eyes searching the clouds for storm, his broad shoulders squared against the roll and pitch of the ship.

She wondered where he was and what he was doing, wondered if he ever thought of her, wondered if he missed her as she missed him. Just that one time did she allow herself to admit the depth of her feelings, though in truth she missed Nicholas Blackwell every single minute of the day. Her heart ached for him. Her body yearned for his touch.

But she hated him, too. More every day. Mostly she just felt numb. And bitter. With an emptiness that could never be filled. She prayed that when the baby came things would be different.

Chapter Fifteen

"Master Brad! Ain't you a sight for these old eyes! Come in, come in." The wizened old black servant motioned Bradford St. John into the foyer of the elegantly furnished town house near Broadway.

"Hello, Isaac."

"The captain's surely gonna be glad to see you." The old man looked down, his bristly white hair unmoving as he shook his head. "He ain't been hisself lately." The worried expression lining his already puckered face told Brad all he needed to know.

"So I've heard." Brad had been worried about his stepbrother. Nicholas had only been back in New York a few weeks, but had uncharacteristically locked himself away. The few friends he'd allowed in the house told stories of his stormy temper, black moods, and bouts of despair. "Where is he?"

"He's in his study. I'll tell him you're here." The old man teetered a few steps down the hall.

Bradford caught the butler's thin arm. "I know the way. Thank you, Isaac." Isaac was a free man of color. He'd been with Nicholas for as long as Brad could remember. The old man knew Nicholas Blackwell's temperament as well as any man alive. If Isaac was worried, things were even worse than Brad had heard.

As he negotiated the dimly lit corridor, which was usually bright and cheerful, Brad wondered if the dark hall mirrored its master's bitter mood. After knocking quietly on the heavy wooden door, Brad lifted the latch and the door swung wide. Embroiled in his thoughts, Nicholas appeared not to have heard the knock. He sat before the hearth, staring into the flames of the fire, his too-thin hand wrapped around a half-full snifter of brandy.

"Hello, Nicholas," Brad said softly.

When he turned, his brother's eyes brightened, his angular features softened for a moment. Then he was on his feet, his long strides carrying him to the door. He extended his hand and Brad shook it, but wasn't satisfied till he'd enveloped his stepbrother in a warm hug.

"You look even worse than I'd heard," Brad teased, more than half serious.

Nicholas almost smiled. "What are you doing in the city?"

"I was in Tarrytown visiting Mother for the Christmas holidays. The city's not that far away, and I've missed you these past few months."

"And I you," Nicholas agreed. "Sit down. I'll pour you a brandy."

Brad took a seat on the tufted leather sofa. Nicholas handed him a crystal snifter, then returned to his overstuffed chair by the fire.

"You're looking fit," Nicholas said, and Brad smiled, knowing he could never look as fit as his stepbrother. Even now, a bit too thin, his face gaunt and a just little haggard, Nicholas Blackwell emanated power and presence. Being eight years younger, Brad had always looked up to Nicholas. It was Nicholas who was paying for his schooling at Harvard, Nicholas who owned the estate in Tarrytown on which he and his mother lived. He'd been more like a father to Brad than an older brother.

"How are you doing in school?" Nicholas asked. "Excelling as usual, I'm sure. You know how proud I am of you, Brad."

"I'm doing just fine. Mother's fine—if you're interested. It's you I'm worried about."

"Me! Why would you be worried about me?"

"You're right, of course," Brad said, not meaning a word of it. "You're much too much of a cad to worry about." He forced a tight smile he didn't feel. "I hear you've been whoring over half the Caribbean."

Nicholas laughed bitterly, a harsh, grating sound like nothing Brad had heard. "For a while," Nicholas said. "Not lately. I'm afraid my interest in the fairer sex has waned."

Brad took a sip of his brandy, seeking the relaxing warmth, and a bit of courage. He noticed his brother stared back into the flames. "I read about the shipwreck," Brad said, easing into the subject he'd come to discuss.

Nicholas turned toward him. "As you can see, I survived."

"Yes." Brad tapped his forefinger against his glass. "That young woman you were stranded with—Gloria Summerfield, wasn't it? She certainly set the tongues to wagging. She must have been some piece of work for you to treat her as you did." He chuckled softly, hoping to spark some emotion from the man in front of the fire. "I felt sure, her being Julian's daughter and all, you'd have married her."

Nicholas's features grew taut, the fire casting shadows into the hollows of his cheeks, making them look almost sinister.

"But then, of course, you've never made any secret of the way you feel about marriage."

Nicholas didn't answer, just stared into the flames.

"The girl was shunned from polite society here in New York, you know. They called her 'the captain's tart.' *Tart.* Such a cruel word to use on a young girl."

Nicholas tensed. Brad noticed the rapid pulse beating at the base of his brother's throat.

"She finally moved to Boston," Brad pressed. "Probably to protect the child."

Nicholas's head snapped up. "What child?"

"Most people don't know about that. Going to Harvard,

I got wind of it and made a point to find out, since the child is yours.''

"Mine! Don't be absurd."

"Ah. Then she *is* a tart, as they say."

Nicholas stiffened, anger boiling to the surface. "Stay out of this, Brad. This is none of your concern."

"It's probably just as well you didn't marry her. After the way she came right out and claimed that Negro half brother of hers. Nathan, was it? Seems there was some trouble on the plantation. Something about returning him to the fields, so she spirited him away. She's got courage, I'll say that for her. The brother goes to school here in the city. Studying to be a botanist, of all things."

The glass in Nicholas's hand shattered into a thousand glistening shards, the amber liquid pooling on the carpet at his feet. He didn't know he was bleeding until Brad leaped from the sofa and gripped his hand.

"My God, man!" Brad pulled his kerchief from his waistcoat pocket and wrapped it around his brother's fingers. "What did you think?"

Nicholas stared at him, speechless. His face looked pale, and his mind seemed far away. He glanced at Brad, saw his concern, read the question on his face that still hung in the air. When he finally spoke, his tone sounded flat, lifeless, dead.

"I thought Nathan was her lover. That she loved him and not me. That she'd tricked me and deceived me. That she was just like all the other women I'd known."

"But she wasn't."

"No."

"You've made a mistake," Brad said. "Sooner or later it happens to us all."

Nicholas shook his head, his face more ashen than before. "It was more than just a mistake. Glory was the best thing that ever happened to me, and I destroyed her."

Brad laid a gentle hand on his shoulder. "There's still time, Nicholas."

Nicholas didn't look up. A fine sheen of perspiration

dotted his forehead, and his hand shook where he braced
it against his knee. "She'll never forgive me, Brad."

"You can't be sure of that. Besides, there's the child to
think of. The child is yours, too."

"I don't know, Brad. I've made such a mess of things."
Nicholas stood up, the bloody kerchief falling to the Tartan carpet. He didn't bother to pick it up.

"The girl needs you, Nicholas," Brad said softly.

Nicholas turned to face him, his mouth hard, as if the
decision he was about to make would change the course
of his life.

"Not half as much as I need her," he finally said. Then
he smiled, that one small gesture making him look vulnerable, as Brad had never seen him before. Nicholas laid
a hand on Brad's shoulder, and the two men walked to the
door.

"Thank you, Brad. For everything. You're the best
friend a man could have." He hugged his stepbrother
briefly. "Now, if you'll excuse me, I've got some packing
to do." He flashed a second wide smile, this one determined, like the Nicholas that Brad had always known. "I'll
be leaving on the morrow. It seems I have some unfinished
business in Boston."

As Christmas approached, Glory felt some of her old
spirit returning. George McMillan was a constant fixture
around the brownstone. Glory found she enjoyed his easy
charm and intelligence. He challenged her in a way no
man ever had. He cared about her opinions, considered
her his equal. More and more he had involved her in the
workings of the Underground Railroad until, inevitably,
he had shown up the week before Christmas with a young
black couple in tow.

"Do you think your aunt would let them stay in the
basement for a few days? There are jobs waiting for them
in Canada, but they need a few days' rest."

"Bring them into the salon, George. I'll speak to Aunt
Flo." Actually, she already had. Her aunt had agreed to
assist in any way she could. Glory suspected the old

woman hoped that by helping others, Glory would be able to forget her own dismal circumstances.

Returning moments later, Glory introduced herself, and the young black couple did the same. Their names were Jackson and Belin.

"Short for Belinda," the pretty dark-skinned woman said. She clutched her brawny husband's arm and looked up at him, the love in her eyes intensified by a smile of trust and admiration. The warm look he gave her in return, mixed with a hint of desire, stirred such poignant memories Glory had to turn away.

"We's mighty grateful, missus," the big Negro said. "My wife and me, we done had a terrible time gettin' this far. But ever' hard day was worth it. Even the air in the North smells free."

Glory smiled and patted his arm. "Come on. You'll be sleeping in the basement. We've been expecting someone to come along sooner or later." They made their way down the narrow passage to the room below. "I'll be back in a while with your supper. There's a nice big bed and plenty of blankets." She smiled knowingly at the young people, so much in love. "I think you'll find it cozy."

Belin gripped Glory's hand and brought it to her generous lips. "Thank you, missus. Me an' Jackson ain't never gonna forget you and the others."

"We're happy to help. Now get some rest. I'll see you in the morning." When she reached the top of the stairs, George stood waiting, a look of quiet admiration on his face.

"You know the danger you're getting into," he warned for the tenth time. Though northern sentiment ran toward the abolition of slavery, the New England Anti-Slavery Society had been attacked on numerous occasions. Their members had been beaten, their newspaper burned, and several meetings broken up.

"I can't stay neutral any longer. My brother is part Negro. How can I believe in an institution that would enslave a man like him?"

"You're an incredible woman, Glory."

She laid a slender hand against his cheek. "And you're a good man, George."

The young black couple left two days before Christmas. No longer fearful of discovery, Glory finally allowed herself to relax and enjoy the holidays. She was over six months along in her pregnancy, her belly round and protruding, though she carried little extra weight anywhere else. The baby moved often, and Glory already loved her precious little burden. Secretly she hoped it would be a boy, a son as handsome as his father.

Again she reminded herself she no longer cared for Nicholas Blackwell. It was impossible to love someone who had treated her so cruelly. The man she loved had merely been an illusion. The man who had left her a ruined woman was the real Nicholas Blackwell, a hard, conscienceless man who used women for his pleasure, then tossed them away as if they were nothing more than the merest of trinkets. The knowledge gave her little comfort on the lonely winter nights.

Determined not to burden Aunt Flo with her troubles any more than she already had, Glory helped her aunt decorate the house. There was holly and mistletoe to gather, strings of cranberries and popcorn to sew, and a wreath to make for the door. George brought over a huge pine tree and they decorated it on Christmas Eve.

In concession to the holidays, she chose a dark gray velvet gown with a high waistline to accommodate her roundness and sleeves that were full above the elbow, then fitted below. She wore the dark clothes not only in honor of her father, but now for her imaginary husband as well. With Nicholas gone from her life, she felt almost as if it were true.

After a supper of roast duckling stuffed with cornbread and pecan dressing, Glory, George, and Aunt Flo returned to the salon. Glory sat in a delicately carved mahogany chair, sipping from a mug of hot cocoa while George hung the last few paper ornaments on the tree. Snowflakes, the first fall of the season, layered the sill outside the window, and carolers strolled the cobblestone streets, their voices ringing with Christmas cheer. George looked handsome in his velvet-collared burgundy tailcoat. The few strands of silver that streaked his light brown hair glistened in the flickering firelight. The room smelled of cinnamon and fruitcake. After hanging the last of the paper ornaments they'd made, George moved to Glory's side, but spoke to Flo.

He seemed nervous and more than a little distracted, and Glory wondered why.

"Florence, I've been trying to find a way to say this all evening. Since you're Gloria's closest living relative, I suppose I should ask your permission first. But I'd rather just give Glory this." He reached into the pocket of his waistcoat and pulled out a small velvet box.

Looking up at him, Glory accepted the box with a trembling hand. When she opened the lid, a delicate diamond and sapphire ring glistened against its bed of muted white satin.

"I know it's too soon after your husband's death to propose marriage," he said, sounding more than a little uneasy. "Until the time is right, I ask that you accept this ring as a token of our friendship—and a promise to at least consider my offer when it comes."

Glory's eyes welled with tears. She looked up at him, her vision blurred, but only moved her head from side to side. She handed back the box. "There's so much you don't know."

"It doesn't matter," he said vehemently. "I love you. If Florence thinks I'm suitable, I want you for my wife."

"I'm afraid that's quite impossible," said a deep male voice from the doorway. Jeremy stood in front of the man, chest high, trying to block his entrance to the room.

"Nicholas!" Glory gasped, but the word came out in a breathless whisper.

"I told him he couldn't come in," Jeremy said. "I tried to make him wait."

"It's all right, Jeremy," Florence soothed from her place on the tapestry sofa. "I've been expecting Captain Blackwell."

"Who is this man, Glory?" George stood in front of her, demanding an explanation.

Glory couldn't speak. Her eyes were locked on the tall dark figure in the doorway. He was dressed elegantly in a black frock coat, pleated white shirt, and snowy white stock that made his tanned skin look even darker. He stood rigid, imposing, just the way she remembered him. Only his face had changed. Tiny lines creased his brow, and his mouth seemed softer, almost vulnerable somehow. His eyes rested on her face as if she were the only person in the room.

"Glory?" George McMillan gripped her icy hands. "Are you all right? Is this man a friend of yours?"

Glory licked her lips, suddenly dry. It was all she could do to concentrate on George's words. Then in her womb, the baby kicked, a reminder of all that Nicholas had done, and Glory's amazement settled to a cold dark rage.

"Captain Blackwell . . . I believe that's how I'm to address you, isn't it?" She held herself erect, her chin defiant. "Captain Blackwell is an acquaintance, nothing more."

"Why don't you come in, Captain?" Florence said. "I'm Gloria's aunt Florence. This is George McMillan." Neither man extended his hand. The air crackled with tension.

"Now that you've so rudely intruded, Captain Blackwell," George said, "would you mind telling me why Mrs. Hatteras and I should not marry?"

"George, please," Glory pleaded. "I'll explain everything later."

"I'll be happy to explain everything now," Nicholas said in his most arrogant tone. "Mrs. *Hatteras* can't marry you because she's going to marry me."

"What?" Glory leaped to her feet. "Have you lost your mind? You don't even like me. Why on earth would you wan't to marry me?"

"Glory dear," her aunt interceded. "Please don't upset yourself. Think of the child."

Florence turned to George, who hovered over Glory

protectively. ''George, I think it would be best if you left us alone. There are some things we need to discuss.''

George turned to Glory. ''Is that what you want?''

She wanted to say no, that she needed him beside her. That being in the same room with Nicholas Blackwell was more than she could bear. She'd already decided to tell George the truth about the child she carried, but she wanted to tell him when the time was right. She certainly didn't want to embarrass him in front of Nicholas.

''It would probably be best if you went home,'' she said instead. ''We'll talk tomorrow.''

He pulled her to her feet, holding each of her cold hands in one of his own. ''Whatever you have to tell me isn't important,'' he said softly. ''I love you. I want to make a home for you and the child.''

Glory squeezed his hands. ''This is all happening so fast. Give me some time, George.''

He nodded and kissed her cheek, then stiffly left the house, stopping only long enough to give Nicholas a warning glance on his way out.

Nicholas watched him go. He hadn't meant for any of this to happen. He'd planned to be gentle, explain what had happened, beg Glory's forgiveness, then offer marriage. He sighed to himself. When it came to Gloria Summerfield his jealousy had always been his undoing. Until he met her, he hadn't believed himself capable of the emotion.

''Won't you sit down, Captain?'' Aunt Flo invited, forever gracious.

''Nicholas,'' he corrected. He moved to the chair next to Glory. ''I know it's Christmas Eve,'' he said, his voice softer now. ''I got here as soon as I could.''

Glory laughed bitterly. ''Where were you? Iceland? . . . Why have you come here, Nicholas?''

How could he tell her? What could he say? How would he ever make her understand? Though he'd prepared for this moment ever since he left New York, no words would come. He felt so damned ashamed he wanted to walk from the room and never look back.

But Nicholas was not a coward. "I came to apologize for what I've done to you. There's no point in pleading with you to forgive me. Either you will or you won't, so I'll say it only once. I was a fool. I believed the worst of you and never even let you explain. Now I know the truth. The baby you carry is mine. I want you to marry me, Glory. I want our child to have its rightful name."

Glory just stared at him. "What makes you think it's yours?" she asked defiantly, and noticed he didn't even blink.

"Because you were a virgin. Because everything I believed about you in the beginning was true."

"I *was* a virgin, Nicholas. How do you know there haven't been others since? How can you be sure the child is yours?"

He wanted to touch her. To pull her into his arms. "Is the baby you're carrying mine?" he asked instead, this time knowing beyond doubt she wouldn't lie.

"Damn you! Damn you!"

"The child is mine, isn't it?"

"Yes."

Nicholas felt a surge of joy like nothing he'd ever known. "We'll be married tomorrow. We'll move to my estate in Tarrytown. My stepmother lives there now, but we'll move her into the town house. She prefers the city anyway."

"How dare you!" Glory fumed. "How dare you come into my home on Christmas Eve and act as if you belong here? Get out of this house, Nicholas. Get out of here and never come back. There was a time when I would have given everything I hold dear in this world to hear those words. But that time is past. I don't love you anymore. There is nothing you can ever say or do to make me marry you."

His mouth thinned, but his eyes looked sad, not hard. "Then you'll marry this man, McMillan?"

She hesitated only a moment. "Yes. He doesn't care who the baby's father is. He still wants me."

"That's easy to understand," he said softly. He rose from the chair, his expression carefully controlled. Glory fought a sudden urge to follow him as he moved toward the door.

At the last instant he turned and looked back at her. "Do you love him?"

Her hand clutched her throat. "What?" she whispered.

"I said, do you love him?"

She swallowed hard. "George McMillan is the kindest, most gentle man I've ever met. He treats me like a lady. He respects my opinion. He's good and he's fair and—"

"Do you love him?"

"I'm going to marry him."

For a moment he stood stock still. Then he smiled, his face lighting up the way it had on the strand. For an instant he looked almost boyish, and Glory felt a tiny chip of ice melt from around her heart.

"You're going to marry *me*," he said. Then he turned and swept from the room.

The clock ticked loudly. Glory didn't move or say a word.

"Are you all right, my dear?" her aunt asked. Silk skirts rustled as she moved to her niece's side.

"Yes, Auntie Flo." It was all she could do to tear her gaze from the doorway. Her voice sounded weak and uneven. "I'm just tired, that's all. So very tired."

"We'll talk about this tomorrow. When you've rested. You'll feel better after you've had some sleep."

Glory nodded. She let her fragile aunt pull her along, guide her upstairs, and coax her into bed.

"Aunt Flo?"

"Yes, dear?"

"Why did you tell Jeremy you'd been expecting Captain Blackwell?"

"Because I had. I knew both you and your father couldn't be that wrong about the same man."

Chapter Sixteen

"Did ye see her, lad?" Mac stepped up beside him. Nicholas stood at the rail of the *Black Witch*, still dressed in his black frock coat, staring out at the smooth surface of the water.

"I saw her." They were moored in Boston Harbor, just across from the navy shipyard at Charlestown. Several ships sat in dry dock, though they were eerily empty, the workers having gone home for Christmas Eve.

"Well, how did she look?" Mac could barely contain his excitement. Nicholas turned toward him, and Mac noticed the pallor that had haunted his friend these past few months had fled.

"She looked beautiful," Nicholas told him. "A little too pale, perhaps, but beautiful just the same."

When he didn't add anything more, Mac prodded, "Go on lad, what did she say?"

Nicholas bristled a little, but his gray eyes were light. "She says she's going to marry George McMillan."

"Who is George McMillan? And how in the devil can ye stand there lookin' so calm about it?" Mac practically jumped up and down upon the deck.

Nicholas smiled, then thought how often he'd been doing that lately. It felt good to be able to smile again. "Because I told her she's going to marry me, and that's exactly what she's going to do." His eyes flashed the determined look that had changed him from the frightened little boy who had run away to sea to the master of a huge shipping empire.

Mac clapped him on the back. "That's my boy! She loves ye, lad. She'll forgive ye sooner or later."

Nicholas's smile faded. "I'm not so sure about that, Mac. But she doesn't love McMillan, so she may as well marry me. She'll have everything she's ever wanted. Besides, the child she carries is mine. I intend to see he's properly raised."

"You're sure it'll be a son?"

"I'd like a boy, of course, but a little girl like Glory . . . how could that disappoint me?"

"You're a good lad, Nicky. I always knew it. It was ye who forgot for a while."

Nicholas nodded. "I think I'll get some sleep. If I'm to face that feisty blonde tomorrow, I'll need all the strength I can muster."

Mac just chuckled. Nicholas took a deep breath, filling his lungs with the salty sea air. Bright stars twinkled above him; the snow had stopped, and the air was so crisp and clear he could almost touch the silver sliver of moon. He felt young and hopeful, happy just to be alive.

"I've spoken with the Reverend Mr. Markham down at King's Chapel. He'll marry us right after the Christmas service." George McMillan gripped her hands, suddenly icy though the salon was warm.

"But I'm still in mourning."

"I'm sure your father would understand. There's the baby to think of. Besides, once you're my wife, no one will be able to come between us."

"I suppose you're right, George. It's just that it's all so . . . so sudden." Glory glanced at her aunt, who sat on the sofa looking worried. "Aunt Flo?"

"Only you can decide what's best for you and the child." She looked at George, her kindly blue eyes resting on his soft brown ones. "You're one of the best men I've ever known, George McMillan. You'd make my niece a

fine husband, and I'd be proud to have you in the family.
But Glory must think of what's best for her, what's best
for the baby. Captain Blackwell is the child's father. He
has asked her to marry him. She must consider carefully.''

''As usual, Captain Blackwell didn't ask,'' Glory countered, ''he commanded. There's quite a difference.''

''You're a headstrong young woman, Glory. Don't let
your anger at what is past decide your future.''

''I can't marry him, Aunt Flo. I could never trust him.
I'd always remember his cruelty and wonder when he might
unleash it again.''

''And George?'' she pressed.

''George is my friend and companion.'' She spoke as
if he weren't in the room. ''He respects me and I respect
him. I'll make him a good wife.''

Florence sighed. ''Then you must do as George asks.''

Glory turned to look at the man with the handsome face
and warm brown eyes. ''Give me a few minutes to change.
A woman has just one wedding day.''

George walked her to the foot of the stairs. ''You're
making me the happiest man in the world.''

Glory only nodded. A hard lump closed her throat, and
tears stung her eyes. She should be smiling, not crying,
she thought, feel happy, not sad. It was all happening so
fast, she tried to convince herself for the hundredth time.
She hurried up the stairs, more conscious of the child she
carried than she'd ever been before. Was she doing the
right thing? The child was as much Nicholas's as it was
hers. Then her mind flashed on the hard sea captain who
had used her and deserted her. A man who could be brutal
beyond anything she'd known. George McMillan would
raise her child, not a man like Nicholas Blackwell. She
squared her shoulders and hurried on up to her room.

''I'm here to see Mrs. Hatteras,'' Nicholas told the tiny
little butler who single-handedly barred the door.

''Mrs. Hatteras is not at home.'' He tried to close the
door, but Nicholas wedged his boot inside the jamb.

''Where is she?''

The little man didn't answer.

Nicholas shoved the door open, nearly knocking the butler off his feet. He strode through the house until he was satisfied the man was telling the truth, then returned to the foyer where Jeremy still stood, ramrod straight.

"I asked you once before. This is the last time I'm going to ask nicely. *Where is Glory?*"

Jeremy glanced at the clock. It chimed the half-hour just as he looked away. "She's gone to church."

"Which church? And you'd better be telling the truth."

"King's Chapel. But you're already too late. She's married to Mr. McMillan by now."

With a curse so low it sounded like a hiss, Nicholas set his jaw and hit the door at a run. King's Chapel was only a few blocks away. He raced down Beacon Street and turned onto School. The old church stood on the corner of Tremont, just two blocks in the distance. Footsteps ringing on the cobblestones, Nicholas rushed down the street, up the stairs, and into the empty foyer. From the back of the church he saw Glory standing beside McMillan at the altar. He could hear the preacher's words—the ceremony had only just begun.

Nicholas gripped the end of a walnut pew to steady himself and slow his pounding heart. Glory clutched George McMillan's arm, her face waxen, her smile fixed in place as if she feared it might disappear. Her plum velvet gown, rich and elegant, only made her seem more frail. McMillan, dressed handsomely in a black split-tail coat and ruffle-fronted shirt, smiled down at her, and Nicholas felt his jealousy flare. He took a deep breath and brought himself under control. Then he walked down the aisle and up to the altar.

"I'm sorry, sir, there's been a mistake," he told the minister calmly. "You're performing the ceremony with the wrong bridegroom."

"Who are you?" the preacher asked, gaping up at Nicholas.

"How did you find out we were here?" George demanded.

All Glory could see was Nicholas Blackwell standing tall and imposing, with light gray eyes and a smile meant only for her. She knew a moment of joy so poignant she felt ashamed. And furious he could still affect her so.

"Mr. Markham," she said, feigning a calmness she didn't feel, "would you please finish the ceremony?"

"Not until we've talked." Nicholas grabbed her arm and tugged her gently toward the nearest pew, just out of earshot from the others.

"Take your hands off her," George McMillan demanded, catching up with them, and Glory wanted to scream. First no one wanted her; now two men fought for her like dogs over a bone. Aunt Flo sat on the opposite side of the aisle and Glory felt certain she caught the hint of a smile on the old woman's lips.

"Let me talk to him, George," she soothed. "It will only take a minute."

George let go of her arm, and Nicholas guided her into the pew.

"I want you to marry me," Nicholas said.

"No."

"The child you carry is mine, Glory. If for no other reason than that, you've got to marry me."

"George will make a good father. He has plenty of money; so do I, for that matter. We'll take excellent care of the baby."

Nicholas felt a flash of anger. "That's not the point, now, is it? I want that child, and even if you don't believe it, I want you. You're going to marry me, and that's all there is to it."

"And just how do you intend to make me?"

Nicholas looked at her hard. He had hoped she'd see reason, and in time he felt sure she would have. But he hadn't counted on McMillan. Time was running out. "If you don't marry me now, this minute, I'll bury you in scandal, just as I did before. I'll tell all of Boston the child's my bastard. I'll ruin any chance of happiness for all of you."

Her look of despair, of utter betrayal, tore at his heart.

"You would do that to your own child?"

"What do you think?" he asked. Then inwardly winced when she replied.

"Of course you would. You'd do anything to get what you wanted. You always have."

He ached to tell her she was wrong. That he would never do another thing to hurt her or their child. That if she had truly loved George McMillan he would have let her go. That once they were married, he would spend the rest of his life making amends for the pain he'd caused her. But the words wouldn't come—there was just too much at stake. His love for her. The love he hoped to rekindle. The child she carried in her womb.

"Then let's get on with the ceremony," was all he said.

Unwilling to face George McMillan, Glory moved woodenly toward the altar. "The captain is right, Mr. Markham. I was marrying the wrong man. Please begin again. This is Nicholas Blackwell—my bridegroom."

George rushed to her side. "Glory, what are you saying? Has this madman threatened you?"

"It's his child, George. There's nothing else I can do."

"Glory, please, there must be some other way."

"No, George. I didn't mean to hurt you. I'm sorry for everything that's happened. I hope you won't think too badly of me."

"I love you, Glory. How could I possibly think badly of you?"

"I think it's best if you leave us now. In time you'll find someone else to love."

George McMillan bristled. He rose to his full height and turned his attention to Nicholas. "Captain Blackwell, I demand satisfaction."

"Oh, Lord, no," Glory whispered. Not this, too! "Please, George," she pleaded, "don't do this. He'll kill you. Don't fight him, I beg you."

"Listen to the lady, George," Nicholas said without a trace of arrogance. "You seem to be a good man. There's no need for you to die."

"I'm asking for satisfaction. Are you a coward as well as a cur?"

Nicholas fought a surge of temper. A month ago he wouldn't have wavered. Now he looked at Glory, who was perched on the edge of hysteria, then at George McMillan, and wished there was some way to spare the lady more grief. McMillan stood erect, waiting for an answer. It was obvious the man would not back down. "Will tomorrow be soon enough?" he said with a casualness he didn't feel. "After all, today's my wedding day."

McMillan's handsome face flushed an angry beet red. "Tomorrow morning at dawn. There's a small grove of trees just below Breed's Hill. Be there."

"As you wish."

George turned and stormed down the aisle, hitting the double doors so hard Glory feared they might splinter.

"Please, Nicholas," she said, her tone pleading, "don't do this."

"Right now the only thing I want to do is marry you." He looped her cold hand over his, then nestled it securely in the crook of his arm. Glory felt the smooth fabric of his black serge tailcoat beneath her cold fingers. She was angry and more than a little afraid. It was all she could do not to turn and bolt for the door.

"Shall we get on with it?" Nicholas said to the minister before she had the chance. His eyes held a gentleness she'd seen only a few other times, and the look, and the strength of his hand, helped to calm her raging fears.

"Trust me, love. Everything's going to be all right."

"I trusted you before," she said and was sure she saw him flinch.

The ceremony went smoothly, what little Glory remembered. Nicholas laced her stiff fingers through his warm ones, and she felt his strength and power. Some of it seemed to flow into her, giving her the courage she needed. Aunt Flo sat quietly dabbing at the tears in her eyes.

When the minister asked for the ring, Nicholas surprised her by pulling a tiny velvet box from his pocket.

"I wanted to propose last night, but . . . I hope you like it."

He slipped the emerald-cut diamond solitaire onto her finger, the fiery lights throwing a rainbow of color against her skin. Glory didn't tell him how lovely the ring was, so simple, so exquisite. It only made her more angry that he had chosen exactly what she would have.

When the ceremony ended, they returned to the brownstone, where a Christmas dinner of roast goose with oyster dressing, fresh steamed vegetables, homemade cranberry sauce, and mincemeat pie waited in celebration of the newlyweds. No one mentioned Glory's substitute groom.

Glory didn't speak to Nicholas at all. She felt angry and resentful. He'd thrust himself into her life, just as he had before. All she had worked for—her independence, the life she'd been building in Boston, her convictions—seemed threatened by Nicholas's intrusion.

She didn't love him anymore, of that she was certain. She'd lost whatever she felt for him a long, long time ago. That he still stirred her blood, she grudgingly admitted. But that was lust, not love. She had already come to grips with her passionate nature. Her father had been a passionate man; she'd inherited the trait from him. She refused to acknowledge the fact that George McMillan never once stirred a passionate chord.

Wherever she went, Nicholas watched her, never standing more than a few feet away, his eyes warm and light. He and Aunt Flo jousted back and forth, and though her aunt had tried and failed repeatedly to discourage Nicholas from meeting with George, Glory feared her aunt was succumbing to Nicholas's powerful charm.

After dinner Nicholas sought Jeremy out. Watching them, Glory wondered what they discussed.

"Jeremy?" Nicholas approached him in the foyer. "I'd like a moment if you please."

The little butler nodded stiffly. He'd been sullen all evening. It was obvious he felt guilty for revealing Glory's wedding plans.

"I know you believe you've done Glory a grave disservice," Nicholas said. "You think she'd have been happier married to McMillan."

The little man just stared, his eyes fixed on the ceiling somewhere over Nicholas's shoulder.

"I can only tell you that I love her. That I want her happiness more than anything in the world. If I didn't truly believe I could give her that happiness, I wouldn't have forced the wedding. I hope you'll believe that and put your conscience at ease. I promise you won't be sorry."

Jeremy Wiggins felt stunned. Never in all his years of service had a gentleman spoken to him as an equal. Never had a member of the upper class deigned to explain his actions to a mere servant—not even George McMillan. As he watched the tall sea captain move back to the place beside his bride and pull her hand onto his lap, he felt a surge of admiration for the man he'd been determined to hate. And a grudging feeling that he had accidentally done the right thing.

As the hour grew late, Glory became more and more edgy. Nicholas seemed perfectly relaxed as he reclined comfortably beside her on the tapestry sofa in the sitting room. He never tried to force her into conversation, just carried on politely with Aunt Flo, speaking as if they were truly the blissful newlyweds they appeared. It was all Glory could do to remain in the room. How dare he look so pleased with himself! My Lord, the man had taken her virtue, ruined her reputation, and forced her into an unwanted marriage! Who knew what other evil intentions he had?

Every few minutes her glance strayed to the top of the stairs. Surely he wouldn't claim his husbandly rights with the baby so close. But there were men who did. If the baby had a tenuous hold on life, as the doctor feared, making love might harm it in some way. If she spoke to Nicholas about her misgivings, surely he would understand. Surely he was as concerned with the child's safety as she.

But when she chanced a look at those light gray eyes she saw the old hunger, and a new edge of worry gnawed at her heart. Would Aunt Flo and the few servants they had be able to stop him? Or would he take her out of the house, demand she share his cabin on the ship? She'd seen his cruelty. She couldn't trust him.

Swallowing hard, she twisted the folds of her plum velvet skirt until she felt the warmth of Nicholas's hand against her cheek. He turned her face toward his, forcing her to look at him.

"Tell me what it is you fear?" he said softly.

"What makes you think I'm afraid?" She raised her chin defiantly. But her eyes strayed to the stairway, and Nicholas's gray eyes warmed.

"You used to enjoy my bed," he teased, but Glory didn't smile.

"I . . . fear for the babe."

"The babe?" He seemed incredulous.

She stiffened, suddenly realizing how ridiculous she must sound. "I'm sorry. You must think me a fool. Obviously you have no interest in a woman whose waistline is as large as a flour barrel."

He chuckled softly, the sound no more than a rumble in his wide hard chest. "To you it may seem so, but I assure you, that is not the case." His eyes moved to the fullness of her breasts, heavier now with the babe. "You look beautiful and womanly, and I desire you just as I always have. But I'll not force myself on you."

"It wouldn't be the first time," she said with a surge of spirit.

"I was wrong to do what I did." He settled his hand on her stomach, the warmth of his touch spreading all the way to her toes. "You needn't fear. I'll not take you to my bed until you're ready." His gray eyes caressed her face. "Never doubt I want this child as much as you do. I shall do nothing to harm it. I'll be returning to the ship tonight. You may have the rest of the week to ready yourself for the journey to Tarrytown. We can be there by the end of the following week. I want you safely installed in your new home before you are any further along."

"But I . . ."

"You what?"

"It isn't important."

"Tell me."

"No."

"Please."

The word sounded so foreign coming from Nicholas she weakened. "I'll sound like a coward."

"Never."

"I was only thinking about . . . about when the baby comes. Would it be all right if Aunt Flo attended me?"

"Of course. Your mother, too, if that's what you want."

Her mother. Funny, she'd hardly thought of her mother since she left Summerfield Manor. Proof they were strangers after all. She'd written several letters, none of which mentioned the child or the circumstances that had taken her so far from home. Superficial letters, meaningless.

The ones she'd received in return had demanded that she return to Summerfield Manor—with Nathan in tow. She had duties, her mother reminded her, responsibilities. Reading between the lines, Glory assumed that meant she should resume her relationship with Eric Dixon. Bring their two plantations together. After what she'd been through, it all seemed senseless to Glory.

She glanced away. "Thank you," was all she said.

"You've had a long day. As much as I hate to leave, I think you'd better get some sleep." He smiled. "Walk me to the door like a dutiful young bride?"

Her head came up. "If you'll promise not to meet George McMillan on the morrow."

His eyes turned stormy. "He gave me no choice. I want nothing more to come between us. I'll not have it said you're married to a coward."

"Nicholas, I'm begging you."

"No."

"You owe me this. I've never asked you for anything. I'm asking you now."

He touched her cheek, took a long deep breath, and released it slowly. "I'll see you tomorrow."

"After you've killed George?" she asked, temper barely in check. "If you harm him, I'll never forgive you, Nicholas."

"Sleep well, love." Long strides carried him from the room.

Glory mounted the stairs to her room, torn between anger and despair. If Nicholas dueled with George on the morrow, George was bound to be wounded or killed. He was a gentleman, not a fighter. She was surprised he even knew how to use a gun. She had pleaded with Nicholas, and, as usual, he'd ignored her wishes. She slammed her hand against the banister, the sound ringing in the empty foyer. Damn him! Damn him to hell! He was every bit the cur George said he was, and yet . . . when she looked at him, she felt that same deadly attraction she'd felt before. What was there about Nicholas Blackwell that sent all reasonable thought fleeing on the wind?

Unable to find an answer, Glory readied herself for bed. By the time she climbed between the pan-warmed sheets, she'd made a decision: George McMillan was a kind and decent man. Beyond that, he was her friend. She wouldn't stand by and see Nicholas Blackwell murder him. Pregnant or not, she'd be at Breed's Hill at dawn.

Chapter Seventeen

"Are you ready, gentlemen?" McMillan's second, a wispy, sallow-skinned man who looked to be a few years younger, stood in front of the dueling men.

"It's not too late to call this off," Nicholas said to the man who faced him, pistol in hand, a look of cold determination lining his handsome face. "Your concern for the woman's honor is well noted. Dying seems a senseless means of proving it."

"In case the thought hadn't crossed your mind, Captain, it's you who will die this day. Glory's husband is already presumed dead. I'll just be marrying the widow Blackwell instead of Hatteras."

Nicholas nodded. "If that's your final word, we may as well get on with it."

The men turned back to back, their feet planted squarely on a thin layer of snow. The sky looked cloudy, the overcast hinting at a storm. A stiff wind sliced the December air and molded Nicholas's breeches even more closely against his thighs. He stood a good three inches taller than McMillan, though the brown-haired man was tall in his own right.

"Raise your pistols," the sallow-faced man instructed. Acting as Nicholas's second, Mac stood tensely beside him, his face ruddier than usual in the biting cold. The two seconds walked some distance away to stand beneath a ghostly, leafless sycamore. The woods around the clearing were eerily silent except for the moaning breeze.

"I will begin counting." The younger man's voice rang with a note of authority across the snow-covered clearing. "One. Two."

"Stop! Stop right where you are, both of you." Glory stepped from beneath a tree on the opposite side of the clearing, pointing an ancient pistol at the men, her arms resting against the sides of her swollen belly, the wind whipping at her heavy woolen skirts. "If either of you take one more step, I'll shoot, and right now I don't care which of you I hit!"

Nicholas felt the pull of a smile. As far as he knew, she had no idea how to fire the weapon. But she'd surprised him before, on more than one occasion. He'd learned from experience not to underestimate her.

"Go back home, Gloria," George McMillan instructed. "When this is over, I'll come for you."

"Don't you understand, George?" She started walking toward them, the gun still pointing straight ahead. "He's going to kill you. You don't know what he's like."

"And you do?" Nicholas put in, just loud enough for her to hear.

"I know enough to be frightened for George's life. I don't want him harmed."

"This is between Captain Blackwell and me, Glory," George said. "Please, just go back home."

Neither man had moved. From the corner of his eye, Nicholas saw Mac circling around the clearing. "Do as he says, Glory," he added, hoping to distract her. "It's out of your hands. Think of the child."

"I'm warning you. Throw down your weapons, or I'll shoot."

Nicholas almost smiled. "It might be worth it, just to see which of us you'd aim for. But then, I guess there's really little doubt."

"That's a very good deduction, Captain, considering what you've put me through these past long months. Now, both of you, drop your weapons and move away from each other.''

The whistling wind hid the sound of Mac's heavy boots crunching on the snow behind her. He reached around her, grasped her wrist, and the gun fired harmlessly in the air.

''Not you, too, Mac!'' she cried, feeling completely betrayed. ''Can't any of you understand? George McMillan is a good man. He's my friend. I can't stand by and let him die.''

''Listen to me, lass. The cap'n's a good man, too. He only wants what's best fer both o' ye. Even if ye stop them now, they'll only meet another time. Come back to the carriage wi' me. Yer place is at home, waiting fer yer husband.''

Suddenly tired, and seeing his words as true, Glory handed Mac the now-empty pistol. She let him lead her across the clearing to the carriage and climbed up inside. Mac said something to the driver, and the carriage rolled away.

Once she'd rounded the corner out of sight, Glory ordered the driver to stop. Pulling her fur-lined mantle around her, the hood up over her head, she awkwardly stepped to the icy ground and headed back toward the clearing. She hadn't been able to stop them, but she wasn't about to leave without knowing the results.

''May we proceed now?'' George McMillan prodded, his voice laced with irritation. ''The sooner we get this over with, the sooner I may return to my fiancée.''

Nicholas worked a muscle in his jaw, but said nothing. The men raised their weapons again. Backs to each other, they began to step off the distance.

''One. Two. Three,'' the second called out. ''Four. Five. Six.''

Nicholas tightened his hold on the pistol; the walnut grip felt smooth against his palm.

''Seven. Eight. Nine. Ten.''

Nicholas turned to face his opponent, saw the man's arm come up, tried to gauge the trajectory, then turned his body slightly at the precise instant flintlock drove against steel. Feeling a sharp sting in his left arm, he muttered an oath, realized he hadn't allowed quite enough for the wind.

Now it was his turn.

George McMillan stood ramrod straight. His face grim. If he ran, his cowardice would be the talk of Boston. Nicholas raised his gun, aiming the sleek metal barrel at his opponent's heart. McMillan didn't move, just stared straight ahead. Nicholas saluted the man's quiet courage. Easing back the hammer with his thumb, the ominous click loud against the early morning silence, Nicholas aimed the barrel well above McMillan's head—and fired into the air.

Catching a movement beside a nearby tree, Nicholas turned just in time to see Glory slump to the ground in a tangle of black wool skirts. Cursing beneath his breath, he raced toward her, Mac, George, and the sallow-faced man at his heels. Blood darkened the sleeve of his coat and dripped onto the snow as Nicholas knelt and placed his hand on Glory's forehead.

"She's just fainted, lad," Mac told him.

"I'll carry her for you," George offered, his voice soft. "You can take her home in my coach."

After a moment, Nicholas agreed. George scooped Glory into his arms and carried her toward his carriage in the distance. Mac checked Nicholas's wound, determined it was only superficial, and they both followed George. When Nicholas reached the carriage and opened the door, he found Glory leaning against the velvet seat, blue eyes open and watching him.

George pulled Nicholas aside. "I'll ride back with my second. Just send my driver home when you have no further need of him."

"Thank you."

"Take care of her, Captain."

"You have my word."

George took a ragged breath, his eyes bleak, but said nothing more. As he turned to leave, Nicholas stopped him.

"I want you to know," Nicholas said, "if things had been different, there isn't another man I'd rather have seen her marry."

"Thank you, Captain." Head held high, George turned and walked away.

Nicholas climbed into the carriage next to Glory. She didn't even look at him. The carriage rolled away, the sound of the wheels muffled by the thin layer of snow. Glory rode along in silence, the rumble and sway of the carriage soothing her jagged nerves.

"Why didn't you shoot him?" she finally asked, her voice no more than a whisper.

"If you knew me better, you'd know I don't go around killing people just for sport. The man only wanted to protect you. I could hardly kill him for that."

She turned to look at him, remembering the man she had loved on the strand. A man she was certain would have felt the same. For the first time she noticed his arm. "You're wounded!"

"Is that wifely concern I hear?" He smiled, then grimaced as he suffered a spasm of pain.

"I'd be concerned for any man who was injured, even a rogue like you. Now, please, lie back and be still until we can summon the surgeon."

"I'm more worried about you. Are you all right?"

"I'm fine, thank you."

"You're sure?"

She felt unaccountably pleased at his concern, but refused to admit it. "I'm sure."

"From now on, madam, there'll be no more traipsing around in the cold. You're to rest and take care of yourself." He touched her cheek with the back of his hand. "That's an order."

She smiled in spite of herself. "You're very good at giving orders, Captain."

"Nicholas," he corrected. "And you're very *bad* at following them."

"I probably always will be."

"Yes. But I suppose that's one of the reasons I love you."

Glory's eyes flew open wide. She rounded on him, pale cheeks suddenly flooded with color. "Don't you dare use that word with me!"

"What word?" he asked, genuinely confused.

"*Love*. You, Captain, wouldn't know the meaning of the word."

His own temper flared. "And I suppose George Mc-Millan would?"

"Yes, he would. George is a gentleman."

"If McMillan is so damned wonderful, why aren't you in love with him?"

Glory clenched her teeth. Refusing to look at him a moment more, she turned away and gazed at the passing row of houses. A door opened and a small boy darted out to fetch the bottle of milk that stood beside the door, then scurried back into the warmth within.

Nicholas turned her face with his hand, forcing her to look at him. "It couldn't be because you're still in love with me?"

Glory stiffened, angered even more. "Not a chance, Captain Blackwell. I may have been young and foolish when first we met, but I'm a wiser woman now."

One corner of his mouth tilted into a smile. "Time will tell, love. We'll just have to wait and see."

The week flew past in a flurry of activity. Glory relayed the story of the duel, and Aunt Florence assured her she'd done the right thing in marrying Nicholas. Glory was just as certain she hadn't. She'd had no choice, she reminded herself. He would have ruined her life again—George's and the baby's as well. She hadn't told Aunt Flo about his threat. Her aunt would only have tried to intervene, and things would have been worse for everyone. No, she'd made the only sensible choice. But the degree of Nicholas's ruthlessness made her feel more wretched than ever.

When the time came for her to leave Boston, it was a sad farewell indeed.

"Here, now, there's no need for tears," Aunt Flo chided, her own voice a little choked. "The baby's due in a couple of months, and I'll be joining you in Tarrytown."

"I'm sorry, Aunt Flo."

"Give him a chance, dear. Everyone makes mistakes."

Glory slumped down on the tapestry sofa. "I don't understand him, Aunt Flo. Maybe I never did. I don't trust him. I certainly don't love him anymore. Nor would I want to."

Aunt Flo patted her hand. "My instincts tell me he's a good man."

"I wish I could believe that."

"Time to go, love," Nicholas called to her from the doorway. "The carriage is waiting."

She kissed her aunt's translucent cheek, wiped the tears from her eyes, and joined Nicholas in the foyer where he wrapped her snugly in a fur-lined pelisse. In minutes the carriage reached the wharf. Nicholas whisked Glory up the gangplank to the deck of the *Black Witch* and into the warmth of the sumptuous officers' wardroom.

Brass and crystal sconces flickered on the wall as Glory pushed open the door. Mac beckoned her forward and pulled out a chair, seating her beside him at the long, carved mahogany table. Gilded mirrors at either end of the wardroom reflected silver candelabra that adorned an elegant sideboard. Memories of Nicholas, their rescue from the island, and the unhappy time they'd spent on board this ship threatened to swamp her. Even with Mac's attentive companionship, Glory felt homesick before they ever left the harbor.

"Give it time, lass," Mac advised. "He loves ye. Give him a chance to prove it."

"I don't want him to love me, Mac. And I don't want to love him. He forced this marriage on me. I agreed only because of the child."

"Ye've a long life ahead a ye, lass. Dinna cheat yerself outta lovin'."

When Glory didn't answer, Mac changed the subject. They continued to renew their acquaintance while her trunks were brought on board and Nicholas readied the ship to make way.

"What's happened to Josh?" she asked. "I didn't see him when we came on board."

"Lad's been promoted to ship's master. He commands *Black Diamond* now."

"And Jago?"

"Dodd is Josh's second mate."

"So much has happened," Glory said with a sigh. She took a sip of her tea, then replaced the cup in its fine porcelain saucer.

"Aye, lass. Some bad and some good." Mac's eyes moved to the bulge of her stomach beneath her black bombazine traveling dress. "Ye've grown up, lass. Ye were forced to do it in a bit of a hurry, but ye've grown up just the same."

Glory smiled a little forlornly. "I suppose so."

Once the ship was under way, Mac led Glory to the captain's richly appointed cabin. She napped for a time, then joined Nicholas in the salon for a quiet supper. Afterward, he returned with her to the cabin. She hesitated only a moment before stepping inside.

"Where will you be sleeping?" she asked, straining to keep her voice even as Nicholas followed her into the lamplit interior. The words struck an unpleasant memory of the first night she'd spent in the room, of a battle of wills, and the humiliation of her body's response. She shivered at the thought.

"With you," he said simply. But his eyes had darkened, as if he could read her thoughts.

Her hand shook as it slid protectively to the life that bulged at her waist. "Is your word so easily broken?" She hoped he hadn't noticed the tremor in her voice.

"I promised I wouldn't make love to you until you were ready. I promised I wouldn't harm the babe." He swept a tendril of pale blond hair from her cheek. "They're promises I've every intention of keeping. But you're my wife now. The sooner you come to trust me, the better off we'll both be.'' He bent and kissed her forehead. ''Now turn around so I can unbutton your dress.''

Glory swallowed hard, a warm blush coloring her cheeks. ''Surely you don't intend to watch me undress.''

''You're my *wife*,'' he repeated almost as if he relished the word. ''You carry my child. The changes in your body are only natural. You have nothing to be ashamed of.'' Before she could protest, he turned her back to him and unbuttoned her bodice and skirt. After helping her out of the top, he pulled the skirt over her head. Next went the petticoats, layer after layer, until she wore only her chemise and simple cotton drawers.

Nicholas turned her to face him, but she wouldn't meet his eyes. ''You look lovely,'' he told her, tilting her chin up. ''There is nothing more feminine than a woman who's with child.''

''I don't believe you. You're just trying to make me feel better.''

''Is that so?'' He cocked a fine black brow. ''Do you know how much I want you right now?''

When she didn't answer, he pressed her hand against the bulge in his breeches, his swollen manhood proof of his desire. Glory's head snapped up. She took a tentative step backwards.

Nicholas chuckled, the merest rumble in his chest. ''You needn't fear, love. I've thought of little except making love to you these long months past. But I can wait till the baby comes—that is, if you'll give me one small kiss.''

Glory shook her head, eyes wide. ''No.''

Nicholas shrugged his wide shoulders. ''As you wish.'' He moved to the wardrobe and opened the carved wooden door. Several of Glory's gowns had been unpacked and hung within. From a drawer he pulled a soft batiste night-dress, helped her remove her chemise, and slipped the gown over her head. While he hung up her dress, she watched over his shoulder, and a flash of curiosity surfaced—along with a spark of jealousy.

"When I was here before. The dresses I borrowed, whose were they?"

He stifled a rueful smile. "I wondered when you'd get around to asking."

"Well?"

"Well, *wife*," he said deliberately, "they belonged to a former . . . acquaintance. One who has long since disappeared from my life. The only dresses you'll find in these chests from now on will be yours."

"Does this *acquaintance* of yours live in Tarrytown?"

"She lives in New York—with her husband."

"A married woman?"

Nicholas only shrugged.

"Oh, yes, I'd forgotten your penchant for other men's wives."

Nicholas strode toward her, his eyes stormy. "That's all in the past. The woman meant nothing to me then. She means less than nothing now."

Glory watched him closely, wanting to believe him, but unsure she should.

"Give us some time, love. For the baby's sake if not mine."

Reluctantly she nodded and the tension eased from his shoulders. "I'm just tired, I guess." *And more than a little confused,* she wanted to add. Instead, she walked to the wide berth and heavily sank down.

"You'll feel better after a good night's sleep." He smiled warmly. Moving toward the bureau, he untied his stock and shrugged off his shirt, leaving his chest bare. His muscles bunched as he unbuttoned his breeches and slid them down his long, lean legs.

Glory swallowed hard, her mouth suddenly dry. The sound of rustling fabric as he stepped free of his clothing sent a tremor down her spine. Conscious of a stirring she hadn't known in months, she tried to turn away, but her gaze locked on the dark hair curling between his flat dark nipples. Too well she remembered the smooth feel of his tanned skin beneath her hands, the stiff bristles of his curly black chest hairs.

Glory's eyes flew wide as she watched him stride naked toward the bed, his footsteps muffled by the thick Tartan carpet.

"Surely you don't intend to sleep like that!" she said.

"Why not? I always sleep in the nude. Surely you remember."

"But . . . but that was before."

"Yes, that was before. Before we were married. Now you're my wife."

"But . . . but—"

"I won't break my promise."

"What if you can't control yourself?"

Nicholas grinned broadly, an expression Glory had rarely seen.

"There's only one way to find out." He wrapped a corded arm just below her breasts and hauled her up in the bed to snuggle against him. She could feel his hard thighs pressing against the backs of her own.

"Good night, love," he whispered, nuzzling his face in her hair.

"Good night, Captain."

"Nicholas," he corrected, a hint of a irritation in his voice.

"Nicholas," she dutifully repeated. Then she closed her eyes and pretended to sleep. Nicholas nestled her close for a while—until, with a surge of alarm, she felt his manhood stiffen. Then he groaned softly and rolled away. With a tiny smile, Glory finally drifted to sleep.

In the morning, she woke to an empty bed, rough seas, and a sharp pain in her stomach. At first she thought she might just be hungry, but the gnawing felt lower, farther down in her abdomen. Soon the tiny needlelike jabs mushroomed into full-fledged knives of pain, and Glory could scarcely breathe. When she rose from the bed to get help, water gushed from between her legs, pooling on the floor and soaking her nightdress.

Shaking with fear, she pulled open the cabin door without even remembering her wrapper. She stumbled down the passageway, encountering Nicholas, who was carrying her breakfast tray. She saw the stricken look on his face, heard the tray crash to the floor, just before she sank into darkness.

Chapter Eighteen

"There's nothing more we can do, lad."

Nicholas glanced from the bloody lifeless bundle he cradled in his arms to the woman who lay on the bed. She looked wan and pale; the covers barely moved with each shallow breath.

"Will she be all right?"

"I know little of women, lad. But by the look o' it, I'd say yes. The problem was wi' the child, not the mother."

Nicholas stood at the foot of his berth, clutching the miniature, blanket-wrapped body of his son. The world seemed tilted, blurred somehow. Outside a wet wind blew across a chilly sea, and the sky was overcast, as bleak and gray as his thoughts.

"Why don't ye let me have him," Mac urged softly. "I'll see the cooper builds him a proper coffin."

Nicholas swallowed past the lump in his throat. It had all happened so quickly. What had gone wrong? Only yesterday the future seemed so bright, so hopeful. With a baby in their lives, he and Glory had a chance to rebuild the love they shared on the strand. But the baby was dead. What would the future hold for them now?

Nicholas fought the burning behind his eyes, the terrible fatigue. "Mahogany," he whispered. "Build him something sturdy. The sea is so vast . . . and he is so small."

Mac laid a weathered hand on Nicholas's shoulder.

"We'll use that lovely old sideboard in the officers' ward-room."

"Yes," Nicholas said, his eyes fixed on a tiny spot of blood on the blanket. "That will make a fine coffin." Mac reached for the bundle and for a moment Nicholas couldn't bear the thought of letting go.

"Life's never easy, lad."

"No, I suppose it isn't." He glanced at the woman sleeping in his berth. Damp hair clung to her temples; her slim fingers clutched the quilt beneath her chin. "How will I tell her, Mac? What can I say?"

"There are no right words, lad. When the time comes, ye'll do the best ye can."

Nicholas carefully handed the bundle to Mac, gently tucking the corners of the blanket around the tiny infant's body. He couldn't meet the old Scot's eyes, knowing the pity he would see. With slow, grim steps, the Scotsman left the room. Nicholas blew out the lamp beside the bed, darkening the room to the same dismal gray as the sky outside.

Heart heavier than ever before in his life, he took up his vigil beside Glory, slipping her cold hand between his warmer ones. He sat that way for hours, until his arms and legs cramped so badly he was forced to stand and stretch them. The room smelled stale with the coppery scent of blood and death. Conscious of the ordeal that lay before him, Nicholas headed up to the deck for a breath of fresh air. He needed to clear his head—and bolster his courage. A few minutes later he returned to the cabin. Glory's eyes flew to his face the moment he stepped through the door.

"Nicholas?"

"I'm right here, love." He knelt beside her and captured her hand, bringing it to his lips.

"The baby?" Her other hand moved to the flat spot beneath the covers, which only hours ago had been round with life.

"I wish there was something I could say, something I

could do to change things, but there isn't. The child is gone, Glory."

"No." She shook her head. "I don't believe you. Just this morning I felt him move. He was alive; he was—"

"He came too soon, Glory. He was just too small."

"A boy?"

"Yes."

"But he can't be dead. Nicholas, please, I'll do anything you ask, just tell me he isn't dead." The pain on her face was so great that Nicholas had to look away.

"I'm sorry," he said. "So sorry."

"Nooo!" she screamed and struggled to get up. As she flailed her arms and thrashed about, it was all Nicholas could do to keep her abed. Finally she stopped struggling. She searched his face for a moment, then slumped back against the pillow. He let her cry out her sorrow, just sat quietly beside her, his head in his hands, his fingers laced through his curly black hair.

She cried for what to Nicholas seemed an eternity. When he could stand to listen no longer, he pulled her into his arms.

"Get away from me!" she shrieked. "Get away and leave me alone! This is all your fault, do you hear me? Your fault!"

"Listen to me, Glory."

She twisted free of his grasp. "Listen to you? Listen to you? Every time I've listened to you, every time I've trusted you, something terrible has happened. I won't listen again. Not now, not ever!"

Nicholas straightened. There was something in her words, some terrible chord of truth. He searched her face, hoping to find some means to reach her, a way to hold on to that tenuous thread of hope. He saw none.

In that moment Nicholas knew any dream he'd ever held of winning her love was as dead as the child they'd conceived. She would never trust him again, never love him again. His chest felt so tight he could scarcely breathe. He stopped near the door for a last long glance. Then slow, dreary steps carried him from the room.

* * *

They buried the baby at sea. Nicholas felt it fitting; after all, the boy was his son. He knew Glory would have preferred a peaceful grave on the slope of a quiet hill. Even that small comfort was denied her.

A week after the burial, they docked at New Rochelle, where Glory and Nicholas disembarked. Nicholas hired a carriage, and they traveled straight to Tarrytown. Glory said little throughout the journey. She looked weak and frail, and wept at the slightest cause.

Arriving at Blackwell Hall, Nicholas found Brad had already moved his mother to the town house near Broadway in the city. Apparently Bradford had no doubt Nicholas would be returning with a wife. A small place in his heart thanked his stepbrother for his thoughtfulness.

Blackwell Hall, a huge estate set at the bottom of a hill near the Hudson, seemed a different place without the bitter presence of Nicholas's stepmother. Brighter somehow, more welcoming. Nicholas had owned the hall for five years, though he'd never been in residence for more than a few days. He sometimes wondered why he'd bought it, since it was more ornate than he preferred. The huge stone house was built in the Gothic Revival style, of marble quarried by convicts from Sing Sing. The interior had vaulted ceilings, figured bosses painted to resemble stone, and huge stained-glass windows. The furniture was mostly European, upholstered in rich brocade and heavy velvet. Elegant velvet draperies adorned the windows.

Though the house was beautiful, it was the grounds that had attracted Nicholas. The beautiful formal gardens, the landscaped lawns sloping to the river, but most of all the handsome paddocks and stables where one day he intended to breed fine racing stock.

Nicholas imagined it would have been the perfect place to raise his child. That his son was dead, would never run through the elegant halls, seemed an even more bitter loss for him here. Looking across the massive salon to the pale face of his wife, who sat staring straight ahead, hands folded in her lap, he wondered how it had all gone so wrong.

"I want an annulment," Glory said, the words ringing hollow and weak against the marble walls. She'd spoken so little since their arrival two weeks ago that Nicholas hardly recognized her voice. She stood in the doorway to the main salon dressed in black, her pale hands clasped in front of her.

"Why?" he asked, shoving back his chair as he came to his feet. The sound grated on the polished hardwood floors.

"Because I don't love you. The baby's gone; there's no reason for us to be bound." She said the words with a casualness that twisted Nicholas's heart.

"If I were to agree, what would you do?"

"Return to Boston," she told him with an equal lack of emotion.

"To marry George McMillan?"

She shrugged her shoulders. "Maybe."

"No" was all he said. When she turned and walked away as quietly as if no words had been spoken, he stormed from the hall, slammed out the door, and headed toward the stables.

Long rides through the countryside seemed his only solace on the chilly winter days. He returned at dusk to find Glory, as usual, locked away in her rooms at the top of the stairs. Each time he saw her, she looked thinner and paler than before. He worried about her endlessly, tried every way he knew to please her, even asked if she'd like her aunt or Nathan to come for a visit.

"No, thank you," she'd said. "I'm sure they have other more important matters to attend to. Besides, I don't feel like entertaining."

All in all there was little he could do. The second time she mentioned the annulment, he considered giving it to her, though it was far from what he wanted. He just didn't believe an annulment was the answer. He wished he knew what was.

* * *

They'd been at Blackwell Hall over a month when Bradford St. John arrived. Nicholas had written him several letters, telling him of the sad state of affairs at the hall and seeking his advice. Instead of receiving a letter in reply, Brad appeared in person.

Nicholas enveloped him in a warm hug. "God, it's good to see you."

"You, too, Nicholas."

"Come on." He beckoned. "I want you to meet Glory."

When they reached her room at the top of the stairs, she was sitting beside the fire, crocheting an antimacassar. Needlework and a little reading were all that seemed to hold her interest. Firelight flickered over her too-thin face, and even her flaxen hair reflected less than its usual sheen.

"Glory," Nicholas said softly. "This is my brother, Bradford. I told you about him on the strand, remember?"

She seemed uncertain. "I . . . I'm not sure."

Nicholas felt a tightness around his heart. "Brad, this is Glory, my wife."

She extended her hand, and Brad accepted it, bringing the delicate fingers to his lips. "It's a pleasure to meet you at last."

"Yes. . . . What did you say your name was?"

Nicholas could have cried.

"It's Bradford. Bradford St. John."

"Brad. That's a nice name." She glanced back down to her lap and picked up her crochet hook.

Nicholas motioned Brad toward the door.

Glory watched his retreating figure. He glanced back at her before he reached the hallway, lingering as if he wanted to speak. He looked as handsome and imposing as ever, and just for a moment she imagined they were back on the strand. Then all the pain and suffering she'd felt these past long months surfaced to weigh her down. Her mind closed off thoughts of Nicholas just as surely as if he'd closed the door. Quietly, he did.

Glory's hands worked the thin ivory hook, forming lacy

patterns with the thread. As she rocked before the fire, she kept her eyes carefully focused on her work. Her mother had taught her to crochet just before she left Summerfield Manor. She still had to concentrate to get the stitches right, but at least the work brought her some solace from her despair.

Glory rested the antimacassar in her lap, determined to keep her thoughts on the intricacy of the pattern. The flames of the fire flickered and hissed, and a stiff breeze rattled the shutters. Outside the sky was dark with the indications of a coming storm. Against her will, Glory's thoughts wandered. She glanced at her surroundings: the high vaulted ceilings, the stained-glass fanlights above the windows. She could almost imagine the small dark-haired boy, so like Nicholas, who might have run to her side and tugged on her skirts. "Mama, won't you come out and play with me? I love you, Mama."

A shiver raced across her flesh, and a hard lump swelled in her throat. Clutching her crochet hook a little tighter, she settled her hands against the folds of her stiff black skirt. Why had it happened? She'd wanted the baby so much, needed a child so badly. Was the baby's death really Nicholas's fault as she had convinced herself? A tiny voice said no. It was your own fault. You should have taken better care of yourself. Glory bit her lip and glanced back at the spidery patterns in her lap. Determined to forget what might have been, she picked up her stitchery and began to catch and pull the thread with her hook.

Nicholas led Bradford down the wide stairway to his walnut-paneled, book-lined study. Ignoring the tremor in his hand, he poured his stepbrother a brandy. Brad seated himself in one leather chair; Nicholas sat in another.

"I don't know what to do," Nicholas said. He took a long, soothing drink of brandy, letting the warmth burn a steadying path down his throat. "She seems to be getting worse every day."

"What have you done so far?"

"I've tried to get her to go out with me, at least for a

ride. I've had lavish dinners prepared; she won't even come down to eat. I've begged, pleaded, apologized. She blames me for the death of the child, and maybe she's right.''

"Do you believe you're responsible?'' Brad asked.

"It's possible. I suppose it *was* upsetting, my arriving in Boston the way I did. As I told you in my letters, I forced the marriage; there was a duel. Maybe that was enough to cause her to lose the babe.'' Nicholas glanced away. "I just don't know, Brad. But Glory certainly believes I'm responsible.''

"Does it really matter?''

"What do you mean?''

"What I mean is, you've suffered, too. I could hear it in your letters, though you didn't come out and say it. The baby is dead. Whose fault it is is unimportant. What *is* important is that woman in there. She's blaming you because she can't bear the thought that she might be the one responsible. She's drowning in grief, Nicholas.''

"Don't you think I can see that! I just don't know what to do about it.''

"What would you do if it were Mac—or me,'' he added softly.

"I'd haul you up by your boot straps and make you face the fact that what's happened is past. That life is full of sorrow, but it's full of happiness, too.''

"So why don't you do that to her?''

"Because I promised myself I'd never raise my voice to her again, never make harsh demands or treat her badly.''

"I know you feel guilty about what's happened, but Glory is your wife, Nicholas, not some sainted virgin. She needs a husband. From what I've learned, she's a headstrong young woman. She needs a man who can handle her. She fell in love with the man you are, not the watered-down image you're trying to become. Be yourself Nicholas. And be a husband to Glory.''

"You make it sound so simple.''

"Nothing's ever simple.''

"No, I suppose it isn't.''

"That young woman needs you, Nicholas. You've got to be strong for both of you."

Setting down his brandy snifter, Nicholas watched Brad for a moment, pondering his words. "How is it, Brad," he asked, coming to his feet, "that you're eight years younger than I and twenty years wiser?"

"Because I'm not in love." Brad stood up, too. "One more piece of advice?"

"Any time."

"Get her back in your bed just as soon as you can. There never was a woman who could resist you in that department."

Nicholas laughed—for the first time in weeks. "You're the best, Brad. The very best." Nicholas clasped his brother's hand. "Thank you. Now if you'll excuse me, I'll see you at supper. I've got some work to do."

Two days later, arms piled high with boxes, Nicholas turned the ornate brass doorknob and burst into Glory's room.

Her head came up, but she didn't say a word, just stared at him as if a stranger had entered her room. She sat before the fire, rocking and reading a book. Nicholas stopped only long enough for a quick glance in her direction. As he strode across the carpet and dropped the boxes onto the bed, she eyed him with a bit of suspicion.

Nicholas muttered beneath his breath. Moving to the rosewood armoire in the corner, he made a great show of opening the carved wooden doors and pulling out one of Glory's black faille day dresses. Just the feel of the stiff material, the lifeless look of the dreary black fabric, made him angry. He set his jaw, caught the collar of the gown between his fingers, and ripped the dress down the front.

The sound of shredding fabric brought Glory to her feet. "What . . . what are you doing?"

"Something I should have done weeks ago. I'm getting rid of these dismal dresses once and for all."

"But you . . . you can't do that! I'm in mourning!"

"Wrong. You *were* in mourning. It's obvious you've

mourned quite enough." He shredded another dress from collar to waist. Glory stared at him in amazement. He ignored her. She made no move to stop him as he ripped a third gown up the seam and it joined the pile of dresses on the thick Persian carpet at his feet. Glory stood stock still, book gripped between her fingers, staring at him as if she couldn't quite believe what her eyes were seeing.

He ripped up another dress, determined to get a reaction.

She took a hesitant step toward him, blue eyes huge in her too-pale face. "But what will I wear?" she finally asked.

"Look in those boxes on the bed. There's a day dress and an evening gown. I hope they'll come close to fitting you." He paused long enough to flash her a smile. "I've always had a pretty fair eye for a lady's figure." Reaching into the armoire, he dragged another black dress from its hanger and threw it onto the pile.

Glory walked toward the boxes on the bed, glancing back over her shoulder. "Why are you doing this?"

"Because I'm sick and tired of all this sadness. You've suffered enough. We both have. If I never see you in another black dress for as long as I live it'll be too soon." He turned to face her. "Speaking of which, I want you out of the one you have on."

Glory gasped, hand creeping to the base of her throat. "You can't be serious!"

"Madam, I assure you I'm quite serious. Take it off."

"Now?" She seemed incredulous.

"Right now."

She stiffened her spine in the first show of spirit Nicholas had seen in weeks. "No."

Nicholas could have leaped for joy. "You'll take it off now, or I swear I'll tear it off."

She glared at him defiantly until he took a long stride toward her. "All right!" she shrieked, backing away. "Send Betsy in."

"You have a husband who is quite capable of helping you unbutton your clothing."

She eyed the door, looking as if she might bolt.

"Don't even think about it," Nicholas warned.

She watched him a little longer, then straightened her spine. Accepting defeat with as much dignity as she could muster, she presented her back, shoulders proud, chin held high. "You know you're acting like a madman," she told him. "What on earth has gotten into you?"

Nicholas grinned so broadly, his cheeks dimpled. If Brad had been there, Nicholas would have kissed him. After unfastening her buttons with his long-fingered hands, Nicholas stepped away. "Now I'll send Betsy up," he told her, not wanting to press his luck. "Then we're going out."

"Out?"

"For a ride in the country. I think it's high time you took a look at your new home." Without waiting for an answer, Nicholas strode from the room.

Glory appeared a few minutes later, dressed in a silver-blue serge day dress that brightened the blue of her eyes. Her hair had been brushed and coiffed in ringlets that curled on either side of her face. Though her skin still looked pale, twin spots of color stained her cheeks.

"If you must drag me out to catch my death of cold, let's get on with it." She accepted his arm and allowed him to lead her from the salon. Her gloved hand rested lightly on the fabric of his gray wool cutaway coat and Nicholas reveled in the contact.

He wrapped her in a fur-lined mantle and presented her with the matching fur muff. "We won't be gone long."

Since a fresh layer of snow had fallen in the night, Nicholas helped her into his black and gold two-horse sleigh. Taking his place beside her, he spread a horsehair robe across her lap. Glory stared ahead, her spine ramrod straight.

"I'll expect you to come down to supper this evening," he told her as he gathered up the reins. "And every evening from now on."

Glory's head came up.

"From now on you'll take your meals with me, not in

your room." He clicked the horses into a trot, and the sleigh slid smoothly away.

"I should have known you couldn't resist bullying me for long."

"I prefer to think of my recent behavior as neglect. I've already *neglected* you far longer than I should have."

"What if I refuse to come down?"

"Then I shall simply come up, toss you over my shoulder, and haul you down. I'm sure the servants will find it a rousing show."

"You wouldn't!"

"Wouldn't I?"

But she knew he would. And didn't know why she suddenly felt pleased.

The sleigh ride passed swiftly. Nicholas pointed out the boundaries of his property, and Glory found herself enjoying the scenery, stark with the hoar of winter though it was. Each tree and hedge was covered with a dusting of fresh snow, and a tiny white rabbit scurried across their path and into its burrow. Glory pointed excitedly, and Nicholas grinned at her obvious pleasure.

Inhaling the frosty morning air, she caught a whiff of hickory smoke from a neighboring chimney. The fresh air felt exhilarating after the long days of confinement in her room.

She wondered at Nicholas's sudden change of attitude, then grudgingly admitted she preferred him this way. He seemed more himself—arrogant, domineering, and downright infuriating. Still, there was something about him. . . . For the first time in weeks, she found herself thinking of Nicholas instead of the child she no longer carried.

As the light jingle of harness combined with the soft tinkle of sleigh bells to lull her, she leaned back against the carriage seat, feeling content. She hardly noticed when Nicholas halted the sleigh in front of the marble mansion. Handing the reins to a waiting groom, he jumped to the ground and rounded the sleigh to help her. A tiny shiver rushed up her spine as he leaned close. He smelled of musk and the leather reins he'd held.

"Now, that wasn't so bad," he teased. Stirring a misty pattern in the cold morning air, his breath felt warm against her cheek. When his hands circled her waist to lift her down, her heart did a queer little twist and hammered uncomfortably against her ribs.

They supped with Brad that night, and Glory found she enjoyed his charming company. He was handsome and intelligent, though a bit frail, it seemed to Glory.

"How was your ride?" Brad asked, hazel eyes light.

"Chilly," she told him, adding, "but I suppose I enjoyed myself."

"Splendid," Brad said. "There's something about the winter air that revives one's lagging spirits."

"I couldn't agree more," Nicholas put in.

Glory noticed he watched her all evening, no longer with that strained, worried look, but with a bit of the old hunger. She refused to admit she felt it, too.

They went into Tarrytown the following day. Glory already felt stronger, healthier somehow. Nicholas surprised her by ordering an entire wardrobe of dresses, gowns, shoes, jackets, and mantles, in serge, flannel, camel's hair, and merino for day; silk, crepe, velvet, and satin for evening, all in rich colors. True to his word, Nicholas refused to let her choose even one gown of dull hue.

By the time they arrived back at the hall, Glory was exhausted, yet she felt an exhilaration she hadn't known in weeks. That night after supper, Nicholas escorted her upstairs to her room. The hallway was empty, lit by flickering candles set in brass sconces. She could feel his hand at her waist, his breath a whisper against her hair.

"Thank you for the clothes," she said softly. "I'm sure they're going to be lovely."

"No matter how lovely they are, they won't do you justice."

Feeling a rush of warmth to her cheeks, she watched him for a moment. With the worry lines gone from his face, he looked roguishly handsome, even a little younger.

Without thinking she lifted her hand to his cheek. Abruptly she pulled away. ''I'd better go in.'' She turned to take her leave.

''Not yet.''

Before she could protest, he pulled her into his arms and captured her lips. Though the contact was brief, Glory's knees went weak. She hoped Nicholas hadn't noticed, but his satisfied smile said he had.

The following morning Nicholas roused Glory early, insisting she ride with him. Dressed in fawn-colored breeches, shiny black Wellingtons, a snowy white shirt, and a cashmere coat, he met her at the foot of the stairs. Glory wore a new sapphire velvet riding gown that Nicholas had paid extra to have finished in a rush. She had to admit it felt good to be dressed in beautiful clothes again. She knew her father would have approved. Then she thought of the tiny infant she also mourned and fought an urge to return to dreary black.

''I have a surprise for you,'' Nicholas told her, taking her arm and guiding her from the room. Isaac, the ancient black butler who had come to the estate from the city, stood in the foyer, holding Nicholas's warm woolen overcoat. He helped Nicholas slip it on. Glory found the old ex-slave a quiet reminder of home, his warm smile and cheerful manner always brightening her day.

Wearing the fur-lined mantle over her habit, Glory clung to Nicholas's arm. They moved through the vaulted foyer and out beneath the portico. The sun shone brightly through the leafless trees, but its heat was lost in the brisk winter air. They headed straight for the stables where several soft whinnies sent a thrill of pleasure up Glory's spine. How long had it been since she'd ridden along the land beside her father's rice fields? How long since she'd felt the excitement riding always stirred?

Nicholas led her to the pasture beside the massive stone barn where a lovely chestnut mare and a tiny foal raced across the snowy fields.

"That's Siren's Song," he told her proudly. The foal is Windsong. They're yours."

"Mine?"

"We can race the colt or you can keep him for breeding stock, whichever you choose."

"Oh, Nicholas. They're beautiful. I don't know what to say."

"How about starting with thank you?"

"Thank you," she whispered.

"Of course a kiss would be better."

Glory hesitated only a moment. She rose on tiptoe to kiss his cheek, but Nicholas turned his face at the last instant, and her lips closed over his. His hard arms pulled her against him, and Glory's heart began to race. She knew it was unseemly to kiss a man—even one's husband—out in the open in the middle of the day, but couldn't persuade herself to end the embrace.

Nicholas coaxed her mouth open with his tongue, then teased the inside, sending shivers along her spine. Glory heard a tiny mewling sound and realized the sound was coming from her. Shaken and more than a little embarrassed, she pulled away. Bright color stained her cheeks.

"Come on," Nicholas said, inordinately pleased with himself, it seemed to Glory. "The groom has our horses saddled and waiting."

They rode along the country lanes, Glory loving the feel of the strong animal beneath her. She nudged the big sorrel gelding faster, and soon they were cantering across the fields. A low box hedge loomed in their path. Before Nicholas could stop her, Glory had taken the hedge and reined up on the other side. He took the hedge with ease, but rode up beside her scowling, furious she had disobeyed his unspoken order to take it slowly this first day.

Frowning, he started to speak, then caught her wide, impish grin—and a look of pure pleasure warmed his light gray eyes.

"Will you never behave?"

"I hope not."

He bent down and captured her lips in a brief warm kiss. "So do I."

They cantered easily back to the house, where Nicholas lifted Glory from her sidesaddle. The brisk air had flushed her cheeks even more than his kiss, and Glory felt more alive than she had in weeks.

That night after supper, Nicholas again walked her to her room. He turned her into his arms before they even reached the doorway. Tonight his gentle kiss turned demanding. He cradled her cheeks between his palms and molded his mouth to hers. When he released his hold, Glory's arms slipped around his neck. She clung to him, the feelings he stirred so powerful her knees felt weak. With practiced ease, he kissed and nibbled and tasted until Glory's mouth parted of its own accord. His breath tasted of brandy and the cherries they'd eaten for dessert.

When he'd kissed her thoroughly, he pulled away and, just for a moment, Glory felt bereft at his leaving.

"Do you have any idea how much I need you?" he whispered, his voice husky.

She only shook her head.

"I want you back in my bed," he said, then turned and walked down the stairs.

Glory entered her room as if she were sleepwalking. Betsy appeared and helped her undress; then she slipped beneath the sheets of her huge four-poster bed. *I'm falling in love with him again,* she thought as she lay staring up at the velvet canopy. She shuddered and felt tears welling. Loving Nicholas Blackwell could only mean more heartbreak. She remembered their time on the strand, how he had gained her trust and finally her love. Then he'd abandoned her, purposely ruined her reputation without a second thought. He'd come to Boston and threatened to do it again—threatened even to destroy his child. She knew exactly how ruthless Nicholas could be.

She tossed and turned fitfully, her body feeling tense and highly strung. Though she fought against it, her mind conjured memories of Nicholas's kiss, the warmth of his lips, the heady male scent of him. Sooner or later he would claim his husbandly rights. Her body yearned for his touch even now. Once he possessed her, his power would be even greater than it already was.

Suddenly restless, Glory shoved back the covers and moved to the window. The snow had melted away, and a full moon lit the leafless trees whose jagged limbs broke the landscape into puzzlelike pieces.

Just like my life, she thought. If only she could fit the pieces together, maybe she could get a clearer picture of what she should do.

Chapter Nineteen

The next morning Nicholas left for the city, stopping by her room only long enough to explain.

"I've stayed away from my business too long already," he had said. "I've got to make certain things are running smoothly. I'll come back as soon as I can." He smiled at her warmly as she sat propped up in bed, the breakfast of warm cinnamon rolls and coffee he'd brought her resting in her lap. "Try to stay out of trouble."

She had smiled at his words, but now, as she readied herself for the day ahead, she wondered why he hadn't told her sooner that he was leaving. Did he have some illicit plans he didn't want her to know about? Was another woman involved? She knew his lusty appetites. It had been months since he'd been with a woman—at least as far as she knew. The first prickle of jealousy, and a stab of alarm, snaked down her spine.

Nicholas returned three days later. Three long, lonely days for Glory. She'd been surprised at how much she missed him. And terrified by what she imagined he'd been doing.

"I'll be gone off and on all month," he told her when he returned. They were seated at the dining table, supping on roast venison, new potatoes, and steaming hot fresh bread. "I've found someone to take over some of the management responsibilities. Max Faulkner. He's a competent man. As soon as we get things organized, I'll be able to oversee the business from here at the hall. We'll have time to breed those racehorses we talked about." He smiled down at her, eyes flicking for a moment to the lush curve of her breasts above her green velvet gown. "With mares like your Siren's Song and a few good stallions, we should have a fine string in no time."

Glory smiled in return, wanting desperately to believe him and happy just to have him home again.

They rode at every opportunity, bringing fresh color to Glory's cheeks and a closeness to their relationship that hadn't existed before. Glory wasn't sure whether to be glad or wary. All she knew was that every day she spent with Nicholas filled her with equal parts of happiness and despair.

Each night he walked her to her room. Each night he claimed a kiss more demanding than the one before. When his hands strayed down the bodice of her gown, his long fingers slipping beneath the fabric to stroke her nipple, Glory moaned and pulled away.

"You said you wouldn't force me before I was ready."

One corner of his mouth tilted in a roguish smile. "Are you certain you're not?"

Glory swallowed hard. Her body was most certainly ready. It was her mind that was not. "I . . . I . . . Yes. I mean, no. I most certainly am not."

He ran a finger along the line of her cheek. "I won't break my promise." He flashed another smile. "But like most women, you may not always know your own mind. I won't be timid in making the decision for you when the time is right."

"But . . ."

"Good night, madam."

That had been two days ago. He'd left again for New York, cautioning her he'd be gone five days. The cold weather had ended and an early spring settled over the land. Now, as Glory strolled through the quiet formal gardens between rows of dormant jonquils, she absently touched the tightly closed buds that awaited still warmer weather. During this, the longest of Nicholas's absences, Glory had begun to realize just how deeply she had come to care for him. Her days seemed endless without him. At night she remembered his kisses, longed for more, then worried that he spent his time away from her in the arms of another woman.

She moved among the green-leafed plants, the white buds brushing against her yellow cashmere dress, her thoughts in turmoil.

"Narcissus jonquilla," came a familiar deep voice laced with a gentle southern drawl. "Beautiful when they're in bloom, don't you agree?"

Glory spun to face him. "Nathan!" she cried, throwing herself into his arms. As he held her against him, she could feel his pleasure at seeing her in the flutter of his heart. Then he set her away, inspecting her from head to foot.

"Well, it seems you're none the worse for wear."

"And you, little brother, it seems you grow taller every time I see you." She hugged him again, noticing how handsome he looked in his dark brown split-tailed coat. For the first time she noticed he wasn't alone.

"These are friends of mine, Glory. Valentine and his mother, Hilly." A tall, thin Negro woman stood at the side of the garden, a small boy next to her, his face buried in her calico skirts.

Glory moved to greet them.

"Hullo, missus," the woman said in a thick black accent Glory hadn't heard in months.

"Hello, Hilly. And this must be Valentine." She knelt beside him, and the boy looked up at her shyly, brown eyes round and a little uncertain. His clothes were patched and worn, but spotless. "I'm Glory, Valentine. I'm happy to meet you." He graced her with a white-toothed smile, then returned to the folds of his mother's skirt.

"They need your help, Glory," Nathan told her. "In your letters, you mentioned your work in Boston. That's where these two are headed."

"Come inside," she said. "Out of the cold."

Once they were seated in the drawing room, sipping hot cocoa, she pressed Nathan about his involvement with the runaways—which obviously they were.

"Actually, it wasn't until I read your letters from Boston that I decided to take action. Of course I'd read about the Underground Railroad in the newspapers. It just seemed like such a risk. After I read your letters, I decided the risk would be worth it." He glanced at the two Negroes sitting on the settee before the fire. "I can already tell you it has been."

"What can I do to help?" Glory asked.

"Where's your husband?" Nathan countered. "I think this is something you should discuss with him."

Glory was surprised by his words. "After the way he treated you, I shouldn't think you'd give a damn what Nicholas Blackwell thought."

Nathan grinned at her surge of temper. "At first I did feel that way. But after you two were married, Nicholas came to the school to see me. He explained what had happened between the two of you. He asked my forgiveness and understanding, and welcomed me as one of the family. I told him I respected him and wished you both great happiness. I assumed he would have told you."

"No. No, he didn't." She glanced at the two by the fire, pleased with Nicholas for having the courage to apologize to Nathan, and wondering why he hadn't told her. But then, that was so like him. It was almost as though he tried to hide the gentle, caring side of his nature. "At any rate, he's gone into the city. He won't be back for three days. Valentine and Hilly can stay here until he arrives."

"That should give them time to rest. A wagon will come by on Wednesday morning to carry them on to the next stop." He looked at her hard. "Promise me you'll tell Nicholas, even if they've already gone."

"I won't promise, Nathan. This work is important to me. I've been looking for a way to help. I'd even thought of writing to George McMillan. I just didn't want him to misinterpret my reasons. Now you've solved my problem. When the time is right, I'll tell Nicholas. Not before. If it looks as though he'll oppose my work, I shan't tell him at all. I think Isaac will help me. Between the two of us, we can manage.''

''I think you should tell him as soon as he arrives. But I'll let you handle it your way.'' He grinned again. ''I always have, haven't I?''

''Thank you, Nathan.'' She turned to Hilly and Valentine. ''Come along, you two. Let's get you settled in.'' She led them to a cozy room off the kitchen. ''This should do the trick.''

They eyed the fluffy quilt, the pitcher on the walnut bureau, and the wide, comfortable-looking bed. ''Thank you, missus,'' Hilly said with an appreciative smile.

''Thank you, missus,'' repeated Valentine, lisping through a missing front tooth.

''You're both very welcome. I'll be back in a while with your supper.'' She closed the door and followed Nathan's tall frame back through the kitchen to the drawing room.

''How long can you stay?'' she asked him.

''I'm afraid I have to return right away. Exams, day after tomorrow.''

''Then let's not waste time. I want you to fill me in on everything you've been doing.''

''How about you? What's it feel like to be a married lady?''

She wished he hadn't asked. How could she tell him she felt far from married. She slept alone and worried constantly that her husband didn't. She glanced away. ''I'm doing just fine. Now tell me about school.''

With that he launched into a thirty-minute monologue on the horticultural experiments he was working on.

The night before Nicholas was due home, Glory lay on her bed beneath its heavy velvet canopy. She had seen the runaways to safety, then returned to her big empty house. Being near the little boy had dredged up painful memories of the child she'd lost. But more than that, Hilly had told Glory about losing her husband, how much she had loved him, how lonely she was without him.

As she stared up at the canopy, Glory tried to imagine what life would be like without Nicholas, forcing herself to remember that day in the harbor when he had abandoned her, her feelings of despair. Would a wedding ring stop him from leaving her again? She'd lost his son; she had no real hold on him now.

All day long she'd walked in the gardens trying to decide what to do. The Hudson flowed past clusters of weeping willows that were just beginning to green while ducks bobbed and dived below the surface in search of food. Maybe she should return to Summerfield Manor, she thought. Her mother's letters had softened over the past few months. It seemed her mother had missed her after all. Or maybe she should return to Boston. Should she ask Nicholas for an annulment again? Maybe this time he would agree. Or should she follow her heart and stay with him, be his wife, bear his children? That would take the greatest courage of all.

Every day she spent with Nicholas wound her deeper into his spell. She'd survived his mistreatment once, even survived the death of their child. But she could not survive his loss again.

By late afternoon Glory had worked herself into a state of nerves that left her moody and on edge. When Nicholas returned from the city that evening, she pleaded a headache and refused to join him for supper. Before he retired, he came to her room to check on her, but she wouldn't face him. She stood at the window in her simple cotton nightdress, determined not to let him know what she was thinking, and feeling totally bereft.

"Are you ill, love?" He crossed the room in long strides to settle a gentle hand at her waist.

"It's just a headache," she said softly, keeping her back carefully turned to him.

"You're sure it's nothing serious?"

A hard lump closed her throat. Just the sound of his deep voice caused her heart to pound. She felt drawn to him, desired him, and loved him, just as she had on the strand. "I'm all right . . . really," she said, her voice soft and strained. "I'll be fine by tomorrow."

He turned her to face him, and try as she might to prevent it, a single tear slid down her cheek.

"Tell me," he said, whisking the tear away with a long brown finger. "Tell me what's wrong."

"I can't. Please, Nicholas, just go away and leave me alone."

"I'm your husband, Glory. You can tell me anything."

She only shook her head. "I'm sorry. I'm making a fool of myself. Please, just go away. I'll be fine in the morning."

"Dammit, Glory. Tell me what's wrong!"

Glory rounded on him, his anger bringing a surge of her own. "I'll tell you what's wrong. Everything! Everything's wrong. I don't want to be here. I don't want to be with you. I want to go home!"

"But why?"

Tears washed her cheeks, but she didn't answer.

"You seemed happy," he said. "I thought . . . If I've done something to upset you . . . tell me."

Still she didn't respond.

"Tell me, dammit! Tell me why you want to leave."

She lifted her chin, her anguish turning to fury. "Because I don't trust you. I never know when you'll walk out that door and never come back." She swallowed past the tears in her throat. "But more than anything else, *I don't want to love you.*"

Nicholas pulled her into his arms. He held her close to him, circling her protectively while she sobbed against his chest. He smoothed the pale strands of her hair with his hand, his voice low and heavy with conviction.

"Don't you understand?" he said. "I love you more than life. For months after you left I grieved, wishing you were with me, believing you were in love with someone else. Do you know what that did to me? Do you honestly believe I could go through that again?"

She turned her face to look up at him. "In love with someone else? I don't understand. Who?"

"We've talked so little, Glory. I can't believe you didn't know."

"Know what?"

"I thought Nathan was your . . . I didn't know he was your brother."

Glory pulled away. "You thought Nathan was . . . ? What?"

"I thought you were in love with him. When I came to Boston, I tried to explain."

"No, Nicholas. You didn't." She looked at him hard. "How could you have believed that of me? That I would make love to you and be in love with someone else?"

"I don't know." He couldn't meet her eyes. "I was a fool."

"Well, I don't know, either. Can't you see? I don't understand you, Nicholas. And until I do, I can't believe you or trust you. Most of all, I can't allow myself to love you."

"Dammit, Glory. I don't know what else to do."

"Maybe it would be best if I just went away."

"No."

"In time things might work out."

"Things are never going to work out between us until you're back where you belong."

She tilted her chin in defiance. "And just where might that be?"

"In my bed. It's time I showed you my love in the only way I know how." He scooped her up into his arms, strode across the floor, and lowered her onto the huge four-poster that dominated the room.

Glory began to struggle as he lay down beside her. "Please, Nicholas. You'll only make things worse."

"I told you once before that I would decide when the time was right. I want to love you, Glory. Maybe my body can make you believe what my words alone cannot."

With that he cupped her chin and kissed her, stilling any further protests. With her hands trapped against his chest, she could feel the rapid beating of his heart. Slanted against her mouth, his lips felt firm and warm, and Glory stifled a moan. She had to stop him. If she didn't stop him now, she would be lost.

"Please, Nicholas," she whispered, pulling away. Again he silenced her with his mouth, kissing her relentlessly. He smelled of musk and tasted of brandy. Plundering her mouth with his tongue, he sampled the velvet corridors within and demanded she respond.

Glory could hardly breathe. Her struggles turned feeble, useless, as if she sensed winning the battle would be losing somehow. In truth, she knew she wanted him as much as he wanted her. Gently, he held her, pulling her nightdress over her head, leaving her bare and trembling beneath his gaze.

"So beautiful," he whispered against her ear. "Just as I've remembered every night these long months past."

"Nicholas," she breathed, wishing she could stop the words, "I've missed you so."

He released her hands and they slipped around his neck. She laced them through his curly black hair. He stroked her upturned breasts, lifting and caressing each one, touching them almost reverently. When he lowered his mouth to her nipple, Glory moaned and arched her back, wanting more and wishing she didn't. He kissed her mouth, her nose, her eyes, trailed tiny kisses along her shoulder.

With shaky fingers, she unbuttoned his shirt and slipped her hands inside to touch his warm skin. The feel of his stiff chest hair sent a shiver of anticipation down her spine and a surge of heat to her core. She moved her fingers to the buttons of his breeches, but he stopped her.

"Not yet," he whispered. While one hand cupped her breast, the other moved downward to gently part her legs. He lowered his body until he nestled between her thighs. His mouth burned a path of kisses from her navel along the smooth flat skin beneath until he reached the source of her passion within its protective nest of pale blond hair. As his lips surrounded her, Glory felt a flash of heat that drove her to madness. She moaned and writhed against him, calling his name and begging for more. With his mouth and his fingers, he brought her pleasure unlike any she'd known. Wave after wave of passion, withheld these long, lonely months, washed over her. Until at last she lay spent and a little embarrassed at her bold response.

She hardly noticed when he left her, only noticed his return as his heavy weight pressed down the thick feather mattress. When she turned to look at him, she saw he'd removed his clothes, and the sight of his lean hard body, his swollen manhood, filled her with a fresh jolt of desire. She watched him for a moment, drinking in the sight of his swarthy features, the hard, powerful body so long denied her. Then she cradled his face between her palms, feeling the angular cheekbones, and brought his lips to hers. Though the kiss began gently, she could feel the power he withheld, the passion he'd denied himself in order to bring her pleasure.

As her hands moved down the muscular planes of his body, the kiss turned demanding, and she heard him groan. Her fingers traveled to the smooth curves of his buttocks; taut muscles bunched beneath her hands. Moving on top of her, he guided his hardened shaft to the entrance of her womanhood.

"Please," she whispered, "I want you so." In answer, he claimed her mouth, forcing his tongue inside at the same moment his hardness eased into her.

White heat flooded her loins. She moaned and writhed against him, calling his name, begging for more. And Nicholas gave her what she wanted. Their skin glistening with perspiration, they rode the crest of their passion. Again and again Nicholas drove into her, filling her, pounding against her, and each time Glory felt sure her pleasure could be no greater. Just when she was certain she could stand the torture no more, a piercing sweetness washed over her, tiny pinpricks of ecstasy that carried her to release. Nicholas followed in her wake as shudders of pleasure washed over him.

They lay quiet for a time, lost in their own thoughts. Nicholas cradled Glory against him. Nicholas, she ached to tell him, I'm so afraid. Please love me as you say. I promise you won't be sorry. But she said nothing.

They made love again. And yet again. Each determined to breach the lonely months. Then she turned her head into the curve of his shoulder and pretended to sleep. By returning her husband's passion, she had made her decision. She was now his wife in every way. Whatever happened, she had chosen the path she would walk. But thoughts of the happiness they'd shared on the strand—and the terrible consequences that followed—kept her from falling asleep. She wondered if Nicholas rested as fitfully as she.

Chapter Twenty

Glory awoke to find she'd slept after all. She blinked against the sunlight streaming through an open window, then remembered the events of the evening. With a start, she turned to find Nicholas beside her propped up on an elbow, sheet bunched at his waist, gray eyes open and watching her. He smoothed a lock of sleep-tangled hair from her face with his hand but said nothing, as if he felt a little uncertain.

"Still want to leave?" he finally said. There was a forced lightness in his voice she was sure he didn't feel. His expression seemed remote, guarded, as if he feared her answer but still had to ask.

"No."

"Regrets?"

She shook her head. The tension in his face drained away, but her answer was only half true. For she truly regretted the nagging doubt, the constant insecurity she felt in loving Nicholas. She'd always been so confident, so sure of herself. Now she faced every day with an uncertainty that never gave her a moment's peace.

"I'm your wife," she told him, with an attempted smile, "for as long as you want me."

He pressed her into the mattress, rolling his hard body on top of her in a single easy motion. "Forever isn't long enough." He lowered his head and kissed her. It was a demanding kiss, a telling kiss, and an apology for the past rolled into one.

If only she could believe it.

They made love again, sweetly at first, then fiercely, passionately, trying to compensate for the time they had spent apart. When they finished, Glory rested her cheek against his chest, listening to the even rhythm of his heartbeat, her pale hair spread across his torso like a gilded blanket.

"Nicholas, there's something I've been wanting to tell you." She shifted, then sat up to face him.

He wound a finger in an unruly lock of her hair. "Yes, love?"

"It's about the baby."

"Glory, we don't have to talk about this now. We can wait until you're ready."

"I don't think I'll ever be ready."

He drew her hand to his lips and kissed the palm, encouraging her with his touch, if not his words.

"I shouldn't have blamed you," she told him. "It wasn't your fault." She swallowed hard and glanced away, feeling a jolt of remembered pain.

"Glory, listen to me." Nicholas sat up on the bed beside her, tightening his hold on her suddenly cold hand.

"Please. Let me finish. I knew there were problems. The doctor told me the baby wasn't sitting quite right. He warned me to take every precaution. I didn't tell anyone, not even Aunt Flo. I wanted the baby so badly, I just couldn't admit the possibility that things might go wrong. I tried to be careful, but I guess I wasn't careful enough. It was my fault, Nicholas. My fault, not yours."

She didn't notice the tears until he pulled her into his arms. Then the wetness dripped from her lashes onto his chest, where it clung in tiny drops, then ran in rivulets till it soaked the satin sheets.

He let her cry for a time, then held her away.

"I want you to stop blaming yourself. We have no way of knowing what really happened. God works in strange ways. There'll be other children. We've already started working on a second baby.''

She smiled at him through her tears. ''We have, haven't we?''

''We certainly have.'' He rested his cheek against her forehead. ''And I intend diligently to pursue that end every chance I get.'' With that he turned her face with his hand and kissed her soundly, beginning to demonstrate the truth of his words. They made love slowly, then slept for a while. It was well past time for the noon meal when they made their way, arm in arm, down the wide mahogany staircase.

''I want your things moved into the master suite where they belong,'' Nicholas said.

Foot poised on the stair, she stopped, half glad for his words, half afraid. Each commitment only buried her deeper. Still, she'd made her decision—or rather as always, he'd made it for her. She was surprised to discover she *almost* felt good about it. A loud knock at the heavy wooden door interrupted her thoughts. Isaac answered just as they reached the foyer.

A woman Glory could only have described as handsome, elegantly gowned and coiffed, clutching the arm of a thin-faced, foppishly dressed gentleman years her senior, swept past a startled Isaac before he had a chance to deter her. Glory glanced at Nicholas, who scowled blackly, then at the woman, who eyed him with a bold stare and an ingratiating smile, then at the gentleman, who yawned and looked bored with the whole affair.

''Nicholas, darling,'' the woman crooned, her voice rich and throaty. Her low-cut ruched-silk traveling dress revealed a great deal of bosom. Her dark hair glistened in the sunlight from the still-open door while her clear skin looked soft and appealing. She was a few inches shorter than Glory, though a bit more full-figured.

''The most dreadful thing has happened,'' the woman continued. ''Our carriage broke down just a few miles from here. We had to catch a ride on a passing hay wagon, of all things. The driver says it'll take at least until tomorrow to fix the awful contraption. I told Arthur I was certain you wouldn't mind the intrusion. I just didn't know where else to turn.'' She spread the painted fan dangling from her wrist, fluttering it in front of her face. ''You don't, do you? Mind the intrusion, I mean?''

Nicholas took such a long time to answer that Glory was embarrassed.

''How could my wife and I possibly object to helping two old friends?'' he finally said. ''Isaac, show Mr. and Mrs Pedigru to the Red Room. I'm sure they'll find it comfortable.''

''Thank you, old boy,'' Mr. Pedigru put in. ''Don't know what could have happened to the carriage. One minute it was fine, the next . . .'' He shrugged his thin shoulders in a gesture of helplessness. Glory chanced a look at the woman and was sure she caught the hint of a satisfied smile.

''Nicholas,'' Mrs. Pedigru put in, ''what has happened to your manners? Introduce us to your lovely wife.''

Glory had been about to make the same request. Then she looked from the woman, richly gowned in rose silk skirts, to her own simple serge frock, thought of her un-coiffed hair, and wished she were someplace else.

''Pardon my thoughtlessness, Kristen,'' he said a bit sarcastically. ''May I present my wife, Glory? Glory, this is Arthur and Kristen Pedigru.''

''Charmed, madam.'' Arthur bowed gallantly, bringing her hand to his lips.

''I'm happy to meet you both,'' Glory told them.

''Isn't she charming, Nicholas?'' Kristen said. ''Why, she's not a bit what we expected.''

Glory bristled, wondering what the woman meant. Nicholas seemed equally displeased.

''Why haven't you brought her to the city? Surely she's tired of this dreary country existence by now.''

''I'm quite happy right here, Mrs. Pedigru,'' Glory assured her, then wondered for the hundredth time whether Nicholas had indeed purposely kept her away.

"Do call me Kristen. I'm certain we're going to be friends."

"All right, Kristen."

"Why don't you two follow Isaac?" Nicholas suggested. "I'm sure you'll both feel better after a rest. You can join us later. Supper's at eight. I'll tell Cook you'll be dining with us."

"That sounds fine," Arthur agreed. "We'll see you then."

Isaac instructed a servant to bring up their bags, then led the couple upstairs to their rooms.

"Who are they, Nicholas?" Glory asked, hoping the Pedigrus would give them some time alone. They were seated in the sunny morning room, though it was growing late in the day, Glory sipping tea, Nicholas a glass of wine while they lunched on cold meats, fruits, and cheeses.

"They're merely acquaintances. People I knew in the city."

"Nothing more?" Glory pressed.

Nicholas met her gaze steadily, as if making a decision. "Are you sure you want to know?"

She stiffened. "Yes."

"I could tell you they're just friends of the family. I could tell you any number of truths, and it would still be a lie. Kristen Pedigru is the woman whose clothes were on board *Black Witch*."

"Oh, God." Glory's hand crept to her throat where a tiny pulse began to throb.

"I told you before, she means nothing to me." He covered her other hand, suddenly cold, with his warmer one. "I haven't seen her in months. I didn't invite her here. I love you, not her. You've got to start trusting me."

Glory stared out the window across the manicured lawns toward the river. Several snowy geese honked and fed along the bank.

"I never professed to be a monk, Glory. I'm a man. I have needs and desires just like any other man. Kristen was willing—no, more than willing—to accommodate my needs.''

''She's beautiful,'' Glory said.

''Not nearly as lovely as you.''

''It's hard for me to think of you with her, doing the things . . .''

''You mean like last night?''

She couldn't answer.

''Glory, last night we made love. I've been to bed with other women, but I've never made love to any woman but you.''

She wanted to believe him, she ached to believe him. She would die if she lost him again. Still, she said nothing.

''You don't believe me.''

''I . . . I don't know.''

Nicholas felt his temper fire. He gripped the napkin in his lap and tried to sound calm, but his voice came out harsh, and colder than he intended. ''For months I've wanted you, loved you, tried to make things up to you. Tried to prove how much I care. But a man can only do so much. I swore I'd never chase after a woman the way my father did, never become so obsessed with loving someone my manhood would be threatened. I've come as close to that with you as I'll allow. I'm tired of trying to convince you of something you should be able to see with your heart.'' He threw his napkin down and shoved back his chair, the sound grating on the flagstone floor.

''Love me for what I am, Glory. Or don't love me at all. It's up to you.'' Without a backward glance, he stormed from the room.

Glory's heart twisted. She watched his tall, retreating figure, the rigid set to his shoulders. In a way he was right. He'd done everything in his power to prove his trust and love. Never once had he failed her—not since the strand. Still . . . If only she could be sure. And now there was Kristen Pedigru.

The rest of the day passed in a blur. Glory thought about going to Nicholas, speaking her heart. But what could she say? She could lie, say she believed every word he told her—the way she had before. But it would be just that—a lie. Instead, she dressed for supper in a sumptuous gown of ice-blue satin, the décolletage indecently low. She might not trust him, but she loved him. She wasn't about to lose him to the likes of Kristen Pedigru! When it came to female competition, Glory had never been a fool. Kristen Pedigru had met a demure country wife this afternoon. Tonight she would meet the belle of Summerfield Manor.

When Glory descended the stairs, Nicholas stood in the foyer. As she had hoped, Arthur and Kristen waited beside him. One look at the dark-featured brunette's hostile face told Glory she'd already won round one.

Nicholas sucked in a breath when he saw her, eyes at first dark as he scowled at the low-cut gown, then turning light with amusement.

"Armed for battle, I see." He whispered the words for her ears alone.

"Some things are worth fighting for." She noticed his look softened even more.

"I see Nicholas hasn't lost his fine eye for clothing," Kristen said. Arthur seemed not to notice her words, and again Nicholas scowled. Glory took his arm, determined to act nonplussed at the intimate exchange.

"I say, my dear," Arthur said, "you look marvelous. Captain Blackwell certainly has a knack for attracting beautiful women."

"I assure you, Arthur," Nicholas said dryly, "my wife is the only beautiful woman I'm interested in attracting." His eyes added a bitter *Even if she doesn't believe me*.

"Such a pity," Kristen said with a sigh. "So many will be disappointed."

Nicholas's gray eyes turned almost black.

An iron band squeezed around Glory's heart as the brunette smiled up at him, and Glory knew a jealousy unlike anything she had prepared for.

They dined on squab and fresh-caught halibut, the sauces rich and creamy, the vegetables crisp, the dessert light. It all tasted like sawdust to Glory. Nicholas was polite and attentive to her, and polite but distant to Kristen. Determined to remain in control, Glory matched quip for quip with the dark-haired woman who fawned for Nicholas's attention.

"Such a lovely gown," she told Kristen, referring to the woman's gold satin brocade. "It seems Nicholas isn't the only one with a good eye—or did you buy this one yourself?"

Kristen tilted her lovely chin. "Madame LaSerre in Paris. Arthur insists I have only the best."

"I'm sure he does," Glory agreed, "at least in those pleasures he's aware of."

Nicholas frowned at Glory, but one corner of his mouth curved and she wondered at his thoughts.

"I've decided to take your advice, Kristen," Nicholas announced toward the end of the meal. "Glory and I are going to spend some time in the city. The Whitmores are giving a ball. I think it would be the perfect place to introduce my new bride."

Glory took a sip of her wine to cover her surprise and still her suddenly trembling fingers.

Kristen seemed surprised as well. "That should certainly make for some amusing conversation."

Remembering the terrible weeks following her rescue from the strand, the way she'd been ostracized and publicly ridiculed, Glory suddenly felt sick. She wondered if Kristen Pedigru knew about "the captain's tart." Her knowing smile said she did. It was all Glory could do to keep from running from the table.

"We'll be certain to look you up," Glory said instead. "Unless of course you'll be too busy." She glanced at Arthur, who looked up from his meringue.

"Nonsense," Arthur said. "My little pet has plenty of time. I'm just sorry I'm gone so much."

"Oh, that is a pity," Glory said. "What on earth do you do with yourself while he's away?"

Kristen smiled tightly. She glanced at Nicholas, whose lips narrowed in warning. "Frankly, I *have* been a little lonely lately." She sighed and batted her long black lashes at Nicholas. "I think I need to see more of old friends."

Glory could have killed her. She took a sip of her wine to calm her temper. They finished the meal in silence, and Glory excused herself with a headache.

"I think we'd both better go," Nicholas said, keeping a firm grip on her arm. It was all she could do to offer polite good-evenings with a smile on her face.

They moved up the stairs together, Nicholas still gripping her arm, Kristen and Arthur close behind. When she tried to stop in front of her room, Nicholas tugged her firmly toward his own room instead.

"Not a chance," he whispered beneath his breath. "I want them to be damned sure you're sleeping with me."

She started to protest, but he covered her mouth with a kiss, pinning her against the wall until Kristen and Arthur rounded the corner and entered the opposite wing. He released her so abruptly she almost lost her balance. Nicholas had to steady her to keep her upright. Temper high, gray eyes dark, he guided her into his room.

"I thought you understood. From now on, you're sleeping in here."

"But what about my things?"

"I didn't have them moved today because I didn't want the Pedigrus to know we'd been sleeping apart. After they leave, we'll move your things."

"Surely you don't expect me to sleep with you when your . . . your paramour is sleeping down the hall!"

"And surely you know me well enough to know that's exactly what I expect. Kristen Pedigru is no longer my paramour, but you, my sweet, are my wife."

"Well, I won't do it, that's all. I'll sleep on the sofa." With that she flounced across the room and, gown and all, stretched out on the plush velvet couch.

"You, madam," came the deep rumble she knew so well, "have a very short memory." He strode across the room, heels ringing against the polished wood floor, scooped her into his arms, and unceremoniously tossed her on the bed.

"Since I bought that gown," he said, "I can do with it as I wish. Right now I wish to see it hanging in the wardrobe. But as you well know, I'll be just as happy to shred it into a pile at my feet.''

Glowering down at her as he shrugged off his coat, he shed his gray woolen waistcoat and wide white stock, then unbuttoned and removed his shirt. ''I'm sick and tired of pleading with you, Glory. From now on you'll do as I say.''

Bare-chested, he towered in front of her, eyes storm gray. He looked sinister and furious—and devilishly handsome. And Glory had never wanted him more. Against her will, she raised her arms to him, encouraging his touch, the feel of his arms around her. When he bent over her, she slipped her fingers through his hair and pulled his mouth down to hers. Nicholas groaned and kissed her with all the passion she could have asked.

When he broke away and began hurriedly to unfasten the buttons at the back of her gown, she watched him over her shoulder. ''Why is it,'' she whispered, ''I cannot deny you?''

''Why is it that you, madam, can make me forget my anger and think only of making love to you?''

She smiled, pleased at his words. He helped her remove her garments, then finished undressing himself. The bed creaked beneath his weight as he settled beside her.

''You are the most infuriating, most desirable woman I've ever known.''

His lips smothered her retort, which settled into a soft, contented sigh. In seconds the sounds became those of passion.

When they had finished, Glory nestled in the curve of Nicholas's arm, the heat of her body cooled by a fine sheen of perspiration. She could feel his even breathing, but sensed he wasn't asleep.

The heavy draperies shadowed his face in darkness. ''Tell me you love me,'' he whispered, his voice soft and low.

Glory felt a tightening in her chest, the sudden pulsing of her heart. When she didn't answer, the muscles of his arm tightened ever so slightly.

"Give me a little more time," she whispered at last.

He made no response. It was a long time before the muscles in his arm relaxed.

In the morning Glory awoke to find Nicholas gone. The sun shone high in the sky, a bright yellow orb that promised a brilliant March day. Glory hurried with her ablutions; Betsy brought a pale yellow cashmere day dress and helped Glory coif her hair into ringlets below each ear. Wandering through the house, she encountered Arthur in the breakfast room, but saw no sign of Nicholas or Kristen.

Next she tried the stable. He wasn't in any of the stalls or out at the paddock, but one of the grooms said he'd seen Nicholas just a few minutes earlier. Glory wandered back through the barn, enjoying the pungent odor of the animals mixed with the sweet smell of hay. Deciding to check the tack room, she pulled open the narrow door just in time to see Kristen Pedigru wrapped in her husband's strong arms. Cursing beneath his breath, Nicholas broke away the instant he saw Glory.

Kristen spun to face her, a guilty flush staining her pretty round cheeks. "It isn't as it seems, I assure you. I simply stumbled. Nicholas was kind enough to catch me as I fell." The smell of her lavender-scented perfume wafted across the tiny room.

"How convenient," Glory said, fingers clutching the folds of her cashmere skirt.

"If you'll excuse me, I have some last-minute packing." Kristen brushed past Glory, who watched her retreating figure all the way to the house.

Nicholas's voice, bitter and low, spun her around. "I'm sure you're determined to believe the worst," he said. "The truth is she came up behind me and I thought it was you. There was nothing more to it than that. I won't spend the rest of my life defending myself for things that didn't happen." His eyes, cool and remote, held hers for a moment in a bit of a challenge; then he straightened. "Now I suggest we return to the house and bid our guests good-bye. Tomorrow we leave for the city." He stalked past her, his mouth a narrow hard line.

Glory watched his tall frame until he'd disappeared from sight. For minutes she didn't move. Then she smiled. She couldn't explain how it had happened, couldn't begin to understand why, but for the first time since they'd left the strand, Glory knew without a measure of doubt Nicholas was telling the truth.

She saw little of him the rest of the day. They bade the Pedigrus farewell, Nicholas cool and reserved, Glory wearing a pasted-on smile; then Nicholas returned to the stables, his mood dark and brooding. Glory left him alone. He joined her for supper, but said little, retiring to his study as soon as they were through with the meal.

Beginning to feel at home there, now that her possessions had been moved, Glory waited for him in the huge master suite with its dark wood paneling and heavy burgundy draperies. She liked the feel of the room, liked the way the fire crackled in the marble-manteled fireplace, the way the velvet curtains could be lowered to enclose the huge tester bed.

The only thing missing from the room was Nicholas.

As the hour grew late, she almost weakened, fighting the urge to go to him. Instead, she dressed carefully in a snowy white French lace negligee, propped herself up against thick down pillows, and tried to concentrate on her book. Heavy footsteps in the hall alerted her to his approach. Setting the book aside, she lowered the wick of the lamp.

Nicholas opened the door without glancing toward the bed. Turning his back to her, he slowly undressed and put away his garments, taking longer than usual, it seemed to Glory. Enjoying the play of firelight against muscle as he moved around the room, Glory watched him from beneath her lashes. At last he turned and walked in her direction, stopping the instant he reached the foot of the bed. For a moment he didn't move, just stared at her in confusion. His gray eyes darkened as they traveled from her face to the fullness of her breasts, the dark circles of her nipples visible through the lacy swirls of the fabric.

Striding toward her with a quickness that had been missing in his step earlier, he drew her into his arms and pressed his cheek against hers.

"You believe me," he whispered, his breath warm against her ear.

"Yes."

As he pulled away to look at her, gray eyes sparkling, a smile softened his mouth. "I promise you won't be sorry." Capturing her lips, he joined her on the bed and spent the next few hours proving she'd made the right decision.

Morning passed in a flurry of activity as they readied themselves for the trip to New York. A driver and groom wearing red and black livery brought around the elegant black brougham, crafted in England especially for Nicholas. He helped Glory inside. She wore a rust and forest green traveling dress, and he looked handsome in his dark gray split-tail coat with its black velvet collar.

As the carriage rumbled and swayed along the tree-lined lanes, Glory wished she could keep her thoughts on the pleasures of the evening past instead of the uncertainties of the next few days. Nicholas expected her to mingle with the very people who had shunned her before. What would they say to her? How should she respond? Would they dare to spurn her as they had before?

"What are you thinking?" Nicholas asked after they'd traveled the first few miles in silence. "You look as though the weight of the world rests on your shoulders." He rode with one long leg propped casually against the empty seat across from them. Glory couldn't help but admire the play of muscle beneath his snug black breeches.

She smiled, distracted from her thoughts by his nearness. "Nothing, really. I'm just enjoying the scenery."

It was obvious he didn't believe her, though the countryside was beginning to turn green and the few scattered houses along the lane seemed cleaner and brighter than they had just a few weeks before. Several farmers worked in the fields, readying the soil for spring planting. An occasional mongrel rushed the carriage, nipping at the wheels and bringing a round of muffled obscenities from the driver.

"You're worried about the ball," Nicholas said a little later.

"I can't help it." She wet her lips, which had suddenly gone dry. "Must we go?"

"I want them to know once and for all that you're my wife. That I love you. That I will not allow another word against you."

Glory closed her eyes and leaned against the velvet seat, pressing herself into the tufts as if she wished she could disappear. "Couldn't we just make a brief appearance and then leave?" Her hand trembled as she remembered the dreadful weeks she'd spent after her return from the strand, the ridicule she'd suffered, the shame she had felt.

"No. I want no doubt left in anyone's mind. We'll still their wagging tongues once and for all."

Glory turned away, her eyes beginning to pool with tears. "I'm not sure I have the courage to face them," she said softly.

Nicholas lifted her chin, turning her to look at him. "I'll be right there beside you every moment."

A single tear slid down her cheek. Her voice came out in a whisper. "They hated me, Nicholas. They said terrible things. . . . They called me . . . 'the captain's tart.' "

Nicholas bristled, his expression turned stormy. "I could buy and sell the lot of them. If they say one word against you, I'll either ruin them or shoot them!" He clenched his fist and scowled as if he would take on the world. Shifting his position on the seat, he moved closer, draping his arm protectively around her shoulders.

Recalling his words and the protective note in his voice, Glory smiled up at him through her tears. Never had she loved him more.

Chapter Twenty-One

They reached Nicholas's town house late that evening, having taken their time and supped along the way. To Nicholas's surprise and delight, Bradford met them at the door.

"It's about time you two got here." Brad grinned broadly, hazel eyes dancing with mirth. "I've been waiting all evening."

"And just what are you doing home?" Nicholas asked with a lifted brow.

"School holiday. Mother told me you were coming."

"I'm sure she was ecstatic."

Bradford rolled his eyes. After giving Nicholas a brief hug, he shifted his attention to Glory. "You look as lovely as ever. No, that's not quite true. You look even more beautiful than you did when last we met. I take it you're feeling better."

"Much better, Brad. Thank you." Brad helped her from the carriage; footmen scurried to unload the baggage while Nicholas led Glory inside. Elizabeth St. John Blackwell stood just inside the door dressed in a simple but expensive gray velvet gown, dark hair parted in the middle and swept into fat curls beside her ears.

"Hello, Nicholas," she said, her tone stiffly formal. She was a short, broad-faced woman of little humor.

"Ah, Mother dear. You're looking well. City life must agree with you." The words were spoken with a touch of sarcasm Glory hadn't heard from Nicholas in some time.

"Agree with me? Why, I've never felt less healthy in all my life." She glanced down her wide nose at Glory. "And whom do we have here, as if I couldn't guess?"

"This is my wife, Glory. Glory, my stepmother, Elizabeth St. John Blackwell."

"Hello, Mrs. Blackwell." Glory extended a slender white-gloved hand.

Mrs. Blackwell eyed her from head to foot. "I can't say I'm pleased to meet you, young lady. Since the day my stepson uprooted me to this house I've suffered nothing but scandal because of you."

Glory let her hand drop heavily to her side.

"That's enough, Elizabeth," Nicholas warned. "None of that was Glory's fault. As to the house. You've been after me for years to move you into the city. I should think you'd be pleased."

"I'd forgotten how dismal the city was. How noisy and dirty. Not at all what I'd expected. But then, I'm sure you're not concerned about my likes and dislikes."

Nicholas clenched his fists.

"Why don't you and Glory get settled?" Brad put in smoothly. "Then come down and join us for a nightcap."

"That sounds like a fine idea, Brad." Taking Glory's elbow, Nicholas guided her upstairs to the suite of rooms at the end of the long lamplit hall. Two black-clad servants brought up their trunks a few moments later.

When they'd left, Glory turned to Nicholas. "Is she always like that?"

"Like what?" Nicholas scoffed. "Biting and rude, bitter and hateful? No, far from it. That was one of her warmer greetings. Sometimes she doesn't speak at all."

Glory's heart went out to him. "But why?" she asked, resting her hand against his cheek.

"She hates me for what my father did to her."

"What could he possibly have done to make her treat you so—"

"He was a failure. She expected so much—wealth, power, position. My father disappointed her."

"But Papa said Alexander Blackwell was one of the wealthiest shippers in the North."

"He was for a time. Then he married Elizabeth St. John and drank himself to death trying to forget the woman he loved."

"Your mother?"

"Yes."

"Oh, Nicholas, it must have been terrible for you."

"I was just a little boy when Father married her. I didn't understand why she loved Bradford and not me. She treated me badly or ignored me completely. Of course, Brad was just an infant. He was the sweetest baby you've ever seen. I used to sit by his cradle for hours just watching him. Elizabeth would shoo me out of the room whenever she caught me, but I'd always sneak back in. I got the birch more than a few times for disobeying her, but it was worth it." His mouth curved in a thin, bitter smile.

"Father felt guilty and began to drink even more," he said. "Things got steadily worse after that. I ran away to sea when I was twelve. You know the rest."

"After all she'd done, you still provide for her and Brad?"

"Brad is a gem. Elizabeth doted on him, but he never became selfish or spoiled. I swear he was born grown up. He deserves everything I've ever done for him. As for my stepmother, she's still my father's widow. I could hardly turn her out in the street."

"Some would have."

"That's the ironic part. She hates being under my protection—at my mercy, she says. She has to take money from me because she has no other way to live. It only makes her hate me more."

Glory slipped her arms around his neck, resting her cheek against his. "I had such a happy childhood," she told him. "Father was always there for me. Mother and I were never close, but I knew deep down that she loved me."

He kissed the top of her head. "I love you, too, Glory. Never forget that." He watched her for a moment, as if he wished she'd say those words to him. Glory swallowed hard, trying to find the courage but still unable to speak.

"I think we'd best descend to the lion's den," he said, breaking the mood, "or should I say the lioness?" He took her arm and opened the door. "It seems different this time. Easier with you here."

She felt a tightness around her heart, a yearning to protect him. She wished she had the courage to speak her feelings.

Arm in arm, they moved into the hallway and down the stairs.

Later that night, after they'd made love, Glory snuggled against him. She lay quietly for a while, but her conscience wouldn't let her sleep. When she rolled to her side, she saw Nicholas was also awake.

She propped herself up in bed. "Why aren't you sleeping?"

"Why aren't you?"

She wet her lips, deciding now was as good a time as any. "Because I've been keeping something from you that I shouldn't have."

Nicholas sat up beside her, the sheet falling to his waist leaving his chest bare. "You lied to me?" Moonlight streaming through a window betrayed the pulse that hammered at the base of his throat.

"No. I just didn't tell you. It's something I feel strongly about, Nicholas. So much so, I was afraid to mention it for fear you'd forbid me to continue. I didn't want to go against your wishes."

Nicholas watched her closely. "Go on."

"While you were gone to the city this last time, Nathan came to see me. He asked for my help. I want you to know he insisted that I seek your permission, but I convinced him I'd speak to you when the time was right."

"And you think that time is now?"

"I think that time was probably when you returned. But you . . ."

"I what?"

She felt a rush of warmth, adding color to her cheeks. Seeing the softening around his mouth, she knew Nicholas had noticed it, too. "You . . . *persuaded* me back to your bed."

He chuckled, the sound no more than the merest rumble. "Is *that* what I did?"

"In a manner of speaking, yes. And then there was Kristen Pedigru, and things got even more complicated."

"So you decided to deceive me."

"No! I wanted to tell you, but I'd waited so long . . ."

"So you're going to tell me now."

She took a deep breath. "This is the most important work I've ever done. I know you don't approve; I'm not asking for your approval, only your permission to continue."

"Now, this *is* a first. Gloria Summerfield Blackwell asking my permission."

"Nicholas, you are making this harder than ever."

"Good. Next time you'll tell me the truth in the first place." The words sounded harsh, but the indulgent light in his eyes said he wasn't as angry as he seemed. "Go on," he urged when she didn't continue.

Glory took a deep, steadying breath. "I belong to the Underground Railroad. I helped runaways when I lived in Boston, and the other day I sheltered two of them at Blackwell Hall." She didn't even move, just waited for his outburst. "Well, aren't you going to say something? I just told you I hid runaway slaves in your house."

"*Our* house," he corrected. "Besides, I already knew."

"You knew! How did you know?"

"Isaac told me. He thinks the world of you, Glory. But he'd never do anything behind my back."

"Why didn't you say something?"

"Because I wanted you to tell me yourself."

She twisted the folds of the sheet, unable to meet his gaze. "It's important to me, Nicholas."

"So you said."

She lifted her eyes to his. The smoky irises didn't waver, but they held no rebuke. "Does that mean you'll let me continue?"

"Could I stop you?"

"I . . . I don't know."

"At least you're honest. I told you before, Glory, I trade with the people of the South. I'd be a hypocrite if I worked against them behind their backs. On the other hand, you'd be guilty of a far greater sin if you didn't heed your conscience. I will not assist you, but I won't stop you either."

"Oh, Nicholas!" She rolled on top of him and covered his face with kisses, smiling and laughing at the same time. "Thank you, thank you, thank you." The hard muscles of his chest bunched as his hand cupped her bottom to settle her more firmly atop him. Her eyes widened as she felt his rigid manhood pressing stiffly between her thighs.

"I'm afraid I won't settle for just a thank-you," he said, his voice turning husky. "It's time you paid the piper." With that he kissed her until she felt breathless and hot all over. Then he slid inside. She could feel the heat, the thickness of his shaft as he filled her, gliding out and then in, stirring a surge of desire with each demanding stroke. Wanting more, Glory arched and bucked against him, but he gripped her flesh and held her steady, thrusting into her again and again. The heat he fired seared her loins. She moaned and writhed, but he didn't let go. Just drove hard and deep until she reached a climax and so did he.

When they'd spiraled down to a comfortable glow, she ran a playful finger along his chest. "If that is my punishment, maybe I should deceive you more often."

"Try it again," he warned, "and I won't be so gentle."

"Gentle!" They both laughed at the same time. Brushing her lips in a last brief kiss, he enfolded her in the circle of his arm.

They lay quiet for a while, then, "Tell me you love me."

She didn't answer. It was still too soon. "I can't, Nicholas," she whispered. "Not yet. Please try to understand."

"I'm trying, Glory. Harder than you know."

"Do you think you can entertain yourself for a few hours while I'm away?" he asked. "I need to check on a few things at my office."

Glory yawned and stretched catlike beneath the sheets. Nicholas was already up and dressed in navy blue split-tailed coat, gray cashmere waistcoat and trousers, white shirt, and stock. Damp black hair curled just above his collar.

"I'm sure I'll manage," she told him with a soft smile.

"I won't be back till late this afternoon. Just take it easy today. I want you well rested for the ball."

Glory's smile faded.

Nicholas leaned over the bed and brushed her lips with a kiss. "It won't be that bad. I promise." He strode to the door. "I'll see you later."

A few minutes after he'd gone, a petite woman in her early twenties knocked and entered the room. She was dressed in black except for a crisp white apron and a white linen cap.

"Mornin', miss."

Glory sighed. "Good morning."

"My name is Cheryl. I'll be your lady's maid whilst you're here."

"Thank you, Cheryl." Cheryl helped Glory with her ablutions, coiffed her hair, and helped her dress. She was extremely efficient, her demeanor almost stoic. Glory imagined the maid had learned the attitude from her mistress.

Glory spent the day reading and resting, as Nicholas had suggested. She walked in the gardens at the rear of the town house, soaking up the early sun, then returned to her room. The day passed far too quickly, though she'd spent the time alone. Nicholas arrived before dark but still had work to do, so she saw him only briefly. She ate a light repast, ordered a bath sent up, and had her gown laid out. She had chosen a beautiful white satin trimmed in blue brocade. The bodice, also of blue brocade, fit closely, ending in a deep-V-shaped inset below the waist. The color matched her eyes; the décolletage was daringly low.

After a rose-scented bath, Glory dressed in a fine linen chemise and demicorset; then Cheryl returned to comb her hair, styling it in long cascading ringlets below her ears. Freshly washed, it glistened in the flickering lamplight as richly as her satin gown. Cheryl finished Glory's toilette by smoothing rose-scented cream over her bare shoulders.

"My, miss, you certainly look pretty. Every man there will have eyes only for you."

"Thank you, Cheryl." Eyes only for her? Glory had no doubt of that. They would be dying to see "the captain's tart." She felt her stomach roll, the color drain from her cheeks. It was all she could do to keep from bursting into tears. She would never be able to face them. Never!

"Are you all right, miss?" Cheryl asked, and Glory felt worse than ever.

Was she that transparent? How in God's name would she be able to fool Nicholas's friends if she couldn't even fool one of the servants? "I'm . . . I'm fine, thank you. That will be all for now." Cheryl quietly left the room.

Glory sank down on the tapestry stool before the gilt-framed mirror. If she gave in to tears, her eyes would be swollen and red, and she would make an even bigger fool of herself. Her stomach rolled again, and for a moment she thought she might really be sick.

Just then Nicholas opened the door. He had bathed, shaved, and dressed in black evening clothes, perfectly tailored to his lean, hard frame.

Nicholas paused in the doorway, his gaze drawn to the beauty who faced him from across the room. Though her cheeks were pale, her blond hair glistened, and her skin looked so soft and smooth he fought the urge to touch it. The creamy mounds of her bosom rose and fell above the top of the gown, tantalizing him, beckoning him—just as they would every other man who saw her. It was all he could do to keep his jealousy at bay. He smiled at himself.

He'd married a beautiful, desirable woman. He would have to learn to accept that. He certainly had no trouble accepting it in bed.

Striding across the room, he dropped a light kiss on the curve of her neck. "Good evening, love." Again he allowed himself the pleasure of watching her. "You look more beautiful than I could have wished." His voice had turned husky.

"Nicholas, I'm afraid I won't be able to go with you after all."

He quirked a brow. "No?"

Nervously she glanced away. "I'm not feeling well. Maybe my monthly time is coming."

Nicholas chuckled softly. "You never cease to amaze me. I was certain you'd be eager for revenge. A chance to show them the stuff you're really made of. That's what your father would have wanted you to do, but if you're afraid . . ." He shrugged his shoulders. "I'd rather you accompany me, but if you're . . . ill, I certainly don't want to encourage you."

Glory chewed her lip, looking uncertain.

"I believe an old friend of yours from Charleston will be there," he pressed. "Lavinia Bond. And of course you know Kristen and Arthur Pedigru."

Cheeks coloring, she lifted her chin. Nicholas took a stride toward the door. "I'll send the maid up to help you undress. I don't want to be late."

She took a hesitant step toward him, hands clenched at her sides. "Nicholas, wait."

He faced her, allowing himself a narrow half-smile. "Feeling better?"

"Damn you, Nicholas Blackwell. You are still a devil of a man!"

"And you, my sweet, are still stubborn and spoiled and in need of just such a man."

They both grinned at the same time. Nicholas extended his arm. "Shall we go?"

"You always win, don't you?"

"Not always. I distinctly remember losing a game of billiards once."

Glory laughed, a soft tinkling sound. She accepted his arm with an impish smile.

"One more thing." Nicholas reached into the pocket of his waistcoat and extracted a small velvet box. He opened the lid and lifted a thin gold chain. A single blue sapphire surrounded by a wreath of diamonds dangled from the end of the chain.

"Oh, Nicholas."

He draped it around her neck and fastened the clasp. "Call it a late Christmas present."

"It's beautiful, Nicholas. I love it. Thank you." She kissed his cheek. He felt the fullness of her lips, the brush of her hair as she leaned forward. He only wished she had told him she loved *him* as well.

His smile a little less wide, Nicholas nestled her hand in the crook of his arm, and they headed for the stairs.

A line of carriages waited in front of the Whitmore mansion. Yellow light beckoned through every window, upstairs and down.

Wrapped in a white satin pelisse lined in the same blue as the bodice of her gown, Glory accepted Nicholas's hand and stepped from the glistening black brougham. His own red satin–lined cape swung out behind them as they walked. Black-clad servants took their wraps as they entered the foyer. Crystal chandeliers flickered overhead, and black and white marble floors glistened beneath their feet. Nicholas kept Glory's hand firmly tucked into the crook of his elbow. He felt a slight tremor in her touch and wished he could somehow make things easier.

Their host and hostess, Morgan and Celeste Whitmore, greeted them just inside the ballroom.

"Captain Blackwell." Morgan extended a hand. "We're so happy you could come. You remember my wife, Celeste."

"Of course." Nicholas brought her gloved fingers to his lips. "May I present my wife, Glory?"

Celeste Whitmore barely smiled. Morgan smiled so knowingly Nicholas wanted to hit him.

"It is an honor to meet the woman who has brought the elusive Captain Blackwell to heel," Morgan said.

"We've been looking forward to meeting you, my dear," Celeste put in. "Quite intrigued, in fact."

"Thank you for inviting us" was all Glory said.

"Why don't you go on inside?" Morgan suggested to Nicholas. "Have some refreshment. I'm sure the others are just as curious—I mean, *eager*—to meet your new bride as we."

Nicholas bowed stiffly, determined to ignore the barbs he knew his wife had not missed. He smiled down at Glory, his gaze purposely long and warm. "Come on, love. I'm sure my *friends* are going to adore you just as much as I do." He caught a glimpse of Celeste Whitmore's surprised expression as he led Glory from the room.

The evening moved with agonizing slowness for Glory. If it hadn't been for Nicholas's reassuring presence, she would have long ago run from the room. He always seemed to be there with just the right words, just the right look to still people's tongues and make them begin to wonder. When he danced with her, he had eyes only for her. Whenever he could, he led her onto the terrace and spoke to her in intimate whispers. Once he even kissed her. She was sure he'd done it to make a point, for she saw several matronly women watching from behind their plumed fans.

By the time he released her, she'd forgotten the ladies' existence, forgotten almost where she was. Breathless and a little dizzy, she pressed a hand against the front of his stiff white shirt to steady herself. "Are you certain you should be kissing me like that?"

Nicholas chuckled, a soft rumble beneath her hand. "It didn't turn out exactly as I intended. It was supposed to be a little more chaste."

Glory blushed to her toes. "You are such a rogue."

"And you, love, are so damned desirable that all I want to do is take you to bed."

"Then why don't you?"

"Not just yet. I want to know exactly where we stand. Will you be all right out here until I get back?"

"I promise I won't desert."

He kissed her cheek and headed back into the ballroom. Lavinia Bond stopped him just a few steps inside the door.

"Nicholas darling, shame on you. Where on earth have you been keeping yourself?" She fluttered her thick black lashes and looked at him over her black lace fan.

"I'm a married man now, Lavinia. Hadn't you heard?"

"Everyone's heard, darling. We all know how you were forced into it, poor dear."

"Maybe *everyone* should take a good look at my wife. I doubt there's a man here who doesn't envy me. I hardly needed to be *forced*. Now if you'll excuse me, Lavinia." He started to leave, then turned. "Isn't that Victor over there? I'll tell him you're looking for him." With an inward smile, he walked away.

Nicholas moved around the room, catching bits of conversation as he passed.

"Apparently the gossips were wrong," one velvet-gowned matron said.

"She certainly doesn't look like the disreputable creature they say," came the voice of a middle-aged man.

"I for one find her charming," a young dandy said, staring toward the terrace with a wistful look in his eyes.

As Nicholas awaited his turn at the punch bowl, he heard Colonel Marcus Wilby, a rotund merchant, and Devon Howard, a thin-lipped importer with wily eyes, in quiet conversation. Devon chuckled softly at something the colonel said. All Nicholas caught was the mention of his wife's name. The next words pumped a surge of anger through his veins.

"I'll say one thing for her, the captain's tart is—"

"Good evening, Colonel," Nicholas said, smiling falsely, temper barely in check. "Oh, excuse me, I hope I didn't interrupt."

"Not at all," the colonel said, clearing his throat. "As I was saying, the captain's . . . bride is one of the most enchanting creatures I've ever seen."

This time Nicholas's smile was genuine. "I couldn't agree more. I'm a fortunate man indeed."

Devon Howard seemed surprised. "Really? Why, we'd heard . . . that is, we weren't quite certain of the circumstances of your marriage."

"That should be obvious, gentlemen. Her father and I were friends. The marriage had long been in the planning."

"I see."

"We all knew Julian Summerfield," the colonel put in. "A fine man."

"His daughter is a fine young woman," Nicholas said softly. "Now, if you'll excuse me, I'd better see to my wife before someone tries to take my place." Satisfied that he'd accomplished his mission at last, he smiled and left them staring after him.

He and Glory left the ball a short time later.

"Now, that wasn't so bad," he teased as the carriage rolled over the cobblestone streets.

Glory shuddered in the circle of his arms. "I'm just glad it's over."

"Next time you'll be able to enjoy yourself."

"Next time?"

"I never intended to turn you into a recluse, Glory. There'll be other parties and balls. Now that people understand the way I feel about you, they'll treat you differently. You've already won most of them over; the others will follow as soon as they get to know you."

"I did enjoy the dancing," she told him.

"I have one more dance in mind just as soon as we get home."

Glory blushed crimson. Nicholas turned her into his arms and captured her lips.

The dance had already begun.

Chapter Twenty-Two

Nicholas left her a few hours after sunup. She wondered how he could be up and dressed so early after their night out and the hours they'd spent making love.

"I hope you don't mind," he said. "I'll be back before noon to take you to luncheon." He headed toward the door, calling back over his shoulder, "Cook will have breakfast ready shortly. I can have it sent up, if you prefer."

"No. That's all right." She had to face Elizabeth St. John Blackwell alone sooner or later. It might as well be today. "I'll see you at noon."

Flashing her a smile, he closed the door behind him.

Glory rose a few minutes later, called for Cheryl, who helped her into a day dress of mint green merino with tiny covered buttons up the front, and headed downstairs. She passed Bradford in the hallway on his way to the dining room. He smiled appreciatively when he saw her, and Glory smiled at him in return.

"My morning's looking brighter already," he said, offering her his arm. They entered the dining room together. Elizabeth perched at the head of the table, back ramrod straight, chubby hands settled in her lap. She wore a navy blue serge day dress; her dark hair, perfectly smooth, hung in ringlets to just above her shoulders.

"Good morning, Mother," Brad said, seating Glory, then stopping to plant a kiss on his mother's pudgy cheek.

"Good morning, Mrs. Blackwell," Glory said. Receiving no immediate reply, she pulled her napkin from its silver ring and smoothed it across her lap.

"I wondered if you'd have the courage to join us without my stepson's overbearing presence to protect you."

"Mother," Brad said, "why don't we give Glory a chance? Get to know her a little before we pass judgment?"

At Brad's use of "we," Glory smiled, admiring his tact and the way he attempted to manipulate his mother. He was indeed the most grown-up young man she'd ever met.

"Huh!" Mrs. Blackwell scoffed. "I don't need to know her. I've already learned far more about her than I need to know." She lifted her head, ridding herself of an extra chin. "Just look at her, sitting there as pious as you please, a rich husband to smooth over her indiscretions. The woman's a strumpet. Did you know she blatantly slept in your stepbrother's cabin on board his ship? Right in front of the whole crew! Shameless, that's what she is. A shameless hussy!"

Glory's temper fired. "I was forced to sleep there against my wishes. Your stepson believed me guilty of deceiving him, which I did not! He purposely ruined my reputation. It's only right he do all he can to repair the damage he caused!"

Elizabeth eyed her coldly. "Maybe you're right, Brad," she said, ignoring Glory and speaking as if she weren't there. "I should have known that no-good stepbrother of yours was behind all this scandal."

Glory shoved back her chair with such force it caught in the folds of the carpet and went crashing to the floor. "How dare you! How dare you talk about my husband like that? Nicholas is a fine man. He made a mistake, that's all. He's been good to you, cared for you, protected you. If you ever say another word against him, I'll . . . I'll—"

"You'll what?" Nicholas asked from the doorway, his

voice heavy with amusement—and more than a little affection.

Glory flushed beet red. When she turned back to Elizabeth, she noted Brad's secret smile along the way. "I'll implore my husband to abandon you and to remove you from his house, which he should have done years ago."

Elizabeth's bravado withered. "Why, I never—" She rose from her chair. "If you'll excuse me, Brad, I have some menus to plan." Without a backward glance, she marched indignantly from the room.

"I'm sorry you were caught up in the middle of this, Brad," Glory said a bit contritely. "None of this is your fault."

"It's all right, Glory. Mother has needed that for some time. Unfortunately, neither my brother nor I have the courage to speak up to her."

Glory glanced at Nicholas, who had picked up the fallen chair and was waiting for her to reclaim her seat. Glory sat down and returned her attention to Brad. Nicholas took the seat beside her.

"I wouldn't really do that," she said. "Encourage Nicholas to throw your mother out, I mean. That's none of my affair. She just made me so mad I lost my temper."

"A wife is supposed to defend her husband," Brad said, causing Glory to blush a second time.

Nicholas grinned but said nothing.

Servants brought coffee and served platters of eggs and bacon. The smells mingled, and Glory's stomach growled. "I thought you wouldn't be back till noon," she said to Nicholas as she lifted her silver fork.

"I came to see if Brad would substitute for me at luncheon. Both *Black Witch* and *Black Diamond* are in port. There are some cargo adjustments I'd like to make."

"I'd love to take Glory to luncheon, if she can stand to be away from you that long." His teasing note made Glory smile.

"I think I can survive for a few hours."

"I'm afraid it's going to be longer than that," Nicholas said. "We have a chance to win a contract with an Albany manufacturer. I want to accompany Max Faulkner to Albany to make arrangements. Make sure he can handle the negotiations. I'll come back as quickly as I can. Then we can return to Tarrytown.''

Glory felt lonely already. ''How long will you be gone?''

''No more than four days, five at most. I wouldn't go at all, but the sooner Max takes over, the more time we'll have together.''

Glory nodded. They finished the meal in silence; then Nicholas stood and bussed her on the cheek. ''I'll pack a few things and be right down.''

He returned with a small carpetbag and Glory walked him to the front door. ''I'll miss you,'' she told him.

''And I you. More than you'll ever know.'' Standing on the wide brick steps, he watched her, his hand coming up to touch her cheek. ''Tell me you love me.''

She wanted to. How she wanted to. ''I . . .'' She wet her lips. It was the final commitment. ''I . . .'' Nicholas kissed her until her knees went weak.

''Stay out of trouble till I get back,'' he teased, but she didn't miss the note of sadness in his voice. Glory watched as his long strides carried him down the brick path to the street where a pair of matched bays nickered in front of the waiting carriage and pawed the cobblestones. Nicholas climbed into the brougham, and the carriage rolled away.

''How about a walk?'' Brad said, seeing her forlorn expression as he walked up beside her. ''The crocuses are beginning to bloom.''

''Yes. I saw them yesterday. They're lovely. I'd enjoy a walk very much.''

Grabbing a light cashmere shawl against the still-brisk air, Glory accepted Brad's arm and walked with him into the garden. Bright sunlight sparkled on the rows of blue and white crocuses. A red-breasted robin perched atop the garden wall. Glory thought of the lovely gardens at Blackwell Hall and realized with a start she had come to think of the estate in Tarrytown as her home.

"Tell me about Nicholas's mother," she said to Brad as they walked along. "His real mother."

Brad led her to a small stone bench at one end of the garden, and they sat down. Brad smiled at her, glad, it seemed, for her question. "Her name was Collette Dubois before she married Alexander Blackwell. She was a beautiful French Creole. Dark, like Nicholas, very exotic. Of course I never knew her. Nicholas knew her only briefly. He was just seven when she left Alexander for a French plantation owner. Alex never got over her. After Nicholas ran away to sea, Alexander would get drunk and talk about her. I'd let him ramble on, fascinated. She seemed the most exciting creature. No wonder Nicholas loved her so much. Alexander said Nicholas used to cry himself to sleep calling her name."

Glory felt a pain in her heart. She could easily imagine Nicholas as a small boy, his dark eyes bright with unshed tears, yearning for a mother's love and never finding it.

"I don't think Nicholas ever stopped loving her," Brad continued. "I know Alexander never did. She was quite a notorious lady. Took one lover after another, right in front of her husband's nose. He just looked the other way. He loved her so much he would have done anything to keep her."

"Did Nicholas know?"

"Other children used to taunt him about her. It wasn't until later that he understood why." They sat silent for a time. The robin flew from the garden wall and winged its way overhead. Then, "Glory, I know what happened on the strand. About Nathan, I mean."

Glory felt the sting of tears, the memory so painful she had to look away. "How could he have believed that of me, Brad? We were so close. I thought he loved me. I trusted him."

"Nicholas has never known a woman like you, Glory. His mother betrayed him; my mother treated him badly. He couldn't trust a woman. Any woman. After he grew up, he was afraid to fall in love, afraid he'd end up the way his father did. He only pursued women who weren't a threat. Women with no loyalties, who required no attachments or involvements, most of them married. Their cheating only perpetuated his mistrust. It was an endless circle until you came along.''

''Me? Why me?''

''Because you loved him. Really loved him. You were honest and sincere. Trustworthy. When he saw you with Nathan, he believed he'd misjudged you. That you were really no different from the rest. By then he loved you so much, he couldn't stand the thought of being betrayed again.''

Glory didn't realize she was crying until Brad handed her his kerchief.

She looked up at him and smiled through her tears, feeling as if a burden had been lifted from her heart. *She understood.* For the first time since they'd left the strand, she understood why Nicholas behaved as he had.

''He loves you, Glory. When he found out the truth about you and Nathan, he felt more miserable than ever before in his life. He realized he'd wronged you. He hoped there was still a chance for the two of you to find happiness.'' Brad squeezed her hand. ''He still wants that happiness, Glory. And even if he won't admit it, he needs you—desperately.''

Glory brushed away the last of her tears. ''Thank you, Brad. You'll never know how much this talk has meant to me.''

''You *do* love him, don't you?''

''More than anything in the world.''

''Have you told him?''

She shook her head. ''But I can now. Thanks to you.'' He helped her up from the bench.

''He still isn't completely sure of you, Glory. He needs to know how you feel. Don't wait too long.''

''I won't, Brad. I promise.''

''He's a good man,'' Brad said. ''The very best.''

''I know. If you wouldn't mind, Brad, I'd like some time alone.''

''I understand.''

He left her there in the garden, alone with her thoughts and wanting more than anything in the world to be wrapped in her husband's strong arms, to say the words she'd said in her heart a thousand times. As she walked among the flowers, she stopped at the end of a row to pick one perfect bud.

The sound of a man's voice and running footsteps jolted her from her thoughts. "Glory!"

Across the garden, Glory saw Nathan racing toward her. His clothes were disheveled and torn, his face wet with perspiration.

The soft petals fell from her trembling hands. "My God, Nathan, what is it?" Eyes searching, she glanced in the direction from which he'd come. "How did you get in here? Where did you come from?"

He answered her in panting, fragmented sentences. "I climbed the garden wall. I didn't want anyone to see me. I got your note. You said you'd be at Nicholas's town house for the Whitmores' ball." He glanced worriedly behind him. "The slave catchers, Glory. They came to the school looking for me. My roommate warned me. He showed me a poster with my name on it offering a reward."

"Oh, my God."

"I've got to get away, Glory. Maybe Nicholas could help. I could go to Boston, then on up to Canada."

"How could Mother do such a thing?" Glory asked.

"I don't know. She always disliked me, but I never thought she'd go this far."

"You'll be safe here until Nicholas gets home and we can decide what to do."

" 'Fraid not, Miz Summerfield. Boy's done broke the law. He's got to pay."

Glory spun toward the heavily accented voice. A tall, thin man with a wispy mustache held a pistol aimed at Nathan's chest.

Glory glanced toward the house. "Brad!" she screamed, picking up her skirts to run. In two quick strides, a second man stepped into her path, cutting her off. He clamped a hand over her mouth and circled her waist with his arm so tightly she could scarcely breathe.

"Let her go," Nathan warned. "I'm the one you want."

"I ain't gonna hurt her," the man who held her said almost pleasantly. He was tall and well built, with sandy hair and an almost boyish face. "She's gonna go with us as far as the docks." Beneath her fingers she could feel the rough texture of his homespun shirt, the muscular chest inside. "We don' want no trouble gittin' you aboard the ship."

"How did you find me?" Nathan asked.

"Figured you'd run soon as you knew we was lookin' for you. Waited outside the school. You led us here."

"But you'll let her go at the docks," Nathan pressed. The tall, thin man stepped forward and punched him hard in the stomach, doubling him over.

"Ain't none o' your business what we do with her, nigger boy. Now, turn around." Eyeing the pistol and gasping for breath, Nathan did as he was told. The thin man bound his wrists, then tied a gag over his mouth.

"You gonna come along peaceful?" the man who held Glory asked with an appraising glance, "or are we gonna have to gag you, too?" His bright green eyes twinkled, as if the thought amused him somehow.

"If it's money you're after," Glory said, "I'll pay you not to take him. More than any reward."

"Money ain't the only reason," the thin man said. "This here nigger put hisself above the law. He thinks he's better than we are, can't you see that?"

"No, I can't. Nathan's just as good as you and I. Not any better. But not any worse."

"Hush now, darlin'," the younger man said. "It ain't fittin' for a white woman to talk like that. Now, get going, or Spence here will have to give your darkie another lesson in manners."

"I'll do just as you say. Just don't hurt him." As they moved toward the gate at the rear of the garden, Glory searched her mind frantically, trying to decide what to do. It suddenly occurred to her that even if she could gain

Brad's attention, he might not be able to stop the two men. The fugitive slave law gave slave catchers the right to return runaways even from the North. These men were determined to take Nathan back to Summerfield Manor. Until they arrived there, Nathan would be at their mercy. Slave catchers were notorious for their cruelty. The only way Nathan was sure to reach the manor unharmed was for Glory to go with him.

But what about Nicholas? a tiny voice warned. She looked at Nathan, bound and gagged, being dragged along like a common criminal. Just as before, she had no choice but to help him. She would do what she must—and pray to God her husband would understand.

Emerging from the alley, Glory spotted a wagon waiting halfway down the block; a third man, with thick muttonchop sideburns and a gray stovepipe hat, sat holding the reins. As they drew near, Glory felt the younger man's hand circle her waist, lifting her up. The feel of his warm breath as he held her a little too close sent a shudder of apprehension down her spine.

"Spence, you get in back," he said to his partner. "We wouldn't want the lady gettin' her skirts dirty." He winked at her as he climbed up on the seat, pinning her between him and the muttonchopped man. The wagon rumbled away, jolting along the cobblestone streets. In a few short minutes they reached the nearby docks.

"What are we gonna do with the girl?" Spence asked.

"Why don't you take me with you?" Glory suggested, and Nathan began to squirm and protest behind the gag. "I've been wanting to go home. My mother would probably pay you quite a bit extra for returning me."

"Gal may be right," the younger man said, eager to agree. "Story I heard was they ran away together. Girl's wanted home, too. Like she says, her ma oughta be real happy to have her back."

"I don't know, Matt," Spence said. "Women ain't nothin' but trouble."

"Money's money," the muttonchopped man put in,

"however it comes. Girl's here. We got no place to keep her till the ship leaves nohow."

"All right," Spence agreed. "But you two is responsible fer her. I ain't kissin' no dolly's behind fer no amount a money."

"Seems to me this dolly's behind'd be real nice to kiss," Matt said, green eyes bright with mischief—and something else Glory refused to name. She felt another shiver of alarm. She might be at the mercy of these three men for more than ten days. Would they keep their distance?

"Come on, darlin'." Matt grabbed her arm. "Wiggle that pretty behind a yours up the gangplank. We got a long ways to go to git you home."

The accommodations aboard the *Southern Star* were less than spacious. Even the tiny cabin she'd shared with Rosabelle on board the *Black Spider* seemed luxurious by comparison. There was a rope bunk with a corn-husk mattress, a barrel for a table, and a single wooden chair. A small whale-oil lantern hung from a peg on the rough plank wall. The moment they boarded the ship, Nathan had been clamped in irons and taken below to join a dozen other runaways.

"*Ship.*" Glory scoffed at the word, the sound hollow in the near empty room. She would hardly call the *Southern Star* a ship. It was a vessel of sorts, more of a scow. The decks were dirty and ill-maintained, the sails grimy and tattered. Nathan would have said the crew was a "scurvy lot." She would have to be careful, stay away from the men as much as possible. Nicholas had taught her about men like these.

Nicholas. Glory sank down on the narrow bunk. Just the thought of Nicholas brought the sting of tears. She could still see his face as he had smiled at her this morning, feel the gentle pressure of his lips as he kissed her good-bye. His touch had stirred sweet longing even before he left. By now he would be on his way to his meeting in Albany. By the time he returned to the city, she would be well on her way back home.

But the South wasn't home to Glory. Not anymore. Now home was with Nicholas, *wherever* he was. If only she could have left word. She should have done something, anything to let him know where she'd gone.

Lying on the sagging bunk, Glory let her mind conjure thoughts of Nicholas, and the one thought she'd held at bay loomed strong: What would Nicholas think had happened to her? Every time the question arose, the answer came swift and hard, bringing a stab of pain: He would think she had run away. He'd think she had betrayed him—just like his mother. She didn't want to believe it, refused to believe it—for now she understood the heartbreak it would cause. Once they reached Charleston, she would send a message to Nicholas by the swiftest packet. Still, it would be weeks, maybe even a month before word reached him. What would he do in the meantime? Would he believe something had happened? Would he try to find her? Even if he tried he would find no trace. Little by little he'd be convinced she had left him.

Glory closed her eyes. She knew what he would do. *Knew,* as she was coming to know him so well. He'd go to Kristen or to a woman like Ginger McKinnes. He'd find comfort in her arms. He'd make love to another woman in an effort to forget her, to be rid of her forever.

And this time Glory wouldn't forgive him.

No matter how much she wanted to, no matter how hard she tried. Because this time the breach of trust would be too great. No amount of love could repair the damage. No amount of forgiveness would bring them together again.

Glory turned her head into the darkness of her bunk. Tears soaked the stiff wool blanket, rough against her cheek. How she missed him. How she needed him. If only she'd told him how much she loved him, he might have believed in her, been able to trust her long enough to discover the truth. But she hadn't said the words, and now it was too late.

She thought of their time on the strand, but that seemed long ago and unimportant. The times that meant something now were those they'd spent at their home in Tarrytown. *Our* home, he had said. She remembered their rides together in the country, the gentleness of his touch as he'd held her in his arms. He was just beginning to confide in her, just beginning to speak his heart.

Now all that might be destroyed.

He would return to find her gone, their room empty, the fire cold. Then his heart would turn cold, too. She couldn't bear to think of it. Couldn't bear to imagine the bitterness on his face as he became more and more certain she'd betrayed him.

If only I had spoken my heart, she thought for the hundredth time. Maybe things would be different. Maybe he wouldn't doubt my love. Maybe he'd wait for me.

But she hadn't.

And in believing she had betrayed him, Nicholas would betray her.

Glory squeezed her eyes closed against pain. She had no choice, she told herself. Nathan was her brother. But her husband might be lost to her, lost to her forever. No words, no amount of justification could make up for that. Not ever.

Please, God, she prayed. You've always been so good to me, given me everything I wanted—or at least thought I wanted. Those things mean nothing to me now, not without Nicholas. Please let him know that I love him. That I would never hurt him. He acts so strong, and most of the time he is. But he needs me.

And I need him.

Glory cradled her head in her arms and wept for all that she had lost—her father, her childhood, her baby. And now her husband. She wished things could be different—and didn't believe for an instant they would.

Chapter Twenty-Three

"I got here just as quickly as I could. Tell me what's happened." Nicholas stood in the foyer, still wearing his overcoat.

Bradford walked up beside him. "Come. Let's go into the study." Brad turned to go, but Nicholas swung him around.

"Where's Glory? Has something happened to her?" It was all he could do to control his voice. His heart pounded so hard he could feel it knocking against his ribs.

"We aren't sure, Nicholas. Please. Let's go into the study. I'll pour you a brandy and tell you what's happened."

"What's *happened*," Elizabeth St. John Blackwell called from the stairway, "is your little tart has followed the same path as your mother. She's run away with another man."

"Mother, please," Brad pleaded. "This is difficult enough already."

"I want to know what's going on, Brad, and I want to know now." Darkness had fallen outside the town house, marking the end of the third day since Nicholas had left home. Three short days—and his world threatened to turn upside down.

"The study," Brad repeated, and this time Nicholas followed. Brad closed the door behind them, helped Nicholas out of his coat, and poured him a brandy, which he accepted with a shaky hand.

"Glory's gone, Nicholas," Brad said simply. "We don't know where."

"How long ago?"

"After you left on Sunday, she and I took a walk in the garden. She said she wanted some time alone, so I left her there. I haven't seen her since."

Nicholas sank down on a leather chair beside the fire. Lamplight bathed the room in a yellow glow that cast shadows beneath Nicholas's high cheekbones. "And Elizabeth saw her leave with a man?"

"I don't believe her, Nicholas. You know she'd do anything to cause trouble between you two. She was upstairs resting. I don't believe she saw a thing. It's just her way of getting even with Glory for the other day."

"What did she say the man looked like?" Nicholas asked with forced control.

"Mother says she didn't get a good look. He was tall. That's all she remembers."

"Any sign of a struggle?"

"No."

"What have you done so far?"

"I've sent a messenger to Tarrytown. She hasn't returned to the estate. We checked with the hospitals, doctors. Nothing."

"Have you spoken to her brother?"

"Only indirectly. His roommate said he was on an extended field trip. He left town before Glory came up missing."

Nicholas took a long sip of brandy, allowing the fiery liquid to burn its way down his throat. "What did you talk to her about? In the garden, I mean."

"Mostly about you. She asked about your mother and I told her all I knew." Brad took a drink of his brandy after warming the snifter between his hands. Nicholas noticed the worry lines around his mouth, the grooves creasing his brow. "The only reason I haven't sent for the constable is because of the gossip you two have already suffered. More would be ruinous for Glory. I hired someone private to look into the matter. The best I could find. I hope you approve.''

"That's fine," he said flatly.

"I won't lie to you, Nicholas. I'm worried. I think something's happened to her.''

Nicholas leaned his head against the antimacassar covering the back of his chair. "Something's happened, all right. She's left me, Brad. Probably for George McMillan or some other man.''

"I don't believe that and neither should you. Glory loves you. She told me so that day in the garden.''

Nicholas cocked a brow. "Is that so? Then how is it she hasn't told me?''

"She was going to, Nicholas. That's what she told me.''

Nicholas released a long, ragged breath and took another sip of his brandy. "I wish I could believe that, Brad, but I don't. She didn't want to marry me in the first place. She wanted an annulment, asked for it more than once. I guess she got tired of asking.''

"If you believe Mother—''

"It isn't just that.''

"What, then?''

"I just don't think she loves me. Maybe she never did.''

"What if you're wrong, Nicholas? What if something has happened to her? What if she needs your help?''

The thought squeezed his heart like a vise. He sat quietly for a time, staring into the flames and remembering Glory's face. "I almost wish it were true. Almost wish something dire had happened, that her life *was* in danger. But I know Glory. She would never have left without a struggle. Somehow she'd have let us know." He finished off his brandy and rose to his feet. Picking up his overcoat, he strode to the door.

"Where are you going?''

"Out.''

"I know what you're thinking, Nicholas. Don't do it. Give her some time. Find out what's happened.''

He didn't answer, just walked down the hall into the
foyer. Brad's footsteps echoed behind him.

"You're wrong," Brad said. "And if you are, she'll
never forgive you. Not this time."

Nicholas's hand paused on the heavy brass latch. He
stood there a moment, poised, his thoughts a jumble of
emotion, his heart breaking in two. Then he opened the
door and headed into the night.

"Join us for supper?" Matt Bigger asked. He stood in
the passageway just outside her door, a hopeful expression
lighting green eyes a shade darker than Glory's dress. She
knew all their names by now. Spencer James was the thin
man; Lester Fields, the older muttonchopped man.

"I . . . I think I'll just eat here, if you don't mind."

"You been sayin' that for days," Bigger said. He
grinned up at her. "Surely you're tired o' being shut up
in this room?"

She felt her defenses weaken. Bigger looked harmless.
She judged he was only a few years older than she. His
manner of speaking put him from somewhere in the South.
Still, she didn't trust him. There was something in his
eyes . . .

"I'd like to. I really would. But I'm tired and I have a
touch of seasickness, I'm afraid."

Stepping inside, Bigger closed the door softly behind
him. The lamp jiggled and flickered against the wall.
"What you need is someone to take care of you. A man
to look out for you and protect you."

"I have a man," Glory said, then wondered where her
husband was right now. She'd been gone five days. Nicholas had surely returned from his trip by now. He'd found
her gone and—*and what*? she asked for the thousandth
time.

"If you've been with a man," Bigger was saying,
"then I don' need to be so careful o' your sensibilities."
He grinned, teeth white, except for one a shade darker
near the front. It made him look almost boyish. "Once
a woman's been broke to the saddle, there's no way to

tell how many riders she's carried. Whey don't you come on over here and let me kiss you? I been told I'm real good at kissin'.''

Glory's heart began to pound. "Please, Mr. Bigger. I'm a married woman."

"Married, is it? Married ladies is my specialty." His hand closed around her arm, and he pulled her against him. His fingers massaged the peak of her bosom through the bodice of her mint-green dress. Though she tried to turn away, he held her fast and kissed her hard. His lips felt warm, his breath tasted of tobacco but was not unpleasant. All she could think of was Nicholas. When his hand moved to fondle her buttocks through the folds of her dirt-stained skirt, she jerked away.

Bigger seemed surprised. He grinned as if he found her refusal a challenge, then stepped toward her again.

"Leave off, Matt." Lester Fields stood in the doorway. "She's goods, same as the darkie. We ain't gonna git top money if the merchandise is damaged."

Matt Bigger stared down at her, eyes dancing. "Might be worth takin' a little less to sample this sweet stuff."

"Me and Spence got a say in this, too, and we say you leave her alone. You can buy all the cock alley you can handle once we git paid. Till then stay away from the girl."

Bigger released her. "I s'pose you're right." He turned his attention to Glory. "Never was one of you sweet-smellin' prisses worth a damn in bed nohow." He grinned till he dimpled, exposing his dark front tooth. "You sure did taste good, though. Lips sweeter'n hard rock candy."

"Come on," Lester urged. "No use dwellin' on it. 'Sides them boys down south kin git mighty nasty, they think you been dickin' one o' their women."

"By, darlin'," Bigger said with a smile.

Glory shuddered as he closed the door, then rolled the heavy wooden barrel in front of it.

Brad awoke to a pounding at the massive oak front door. So did the rest of the household. Servants scurried into the foyer, each trying to beat the other to the door to quiet the raucous sound. Brad had made it only as far as the top of the stairs when the door swung wide. Nicholas stepped inside, clothes disheveled, black hair mussed. Several days' growth of beard darkened his swarthy cheeks. He took the stairs two at a time. Brad grimaced as he passed, smelling stale alcohol—and the scent of strong perfume.

"Where the devil have you been?" Brad demanded. "I've been worried sick."

Nicholas continued down the hall and into the room he had occupied with Glory, Brad trailing behind.

"I said, where the devil—"

"I heard you the first time. I've been in half the sleazy taverns in New York."

"And Kristen Pedigru's bed?"

"No."

"Well, you certainly smell as if you've been in someone's bed."

Nicholas stopped only long enough to throw him a sidelong glance. "It isn't what you think. I've been trying to find out what happened to Glory. I started in the taverns, then decided to go back to see Nathan's roommate. After a bit of persuasion, he showed me this." Nicholas fumbled in the pocket of his rumpled waistcoat, then handed Brad the poster that offered a reward for Nathan's capture and return to Charleston.

"My God!" Brad exclaimed.

"Nathan wasn't on a field trip. He was headed here to find me and get help." Nicholas tossed several clean shirts, some breeches, and his boots into a carpetbag. "They've taken her, Brad. I'm sure of it."

"Two days ago you were just as sure she'd left you. What happened to change your mind?"

Nicholas snapped the latches on the bag. "After I left here, I wandered the streets for a while, trying to clear my thoughts, remembering your words and what happened on the strand. I knew you were right about one thing: If I accused Glory unjustly, she wouldn't forgive me a second time. Still, I wasn't sure. I drank too much, ended up sleeping in some dingy room above the Fraunces Tavern.

I dreamed about her all night, couldn't stop thinking about
her, about our times together, the way she made me feel.
When I woke up, I knew she wouldn't have just run away.
She's too damned honest, too sincere. She'd have told
me, Brad. I knew it without the slightest doubt. After that
I went to work to find out what happened. Once I saw the
reward poster, the rest was easy. I had to bribe half the
drunks in town to find out which ship she was on, but I
finally found out.'' He grinned. ''There aren't many sailors who would forget a woman like Glory.''

''What are you going to do now?''

''The *Black Witch* is in port. So's the *Black Diamond*.
Their crews are on leave, but I found Mac, Josh Pintassle,
and Jago Dodd at the Tontine Tavern. They've rounded up
enough men to make way. We'll take the *Black Witch*.
She's the fastest. We should make Charleston damn near
as fast as that leaky tub, the *Southern Star*.

''I'll go with you,'' Brad offered.

''Not a chance. You've got school to think about.''
Nicholas set his jaw. ''I'll bring her back, I promise you.
And they'd better not have laid a scurvy hand on her.''

Even at night the marshes along the pine-covered shores
looked familiar. Glory felt a rush of nostalgia as she stood
on the deck, wind whipping her skirts, watching the coastline slip by not far off the starboard rail. She'd forgotten
the fragrance of azalea that tinged the air, forgotten the
warmth of the southern breeze. If circumstances had been
different, she'd have been eager to see her home, visit
family and old friends. Now all she thought about was
what would happen to Nathan once he was returned to
Summerfield Manor—and what had become of Nicholas.

Every waking hour she spent without him seemed an
eternity. Every moment of restless sleep was beset by
memories, fantasy dreams in which Nicholas appeared beside her or kissed her until she was breathless and warm
all over.

In her dreams he made love to her, time and time again.

Then she would awaken to a rush of despair, her body hot
and tightly strung, achy, and tense.

Glory stared down at the water sweeping beneath the
hull, an iridescent froth glistening in the moonlight. By
tomorrow night, Spencer James had told her, they'd be
docking in Charleston. The trip had taken even longer than
she'd imagined. They'd stopped twice to drop off or pick
up runaway slaves, and on top of that the *Southern Star*
was a wide-keeled slow-moving old boat. Glory thanked
God the trip was almost over—but Nathan's ordeal was
just beginning.

It still seemed out of character for Louise Summerfield
to carry a grudge this far. She was too practical, too concerned with the everyday problems of running the plantation, to get caught up in revenge. Still, there was the
poster to consider. Nathan's roommate said a reward had
been offered to bring Nathan home.

Glory shuddered against a gust of cool wind that tore
at her hair and whipped at her skirts. Somehow, some
way, she had to make her mother see reason.

"Evenin', darlin'."

Glory turned with a start. Matt Bigger stood beside her,
eyes fixed on the gentle curve of her bosom hidden beneath her soft cashmere shawl. She pulled her wrap a little
closer around her shoulders as she faced the sandy-haired
man. "Good evening, Mr. Bigger."

"*Mr.* Bigger. I like that." He teased the edge of her
jaw with his finger. "I like my women polite. Polite and
pretty—just like you. I been doin' some thinkin'. 'Bout
what Spence and Lester said, how you was goods and all.
I figure my share of the take this trip to be a good bit of
cash. I could make it up to 'em for their share of the profit
on you. You and me could go away together. Go some-
wheres and make a fresh start."

"I'm flattered, Mr. Bigger," Glory said, straining to
make her voice sound even, "but as I told you before, I
already have a husband."

Matt's green eyes rested on her face. "Makes no difference to me. I got a powerful need for you, Glory." He

placed his hands on her shoulders, drawing her just inches away from his face. "Come downstairs with me. I'll show you how good a real man can make you feel."

Glory fought against the tremors she knew were just moments away. "Please, Matt. You're a nice boy. But I—"

"You're gonna come downstairs with me," he told her, all the softness gone from his voice. "You're gonna entertain me proper like, and you ain't gonna say a word about it to nobody. 'Cause if you do, I'm gonna see that nigger boy of yours has a little *accident*."

Glory swallowed hard, fighting back tears. What on earth could she do? Bigger tugged her toward the passageway. It was dark and musty in the narrow corridor. Wildly, Glory glanced around, looking for some means of escape. If she screamed, other men would come to her aid, but from the looks she'd been getting these past few days, she might have more than one attacker to defend herself against. Bigger swung open his cabin door and forced her inside, closing the door with a soft thud behind him.

"Don't you understand, Glory? I gotta have you. Don't make this harder than it has to be."

"Matt, please, listen to me."

"Shut up! I'm tired o' listening. After we make love, you'll feel different. We can go away together. Now, take off that dress."

"You know I'm not going to do that."

He stiffened. "If you want that nigger boy to get back home alive, you will."

Glory swallowed past the lump of tears in her throat.

"I don't want to hurt you, Glory. You're about the prettiest, sweetest little thing I ever seen. No one's gonna know." Bigger advanced on her. "Now, take it off."

Glory took a step back. "All right. I'll do as you say." Stalling for time she turned her back to him and removed her shawl, then began to unbutton the front of her dress. Her eyes searched madly for something she could use as a weapon.

"Turn around. I wanna watch."

Shaking all over, Glory did as he asked. Glancing about, her eyes locked on exactly what she needed. Resting on a barrel next to Bigger's arm, the antler handle of a small, thin-bladed knife protruded from its sheath. If she could just distract him long enough, she could loose the knife and use it to gain her freedom.

Glory unbuttoned each button with care until she'd reached her waist. Bigger slid the material off her shoulders. His hands felt rough against her skin, and Glory fought the urge to run. The skirt of the dress buttoned down the back.

"Would you mind helping me?" she asked.

Bigger's one dark tooth flashed as he grinned. "My pleasure."

Glory got as close to him as she dared, then again turned her back. While Bigger fumbled with her buttons, Glory carefully freed the knife. She slid the blade out just as the sandy-haired man realized what she was doing.

"Why, you little minx!" He spun her around and slapped her, sending Glory sprawling and the knife flying. She saw where it landed and rolled to grab it just as Bigger lunged. She'd moved the knife only inches—it was enough.

Bigger fell on the blade, his weight heavy on top of her. She heard the breath leave his lungs in a rush, felt something warm and slick between her fingers. The door burst open and Lester Fields raced in.

"What the hell's goin' on here?"

Glory couldn't answer. Her teeth were chattering, her body shaking all over. Fields pulled Bigger off her, and he rolled into a protective ball, clutching his injured shoulder.

"I didn't mean to," she whispered. "It was an accident."

Lester Fields helped her to her feet. "You did what you had to, ma'am."

To her surprise, Bigger grinned up at her. "You got grit, darlin'. I'll say that for you."

"Leave her alone, Matt," Fields said.

Glory pulled the bodice of her dress up over her chemise, buttoned the soft merino with shaky fingers, then let Lester Fields guide her from the room.

"Don't you worry, ma'am," Lester told her. "I shoulda kept a closer eye on him. He really ain't such a bad sort, 'cept when it comes to women. Then he sorta goes crazy. Women's always been Matt's downfall, and you're way pertier than most."

"I'm afraid he'll hurt my brother."

"Matt's no fool. Nigger means money. He likes money almost as much as he does women." He flashed a reassuring smile, gray muttonchop sideburns pulling wide with the expression.

Hoping Lester Fields was right, Glory let him lead her down the corridor to her room. That night she propped the barrel *and* the chair against the door.

"We've made good time, lad. With any luck at all, we'll make Charleston right behind 'em." Mac leaned an arm on the mast, watching the coastline in the distance. Nicholas stood a few feet away, hand gripping the shrouds, black-booted foot propped against the rail. The warm southern breeze ruffled his clean white linen shirt and curly black hair.

"You and the men have done a fine job," Nicholas said, "but I can't help worrying."

"Aye. She's a beautiful woman, lad. A temptation to any man. But she's a fighter. Smart, too. She'll take care of herself. Ye have to believe that. Besides, they wouldna be takin' her along if there were no profit in it. They expect to be paid. She'll do 'em no good if she's not returned unharmed."

"I hope you're right, Mac."

"Excuse me, Captain." Josh Pintassle walked up beside him looking as handsome as ever, if a bit more mature. "Any special orders before I turn in?"

Nicholas smiled, "No, Josh. We're making record time, thanks to your efforts. You know how much I appreciate it."

"We should make port late tomorrow night. Knowing the *Southern Star*, she won't be far ahead of us."

Nicholas nodded. "It depends on whether she's made stops along the way."

"Most likely she has. Wouldn't make sense for her not to." Josh glanced toward the wheel. Jago Dodd manned the helm, his knife-scarred face set to the task. They'd run with a spare crew, put in twice the normal hours, but it felt good to be back with old shipmates. Josh turned toward his friend and mentor. Captain Blackwell looked different somehow. Certainly he looked worried, but a new sureness, an inner strength, had stilled the restlessness that had plagued him before. Loving a good woman could do that for a man. Or so it was said. Josh hoped one day he'd find out for himself.

"Think I'll go below, Captain."

"Good night, Josh."

"Ye had best git some sleep yourself, lad," Mac told Nicholas.

"I will, Mac."

" 'Night, Cap'n." Mac's heavy footfalls receded across the deck, leaving him alone with his thoughts. Moonlight glistened on the crests of the waves, reminding Nicholas of the lights in Glory's flaxen hair. God, how he missed her. When they got home, he vowed, he wouldn't let her out of his bed for a week!

When they got home. He pulled a thin black cheroot from his pocket, struck a lucifer against the rail, and lit up, inhaling the pungent smoke. Let her be all right, he thought for the hundredth time. Let her be safe and unharmed.

And make her want to go home.

Chapter Twenty-Four

The *Southern Star* reached the Charleston docks early the following afternoon. Glory had stayed in her cabin, letting no one in except Lester Fields, who brought her a tray of food.

Now, as she climbed the ladder to the deck and caught her first glimpse of home in almost a year, Glory felt a tightening in her chest. She'd missed this place. Missed seeing the old Negro women braiding baskets from sweet grass, palmetto, and pine needles as they'd been doing for decades. Missed summers on Sullivans Island. Missed she-crab soup and oyster and sausage pie.

But now above all else she missed Nicholas. Even the beauty of Charleston couldn't stay him from her thoughts. Again she wondered if he'd been true or if he had been driven to seek comfort in another woman's arms. Whatever had happened, somehow she had to get word to him.

She moved toward the rail where Lester Fields, gray stovepipe hat in hand, stood beside Spencer James. Matt Bigger waited with Nathan and a string of glossy black-skinned slaves all chained together. Glory's heart went out to them. Except for his cocoa coloring, Nathan looked like the others—gaunt and haggard, tired and bedraggled—older than their years, it seemed to Glory. Nathan's elegant frock coat was missing, his white shirt and fawn trousers no more than a tattered mass of brown-stained rags. His feet were bare and dirty. She moved to his side and put her arms around his neck.

"Oh, Nathan, what have they done to you?"

"Hush, now," he soothed. "We're almost home."

"Are you all right?"

"I've felt better." He took a deep breath of the salty sea air. "Feels good just to breathe clean air again."

"Git away from the darkie," Matt Bigger warned. "Ain't seemly for a white woman to be talkin' to a Nigra, let alone touchin' 'im."

"Do as he says, Glory," Nathan told her, seeing her stiffen, ready to do battle. For once she did as her brother asked.

"I'd like to get word to my husband," she said to Lester Fields. "I need to let him know I'm all right."

"That'll have to wait till you get home," Matt put in. His mood had darkened the minute she mentioned her husband. "We ain't got time for your socializin'."

Glory squared her shoulders, once more ready to fight. Then her proud bearing sank. What difference would another day or two make? By now the damage was done. Or at least so she imagined. Last night her dreams had been of Nicholas wrapped in Kristen Pedigru's arms.

"She's gone, Kristen," he'd said to the dark-haired beauty. "She never really loved me anyway."

"*I* love you, Nicky. Let me show you how much."

Glory had awakened in a cold sweat, images of Nicholas kissing Kristen's heated flesh imprinted on her mind. She closed her eyes against a sudden rush of pain and headed down the gangplank.

Four horses were waiting on the docks for the ride to the plantation. None carried a sidesaddle. Glory had never ridden astride, but she didn't protest. Instead she let Lester Fields lead the animal over to a small wooden crate so she could mount. She settled herself onto the low-cantled man's saddle and dug her soft kid shoes into the metal stirrups, skirts hiked up on her calves. Her stockings had gotten so torn and ragged that she had discarded them long ago.

Matt Bigger stared at her with a hungry look in his eye and a wide grin on his boyish face. The bandage on his shoulder protruded from the open front of his homespun shirt. "Let's get goin'," he said. "We'll take the girl and the fine-talkin' darkie home first, then deliver the rest."

Glory didn't argue. She just hoped no one would recognize her. Her hair was a mess, her clothing a blood-stained shambles. She wanted this whole sordid business settled with as little notoriety as possible. Her family had lived in Charleston for years. The Summerfield name did not deserve to be sullied; her father's memory did not deserve it.

They rode all afternoon, the pace a fast crawl that forced the slaves to keep moving in a long forlorn column stretched out behind them. The sound of their clanking chains broke Glory's heart. Matt Bigger rode beside her, green eyes glued to the smooth skin bared between ankle and hem. Once he ran his hand all the way up to the curve of her bottom, and Glory wanted to scream. Instead she jerked on the reins, bringing the horse to a halt and nearly unseating Bigger from his. He chuckled and winked at her. God, she wished she were home.

"There she is, lad. The *Southern Star*." They stood at the rail, Mac beside Nicholas. The Charleston dock swarmed with activity even though dusk had set in. Wagons and drays rumbled past, and raucous laughter bubbled from nearby taverns.

"Back the sails smartly!" Nicholas ordered as the *Black Witch* pulled alongside the dock. The ship was made fast in minutes, and Nicholas, Mac, Jago, and Josh headed down the gangway. Mac stopped to speak with a passing sailor, then caught up with the others just as they entered the livery.

"That was Timothy Jones from the *Star*," Mac told them. "He says she put in early this afternoon. The slavers were leading a string o' Negroes, so there'll be a bit o' time afore they reach the plantation."

"Was Glory with them?"

"She sure was, lad. Timothy says he couldna miss a face like hers. Says she was fine, last he saw her." Mac slid his eyes away. Nicholas didn't miss the look.

"Tell me the rest."

Mac took a breath. "Seems one o' the slavers took a shine to her. Tried to force himself on her. Glory stuck him wi' his own knife."

Nicholas set his jaw. "What else?"

"Timothy said Bigger—that's the mon's name—was braggin' to the crew he was gonna bed her, one way or another. Says she owes him. For what she done to his shoulder."

"Damn!" Nicholas stormed, gray eyes dark. "Let's get going. We haven't a moment to lose." He swung into his saddle and the others followed suit. Threading their way through the noisy throng of people along the wharf, they picked up the pace as they headed out of town.

By late evening the slavers had reached the far boundaries of the Summerfield plantation. Glory recognized the lane beside the rice field she'd ridden with Nicholas. How long ago that had been. The slaves had begun to sing as they trudged along the road, their deep voices sweet and low on the still evening air. Nathan's voice mingled with the others, but Glory could easily discern his flawless speech pattern, so different from the lowland drawl of the rest.

She was surprised when they passed the road to the main house and headed instead up a back lane that led to the residence of the overseer, Jonas Fry.

"Why aren't we going to the manor?" she asked Spencer James.

"Fry's the man we come to see."

Glory felt a shiver of apprehension, but brushed it away. They were on Summerfield land now. Everything was going to be fine. Bone-tired, she kicked her feet free of the stirrups to stretch her sore legs, raw and strained from so many hours in the unfamiliar saddle.

"You need those pretty long legs o' yours rubbed,"

Matt Bigger told her. "I'd be happy to stop here an' oblige." He grinned wickedly.

"I'm fine, thank you. I just want to get home."

"Oh, you're gonna git home," he said, just loud enough for her to hear. "But not before you and I finish what we started on the ship."

"We started nothing on the ship."

"Oh, I wouldn't say that. I can still remember the taste of those perty pink lips of yours. I never wanted a woman the way I want you. I'm gonna have you. Sure as my name's Matt Bigger."

"Mr. Fields," Glory called out. "Would you mind if I rode beside you?"

"Won't do you no good," Matt said with a soft chuckle. "You're gonna warm my bed sooner or later."

Glory urged her horse forward, fighting down a rush of fear. Why did Bigger sound so sure of himself when they were already on Summerfield land? And what about the other two men? Surely they'd be able to defend her. Bigger must be bluffing.

But something told her he wasn't.

They skirted the main house and rode straight to the Fry place. Jonas heard their noisy approach and sauntered through the front door dressed in a red flannel undershirt and cotton twill trousers.

"So you brought the runaway home," he said as Lester Fields broke Nathan loose from the others. "And his sweet sister, too. I got the word you was comin'. Got yer money right here, includin' some extra fer Miss Glory."

"Shouldn't we return Nathan to my mother?" Glory asked, heart pounding. "After all, she's the one who offered the reward."

"Your mama don't know a thing about this," Fry said. "But you kin bet she'll be real pleased to git her nigger back."

"If my mother doesn't know about this, where did you get the money?"

"Miz Louise's been handin' more and more of the business over to me. Seems it were more'n she could handle, you leavin' an' all.''

Glory felt a twinge of conscience. "What are you planning to do with Nathan?''

"What shoulda been done long ago. But don't you worry your pretty little head about it. That's man's business.''

"But I *am* worried, Mr. Fry. Whatever you're planning, I won't let you. We're going to take Nathan to my mother. That's an order, Jonas.''

Jonas just smiled. "Sorry, missy. You don't give orders 'round here no more.''

"Why don't I take her on up to the house for ya?'' Matt Bigger offered.

"Good idea,'' Jonas agreed.

"No! I'm not going anyplace with that horrible man. Tell him, Mr. Fields.''

"Tell him what, Lester?'' Matt asked, grinning, face all boyish and innocent.

Neither of the two men answered, just kept their eyes fixed on the ground, and Glory suddenly understood why Matt Bigger had been so sure of himself all along. Both Lester Fields and Spencer James were afraid of Matthew Bigger.

"Listen to me, Jonas,'' Glory said. "This man means to . . . he intends to force his intentions on me.''

Matt Bigger chuckled. "She sure has an imagination, don't she? Why if I'd wanted to take you, darlin', I'd've done it long before now.''

Jonas relaxed. "I know you, Miss Glory. You're used to gittin' yer way. Well, not this time.'' He returned his attention to Bigger. "Already sent word to the committee. They mean to see justice is done.''

"No!'' Glory gasped, jumping down from her horse. Bigger was out of his saddle in an instant.

"Tie her up and take her home,'' Jonas ordered. In seconds, Glory felt Bigger's large hands tying her smaller ones in front of her, then shoving a gag into her mouth. The next thing she knew she was hoisted into her saddle, and Bigger was leading the animal away.

"Make sure you untie her 'fore you take her up to the door. Her mama might not like us manhandlin' her little girl."

Matt waved back over his shoulder.

"You boys can camp right here tonight," Jonas told the other two men. "Do these niggers good to see what happens when they try to run away."

Feet dangling outside her stirrups, Glory gripped the horse with her knees to keep from bouncing up and down on her already sore legs, protesting against the gag as Bigger led her horse farther and farther into the darkness. By the time he stopped, she could no longer hear the voices of the others. Reining up beside a huge live oak shrouded by Spanish moss, he pulled her down from the saddle. Glory felt the metal stirrup pressing into her back, smelled the horse's musky scent as she leaned against the animal's warm flesh.

Matt slipped the gag from her mouth. "It's time we finished our business."

"You're on my family's land, Mr. Bigger. If you harm me, they'll see you hang."

"I ain't gonna hurt you. I told you that before. But I gotta have you. My breeches is bustin' with wantin' you. You ease my need, I'll let you go."

"And what if I don't?"

"I'll take you anyway. Never took a woman against her wishes before." He smiled, looking almost handsome. "Never had to. But I will if you make me."

"You'll be hunted down."

"If I gotta give up my share and leave this part of the country, that's what I'll do."

Glory felt sick with dread. She licked her lips, now dry. "I'll do as you ask. Untie me."

"I knew you'd see reason. You're a smart girl. Got guts, too." He chuckled as he worked the knot at her wrist. "Stickin' that knife in me. That took courage. Never knowed a woman with courage like yours. Made me want you even more."

"Why did you wait until now?" she asked, stalling for time.

" 'Cause I didn't want to share you. Figured those sailors would want a piece of you, too. I don't like to share my womenfolk. I like you, Glory. I like you a lot. I'd take you with me if you'd just say the word." He turned her to face him, one rough hand beside her cheek.

"I never seen skin like yours. Like cream it is." He dropped his head till his mouth touched her lips. The sensation was not unpleasant; still, her stomach rolled. She tried to remain calm, tried to blot the thick feel of his tongue as he forced her lips apart.

She waited till she felt his hold ease, then with a quick turn, brought her knee up between his legs. Bigger swore as she made contact, but she knew her skirts and petticoats had kept her from doing any real damage. Twisting away, she tried to run, but got only a few steps before Bigger's arm snaked around her waist. He brought her up short, forcing her back against the muscles of his chest. While she fought to still her trembling, he pulled the pins from her hair and let the soft strands cascade onto her shoulders.

"Please let me go," she whispered. "I can't do this."

Bigger stiffened. "Have it your way." He scooped her into his arms and carried her, struggling, to the base of the oak tree. Pinning both her hands above her head with his larger one, he used the other to work the buttons on the front of her dress. Achieving only minimal success, he growled in frustration and ripped the dress away.

"I hate doin' it like this, but you ain't leavin' me no choice." She squirmed against him as he tore away her chemise, leaving her breasts bare above her demicorset. With an appreciative groan, he cupped one in his free hand and caressed her nipple with his thumb. His mouth stilled her protests, his tongue slick and moist between her teeth.

Fighting to twist away, Glory felt herself freed so abruptly she jerked backwards, hitting her head with a dull thump against the tree. When she looked up, Nicholas stood in front of her, booted feet spread apart, chest dark beneath the open front of his white linen shirt. Matt Bigger moaned at his feet. Nicholas's gray eyes looked so stormy they appeared almost black.

Glory felt a surge of joy so powerful it made her dizzier than she already was. Clutching the tree, she shook her head to be certain her husband's image was real.

Nicholas lifted Bigger off the ground and punched him again, sending him sprawling. He gained his feet, staggering. Nicholas spun him around and hit him in the stomach, doubling him over. A last hard blow glanced off his chin. The young slaver slumped unconscious to the ground.

Eyes dark with worry, Nicholas turned to Glory. Long strides carried him to where she sat leaning against the tree. Kneeling beside her, he pulled her into his arms, cradling her head against his shoulder.

Glory felt the sting of tears. "I thought you'd gone to Kristen," she whispered. "I was afraid I'd lost you."

"Hush," he said, drawing her dress together over her bare breasts and fastening the few buttons that remained. "You're all I care about. All I've ever cared about. Not Kristen. Not anyone else." He kissed her eyes, her nose, her mouth, showing her his love, proving it in a way no words ever could. He smelled of leather; his shirt felt crisp beneath her fingers. His breath tasted warm as their tongues met and he teased the softness inside her mouth.

When he pulled away, they were both a little shaken. "You're *sure* you're all right?" he said.

"I am now. How did you find me? How did you know?"

"Jonas Fry's name was on the poster. We followed you to his house. Fry told us Bigger had taken you on up to the manor. We split up to look for you." He grinned. "Considering your state of undress, I'm glad I'm the one who found you."

Just then Mac, Josh, and Jago burst into the clearing, horses lathered with exertion.

"You found her!" Josh called out.

"Thank the Almighty," Jago agreed, making the sign of the cross.

"Aye. It's good to see ye, lass," Mac told her.

Glory flashed a grateful smile, clutching the front of her dress. "It's good to see you, too. All of you."

"Jago," Nicholas said. "Take care of this—*gentleman*, will you?" Matt Bigger still hadn't moved.

"Be a pleasure, Cap'n."

"Come on." Nicholas clutched Glory's arm. "I'll take you up to the house. Then the men and I will see to Nathan."

Head still fuzzy and spinning, Glory pulled away. "I'm going with you. I want to be sure he's safe."

The sound of a gunshot echoed across the darkness. Glory's head snapped up. "Nathan," she breathed. Grabbing up her skirts, she raced back in the direction they'd come. Nicholas caught up with her in three long strides.

"We'll take the horses," he told her, spinning her around.

Glory let him lead her back. Nicholas helped her into the saddle, and they dug in their heels, urging the animals into a run.

They reached the cabin to find a circle of men holding torches aloft, flanked by the chain of wide-eyed slaves along with Lester Fields and Spencer James. In the center, Jonas Fry stood beside Nathan, who was tied to a post, his ragged shirt ripped away to expose his broad muscular back.

Nicholas swung down from his horse before it slid to a halt. "Let him go, Fry," he ordered.

"The devil you say."

Jago Dodd tossed Nicholas his pistol. Nicholas caught the weapon and swung his arm toward the overseer in the same easy motion, pressing the muzzle of the gun behind the man's ear.

"One of you men cut him loose," he directed the circle of slaves, motioning toward Nathan. "The rest of you go on back home."

"The boy's a runaway, sir. Law's clear on that. He's bound to be punished." The heavy male voice bore the smooth accent of a well-bred southern gentleman.

"And just who might you be?" Nicholas asked, still holding the pistol to the overseer's head.

"I'm Thomas Jervey. I own Magnolia Gardens plantation just south of here, and I'm head of the Committee for the Preservation of Southern Society." Jervey sat astride his big bay, flat white hat perched atop his head—the epitome of the southern planter. Like most of the southern aristocracy, Jervey was obviously a man of conviction. A man who believed in what he was doing.

"All right, Mr. Jervey," Nicholas said. "We'll return Nathan to Summerfield Manor. Tomorrow you may come and speak with Mrs. Summerfield. If she gives you permission, the punishment will stand."

"No!" Glory screamed, sliding down from her horse. Already on the ground, Josh caught her up before she could reach the circle of men.

"Let the captain handle this, Glory," he whispered. "He knows what he's doing."

Trembling all over, hard-pressed just to stay on her feet, Glory nodded and felt Josh loosen his hold.

"Do we have a bargain, Mr. Jervey?"

"I don't like bein' coerced, Mr.—"

"Blackwell. Nicholas Blackwell."

"Ah, Captain Blackwell. Yes. I've heard of you. I believe we may have even met on one occasion. I'm surprised a man of your stature would interfere in local jurisprudence."

"I don't normally. But Glory's my wife now. What's important to her is important to me. Besides, Nathan's a relative of sorts."

"It's a sad day indeed when a white man comes out with an admission like that."

"I'm sorry if I've offended your sensibilities. Now, do we have a deal?"

"Jonas?" Thomas Jervey asked.

"Don't do it, Mr. Jervey. Ain't right bargainin' with no nigger-lover."

Nicholas cocked the pistol, pressing the cold metal even harder behind the man's ear. "You sure about that, Fry?"

Jonas Fry spun and jerked at the same time, grabbing Nicholas's pistol hand. A shot was fired; then several more sounded. Josh pushed Glory to the ground, his own spent weapon acrid with the smell of burned powder. Jago crouched as he drew his blade and held it menacingly. Mac pointed his spent weapon at the dirt. When the smoke and dust cleared, the circle of men had scattered; some had flattened themselves against the earth. One moaned softly.

One lay silent.

Stifling her terror, fighting the beckoning dark of unconsciousness, Glory rushed to Nicholas's side. At first she thought he was dead and it was all she could do to breathe. As she knelt beside him and carefully shifted his head into her lap, blood from the wound in his chest oozed through her trembling fingers.

"I'll go for help," Josh said, darting for his horse.

Mac knelt beside her, his ruddy face grim. He opened Nicholas's bloody shirt to look at the wound. Mumbling something beneath his breath, he stepped away, eyes fixed on the ground. "I'll get some clean rags," he said softly. "We need t' stop the bleedin'."

Glory brushed damp tendrils of hair from Nicholas's cheek. His breathing sounded hollow; his chest rose only a fraction with each uneven breath. A weak pulse throbbed at the base of his throat. He hadn't moved at all.

Glory leaned over him. Tears welled and slipped down her cheeks. "Nicholas, please don't die." Her hand trembled so badly that she clenched her fist to still the motion. "You can't die now. We have our whole lives ahead of us."

His fingers closed over hers, brown against her fairer skin. His eyelids fluttered open. He ran his tongue over his lips and swallowed, straining to speak.

"Don't try to talk," she pleaded. "You have to save your strength."

He lifted his head, determined to make himself heard.

"Please, Nicholas. You've got to lie still."

"Tell me . . . you . . . love me," he whispered. "Tell me. . . ."

"Oh, God." Glory closed her eyes against the pain. Touching his cheek with her hand, tears blurred her vision and ran in rivulets to dampen the front of his shirt. "I love you, Nicholas. I wanted to tell you so many times. I've loved you since the first day we met. I loved you the night you saved my life on the *Black Spider*. I loved you on the strand. I loved you in Boston and at Blackwell Hall. I couldn't stop loving you. Even when I wanted to, I couldn't. I've always loved you, my darling Nicholas. I always will."

But Nicholas couldn't hear her.

His eyes had closed. His fingers relaxed their hold and slipped from between her own. His head slumped softly against the folds of her skirt.

" 'The Lord is my shepherd, I shall not want. He maketh me to lie down in green pastures; he leadeth me beside the still waters. He restoreth my soul.' " The minister's voice droned on, soft with sympathy above the bowed heads of the people who had gathered to pay their last respects.

" 'He leadeth me in the paths of righteousness for his name's sake. Yea, though I walk through the valley of the shadow of death, I will fear no evil, for thou art with me; thy rod and thy staff they comfort me.' "

Glory stood facing the oak coffin that rested on the mound of fresh earth in the tiny cemetery on the hillside below Summerfield Manor. A cloud blocked the sun. A single cloud, casting rays of shadow over the mourners in the graveyard. A damp breeze whipped her skirts and ruffled the black tulle veil she wore.

No tears wet her cheeks.

The time for tears had passed.

" 'My cup runneth over. Surely goodness and mercy shall follow me all the days of my life, and I will dwell in the house of the Lord forever.' "

Glory twisted the folds of her dark gray bombazine skirt

and stared straight ahead, eyes fixed on the garland of yellow roses draped across the coffin.

"Earth to earth, dust to dust, ashes to ashes."

Not long ago she had stood in the same spot, staring at another casket, one of fine mahogany, which held the remains of her father. She swallowed past the lump in her throat.

"Are you all right?"

She felt the pressure of his hand as it nestled atop her own in the crook of his arm. Nicholas still looked wan and pale, but he was alive—unlike Jonas Fry who lay cold and still in his coffin.

Glory nodded. "I'll just be glad when all this is over and we can go home."

"So will I."

Across from her, Glory saw her mother watching her through her own dark veil. She'd changed since the last time they'd been together. She seemed more vulnerable now. Glory had been right about her mother: Louise Summerfield had been just as upset as Glory when she learned of Jonas Fry's scheme to have Nathan returned. Her mother had come to terms with the past, it seemed. She just wanted to get on with her life, someday make a home for the soft-spoken, graying man who stood beside her—Caleb Harcourt.

She and Glory had talked for hours after it was certain Nicholas would live. They'd become closer in these past few days than they had been in years. Louise had spoken to Glory about Caleb, seeking her approval. After Glory had left Charleston, her mother had met Caleb Harcourt through Eric Dixon's family and the two had fallen in love. Since the period of mourning for Julian had not yet ended, Louise and Caleb had been unable to wed. In order to spend time with him, she had delegated more and more tasks to Jonas Fry. But all that would change now. Soon Caleb would be helping her run the manor.

Glory liked the quiet older man, so unlike her father. He'd spent most of his adult life as a merchant in Charleston, but he'd been raised on a plantation.

"I can learn again," he'd said with a wry grin. "For a woman like Louise it will be worth it."

Louise had blushed like a schoolgirl.

Glory was happy for them. Her mother deserved this chance at love.

Louise had even made peace with Nathan. To Thomas Jervey's chagrin, she'd given Nathan his freedman's papers, and he had already embarked on a ship heading north.

"You've always been there for me, Glory," he'd said. "Someday it'll be my turn."

"Pay me back by helping your people." She had hugged him and waved till he rode out of sight. This time when he reached New York, he would be safe there.

Nicholas's wound had been less serious than it had appeared at first. The bullet had passed all the way through his chest, a safe distance above his heart and lungs. Now it was just a matter of rest and recovery. He'd been abed three days, but today he had demanded she let him accompany her to the funeral, determined to lend his support.

Her mother seemed quietly pleased at his sense of duty. "Jonas Fry was a loyal employee of this family for over twenty years," Louise had said. "It's only fitting he be buried on Summerfield land and attended by family."

And so it was.

Mac, Jago, and Josh had turned Matthew Bigger over to the Charleston authorities. Since he'd been in no other trouble, there was a chance he would receive a light sentence. Glory hoped so. In some ways, as Lester Fields had said, he wasn't a bad sort.

"Bye, darlin'," he'd said with a grin, his face still battered from Nicholas's beating. "I wouldn't mind goin' to jail if I could've tasted that sweet body of yours just once."

Josh had been outraged. Jago grinned as if he understood, and Glory was just thankful Nicholas hadn't been anywhere near.

Mac and the crew of the *Black Witch* had left for New York as soon as the doctor was sure of Nicholas's recovery. *Black Neptune*, another of Nicholas's ships, would be at the Charleston docks in three weeks. By then Nicholas would be well enough to travel, and Glory would have had some time with her mother and a chance to visit old friends.

The funeral service ended, and Nicholas led Glory back up to the house. For propriety's sake she'd made an appearance, but she felt no grief for Jonas Fry. She wouldn't have wished him dead, but the fact that he was brought her little pain. She hoped the man her mother hired to replace him would be more sympathetic to the Negroes' plight.

"You look a little peaked," Glory told Nicholas, laying a hand on his brow to check for fever as they climbed the sweeping staircase to their third-floor room.

"I believe you may be right, Mrs. Blackwell. I'd better get back to bed right away." His eyes moved from her face to the swell of her breast beneath the dark gray mourning dress she'd worn after her father died. They darkened to that heated, hungry look she knew so well.

"You'd better come with me," he told her. "Just to be certain I'm all right. Besides, I want you out of that dismal dress." His look said the dress wasn't all he wanted her out of, and Glory felt her own desire swell. They moved along the hall and into Glory's bedchamber. She'd put Nicholas in the wide four-poster to convalesce, but so far she'd slept on the narrow settee each night for fear of opening his wound.

"Turn around," he ordered, as soon as they'd closed the door.

Glory did as she was told and felt firm fingers unbuttoning the back of her dress, then releasing the tabs holding together her petticoats. She stepped free of the frothy folds, pulling the dress off at the same time. She turned to face him in snowy corset, chemise, and lacy drawers.

Nicholas groaned. "I'd almost forgotten how lovely you are."

"I love you," she whispered.

"I don't think I'll ever tire of hearing you say that."

"I love you, I love you, I love you." A bubble of soft laughter escaped.

Glory smiled seductively. She slid down her drawers and faced him clad in dark gray stockings and velvet garters, a demicorset, and a lacy chemise that barely covered the curves of her bottom.

"Vixen," hc whispered, pulling her against him. He kissed her soundly, until she felt him sway.

"I think we'd better get you in bed."

"Not unless you're coming, too."

"Try to keep me away."

He let her remove his clothes, first his dark brown coat, then his pleated white shirt. He sat on the bed while she worked open the buttons of his breeches. Bending over, she felt a rush of heat, first to her cheeks, then to her loins, as Nicholas's hand moved up her thigh to tease the rounded curves of her bottom.

She slid his breeches down his long hard legs and felt his muscles bunch as her hand brushed against the now-stiff shaft between his legs. Licking her lips, she let her fingers play over the rigid flesh, fascinated as always by the size—and the promise of pleasure it held.

Nicholas eased himself up against the headboard. "Come here."

"Not yet." Giving him a seductive glance, she wet her lips and lowered them to the tempting flesh at the juncture of his sinewy legs. She teased and caressed him with her mouth and tongue, wanting to give him pleasure, delighted by his soft low groans of passion. She licked and sucked and drove him to near distraction, finally bringing him to shuddering climax. As he lay spent and more than a little surprised at her boldness, she finished undressing and joined him on the bed, careful not to touch his injured chest.

"You're even more of a vixen than I imagined," he whispered, cupping an upturned breast. He teased the nipple with his teeth, then circled the hard bud with his mouth. Glory felt a rush of pleasure that went all the way to her toes. When he pulled away, she traced a finger down his chest to the flat spot below his navel, then was surprised to feel his shaft hot and pulsing again.

"And you, my handsome husband, are even more of a devil."

He chuckled softly and captured her lips, his tongue teasing and warm as it slid inside her mouth. He settled her astride him, and Glory slipped easily onto his hardened length, her body long ago wet and ready to accept him. She moved sensuously, until he cupped her buttocks with practiced ease and set up a rhythm that made it hard for her to concentrate.

Soon she was lost in the pulsing motion, melting with the liquid sensations that washed over her. She kissed him, laced her fingers through his hair, and mewed softly against his mouth. Once she felt him flinch, as she accidentally touched his wound, but he didn't stop. Just kept thrusting into her, slowly and deeply, until a wave of pleasure broke over her, curling her upward and forcing his name from her lips. Nicholas followed her to release.

He nestled her beside him and they drifted to peaceful contentment.

"Tell me—"

"I love you," she interrupted before he could finish the words.

He traced the line of her cheek. "And I love you." There were no more doubts, no lingering fears between them. From now on Glory would speak her heart to Nicholas. And Nicholas would spend the rest of his life proving his love in the age-old manner he'd demonstrated only moments before—and was eager to show her again.